KNUCKLE DOWN

DAVID TEMPLE

82 MERCER PUBLISHING

82 MERCER Publishing: 1160 N. Coast Highway 101, Encinitas, CA 92024

Cover Design & Book Layout by Jack Poppy

Editorial by: Tammy Lynn

Images: Shutterstock

ISBN: 978-0-9891865-9-9 (*Paperback*)

Proudly published & manufactured in the United States of America.

ALSO BY DAVID TEMPLE

Carter Matheson Series:
BEHIND THE 8 BALL
LUCKY STRIKES

Detective Pat Norelli Series:
THE POSER

Stand-alone Thriller
DEVOUR

Book & Film:
CHASING GRACE

For my wife and partner, Tammy,
whose gracious encouragement allows me
to pursue my dreams with reckless abandon—
your love has set me free.

To all the brave men and women who protect
this great country we call home—Thank You.

America will never be destroyed from the outside. If we falter and lose our freedoms, it will be because we destroyed ourselves.

— *ABRAHAM LINCOLN*

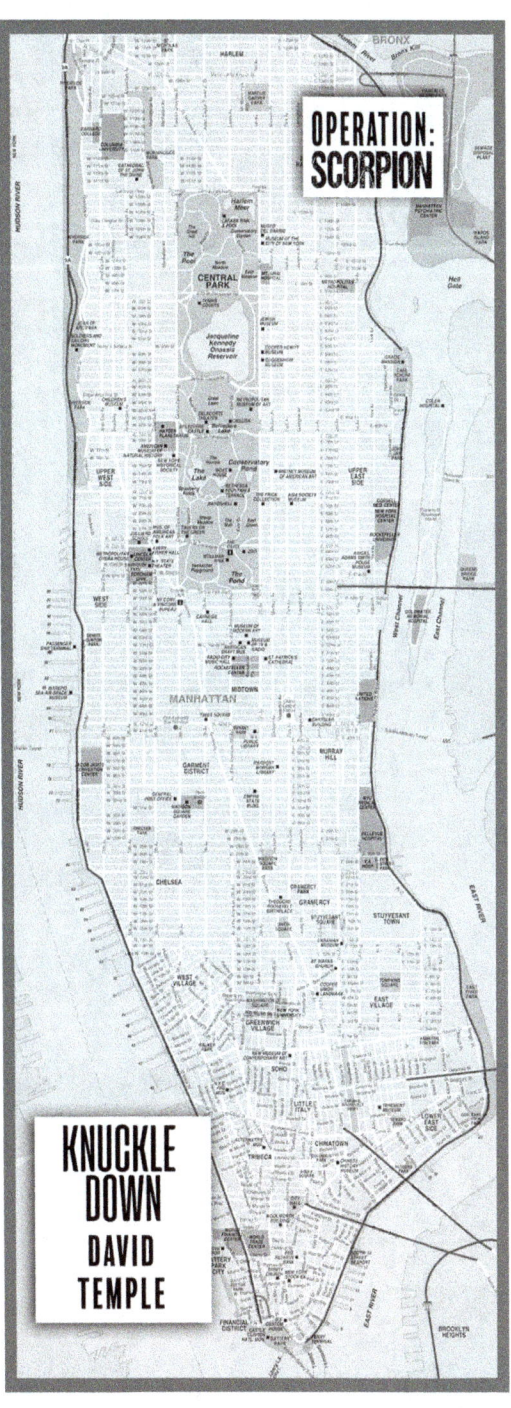

OPERATION:
SCORPION

KNUCKLE
DOWN

DAVID
TEMPLE

PART ONE:

THE SNATCH

MIDTOWN MANHATTAN, 11 A.M.

Donovan focused on the body lying on the table in front of him as though it were the last thing he would ever see. His concentration was unfaltering. His hands moved delicately yet precisely.

"This is taking longer than expected," his assistant Mo said quietly.

"Perfection takes time," Donovan grinned.

While most people conducting this procedure would be sweating bullets. Not Donovan—even though she wiped his brow every few minutes.

"You good?" she asked, already knowing the answer.

"Very."

"Nervous?"

"Never."

Maiko "Mo" Wang was Japanese and had been Donovan's assistant and girlfriend for the past ten years. She knew him well, and could tell when he was bluffing. Today, she wasn't sure. Attentive, she admired the skill with which his hands worked and the effortless way the razor sharp tool sliced through tender skin.

"Have you decided what pattern you'll use?"

"What?"

"Pattern, you know—" she hesitated.

"Three loop pulley."

She nodded.

The temperature in the warehouse had lowered considerably, and had to be in order to keep the meat fresh and the surgeon sharp. The area doubled as a temporary refrigeration station for a nearby restaurant. Being underground also helped keep noise and interruptions at bay.

"High tensile strength. Less gap," he quietly said. "Prevents ripping."

"Of course."

As the blade glistened from the bright overhead lights, Donovan caught himself staring at the angelic face of the child on his operating table—marveling at her porcelain skin and golden, soft hair. It was a sharp contrast to what lay in front of them.

"This is certainly one of your more…" Mo hesitated. "Ambitious scenarios."

"Drastic times. Drastic measures."

Making a last deep cut, he was careful not to lacerate internal organs. He likewise wanted to keep the scar minimal, although he knew the girl would be reminded of this moment, and the maniac performing the procedure, for years to come.

Donovan whistled, keeping his spirits up and nerves down.

THREE HOURS EARLIER—

Young Abigail Burton was strolling through Central Park with her Nanny—french-born Stephanie Marcheaux, just as they did every weekday. Having just left the Zoo, the two were making their way to the Dairy Visitor Center & Gift Shop, when the distance between them stretched.

"Abigail, stay close!" Stephanie shouted, as the nine year old ran toward balloon artists who were busily making free souvenirs for a large gaggle of children.

"Oui, oui, Miss Stephanie," Abigail giggled, as she joined other children who were likewise mesmerized by the colorful and animated clowns. Abigail was the only child of New York Mayor, Lukas S. Burton, one of the most admired leaders of New York—perhaps the entire country. He had been commended for dramatically lowering both crime and tax rates for three years in a row, and rumored to be considering running for President of the United States.

Summer had arrived early in Manhattan. The flowers were in full bloom and people were out in droves. That, and a 5K race for Breast Cancer Awareness, made for a packed park. The race was to begin in the middle of the park—where 65th Transverse intersected Center Drive, and would end a city block north of the Columbus Circle entrance—where 59th met Central Park West.

Stephanie was completely engrossed in her cell phone, when she glanced up to find Abigail missing.

"Abi?" she screamed, whipping her head around in all directions.

"Over here," Abigail shouted, waving to her friends, as she ran toward her nanny.

Stephanie's shoulders relaxed just as a woman approached from behind. She pulled on Stephanie's sleeve.

"Please help me. I've lost my little girl," the woman cried first in French, then in English.

Distracted by the hysteria, but pulled in by the stranger's familiar accent, Stephanie first checked to see that Abigail was still nearby. There she was, alongside several children petting a large rabbit which was being held and stroked by a tall circus clown with yellow hair and a red nose.

"Please help," the stranger shouted, still pulling at Stephanie's sweater. "My little girl has run off and…"

Stephanie asked, "Where did you see her last?" Then abruptly stopped as the eyes of the hysterical woman suddenly shifted from terror to neutrality.

Confused, Stephanie whipped back to scan the crowd. She gasped aloud when she couldn't find Abigail.

Also, there was no clown.

As well as no rabbit.

And no Abigail.

Shocked and distracted by the continual pulling at her sleeve, Stephanie spun back around to the hysterical stranger. However, he was suddenly face to face with a blind man wearing sunglasses and holding a cane. He appeared disoriented.

"*Putain de merde!*" Stephanie screamed in French, frantically fumbling for her cellphone, while scanning the park for help.

"Holy shit, indeed," said the blind man.

Ignoring the man, Stephanie saw a police officer in the distance and felt momentarily hopeful.

Now as she turned back to the second stranger, *he* was gone.

In a flash, her tears turned to sobs, as her head buzzed with confusion and her heart sank with guilt. Standing amidst a throng of runners and sun-worshipping strangers, the Mayor's number one employee of the past dozen years was paralyzed with fear, afraid she would be fired.

Or murdered and dumped in the East River, she sobbed.

Either solution would be better than being responsible for the loss of Abigail Renee Burton.

As HIS DAUGHTER was being snatched from Central Park, Mayor Burton was hosting a televised conference about a new super train he was promoting which would run the distance of Long Island. At the game time, Abigail's socialite mother, Clare Marie, was hosting a fundraising event atop the elegant Frick Museum on the upper-crusty East Side.

SIMULTANEOUSLY, Donovan's other assistant and second girlfriend, Margo "Hysterical Mother" Wheeler, along with Donovan's body-guard, Ken "Park Clown" Dawson, and sidekick, Sean "Blind Man" Combs, were racing down the Westside Highway in an all black SUV adorned with police license plates, strobing lights, and a blaring siren.

By the time the nanny had cleared enough headspace to call 911, they were in the underbelly of a subterranean warehouse in the Chelsea district of Midtown—disappearing without a trace.

2

THE PREP

DONOVAN HAD the attention of his crew who were watching their leader pace like an expectant father. Periodically scanning mid-town Manhattan, his eyes shifted from the city, to his team. The constant motion was not nerves, but energy. Staying fit with daily exercise kept him at the front of the pack. In every situation. His confidence, plus the drive to win at any cost, had always made him one of the elite in any of his former units. But his days of military service had run off the rails, evolving into a new mission.

His current squadron included Mo Wang—a woman he had known the longest. She was expert in computers and electronic surveillance. Besides being one of his two girlfriends, she was the only person he trusted with his life.

Another he trusted nearly as well was Ken Dawson—a comrade of twenty years. They had grown up together in their old Brooklyn neighborhood. That was before one turned to the military, and the other to law enforcement. Ken became Donovan's bodyguard about seven years ago, when Donovan found himself in the wrong place at the wrong time; something that didn't happen often. Ken was there to save his ass. It also became the tipping point where Ken exchanged his "life of Blue" for a life of crime.

When Donovan showed Ken his future could be infinitely more

lucrative if he helped get his pal out of a tight spot, it was Game Over. Their secret sauce was how they had managed for Ken to keep one foot in the blue camp and the other working for *Team Scorpion.*

"It won't be long," Donovan said, checking his Tag Heuer, "Before the shit hits the fan."

"But you've planned meticulously," Mo smiled. "As always."

"She's right, Donovan," Margo added. "We've gone over the mechanics a dozen times. The snatch was flawless."

Sean nodded. "Copy that, boss. I'd beg anyone to put a bead on us."

"That's not my concern. You all performed perfectly. It's the unknown I'm always overly cautious about."

Donovan wanted his team always happy and ever loyal. Which is why he spared no expense in providing luxurious homes with a state-of-the-art fitness center and pool on the penthouse level of the building the entire team occupied. Add to that handsome salaries, huge bonuses, and all the toys one could want, and it was a win-win.

Avalon Tower was a glass and steel tower that skyrocketed toward the sky, passing all surrounding high-rises by dozens of stories. Among the best in the city, it offered modern construction, European amenities like a full-blown concierge service. The 1,225 foot residential tower placed it among the five tallest buildings in New York City—in between the Empire State Building and Bank of America tower. The only taller residential tower was 425 Park Avenue, climbing nearly as high as One World Trade—the proud replacement to the two World Trade Center buildings that collapsed on 9-11, which rose to 1,776 feet.

It was nearly five years ago when Donovan and his investors began erecting the modern structure on Eleventh Avenue. Being located in the heart of Hell's Kitchen, it practically sat atop the Lincoln Tunnel, had instant access to Air Pegasus heliport on 30th, was within minutes of Penn Station, and not much further from Grand Central Station. The location, and more specifically Donovan's penthouse, provided perfect visibility of the George Washington Bridge to the north, the Holland Tunnel and Brooklyn Bridge to the South, and both the Queensboro Bridge and Midtown Tunnel to the East.

Having a bird's eye view of the island was not only a luxury, but a necessity. The office, and home to their underground labs, sat directly across the street in a nondescript eight-story brick building. Built in 1905, Donovan had purchased it a decade ago when his drug business was young and prosperous. The building had remained unchanged, with one exception. The building maestro had created construction magic by leaving alone all the office units which faced Eleventh and 45th Avenue, while the two sides which faced neighboring buildings were retrofitted like a Hollywood back-lot, showing what appeared to be a live office. Lights turned on and off all hours of the day and night which provided a perfect cover for his underground business.

The center of the building had been cut out like an enormous tube, extending from the basement to the roof's skylights. This allowed any airborne byproducts to filter from the basement before dissipating through the roof. Thanks to advanced filtering systems, it called no attention. The subterranean warehouse was three stories deep, underneath two parking decks, and apart from hiding a monstrous drug lab, the depth of the building masked tremendous technology for all the monitoring that happened in Donovan's penthouse.

"This is why I chose you guys long ago. And why we're working together today," Donovan said, looking at each of his team.

"And we will see this through, just as we have from the start," Mo said quietly.

Taking a remote, he aimed it at a large piece of art on the wall. A panel quietly lifted into a pocket in the ceiling, as a bank of tall doors quietly opened and seamlessly pivoted before disappearing into the wall. All eyes were on a wall of TV screens which were monitoring most of the major intersections in Manhattan.

The team clapped as though he just dropped a winning putt. The technology, along with an enormous arsenal of weapons, made for one of the most expensive bank of toys Donovan had ever created.

When Donovan's underground lab at the former Nuclear Power Plant outside Havana was demolished—thanks to misplaced operatives who got embedded with a business partner of his, he needed an alternate place to expand his business, without having to travel overseas. Plus, the hometown boy wanted to make his mark in his own backyard.

"Is that the Governor's—" Sean began.

"Mansion? Yes," Donovan grinned. "And the Mayor's home," he said, pointing at another screen. "Over here is the home of our esteemed Chief of Police." Pointing to another screen, he added, "And just outside the *secret* entrance to the United Nations," Donovan said, crossing the room, "Is the Federal Reserve Bank. Oh, and we can't leave out the Central Park Zoo."

"Looks familiar, right kids?" Margo joked, punching Sean in the shoulder.

"And Times Square, One World Trade, The Stock Exchange, Penn Station, Grand Central," he continued clicking screens, "And all the tunnel and bridges, with entrances *and* exits."

"Talking about Big Brother," Mo chuckled. "Jesus."

"Nah," Donovan grinned, "You can just call me *Scorpion.*"

3

THE BEAST

DONOVAN BLAIR, known in many dark corners of the world as *Scorpion*, never tired of thinking of inventive ways of getting his products from lines of impasse to lanes of progress.

With a life packed with determination and drive, he was a man of clarity and focus—wanting nothing more than to make enormous amounts of money which would give him massive amounts of control. The passion to be rich superseded anything else and represented what few genuinely knew: Freedom. Power was a close second. And Donovan made certain nothing stood in the way of his achieving both.

He also enjoyed savoring the bitter taste of revenge—an emotion he had nurtured over many years. And given his primary target was largely responsible for the maturation of such a vehement passion, he wanted to take as much time as was possible to devour such an evil dish.

"What's her BP?" Donovan quietly asked Mo.

"110 over 60."

"Perfect," he smiled.

The rogue surgeon had worked diligently for hours. Carefully slicing Abigail from sternum to abdomen, he had opened her stomach cavity—pushing aside internal organs, only to place several small balloons of synthetic explosives inside the healthy and delicate body. She was being perfectly monitored, as to remove any potential infections or complications.

"Roll another one, will ya?" Donovan smirked, motioning for Mo to fill another balloon. "I've got a bit more space."

Mo tapped a small glass vial of explosives into a balloon, careful to keep the material from contaminating the area. Or risking possible devastation.

Taking the last tube from her steady hands, he filled a remaining space and whispered, "Nicely done." Admiring her precision, he added, "Now, let's see how my seam work goes."

Years earlier, Donovan's original synthetic mixture of explosives was called *K5*. Similar to *C4*—which was a popular product for dropping buildings in cities nationwide, or destroying enemies in battle around the globe, he had developed the deadly concoction for his construction business. The difference between C4 and Blair's latest proprietary material was its lower toxicity, yet higher combustibility factors. Terrorists had made headlines in Brussels by using a similar product in the form of *TATP*, a crystalline power. *Nightmare Dust*, as authorities had come to call it, was quickly becoming the new method to wreak havoc.

While Donovan's usual fare of mayhem included kidnapping, drug trafficking and murder, his latest endeavor would gain higher access, using lower resources, reaching into deeper pockets, for shallower reasons.

Ken Dawson, Donovan's bodyguard and ammunitions specialist, had been watching from a distance, balancing calls on two separate cellphones.

Approaching the table, he quietly said, "Hey, boss?"

"Yeah?" Donovan didn't look up.

"Burton and his wife just got the news. They're both heading to his office now."

Donovan glanced at a bank of oversized clocks on the far wall. "Perfect timing," he said, closing the last stitch. Nodding toward a case at the end of the table, he said, "Put that next to the patient."

Opening it, Donovan retrieved a transmitter one-fourth the size of a watch battery, and connected it to a tiny wire protruding from the stitches in Abigail's lower abdomen.

Nodding to Mo, he said, "Get her dressed and upstairs." Turning to Ken, he added, "Upstairs. Time to plug in Part 2."

DONOVAN HAD CHOSEN to set up shop in the Meatpacking District years ago, when meat was the currency of the day and rents were affordable enough to buy entire buildings for less than six-figures. Today, things were different, as buildings were going up in months, not years, and access to and from the island was much more sophisticated than it used to be. Another selling point was the proximity to not only the Holland and Lincoln Tunnels, but a Helipad on 30th. Having those avenues of egress so close, and a Bell Ranger helicopter mere blocks away, provided him easy access to the island and wherever else he needed. Donovan capitalized on the accessibility, as well as his expertise in military warfare—all of which combined to provide him the control and power he so desperately craved.

Upstairs, Abigail was being filled with a variety of antibiotics and vitamins to keep her body functioning as normally as was possible. Mo was administering a buffet of calculated drugs—mainly benzodiazepines. One would wake her, another control her, and yet another to help erase her short-term memory.

Leaning against a wall of floor-to-ceiling glass, Donovan admired the High Line revitalization below. The location of his Hell's Kitchen tower afforded him a panoramic 360-degree view—allowing him to keep an eye on an enormous portion of Manhattan. The live-work building was a fortress of steel and glass, with the best of security.

"This is your best plan yet, babe," Margo whispered in Donovan's ear.

He leaned into her, allowing a kiss on his neck. "Feels wickedly good," he smiled, kissing her cheek.

Entering the office barefoot and quiet, Mo said, "I expect her to wake up in about 20."

Quiet before the storm, he thought, waving both women close. He kissed Mo, then Margo, as the three shared a warm embrace.

Ken and Sean entered the room, taking a seat at an enormous marble dining room table.

Rubbing his hands together, he said, "Okay, kids. Let's go over the plan once more before our surprise package wakes up. With so many pieces to our puzzle, everything must come together perfectly."

Young Abigail would soon be part mule and part incendiary device; a dangerous conduit aimed at bringing down a prominent political leader in the most powerful city in the world—a family man who crossed a mad man one too many times.

Scorpion's upcoming attack would soon provide an explosive sting Manhattan would never forget.

4

THE HYSTERIA

MAYOR LUKAS BURTON and his entire security entourage completely commandeered the front of the New York Mayor's Office of Operations. The long line of black SUVs stretched the length of the building along Broadway, wrapping around to Murray. The parade of vehicles resembled a funeral procession. Burton's heart sank at the thought of that being an omen. A random gaggle of press had followed the pack of politicos from Long Island—wondering where the fire was.

Pushing aside fear, Burton stormed down the hallway toward his office, having multiple and simultaneous conversations with members of his staff along the way. Staff who were not in attendance at the Super Train media circus on Long Island joined others in preparation for an impending media conference. The press was already a pack of salivating dogs awaiting a meal of gossip. Burton could only imagine how the news had spread so quickly.

"Where in the hell is my wife?" Burton barked to his small pack of personnel.

"She's in your office, Sir," Margaret Childress, his secretary of two terms answered. "She arrived within minutes of being notified by your Nanny that—"

"And where in God's name is that *moron!*" he shouted. "I want her in my office now and I—"

Childress pulled up close to the Mayor's ear, lowering her voice and nodding to the security director. "Sir, might I suggest that Ms. Marcheaux wait in your private lobby?"

Mayor Burton slowed his pace and taking her by the arm quietly said, "Yes, good idea. Otherwise, I'll kill for—"

Knowing everything he said was being monitored, he stopped and planted a smile across his face. "Thank you, Ms. Childress, that's fine. I'll be in my office, talking to..." He stopped in mid-sentence, catching the piercing look of his Chief of Police crossing the expanse of marbled hallway.

Red-faced and overweight, Chief Jacob Davis looked petrified. He had been elected to the office two years before the Mayor was elected, and while they hadn't started as friends, both had grown to respect one another. Burton was known to be a bear—demanding complete loyalty from his staff, and Davis could be a dick—disregarding his staff when he wasn't revered. Both understood one another's need for loyalty. Their heads had butted a dozen times along the way; that was until Burton found Davis' soft spot.

Cash.

"What's up, Jake?" Burton asked, likely knowing the results—judging from the man's expression.

"Not good, Mayor," Chief Davis said, nodding toward the office where they were heading.

"Right," Burton said, taking a deep breath and pushing the nightmare down as far as his mind would allow. He handed Margaret his briefcase. "Can you take this, brew a pot, and give me..." he hesitated, looking to The Chief who held up five fingers. "Five minutes. No, make that ten. I gotta pee. The drive on the L.I.E. shook my kidneys into my back pocket."

RELIEVING HIMSELF AT THE URINAL, the Mayor listened to his Chief rattle on. "First, I'm sorry, Luke. Seriously. Oh my god, I wouldn't know what..." he stumbled, shaking his head. "Anyway, we have no idea where she is. I mean, I've been drilling your nanny down-stairs for the past half hour and all I've got outta that fuckin' immi-grant is…" He took a deep breath, checking the Mayor's reaction. "Sorry, but she's fuckin' hysterical and I can't for the life of me figure it out."

Zipping up, Burton raised a hand for Davis to slow down. "I get it. She's an idiot. And trust me…" he looked around the stalls. "If you, I mean if *we* don't find my daughter inside the next 24 hours, *you* will make that fuckin' moron disappear. Hear me?"

Davis nodded, handing the Mayor a towel.

"What else?" Burton barked. "There's got to be *something*."

Davis shook his head.

"No clues?"

"Nothing."

"Ransom note?"

"Zilch," Davis answered.

"Fuck!" Mayor shouted at himself in the mirror, adjusting his tie.

"We're on it, though. Full force. We'll find these pricks."

They shared a look.

Davis growled, "You and I've been in some tight places, Sir. I've never let you down. And I won't this time."

Opening the door, Burton waved him through before being approached by a half-dozen staffers. "We had better," he said quietly. "Or heads will roll. Get it?"

"Got it."

"Good, now let's get to it."

CLARE MARIE BURTON was the quintessential socialite: perfectly coiffed, demurely outfitted, and elegantly poised in every situation. However, today the First Lady was anything but poised. In fact, she had become unraveled, and having a difficult time not showing it.

"What in God's name is happening, Lukas?" Clare whimpered, as her knight approached.

The Mayor took his wife by both shoulders and kissed her

cheek. "We are doing *everything* possible to find our little girl," he said softly.

Her heavy breathing slowed, calmed by his words.

"And trust me, love, we *will* find the perpetrators of this heinous crime, and prosecute them to the *fullest* extent of the law."

"Prosecute?" she spat a nervous laugh. "How about permanently disfigure? Or even—"

Taking her arm, he moved to the window—knowing ears would enjoy taking statements like that. Under duress or not, the press would love to whip anything they could get into a rumor-spinning headline. "Can I get you some water?" Burton asked, looking to Margaret, who practically sprinted across the room in response.

"I want my baby," Clare began to sob, grabbing Lukas' arm before melting into a chair.

As Margaret handed Clare the glass, Chief Davis entered the room, holding his hat in his hands.

"Mrs. Burton, we have the very best minds on this. We *will* find your daughter. And we'll find her *soon.* You have my word."

Clare smiled as sincerely as possible, holding his stare. "I certainly hope so, Jacob."

He didn't budge. "Yes, ma'am." Nodding to Lukas, he left the room.

"Dear, I've got to meet with my team to design a message we can release in order to get this moving, okay?"

Regaining some composure, she gave a tiny nod.

"Now, why don't you go home and get some—"

"Not on your life, Lukas. I'm not moving an *inch* from this office until—"

"Hon, trust me when I say that we're going to be doing *every-thing* in our power to find her, but your being here won't do either of us any good."

"Lukas Burton, I'm not moving until you can assure me—"

"Clare, listen to me," he began, turning to Margaret and nodding toward to the door.

Margaret offered a smile, squeezing Clare's hand, then gathered the team and quietly left.

As the door closed, Clare let out a deep sigh. "Of course you're right. I'll get home. And pray."

Lukas looked at her and smiled. "That's my girl. And a good idea."

Sharing an embrace, she whispered in his ear. "You're right. You have a lot deal of pressure, and well, I'll be fine."

Kissing her cheek, she whispered, "Luke, I don't care what must be done, but I'm sure you'll do *everything* possible to get our girl back."

"*Everything.*"

"Okay, I'm leaving. Call me the instant you have anything."

"Of course."

Stepping out through a private exit, Clare was joined by her two waiting assistants. At the door, she turned to blow a kiss to Lukas, and as she left, Chief Davis stepped in.

"Okay," Burton said, taking a deep breath. "Let's prepare a statement."

CLARE RODE in silence on her way to Gracie Mansion—the old Federal homestead that had been home to New York City Mayors and their families for nearly seventy years. She enjoyed living on the East side. This part of Manhattan had a certain civility she admired—not to mention shopping along the rich Park Avenue corridor.

However, right now, all she could focus on was her little girl—her mind rapidly shifting images of where she might be, of who could have abducted her, and what condition she might be in. As tears streaked her cheeks, her heart raced and her breathing became labored.

Her driver Jerry kept checking on her—his eyes shifting back and forth from the East Side Highway to her.

"Are you okay, First Lady?"

Fighting tears, she nodded, then rode in silence for most of the journey. As her fears began to subside, her emotions gave way to anger, and in minutes, she was simmering, as her imagination ran a dark course. Reaching into her purse for a silk handkerchief, something caught her attention.

She stopped—getting lost in thought for several minutes, before snapping out of it.

Looking to the driver, she said, "Jerry, would you please close the window? I've got a private call to make."

"Of course, Ma'am."

As the window between them began to close, she said, "And I don't want to be disturbed. For *any* reason."

She waited a moment, before taking two cell phones from her purse. One was silver and decorated with a New York City emblem. The other was black and nondescript. She laid the silver one aside, and pressed a single button on the other. After a series of tones, she entered a four-digit pin and waited for the connection.

A voice answered. "I wondered how long it would take before you called."

Smiling, she started to speak, before the voice continued. "Okay, now leave a message and I'll get back to you. When I feel like it."

She hesitated, then hung up smiling.

5

THE PLAN

DONOVAN KNEW this was destined to be one of those once-in-a-life-time moments. He relished holding something that his longtime adversary wanted. And he possessed the one thing his opponent could not have. For right now. As he momentarily owned the very apple of her father's eye, the Scorpion's adversary couldn't do a damned thing about it.

Young Abigail sat in a large chair between Donovan's legs. With her back to him, he brushed her hair with all the tenderness of a loving father. He smiled the entire time, combing and smoothing each strand, as though preparing her for a young beauty pageant. His crew had never seen this side of him. Both Mo and Margo were moved, but wondered how long the tender moment would last. Ken and Sean also watched, witnessing how he could be ruthless at one moment, and at another—gentle as a new father.

"How are you feeling, Abigail?" Donovan asked.

Still groggy from the operation, she batted her eyes in slow motion. "Fine, I guess."

"Are you hungry, or thirsty?"

"I'm kinda thirsty," she whispered.

Margot looked to Donovan for approval, got a nod, then went to the kitchen, while Mo leaned forward and took Abigail's hand.

"Abigail, my name is Mo. Short for…Maureen," she smiled.

"Hi, Mo. You have pretty hair," Abigail smiled.

"Thank you." Taking it down from a ponytail, she shook it loose, she said, "Would you like to feel it?"

Abigail looked to Donovan.

"Sure, Abigail, go ahead."

Abigail softly stroked her hair. "Wow, it's so soft. And dark."

"I'm Japanese. We all have black hair."

Twirling a strand between her fingers, she said, "Mine's blonde. Mommy calls it strawberry blonde 'cause it's kinda pink."

Margo arrived with a glass of water. Abigail drank slowly.

Mo and Margo leaned close, as instructed by Donovan—to bond with her. It was important for the entire team to make Abigail feel like family. Donovan was no psychologist, but his training had taught him how in high stress situations it was better to focus on the client with such gentle attention to detail that they're distracted from thinking anything to the contrary.

Taking the glass from her, he didn't want her stomach to expand any more than necessary. The stitches—while strong and internally sewn, needed more time to heal. The numbing agent she had been given would prevent her from feeling much of anything.

"Abigail, do you know why you're here?"

She shook her head.

"Do you remember when you and Margo were playing in the park—with your nanny?"

"Sure, you were with a big happy clown," Margo said, glancing toward Ken. "He was making you a balloon."

She began to smile.

"And Ms. Marcheaux wanted you to go play with some new friends," Mo said.

As Abigail frowned, Donovan motioned to give her a second. Her frown slowly morphed into a smile.

"I like the park. And the clowns and—" she looked around.

Sean took a balloon from behind a chair, and her face brightened.

"Your nanny is taking a vacation and wanted you to visit with us a little while before we take you back home to Mommy and Daddy. Okay?" Donovan asked gently.

"Sure," she said, looking around. "You have a nice house, Mr. Smith. I know Daddy would like it."

"Yes, I bet he would. I built this, along with lots of buildings for lots of people. Maybe I can build your Daddy and Mommy one some day."

Looking around, she said, "There are so many windows."

"Yes," Margo said. "That's because—"

"But why are the curtains closed?" Abigail asked Margo.

Curtains had been drawn before Abigail entered so she wouldn't be tempted to look out. Future questions would help reveal their location.

"It's pouring down rain and well, rain makes me sleepy," Margo snickered, waiting to see the little girls reaction.

As Abigail yawned, Donovan looked to Margot. Stretching, she faked a yawn. "Abigail, I need to take a nap. Would you like to read me a story?"

"Okay."

Standing, Margot took her by the hand and crossed the enormous room to an adjacent bedroom.

"Bye Abigail. We'll see you in a little bit, okay honey?" Donovan waved.

Looking over her shoulder, she said, "Okay, Mr. Smith."

Looking up to Margot, she said, "I have some favorite stories Mommy reads me."

"Like what?"

"Where is Mommy?"

"She's at the beauty parlor, getting pretty for you and Daddy. She'll be here real soon and we'll go back to the park to play. How's that sound?"

Donovan waited until they were out of range before he said, "Cute kid."

"And not nervous at all," Sean said.

"No kidding. Sitting on your lap, for crap sake," Ken added.

Grinning, Donovan stood and motioned for Sean, Ken and Mo to join him in the kitchen.

"Simple psychology. If only the buffoons we're up against would be so docile, huh?"

Without waiting for a response, he took a sparkling vitamin water from the fridge and emptied it before continuing.

"It's a waiting game now," Ken said, walking to the sliding doors. Touching a button, a wall of window treatments quietly lifted into the tall ceiling. He looked at the pool below.

"But not for long," Donovan said. "Too much on the line. Anybody in this racket knows if you don't find someone inside the first 48 to 72 hours, the chances of finding them decrease."

Sean asked, "How long?"

"Soon," Margot said, without even thinking.

"Yeah, what *she* said," Donovan grinned. "Always *trying* to run the ship, huh?" he added, grabbing her arm to spin her around and place her in a body lock.

"Hey!"

"Relax, I'm playing," Donovan said and let her go. "And you're right. Like I said earlier…" he stopped to frown at Sean. "If *someone* was listening…"

"I know, I know. I was just anxious," Sean said.

Donovan checked his watch. "Let's give 'em an hour or two. Make the move at cocktail hour. They'll still be getting adjusted to the initial shock. Next, they'll hit anger, and then it shouldn't take long before they pull together the troops." Walking back to the kitchen bar, he pressed a button for a cappuccino. "We'll send out the first message then."

Donovan was enjoying this. Waiting for the coffee to brew, he pulled Mo close, giving her a deep kiss. As she moaned, the guys shifted their attention to the pool.

Pouring his drink, he asked, "Are we 100% tight on the message boards in midtown?"

"One hundred and *one* percent," Mo said, rubbing her fingers together. "My boys are *golden*. We've set up…" she motioned air-quotes, "A *glitch* to hit thirty seconds before we go live. That will be our visual trigger for all hands on deck to be prepared to push their respective buttons...or whatever means of launch that may be."

"Good."

"I'll be with my pal from the 13th Precinct flying over 42nd in his Ranger," Ken said.

"Wait, there's only 8 *official* birds in town, how'd you manage —" Donovan interrupted.

"Boss, you worry about your shit. I'll worry about mine," Ken smirked. "Like I said, we'll be just outside of the epicenter at that time, but close enough to allow Mo to send a feed to me, we'll scramble and bounce it to our boy, Sean, back to the office on 11th."

Donovan slowly nodded, sipping another coffee.

Waving the conversation back to herself, Mo said, "When the first images appear, they'll think it's a commercial. It looks like one. The guys at any of the boards will assume it's a takeover from an *outside* source. However, we've installed a switch to an *inside* source on several of the program centers.

"More details," Donovan said, motioning for more.

"Sure. There are 17 primary screens on 42nd and I won't bore you with *all* the deets—and we can't control *all* of them, but suffice it to say we have control, or at the very least, *partial* control of more than half of them."

"Like?" Donovan said. "You know how details give me a boner."

She rolled her eyes. "We have the biggest three: The ABC *SuperSign*—thanks to my former broadcast connections. Couldn't get the Fox screen though. Bitch wouldn't help. Second biggest, the Walmart screen. I've managed some chaos during their shift change. And the third biggest—the *SilverCast*, is smack dab in the middle, covering the whole block."

"That's it?" Donovan made a face.

"Are you kidding?"

"You have more than three, right?"

She reached over to punch his arm. "Yes, we have three more.

The one next to MTV—that was the easiest. And the Clear Channel, well, let's just say I cashed in favors from my radio days. Last but not least, we have the one on Broadway, known as the *Express*. Super impressive. Seven screens, 8,500 square feet and the highest-resolution screen of most of them. You can see this screen from space!"

"What about the Reuters Ribbon and the NASDAQ tube," Donovan said with a straight face.

"Are you high? What we have is awesome. Besides, the *security* on those bitches—"

Holding up both hands, he shook his head. "All good. I'm just busting your nuts. Really. I'm impressed."

She stared at him. "We've been putting these deals together for months, Donovan. I mean, *months*. It takes a lot—"

"I got it. So, run me down—real quick like, the rest of the process."

Taking a deep breath, she continued, "That relay we talked about will kick to our primary source. The firewall is tight, the connections are solid, and the signal is redundant to, oh about...*forty-five* times. So, try as they may, they'll never be able to trace it—certainly not in the amount of time we'll be *live*, anyway."

"Which is..." Donovan leaned forward, waving a finger in circles.

"About one-minute-forty-five seconds. That's from the time the slate starts, followed by the shot of her...until the *clown* is out of the picture."

-She looked to Ken.

"Don't look at me," he laughed. "I'll be in the air."

"The beauty of pre-record," Donovan smirked.

"*Anyhow*," she continued, "The glitch kicks back off just shy of the two-minute limit. It's a safety valve of sorts, put into place for something exactly like this." She smiled, pleased with herself.

"About?"

"No. *Exactly* at one-minute-forty-five seconds, we dump the feed," Mo confirmed with a smile.

Ken added, "It will take most anyone about thirty seconds to fully comprehend what's happening. This way, the meat of the message—nearly a full minute, will be seen while they scramble to *pull the plug*."

"Nice," Donovan slowly nodded.

"Perfectly choreographed and untraceable," she said.

"Audio?"

"Yes," Mo high-fived Margo. "While there isn't *usually* audio, we're providing a wireless feed to several rented speakers placed in the area—basically, a handful of windows at a variety of locations. And yes, untraceable."

"*Plus*, we're taking the signal and relaying the message via a special Wi-Fi satellite to all television screens within a square block...oh, only every single square inch where our cameras are watching," Margo said with a grin.

They all looked at her.

"Hey, I've been quiet this whole time, letting y'all swing your..." she looked to Mo, "Well, *show* your goods," she said, leaning over to kiss Mo.

"Thank you, baby," Mo said. "Better go check on our girl."

As Margot left the room, Donovan nodded to Mo before turning to Ken. "How many cameras have we managed to accumulate?"

"Dozens." Ken said, looking to Sean.

"Oh, uh, last count, we have...almost 300. Okay, 291, to be exact. We'll hit 300 inside the month and are on track to have something like 600 by fall."

Donovan drained the last of his cappuccino and licked his lips. "Perfectly *delicious*," he smiled.

Margot returned, barefoot and smiling. "She's still out. I put enough solution in her water to drop Ken," she said, raising an eyebrow toward the well-built bodyguard. Then, checking her watch, added, "I'd say she'll be out for maybe another hour. It was a good call to see her up and around; proved your handiwork was all sewn up," Mo grinned.

"Yeah, to see if she..." Margot said, holding her index finger up so they'd wait for it, "Could *stomach* the process."

They laughed.

"Damn girl," Donovan said. "A herd of cattle wouldn't wake her. In fact, it'd damn near take an *explosion.*" Opening his mouth, he raised his eyebrows—feigning surprise, as both girls smacked Donovan.

"I'm just f'n evil," he sneered.

6

THE NANNY

THE INTERROGATION ROOM looked like it did on television; cold, bland and nondescript. The only thing that wasn't like TV was a respectable amount of daylight—albeit partially hidden behind a small frosted window. A tired coffee-maker on a table in the corner completed the homey look.

The odor of burnt coffee hung in the air, as nanny Stephanie Marcheaux nervously fiddled with a child's bright pink hair band. The only joy in the room appeared to be the rhinestones that encrusted the ornament. Abigail was wearing it shortly before she disappeared.

A uniformed police woman stood motionless at the door, staring at the window like she could see out. She couldn't.

The silent room was suddenly jolted to life when the Mayor, his aide—Chief of Police Davis, and a man in an expensive suit entered. No one spoke, as Stephanie looked at all of them one at a time. Fear radiated from her, and she began tearing up the minute Mayor Burton sat down across from her.

He began speaking softly and emphasizing several words. "Stephanie, *don't* cry. I'm sure it was an *accident*. Just tell me *exactly* what happened. And *please* do not leave out a *single* detail. Okay?"

For effect, he patted her hands which were clasped together so tightly it appeared she could break the plastic band she had been holding in a choke-hold, since she had arrived.

"Mayor Burton, I'm so sorry. Really. I had no idea what happened…" she said with a squeak, unsuccessfully choking back tears.

"I understand," he whispered, looking around for tissues. "Just take a deep breath."

His assistant grabbed a box from a corner table and handed the box to Stephanie.

"Thank you. Okay, here is exactly what happened," she said, slowly composing herself. However, she just sat, saying nothing; perhaps trying to catch her breath.

"Don't worry, Stephanie; you're among friends," Burton continued with the calm approach. "Take your time and collect your thoughts. This is very important. Understood?"

"Yes, of course. I took Abigail to the park, just as I do every single morning. We were minding our business, watching the ducks in the pond, we stopped by the zoo to see the panda, and…you know, just enjoying the day."

Burton's patience, though pushed, was holding. "Go on."

"We had just arrived to the Dairy Visitor gift shop…after leaving the zoo. There was a race, I think…because there were a bunch of runners…and some *circus* type event going on. A couple of clowns were tying balloons for the kids."

"Clowns? Like circus clowns?" Chief Davis finally spoke.

Caught off guard, Stephanie turned and stared, before regaining her composure. "Yes, circus. And that was when this stranger—a woman, came up to me. She was yelling *Help me, help me…I've lost my little girl!*'"

Burton looked from one person to the other, while the Chief squinted. He appeared deep in thought, but said nothing, and let the Mayor try his method.

Burton's aide took notes, scribbling down every word.

The suit said nothing.

"I've lost my girl? Burton asked. That's what she said?"

Stephanie nodded.

"And where was Abigail at this time?"

"She was right in front of me," she sniffed, wiping her nose. "Needless to say, my instincts kicked in and I turned my attention to the woman."

The Chief nearly barked, "But you were turned facing this stranger, correct?"

"Yes, well, I was facing Abigail...because I was following her—"

"Wait!" Burton said. "Isn't she usually either on her bike, or at the very least...holding your hand?"

Startled, she said, "Oui. I mean, yes, yes, of course. But you know, often, I'll let her stroll out in front of me."

Davis asked, "How far?"

"How far...what?"

"How *far* would you *ordinarily* allow her to...*stroll ahead of you?*" Davis impatiently asked.

Burton raised a hand toward Davis then patted her hand. "It's okay. Just answer, Stephanie."

"Ordinarily, I would say that she is sometimes ten or twenty yards in front of me."

"Okay. And how far would you say that she was...in front of you *before* she disappeared?" Burton asked.

She took a moment to visualize the scene.

"Thirty, maybe forty yards ahead."

Burton's patience was thinning. "So, *forty* yards," he said, looking to Davis. "And where was your cellphone at this time?"

Looking down, she swallowed hard.

After a long silence, Burton said, "I'm waiting."

"In my hand," she whispered.

His nostrils flaired. "Why?"

"I was...checking my..." he hesitated, dropping her head toward her lap. "*Soap Crush.*"

Burton slammed the table with both fists, as pens flew and a cup of coffee spilled. He ignored it—his eyes, not budging from her. "If I've told you once...I've told you a hundred times...you are NOT allowed to…to surf the web, check your email, or do one *goddammed thing except*…take calls from either myself *or* Mrs. Burton!"

She fought hard not to burst into tears, but felt confident it wouldn't get her any sympathy.

Burton's aide cleaned the table and was tossing the remnants in a trashcan when her phone buzzed in her pocket. Burton whipped his head in her direction.

Reading the screen, she said, "Sorry, sir. It's your secretary. They're ready for you in the press—"

"TEXT her that…" he hesitated. "Sorry. Please text her that we'll be there shortly. Thank you."

Turning back to Stephanie, he worked to regain his composure.

"Okay. We will forget…for the *moment*…that you directly disobeyed the ONE order I've *ever* given you. So, allow me to refresh. This stranger comes up to you…and screams for you to help her find her child."

"Sorry, Lukas," Chief Davis interrupted. "You said the stranger came up to *you*. Not anyone else, correct?"

Stephanie looked confused. "Um, I'm not sure if it was *just* me, but…" she's searching, "But as far as I know, she was just asking me. It happened so fast. All I know is one minute Abigail and I are walking through the park, the next minute a strange woman—not that she was strange, just…anyway, she screamed hysterically that her daughter…"

Suddenly, she stopped and frowned, looking at her trembling hands.

"What?" Burton barked.

"I can't say for sure that it was her *daughter* she was screaming about…just her little girl. But the odd thing was what happened after. I turned around to see Abigail was fine."

"What?"

"I remember turning around to see her with two or three other children. I think. They were with this clown who was twisting up balloons. But I remember the woman was pulling on my sleeve, but when I turned around, it was as though…nothing mattered."

"What do you mean, Ms. Marchaeux?" the Chief leaned forward on both elbows, "By nothing mattered."

"What I mean is…when I turned back around to attend to her—knowing that Abi was fine, he expression was…*innocupe*. Uh, vacant. Her face was just…vacant, like suddenly, it didn't matter."

Burton looked from Davis to The Suit—who had yet to say anything.

"She looked…*vacant,*" Burton said with little emotion.

"Yes. I know it seems, well, odd, but her expression just seemed to, I don't know, be like…*it doesn't matter*. That's when I turned back around and wondered what she was looking at."

She stopped speaking again, and nearly stopped breathing, as she stared at the band still in her hand.

Burton shouted, "What?"

She snapped back, but this time, she was spent. Her lack of reaction confirmed as much. "When I turned back around the clown and the balloons were…gone. But Abi was coming towards me…with a pink…" She looked at the pink hair band in her hands. "A pink giraffe balloon."

Clearly on the edge of losing all patience, Burton said, "And?"

"And as I turned back around to attend to the woman still pulling on my sleeve, she wasn't there."

"What?" Davis snorted—accidentally spitting on the table. "Sorry. But wait, you said she had *just* been pulling on your sleeve!"

"No, it was a blind man. A man with a cane and sunglasses. He was disoriented and—"

"What in the *hell* are you *talking* about, Stephanie," Burton shouted. "A BLIND MAN…is replaced by a…screaming *vacant strange* woman…with *no* little girl?"

The room was silent.

Standing, Burton barked, "What the *fuck,* Stephanie?" Pacing, he ran a hand through his hair then across his sweaty forehead.

"Wait," she said, cocking her head to one side. "The blind man, I assume…came from nowhere," she said, "I was so confused, so I turned back around and that's when…Abigail was gone!"

Burton sat down, and just as she was about to start crying again, he tried to level the moment with a long, deep breath.

"I swear to Holy God above…if you start crying, I will slap you so hard, you'll *WISH* it were the *clown that kidnapped you.*"

Davis snapped his fingers. "Wait!"

Turning to the Chief, Stephanie whispered, "Qu'est-ce que c'est?"

"We're asking the questions," Burton spat, holding up a hand.

"I know you were just joking, Lukas, but…" Davis said, turning to her. "But let me get this straight. You said, a hysterical woman is screaming and pulling on your sleeve, you turn to see Abi—who is fine, then you turn back and she's…nonplused. You then turn *back* and the clown is gone, but Abigail's coming toward *you*…then, as you turn *back* around, you come to find a blind man…but since you're further confused, you turn *back* around to see no clown…and no Abigail."

She managed a tiny nod.

"So…" Burton said slowly, "When you turned back *again*…where was the blind man?"

Squinting, she bit her lip, trying not to cry. After a long beat, she whispered, "Gone."

7

THE CALL

CLARE WAS STUCK—EMOTIONALLY and physically. Construction on the FDR, near Roosevelt University, had traffic at a standstill. She looked through the darkened windows which separated she and the driver. His animated hands threw exclamation points to other drivers who were trying to cut him off.

Her stomach was in knots and her heart was pounding. Her hands were shaking and her head felt slow—like she was underwater. Tears began to pool in her eyes and she wanted to scream. But deep inside, she knew that while screaming may not help, it would certainly make her feel better.

Or, would it?

All she could focus on was holding her *baby*. She wanted her life to return to normal and become real again.

And she wanted a stiff drink.

Feeling the small confines of the vehicle closing in on her, she tried to keep from feeling that she was being suffocated. Lightheaded, her vision was narrowing.

Get yourself together, Clare, she shouted in her head. *You won't be doing anyone any good if you loose your mind.*

She tried counting to ten, wishing the heart-wrenching situation would end.

Not the case.

Squeezing her eyes closed, she tried picturing happy memories. But all that appeared were moments with her little girl in her arms.

At the beach, playing.

At a friends home, playing.

At a birthday party, singing and playing.

Doesn't help, dammit, she cried silently. *This is the worse nightmare I can imagine. Someone please wake me up!*

Taking a long, cleansing breath, she opened her eyes, picked up the private cellphone and dialed again.

A voice answered.

"Well, hello stranger. What's up?"

Her heart fluttered for an instant. She was surprised, yet grateful he had picked up. "I've rung you five times."

"Six, actually," he said. "I was out back. Working."

"Chopping wood?"

"You bet. Best therapy you can get. Without babbling to a stranger on a couch."

"No doubt."

"You okay?"

"No," she said, taking time to breathe and reconcile her mixed emotions. *Keep yourself straight,* she thought.

He let the silence pass without a push.

Finally, "Abigail is missing."

Now, his heart skipped a beat, and for an entirely different reason, because he knew what that meant.

"How long?"

"A few hours."

"Could she have wandered off?"

"Doubtful."

"Really?"

"Certain," she said, nearly holding her breath. "A mother just knows."

"Understood."

He reached for his pocket, took out a cigarette and a Zippo.

"Maybe this call is premature," he said, with a question in his statement.

"Maybe you're being insensitive," she said, meaning more than she said.

Blowing rings into the air, he absently watched them drift toward the porch roof. "Could be," he said, after letting a dozen seconds hold her attention. "Your husband must have the best in the biz on this by now."

"His heart's in it—just not sure his *balls* are."

They shared an uncomfortable chuckle.

"Not sure I should say this," she stuttered. "But I'm not certain he'd do...*whatever* it took...to find her."

"Sure he would."

"Not like you."

Taking a drag before crushing the butt, he tried to imagine what she was implying.

And what he could be in for.

"Not *whatever* it took," she added.

"Perhaps."

Silence.

"What would he think if he knew you called me."

"You mean...before giving *him* a chance to be the hero?"

"He's a man. That's his daughter. He will certainly move heaven and earth—"

"He's so goddamned *political*...that he would have have to precisely measure all audience reactions and see if the data..."

"Clare?"

Taking a slow, deep breath, she tried desperately to keep from saying or feeling too much. "Yes?"

"He will. Maybe not as fast. But...just give him a chance."

More silence.

She fidgeted with her expensive necklace.

He fumbled for the right words.

"That doesn't mean..." he paused, "I won't help. Because you know I'd do anything for you."

"Thank you."

A horn blasted outside, and Jerry slammed the brakes—throwing up a hand to apologize to Clare. She ignored it.

"What is she now...seven?" he asked.

"Nine."

"Geez time flies."

"You have no idea," she said, reaching for a cigarette from her purse. Pushing the lighter in the center console, she waited—staring for it to pop up.

"And you've passed the point of the itch."

Inhaling a long drag, she enjoyed the rush and the smile on her face—both of which felt strange at the moment. "Cute. And maybe true," she said, taking a second and a third drag—doing everything she could to numb her senses. "No, I'm happy. She's wonderful... and the city's great."

"And Lukas?"

"Same. Scrambling for the top."

"What's the gold ring *this* time?"

"President."

"Of the Country Club?"

She chuckled and cleared her throat before answering. "The United States."

He whistled. "Cheese whiz."

"Cornball."

"Sassy-pants."

While they enjoyed the levity, the heft of the call continued to weigh deeply.

She sighed, "Carter, I need you."

He stopped twirling his silver lighter. "You need...my *help*."

The inference felt palpable.

"Yes. Your help."

"Why me?"

"Don't be coy. Why else would I call you," she said, grinding out the cigarette. "You're ruthless."

"And you're heartless."

There's a long sigh on the other end. "That was a summer fling," she said, feeling a second flutter.

"It was more," he said, feeling exposed.

"No, it wasn't. And you weren't going any further."

"Maybe."

"Doubtful."

"True," he said. "Probably."

Traffic had cleared and they were nearing Gracie Mansion.

"Sorry. I shouldn't have…" he stuttered. "I don't even know what I was—"

"Carter, that was then. And not to be corny, but we'll always have those memories. But right now—"

"Of course," he interrupted. "Silly."

"Not silly," she said, taking a moment to gather herself. "Okay, it took everything in me to call you. And I did. So, you *have* to know I wouldn't have called you if it weren't *extremely* important." She fought to keep from crying.

"I know it did. And you wouldn't. And I will."

"Will what?"

"Do whatever I can to help."

"I know. Thank you. And let's keep this quiet. For the moment, anyway."

"Of course. I'm just a call and a flight away," he said. "And Clare?"

"Yes, Carter."

"She'll be fine. Trust me."

"I do. With my life."

The silence felt deafening, as she stopped to let that sink in. "With *our* lives."

"Call me."

"I will," she smiled. "Probably tonight. Certainly tomorrow."

"And you'll want to let him know. Before too long. Nobody likes surprises. Especially the competition."

She tried to ignore that. "You know how ugly this world has gotten, and how calculating this office is. As disturbing as it may be, I have to imagine the worse."

He didn't have a comeback, so he left it alone.

Approaching the mansion, she saw the Press setting up along the gates surrounding her home. "Shit," she blurted.

"What?"

"The vultures have landed. At the house. I've gotta go. Thank you, Lucky."

"You got it," he said, listening for the phone to disconnect. Next, he let his mind fight with his heart.

But only for a moment.

8

THE INTERROGATION

MAYOR BURTON, his aide, Chief Davis, and the quiet attorney stood huddled on the other side of the two-way mirror, while Nanny Marcheaux sweated it out in the interrogation room. Her head was in her hands.

"Can you believe this *shit*?" Mayor asked no one in particular.

"Not exactly," Davis mumbled.

"Perfectly, actually," Attorney Steven Glass finally spoke. "Classic case of too much pressure, too much information. She was sidelined. Hoodwinked."

The four looked at one another, as Burton said to his aid, "Go help set up the press. Tell 'em I'll be there in five."

She disappeared with a nod.

When the door was closed, Steve Glass spoke again. "Damage here's minimal. She'll take the fall for irresponsibility. You'll explain it was…an orchestrated operation, not her fault, etc."

Davis slowly gave a nod. "Agreed. This was well-planned. Using a crowded park, an enormous event, and some crafty acting."

"No shit," Burton mumbled, absently staring at his train wreck for a nanny through the glass.

"A bat-shit crazy woman, a circus clown, and distracting a kid with *balloons,*" Davis said. "Jesus, why not add a bowl of candy and a video game?"

Burton snorted.

"That's a trifecta, gentlemen. And stacking all that crazy inside a well-publicized and heavily attended 5K race? But adding the blind guy? Brilliant," Glass chuckled.

Burton cut him a look. "Can we stop praising the assholes who dreamt this scheme up and get out and catch 'em?"

"Sorry, Lukas," Glass said, "You're right." Turning to Davis, he added, "And we will, right Chief?"

Davis gave a lazy salute.

"I don't know what they want...and I'm sure it's gonna hurt... but for the love of Christ, let's not forget my girl's out there somewhere in the hands of a *fucking maniac!*"

Davis tapped the brakes. "One thing at a time. Now, all we have to do is..."

Burton waited.

Glass asked, "Yes?"

Burton leaded forward. "*Aaaand...*"

"Okay, so clowns are out there every day at that freaking fair. It'll be hard to identify that one, but I'll ask about any 'extras' around that morning. A shouting woman and a blind guy? That'll be tough," Davis scratched his chin.

"Right. So, the way I see it is—" Burton began.

Davis interrupted. "We've got surveillance all around the park. And there has to be *someone* who saw *something* out of the ordinary. All those people? We'll put it together," he said with confidence.

"And we wait..." Glass added, "For the ransom note."

Burton's head whipped around. "Right. There's that." Checking his watch, he said, "I've got to get out there. The press'll have a hey day with this."

"And on the cusp of your running for—"

"Don't remind me."

"No, this is good," Glass said. "We'll use this to our favor. When the time comes, tug at the heart...family values 'n shit."

"Twisted, as always, Glass," Davis said, shaking his head. "But pretty much true."

Burton started toward the door, "Alright…"

Davis tapped his shoulder, nodding toward the glass. "What'ya want me to do with her? Well, besides the obvious."

Burton's hesitation and accompanying icy stare got their attention. "Tell her she can go. She needs to get home. And sit. I'll, rather, Clare and I will figure it out later. Can you do that for me, Jacob?"

Putting on his cap, he said, "Sure thing," then left.

Burton was about out the door when Glass grabbed his arm. "No really. What about her?" he stared in Burton's eyes.

Burton stared for a long beat before answering. "What do *you* think?"

9

THE PRONOUNCEMENT

MOMENTS LATER, Burton and his team were on the front steps of City Hall—a usual vantage point for any number of political occasions, but this time, it was an announcement that the Mayor not only hated making, but one his New York family would hate to hear. As the Mayor's only child, and a familiar face to the city, Abigail had become very special to her hometown.

A sizable crowd had collected, and cameras and lights from all local news stations were in place. Reporters pressed toward the front, hoping to be the first to break the story. Chief Davis held up both hands.

"Quiet please. The Mayor will make a short announcement and then we have work to do."

The crowd murmured, closing in.

"And there will be *no* questions at this time. There's too little information thus far, but trust us...we'll give you all the information you could possibly need...the *minute* we get it."

He gave a nod and a smile to Burton who was talking close to the ear of his aide.

"New York City's Mayor Lukas Burton," Davis said, stepping aside.

"Thanks, Chief. As Chief of Police Davis just said, we have

very little *substantial* information to report at this very moment. However, it's become painfully clear that my daughter, Abigail is missing. And we currently assume—we have to assume it's a…kidnapping."

The crowd erupted into shouts and questions. Burton held his hands up, waiting for the noise to stop.

"At approximately, 10:15 this morning—while playing in the park with our nanny, Abigail disappeared. In plain sight. Within moments, we had an entire battalion of our city's finest, scouring Central Park and the surrounding areas. Unfortunately, inside these past…" he hesitated—not only to check his watch, but to buy the time he needed to regain his composure.

Cameras clicked furiously, catching an unguarded tearful moment certain to make the front page of all the local newspapers. Clearing his throat, he continued.

"Inside these past several hours, we've looked, we've asked, and we've set into motion…a process to locate my little girl. If *anyone* has *any* information leading to her disappearance and… assumed abduction, we want to hear from you."

"Is there a reward?" A voice shouted from the pack of reporters.

Chief Davis expected this—as did everyone at the Mayor's office, and as he scanned the audience, he saw the voice was a reporter from the Post. Looking at one another, Davis and Burton realized that in all the frenzy they hadn't discussed that issue. It would be the Commissioner's call—given he would have to approve the deal.

"We'll have details on that inside the hour. That's it for now. Thank you for your time. And your prayers."

With that, Burton was off the steps and down the hallway, leaving a crush of shouting questions behind.

MAYOR BURTON SAT QUIETLY at his desk, staring out the window, trying to imagine what his little girl might be going through at that very moment. And how scared she must be.

Gritting his teeth, he thought, *If anything happens to her, I will take whomever is responsible and tear them limb from limb. Then kill them.*

Having served in the United States Marine Corp, he had seen his fair share of terror. The blood, guts and travesty of warfare had scarred and numbed his sensibilities. His *modus operandi* was more about "doing what's needed" rather than considering "doing what's right." That vicious tenacity had served him well in any number of situations. And he was sure the same would become available, as the opportunity arose.

He stared at a picture frame on his expansive mahogany desk. It had been sitting at that same spot since he had come to office. While he had many other photos—highlighting all sort of dignitaries who had visited his great city, this one three-paneled frame contained some of his favorite and most memorable photos.

The first displayed he and Clare's wedding which took place in her hometown of Charleston, SC. It was a classic wedding with all the bells & whistles. He had been married before and would have been perfectly happy with a quick stop at the Justice downtown, but Clare wouldn't hear of anything but the very biggest wedding possible. He allowed his memory only one brief moment to reflect upon his first wife—his high-school sweetheart, who died much too young from breast cancer.

The middle photograph was taken during a celebration of Abigail's eighth birthday a year ago. Clare and Abi were both wearing pink tiaras and vamping for the camera. He smiled, recalling having captured that moment just before she blew out the candles on an enormous cake shaped like a giraffe—her favorite animal. It was Burton's favorite picture of both of his girls.

The last photo was from his Marine Corps days, back in the late '70's and early '80's. His buddies, from a wide variety of backgrounds and levels of rank, were inseparable, living every day to protect one another. They were nicknamed: *Radio, Bulldog, Hollowpoint, Tequila* and *Snake*—Burton's nickname. A gunner, Hector Gonzalez, aka *Tequila*, was the only one from the crew who didn't make it back.

He sat there thinking of everything he had to be grateful for.

And how lucky he was to have accomplished what he had. As he looked back at the photo of Clare and Abigail, his heart was heavy. Reaching for the phone, he dialed the Mansion, assuming that their maid, Francine, would answer.

It rang four times before Clare came on, "Hello?"

"Hon, it's me. Are you all right? Well, considering everything," he asked with a smile.

"Hello love. And yes, I suppose so. Just waiting. The hardest part…I guess."

They shared the safety of silence.

"Yes, it is. But we are doing *everything* in our power…" Trailing off, his eye caught one of the six television screens which adorned the wall across the room.

"Ho-lee-shit!" he blurted—his eyes nearly popping from his head.

"What?"

Leaning forward and not fully comprehending what he was seeing, his mouth hung open, as he slowly stood.

"Lukas, is that what…" she whispered, seeing the same thing that had grabbed his attention. The television at the end of her kitchen counter was on but silent.

She choked back tears at the image and gasped, "Lukas, no!"

"Oh my God," he whispered—the sound crawling up from his chest like an angry dog.

Just then, the door burst open as Chief Davis, Burton's secretary and other personnel poured into the room. The look of panic on their faces expressed pure terror. Davis ran to the screens, searching for the remote.

Approaching the screen, Burton barked, "Turn up the sound *now!*"

10

THE BROADCAST

TIMES SQUARE WAS one of the busiest, most congested intersections in all of New York City. In the country. Millions passed through the several block corridor every year, shopping, eating, people-watching, taking selfies, and staring up at the bright, colorful images that covered literally acres of digital landscape.

Today was no different, as those flashing boards of 24-hour advertisements displayed something altogether different. The images on the screen were at one moment, tender—at the next, horrifying.

There, on seven of the biggest, brightest screens in the world, a countdown simultaneously began. The numbers were enormous and in blood red, set against a black background. A thunderous boom sounded from the area, bouncing off the towering high-rises and in sync to the numbers being flashed.

5...4...3...2...1

The first image was a sleeping Abigail. The camera was so close the people on the street could practically count her eyelashes. The music that accompanied the scenes was a mixture of classical and techno, making for a nerve-wracking combination.

Suddenly, the scene cut to her playing in the park. Smiling, she walked alongside a woman, holding her hand. The background and surrounding people were blurred so only she and the woman were in focus.

Cut-to: Abigail, standing alongside several other children, surrounded by what appeared to be circus clowns. The video was cut sporadically and the camera work, while shaky, was well edited.

Cut-to: Abigail whipping her head, as though being called.

Cut-to: Abigail's frightened expression, as he started to run, before the image shifted into slow motion.

Cut-to: Abigail appeared to be pulled from the picture frame.

The scene returned to a sleeping Abigail, surrounded by lots of large pink pillows. Beside her was a pink giraffe-shaped balloon.

The camera then cut to a large clown sitting in the middle of a nondescript space. The room was dark. His eyes were wild. His mouth seemed to move mechanically, making it hard to determine whether it was a machine or a man.

The clown looked surreal and oddly terrifying—similar to the wicked clown in Stephen King's film, *It*.

People in Times Square stopped and watched—their faces, frozen in doubt and fear.

While the maniacal clown spoke, closed-captioning on the bottom of the screens transcribed what was being said:

Mayor Burton we have your beautiful daughter. We want her to remain that way. As do you. You have 48 hours to meet our demands, or your little girl will literally vanish into thin air. Those details will arrive at your office inside the next 15 minutes. Be careful. Don't be stupid. We are watching your every move.

The video dissolved to a sleeping Abigail, then morphed into old newsreel footage of a mushroom cloud during the bombing at Hiroshima, then slowly faded to black.

The various ads, which had been running just moments ago, resumed, and faces by the hundreds went from staring at the screens above their heads, to cellphones in their hands and pockets—dumbfounded by what they had just witnessed.

11

THE PARENTS

LUKAS BURTON WAS SPEECHLESS. Clare, still on the other end of the phone, was sobbing. Their maid, Francine, had her hands on Clare's shoulders trying to comfort her.

"Honey, please try and remain calm. We are going to find these maniacs and bring them down," Burton said, waving for the Chief to cut the sound and clear the room.

Davis followed the orders, shuffling them out the door.

Burton snapped his fingers, pointing to both his secretary and Darcy McMillan—his Communications Director and Press Advisor, motioning for them to stay. They took a seat, as he walked to the window to stare at his city.

"Lukas, *please* tell me she was just sleeping," Clare sobbed.

Lukas didn't have all the answers, but he had instincts. And both of those elements—while crucial, didn't need to be discussed in grand detail right now.

Not with a hysterical wife in the mix, he thought.

"She was just sleeping, love. They haven't harmed her. They are certainly thugs, but all they want is money. And we will give it to them."

Catching her breath, she whimpered, "You haven't heard anything else?"

"No. What you and I just witnessed is all I know. But according to the message..." he checked his watch, "That information should be here soon."

He listened to her cry—trying to remain strong, and felt so badly for her. For them.

"You go. I know you have your hands full," she said, "Just keep in touch? Let me now *anything*."

"Of course, love. The *minute* I get word, you'll be my first call. Love you."

Hanging up, he clenched his jaw, took a deep breath, and joined his team across the room.

"I don't need to tell you just how *grave* this situation..." he frowned, "Well, that's not the best choice of words."

"We understand," Chief Davis said.

Looking from his team to the screen, he saw that both ABC and FOX affiliates had already cobbled together a story consisting of surveillance camera footage and cellphone video from tourists. Thanks to a CBS reporter already on location doing a story on the animated characters in Times Square, the story was live on their network in the time it took for Lukas to hang up with Clare. Shaking his head, he mumbled, "This is *one* time I'm glad those vultures were nearby. We'll be able to use that footage to decipher who's behind this."

"Yes, sir. It will be a tremendous help," Davis said. "While you were on the phone, I was putting in calls to our best teams. We are assembling at HQ. As soon as you've...given us your orders, I'll head over."

Burton nodded. All eyes were on him. "I suppose..." he began, working diligently to keep his emotions in check. "I suppose the best thing to do is to pray that she's okay. After that, I think we have some serious ass-kicking to perform."

The levity was a weak attempt to remain strong. "I don't get the significance of Hiroshima. I doubt this is some form of...political retribution or..." Burton trailed off.

"Sir, it's money," Davis said. "That was just...dramatics."

"After all, sir, it is the *theater* district," Darcy added with a tight smile.

Everyone looked at her.

"Sorry, sir. That was…ridiculous. My nerves. I was just…"

"Understood," Burton waved it off. "We're all on edge."

"Sir," Margaret interrupted, "Let Darcy and I begin crafting what we need—what *you* need the public to know about this. Between the time we get that started and when any instructions arrive—"

"Thank you, Mrs. Childress," he said with a wave. "That's a fine idea. And Darcy?" Burton turned to his new Press rep. "Needless to say, we'll need to contain any *fear* this may cause people. What I mean is, we want to be sure everyone knows this is aimed at me and our family. Not the city. We don't need mainstream panic hitting the streets."

"Yes, Sir. Of course."

Removing his sport coat, Burton loosened his tie, then looked to the two standing there. "Well? That release isn't going to write itself. Get the draft started and I'll punch it up when you're done."

Eagerly nodding, they left. The Chief joined Burton as he sat behind his desk, looking ten years older since just this morning.

"Lukas, those bastards will slip up. They always do. It's just money, and there's plenty of that. You and I just need to keep our heads about us."

"Thanks, Jacob. I know they do. And we will," he said. "That bomb has me puzzled. And what's with the clown suit?"

"Like was said, theatrics. We've seen it before. Remember the bank heists last summer? The idiots dressed like nuns?"

"Those guys were idiots," Burton nodded, breaking the first smile of the morning. "Remember the one guy who tripped on his skirt running from the scene, only to stumble over his buddy? We had 'em before they hit the Holland Tunnel."

"Botched, right?" Davis laughed. "How about the moron who dressed like—what was it, Superman or Batman…who walked into the jewelry district and held up that diamond joint on 47th Street?

Remember how the owner pulled a *bigger* shotgun on the perp, blowing a hole through the idiot's cape, taking half his arm with it?"

Burton shook his head. "I appreciate the diversion, Jacob. And you're right, theatrics. But until we know more, well, we're just swinging at the breeze."

Davis watched Burton chew the inside of his cheek. He waited, knowing something significant would pop up shortly.

A knock at the door jarred them both.

It was Margaret. "Sir, a package just arrived at your home."

"Okay. Clare's there, she can—"

She interrupted, "It was delivered by a *drone*."

Confusion crossed his face. "What?"

"Evidently one of those delivery drones that online companies use. Sadly, it was gone before anyone could grab it."

Davis snorted, "Sneaky bastards."

"Where's the package?" Burton asked.

"On the front steps. Bomb techs have been called in to…" she stopped as Burton and Davis nearly knocked her down running out the door and down the hallway.

12

THE DELIVERY

DONOVAN and his team sat comfortably in the enormous and expensive leather couch. They were high atop the recent chaos, watching a wall of screens. The story had already begun running by all the local news stations. In fact, they were stepping over each other to put their particular spin on a headline that was certain to capture the attention of the city—and the world, in no time.

On another screen, Donovan watched the closed circuit feed from a camera that was perched atop a building at 88th and East End Avenue. It was hidden from view and had a bird's eye view of the Mayor's home.

Donovan enjoyed the chaos of the moment. Looking to the live satellite feed which was being uplinked from the drone, he saw the view as it left Gracie Mansion. Soon it would be out of visual range. Fortunately, he had a second team who released the drone from a nearby rooftop and instantly disappeared.

"Play that back, will ya?" Donovan asked Sean who was busy typing on two different laptops.

"Sure boss. *That* screen will stay live," Sean pointed to one screen, while typing with his other hand. "But watch screen twelve, right about…now."

The video feed blurred—as it sped in reverse. Seconds later, it was playing in real time.

The room watched as the drone launched from a rooftop directly across the street from Gracie Mansion. It shot straight up to hide itself, hovered over the house—locating the drop zone, and quickly descended. The camera saw two arms detach and release a black box, then retracted the arms and shot straight up, just as two uniformed policemen came running across the driveway. Attempting to jump and grab the landing gear, they weren't able to catch it, as the drone was too fast. They continued to watch as the treetops of the park surrounding the mansion quickly dissolved into murky brown water of the East River. The wide angle of the camera captured the small Mill Rock Island as it whizzed by.

"Quality's great," Margo said. "And you're good at that."

"It's 4K," Sean replied with a smile. Returning to his laptop, he prepared his next act. "And thanks. I love these things."

As he hit pause, Mo looked at him and frowned. "Hey!"

"Hold on. I've got the feed paused. Now, watch this..." Sean said, controlling the flight of the drone from his other laptop.

"This is live. I'm controlling it via satellite."

"The feed's so clear," Mo mumbled.

Sean manually spun the camera in a 360, so the group could see Manhattan disappear into the distance.

"View's as good as from my Bell Ranger," Donovan said.

"True. But this baby can get much closer and into much tighter spaces," Sean said, typing something on his laptop. A second later, the drone spun back around, just in time to fly right over the top of the Triborough Bridge, missing it by feet.

"Show off," Margo chirped.

Rikers Island came into view, and as the drone's camera panned to the right, LaGuardia appeared in the distance.

Donovan snapped his fingers, and the screen went black. He looked at Sean and smiled. "Nicely done."

"Hate to see it go, but the best way not to track it..." Sean began.

"Is to blow it," Donovan finished. "And preferably over the deepest part of the East River."

"Hashtag *Boom!*" Sean laughed.

"It's what we do," Donovan said, looking up to see Ken exiting the elevator to join the group.

Setting down a large duffle bag by the door, he greeted the group. "S'up?"

"Just watching Sean's home movies," Margo said, smacking him on the arm, as she headed to the kitchen.

"I'd ask how it went, but I can see," Donovan said, reaching for a high-five. "Flawless."

Ken smacked Donovan's hand, then Sean's and took a seat on the couch. "Yeah, not a hitch. Lifted off from the Heliport on 30th and was there and back without incident. Like nothing happened. The *distraction* on 44th was a nice touch."

"Nothing like a dumpster fire," Donovan grinned. "Big flames —nobody gets hurt."

"Copy that."

"Needed some *justification* for a chopper to be overhead, right?" Ken nodded with a grin.

"Good to have friends in all places," Mo said.

"Hey, Sean, do me a favor and replay the video," Donovan said.

"Sure." Typing a few strokes on a wi-fi keyboard, he said, "It'll be up on 7."

The countdown played, followed by the images.

"You wanna hear it too?"

Donovan shook his head. "Just watch it."

"For the *twentieth* time," Margo joked entering the room with a bottle of water.

The images are perfect, Donovan thought. *Heart-warming. No details to give us away. Just enough close-ups to unnerve, but not enough to convict.*

Looking to Ken, he said, "Nice work…*clown.*"

Ken smirked.

"And the makeup?" Donovan gave a thumbs up to Margo.

"It's what I do," she smiled.

"It's hard to tell if he was real or a mannequin," Mo said.

"In real life, too," Margo laughed.

Ken swung behind him, trying to catch Margo, but missed. Donovan leaned forward, enjoying the performance. Holding up his hands, he said, "Here comes the best part."

The group settled.

"Wait for it."

All eyes were on the screen, as the camera zoomed in extra close to Abigail before morphing into a mushroom cloud explosion.

A sniffle from across the room grabbed everyone's attention, and all heads turned to see Abigail huddled in the corner of the room, staring at the large screen.

A tear slid down her cheek, as she quietly said, "Am I going to explode?"

13

THE DILEMMA

MAYOR BURTON STOOD in the living room of their home—his arm around a shaking Clare. The Chief and his crew waited a good distance from the spot where the black box was delivered. Given the recent spectacle in Times Square, they couldn't be too careful. NYPD Bomb Squad had set up along the long, circuitous driveway, putting up several barriers to protect the 217-year old Federal-styled mansion.

Jack Klinger, affectionately known as "Trigger," had donned a padded suit, and was slowly commandeering his six-wheeled robot toward the box. It was a long and nerve-wracking fifteen minutes while the remote-controlled machine rolled up to the device, opened and engaged it, trying to ascertain the danger level.

Minutes later, he confirmed there was no bomb threat.

The box turned out to be nothing more than a basic cash box found at any big-box office supply store. They removed a single note which had been created on standard copy paper and printed on a generic printer.

Klinger undid the top half of his bomb suit and took the box to the front porch, handing it to the Mayor who was joined by several of his staff.

"Here you go, Mr. Mayor. Pretty harmless."

Frowning, Burton took the box. "Harmless, maybe. But frightening for sure."

"Yes. And sorry, Sir. We'll get this muther..."

Ignoring the cop, Burton unfolded the paper and read it aloud:

"Mayor Burton, you will deposit $100 million US dollars into the offshore bank account listed below. The moment it is deposited, your daughter will be returned safely. Check the time; it should be approximately 6:00PM/EST. You have 48 hours from now to make this transaction. If you do not, your daughter will vanish into thin air. Currently, she is safe and will not be harmed in any way *unless* you fail to meet our demands. You have the money. We have your daughter. Do not be stupid, it won't end well."

Handing the paper to Chief Davis, the color had all but disappeared from Burton's face.

"You were right. All they want is money," Burton said quietly.

Davis re-read the note. "100 million. We can do that, right?"

"*We?*"

"Sorry, Lukas," Davis said, flipping the paper over. Even though he knew there would not be any, he still looked for any potential clues.

"Okay, let's get inside, put the finishing touches on the press release..." Burton said before stopping mid-sentence to see Sarah Ferguson, a local CBS anchor, make her way through the crowd to them. "Holy shit," he said so quietly only Davis could hear him.

Davis followed his look. "Oh boy. I'll take care of this. That's the last thing—"

"No, it's okay. You know how she is—nothing'll stop her once she sets her mind to it."

"You're the boss."

Burton looked to Margaret Childress and nodded her over. Glancing back, he saw Sarah approaching the end of the driveway. "Marge, do me a favor, head inside, then in exactly 2 minutes, come back out—with whatever release you have in hand, and *insist* that you get me into a meeting with everyone."

They watched as Ferguson talked to her cameraman setting up a camera and lights.

"And take everyone, okay?" Burton added.

Before she could answer, Burton took the offensive by walking toward Ferguson, patting Davis' shoulder for him to follow. Childress shuffled inside, taking co-workers with her.

"Hello, Ms. Ferguson," Burton smiled shaking her hand. Waving the cameraman away, he pulled her close enough so only she could hear. "I told you to keep your distance, *Fergie*."

"Hello, Mayor. I'm *so* sorry about this news," Sarah said loudly enough for anyone to hear, quietly, adding, "I don't give a shit what you told me. *This* is government property, *you're* at the center of an enormous story, and *I'm* going to have the exclusive on our network...*inside the hour.*"

Smiling, she pecked him on the cheek, "And *don't* call me *Fergie*. I'm not your girl anymore!"

Margaret Childress exited the front door and was down the steps just as Sarah spun around, taking a microphone from her cameraman.

He waved a signal and she began, "Five, four..."

Burton waved Margaret to head back up the stairs. "Too late, Margaret, her *highness* has a news report to do..." he said, staring at the reporter before walking away.

"And funny how she didn't ask a single thing about Abigail's disappearance."

CLARE BURTON STOOD at the window, sipping a second glass of wine. Besides worrying about her little girl's condition—both mental and physical, she had been watching the charade unfold. She also saw the cozy exchange between the reporter and her husband. Everyone knew the reporter, but Clare also knew the significance of her being there, and was all too aware of the history the reporter shared with her husband.

She's got a lot of nerve getting cozy with my man in front of my home.

Catching Lukas' sheepish glance back toward the house, she wasn't sure if he could see her, but she certainly saw him. Moreover, she was trying with all her might, not to allow anything to get in the way of finding their little girl—the single most important person to her on the planet.

Finishing her wine, she walked the empty glass to the sink, then made her way to her home office. Going through her purse, she located the two cellphones. One was all business—a line shared between she, her husband, nanny and friends. The other one was also business—albeit, a different sort.

She thought of it as her Plan B; a connection to the past. Some of that past was good, with delicious memories. Other parts of were dark, with secrets few knew about.

The only number in the phone belonged to a man with whom she had shared a hot summer, long ago. The time had been filled with fantasies, and included a romance that seemed to haunt her nearly a decade later.

She fought the urge to push the button. In her mind, she knew placing that call could take long strides toward bringing her girl home. It could also just as easily make short stabs toward bringing her marriage down.

In the stillness of the moment—that schizophrenic calm before the storm, she asked herself, *What do I have to lose?*

14

THE DECEPTION

THE PAST SEVERAL hours had involved placating Abigail's anxiety and making her feel safe and secure. With a snack, juice and play-time with her pals, Mo and Margot, the nine-year old *hostage* was feeling very welcome. They had explained how her parents had asked "Mr. Smith and his friends" to play with her while her parents prepared a birthday party the day after tomorrow.

She had settled into the notion that all was well.

"Saturday is the *perfect* day to have a birthday," Mo sang to Abigail, adding how her daddy was going to open the zoo to all her friends—which made her ecstatic.

Donovan, Ken and Sean had watched replays of all the news stations. One by one, the local affiliates had broken in with a consortium of details concerning the recent kidnapping of Mayor Lukas Burton's daughter. Given that New York City had watched Burton's little girl grow up over the last nine years, the timing of her upcoming birthday party proved to strike an even deeper emotional chord.

Donovan needed space and time to think. Retiring to his office, he sat alone, watching the day close. It was the first time in all this chaos—perhaps the first in recent time, that *Scorpion* felt guilty.

The guilt would be from the pain that *could* result if Daddy didn't make the dream birthday party come true.

As in: deposit $100 million to Donovan's off-shore account.

He had done his part; he'd had enough of the preparation. After all, the orchestration of this deal had been in the works for months. Actually, the big picture was put into place decades ago.

His massive office was not only the nerve center of his real estate development and construction business, but also his banking business. He owned large pieces of small banks in a number of foreign countries. He also owned, or had partial share in, an international drug ring. This investment was thanks to a debt he owed drug czar Manuel Navarro, the wealthiest and perhaps most notorious drug dealer in the world. His territories started at the top of Mexico and covered to the bottom of Argentina; basically, most of South America.

Known as *El Diablo,* or "The Devil," his fortune and reach made Pablo Escobar's kingdom look like child's play. In his day, Escobar was said to be worth $30 billion dollars. Rumor was Navarro was worth upwards of $50 billion. Coming in at around $10 billion, Scorpion, was well behind those men. But with that amount of money, one could do anything they wanted.

From his window, he had an excellent vantage point of his beloved city and all that made it tick. He loved being at the center of the universe. But what he enjoyed most was being completely immersed in the financial part of this city. Yet, he could also hide behind much of it, playing a skillful role on both sides of the proverbial fence.

That reminded him of his favorite game, and looking at his prized chess board, he pondered his next move.

He enjoyed chess; not only for the intellectual stimulation, but for the taste of competition. He loved to win. But it was *what* he won that played a higher role. Stakes were his way, as with many powerful men, to keep score.

Whenever and with whomever he played, there had to be a price attached. Preferably a handsome one. When his adversaries didn't play fair, or brushed aside competition *after* they engaged in the game, he would bite back.

In one moment, Donovan was imagining his next move—in another, he was imagining Burton's next move. He had to assume the Mayor wouldn't blink any eye at paying the ransom. His daughter was certainly worth whatever funds he had. And it wasn't the $100 million that interested Donovan most; it was the second part of his plan which he felt confident would set him apart from all the rest.

He wanted to stand as one of the world's most notorious men.

One thing was certain: Burton needed to *feel* the pain. Donovan doubted the amount of money he was requiring was stashed in Burton's private reserves—secured, no doubt, by any number of "appropriations" over the years.

Donovan felt the particular amount was due him. He figured that more than a dozen such *appropriations* were depleted from his construction business, as they became stacked into another man's investments.

One man played by the rules; albeit, from a handbook most couldn't respect. The other, played by a set of rules handed down by generations, but circumvented to meet his wishes.

Both men had their secrets. Both men could be seen as different sorts of tyrants, using different methods. One wanted to grow city skylines, while creating absurd wealth. The other wanted to grow councilmen's securities, while compounding awesome wealth.

Having businesses in Havana, Nicaragua, London, and Stockholm, as well as in his home country that included Los Angeles, San Francisco, Miami and New York City, Donovan Blair had his mind set on global domination as one of *the* real estate developers in the world. And while he enjoyed the enormous wealth his empire had built upon illegal drugs and arms, there was nothing as invigorating as owning parcels of property in cities and countries where it was becoming increasingly difficult to build and own the prime spots.

Donovan took a sip of *Louis XIII Black Pearl Cognac,* as he studied the extravagant board.

The cognac was among the finest in the world. The Victor

Scharstein's *Art of War* chess set was a masterpiece of solid gold pieces studded with diamonds, sapphires, emeralds and rubies.

Money bought such things.

But power bought much more.

It was time to make two moves. The first move—referred to as the *Sicilian Defense,* one of the most complex yet classic defenses in chess. The second move involved checking on the Mayor first thing tomorrow.

It would become Donovan's most strategic move.

He smiled, admiring the elaborate statues opposite him, and contemplated what his adversary and his bride were doing right now. One thing was certain—they wouldn't be expecting his next moves.

15

THE BACKUP

THE NEXT MORNING found Lukas and Clare sitting at the breakfast table in silence. He sipped coffee, while reading the headlines of several newspapers. He needed to be kept abreast of all that was happening in the world *before* he got to the office. Clare held her coffee mug with both hands— the warmth providing her comfort from a sleepless night.

They looked years older than when they had gone to bed.

"Have you a plan today?" Clare asked, absently staring out the window at the grounds leading to the East River.

The elaborate flower gardens provided her happiness, as it was a place to ground herself with Mother Earth, amidst the dirty city.

Lukas set aside the paper, finished his coffee and followed her gaze out the window. He knew she was facing the fear of any number of scenarios.

"Of course, love. I doubt I slept any more than you did."

"I'm not so sure," she said, snorting a nervous smile. "You were snoring, as always. While I was pacing."

"I'm sorry. It was an exhausting day."

"Me, too," she whispered, looking at the clock. "I'm just…petrified."

"We have 24 hours. And we have the money. It will be—"

"*Please* don't tell me it will be difficult to pull it together," she spat through gritted teeth.

With a deep frown, he said, "I was *going* to say, it will be easy to pull that together; however, it will take a bit of time *liquidating* the proper assets. We just have to be smart."

Whipping her head to him, she barked. "Smart? You're trying to be *smart*, while our *baby* is in the hands of a fucking maniac!"

She rarely swore, so he knew she was approaching a breaking point.

"Clare, I'm sorry. I know the situation, frontwards and backwards. And I'm not being insensitive to our daughter. It's just details...of *reality* I must face."

"It's just money, Lukas."

"Understood. But remember...there are several things which have tied up a larger *part* of our money."

"Such as?"

He didn't like to be pushed. Swallowing his angst with a consoling breath, he managed an awkward smile. "Such as when we, rather, *you* decided to build the Hamptons house *you couldn't live without*—"

"Please do *not* push that in my face. *We* wanted that place. To relax...during the *rare* times you weren't pulling 18 hour days. I seem to recall a time you actually *wanted* to spend time with your family."

He started breathing heavily. She started digging deeply.

"That's right, when you weren't trying to *rekindle an old flame*," she spat.

"What?"

"I saw you and *Fergie* last night, making eyes during the press spectacle."

"Clare, before you start picking a fight by drudging up *old news*," he interrupted, "Please let me remind you we have *more than enough* money. It's just so much of it is tied up in investments. That's all. I'm meeting with Phillip McDonough today to discuss moving some things around."

She looked at him, knowing he was serious. At $3,000 an hour and a penchant for getting business deals closed quickly, Phillip was one of Manhattan's most powerful and notorious attorneys, as well as the Burton's counsel on all matters legal and financial.

She liked "PM" because he was a man's man, didn't take grief from anyone, and always got the job done. He won 99% of the time —no matter what. She wasn't sure how he did that, but she was impressed that he did. He always was kind to her—something he wasn't known for, as he was a notorious womanizer. That made her feel protected. Her therapist was always reminding her that protection, or a strong nurturing behavior, was what she always searched for in men. Consequently, it was a characteristic she found difficult to count on in her husband.

Lukas was at the kitchen counter, pouring his fourth cup of coffee, wondering how deep Clare wanted to go for this fight. He had neither the desire, the energy, nor the time. Checking his watch, he saw it was nearly 8 o'clock. Ordinarily, he would be at the office by now, but he knew he needed to play along, to keep the peace.

"I'm sorry, Lukas," she said again. "I'm trying…I really am."

He felt for her. Amidst all the feminine bravado, she was just a hurt little girl from a small southern town who had a less-than-charming upbringing with a largely absentee father, and a charming southern mother who suffered bipolar issues.

"Clare, all I want to do is find our girl," he said, joining her at the table, taking her hand. "Trust me when I say, I will move heaven and earth to get her back. I will. And before you know it, we will all be together again…and this nightmare will be over. Okay?"

She fought back tears, forcing a smile she wanted him to believe, but one even she couldn't buy. Taking a deep breath, she forced a smile. "Of course you will. Now, go ahead. Be my prince in shining armor, and I'll rally my girls for a support group, if nothing else."

"I think that's a fine idea. You need that support and they're your rock," he said, kissing her forehead, then heading for the door.

"Lukas?"

He stopped. "Yes, love?"

"You're not really…interested in Fergie again. Are you?"

He rejoined her at the table, realizing the peck on the forehead wasn't the right message, so he kissed her. Pulling apart, she raised her eyebrows.

He smiled. "Does that tell you anything?"

Nodding, she leaned in for another. The second kiss, while not as passionate, certainly told her he was her man. "I love you, Lukas."

"And I love you. Now, let me get out there and slay this damn dragon. So this Queen and her prince can live happily ever after."

AFTER HE HAD GONE, she sat and revisited her raw emotions, and her mind drifted to another time—in another place, and with another man.

What is wrong with me? He's just professed his love and is going to handle everything.

She shook her head, and with it, perhaps her doubts. Gathering dishes, she took them to the kitchen sink, and put the milk away. That's when her eyes fell on an ample supply of Chardonnay. After a prolonged hesitation, she looked at the clock and closed the fridge.

Yeah, Clare, there's a great way to start the day.

MOMENTS LATER, she was in her office taking the private cellphone from her purse. Stopping to stare out the window, she caught herself waiting for a small voice inside to tell her not to make the call.

No such luck.

So, she lit a cigarette and dialed the phone. Waiting for the phone to connect, she opened a window.

"Hello?"

"About that Plan B," she said quietly.

"Talk to me."

"It's not happening fast enough."

"Much seldom does."

"I want my girl back, Carter," she said through gritted teeth, trying not whimper.

While he enjoyed hearing his name—especially spoken by her, he wanted to be cautious to keep his head out of drama. Yet in the game.

"Haven't heard anything?"

"No," she sighed, wanting desperately to run away.

He let her absorb the moment.

"I want Abigail's return more than anything."

"I know that," Carter calmly replied. "We all know that."

Looking around the room, all Clare saw was memories. They were both new and old; however, there were no memories—visible anyway, of her past love affair with Carter.

"What's Lukas doing?"

She hesitated, trying not to play the victim. "Not enough."

The minute I put this into motion, he thought, *There's no turning back.*

"Are you sure?" he asked.

"No," she sighed heavily. "Actually, yes, I'm sure he is. And I'm sure the ransom will be painful."

That got his attention. "Have you heard anything about that?"

"It won't matter. We have plenty."

"Plenty?"

She began to answer, but panic flipped her stomach. She placed a hand over her mouth.

"Clare?"

Breathing through her nostrils, she tried to will the nausea and fear away.

"You do realize...the *minute* you pull the trigger..." he caught himself. "Sorry. Once you get this ball rolling...there's no stopping it."

She said nothing.

"Right?"

"Yes," she whispered. "I understand."

Carter waited another beat. Then two.

Before he could speak, she interrupted. "But that's okay. I'm ready. For anything."

"Okay. I'm on the next flight out," he said, then stopped—giving her a chance to back out.

After a long breath, she smiled. "Good."

He also couldn't help but smile—for any number of reasons.

"Carter?"

"Yes, Clare."

She bit her lip. "It's not that I don't think…that he will be *strong* enough, it's just—"

"You don't owe me an explanation."

"Yes, I do. I want this to work."

His eyebrows raised.

"I mean…with Lukas," she said.

"I know. Always have," he let out a breath. "And that's okay."

"Okay," she whispered.

Silence.

"This is business, Clare. Nothing else."

She smiled again. "Thank you."

16

THE PUSH

DONOVAN FINISHED MAKING love to Mo, while Margot fed Abigail breakfast. Having already taken care of Margot an hour earlier, he was proud of the fact he could keep not one, but two women happy. It wasn't always easy, but it seemed to work for all of them—for different reasons.

Bypassing Margot's "mother/daughter moments" in the kitchen, he headed down a flight to work out on the treadmill where he would make plans for the day.

Downstairs, he found Ken who had begun his workout two hours earlier.

"Morning, Boss," Ken said, guzzling some concoction at the juice bar.

"Yes, it is," Donovan smiled.

"Busy morning?" Ken asked, not expecting an answer, but exercising the pleasantries.

"What do you think?" Donovan smirked, moving on to business. "I need about an hour, then how about you and I meet in my office at…" he looked to the digital display on the wall over the reception desk. "9:30? We've got less than a day, but he won't take that long."

"Copy that."

"Gonna be a killer day. Have a lot on my mind...and need you behind me."

"Whatever it takes, Boss. You know that."

Donovan had always liked Ken. His loyalty was profound.

He recalled the time he plucked Ken fresh from the academy-back when he was blinded by some sort of *Blue Loyalty*. But that was the one thing Donovan looked for most in a person: loyalty.

"Tell me something, Donovan, and I'm just spitballing here, but if you were Burton, and your *only* daughter disappeared, wouldn't you get on television and...plead, or something?"

Donovan took a swig of Ken's concoction, and stared off into the distance, slowly nodding.

"Yeah, probably. Especially if I had that sort of power. And position. Frankly, I'd play on the emotions of the people. Try to get them to help."

"Not like they can *actually* do anything to help," Ken said.

"Exactly. Hey, we've laid the snare. It's his move. And if I know Lukas—and I most certainly do, he'll pull this thing together *pronto*."

"And we crank next steps."

"You bet. Now, get going. And I'll see you shortly."

WHEN DONOVAN HAD COMPLETED enough training for a marathoner, he was showered and at his desk by 9:29. All the television screens in his office were lit up with the sound muted. Standing behind his desk and sipping coffee, he scanned both the news channels and his stock market screens. Wall Street was about to open for business and he was sure to make a killing today—both in the opening market, as well as the upcoming melodrama.

His attention drifted to the chess game across the room, where he had made his move last night.

Now, it was his opponent's turn.

That play would show up either in an email, or on his cell phone, sometime during the day. The opening move was called the *Ruby Lopez* and would begin something like this: One: ef e5, Two:

Nf3 Nc6, Three: Bb5. Perhaps one of the most complex openings in the game, the move was invented in the 1400's by a Spanish priest named Ruy Lopez de Segura.

Donovan found the opening choice oddly coincidental, considering the ethnicity of his opponent.

A tap at the door startled Donovan. "Yo, come in!"

Ken entered, dressed in all navy.

"Who died?" Donovan grinned.

"Funny," he said, taking a seat. "What's the plan?"

Donovan cut the small talk, grabbed a grip crusher—a tool for building grip strength, and took a seat on the edge of the desk.

"Today's about precision. It's going to be one of those *seminal...* groundbreaking moments you and I'll be talking about for years to come."

Ken smiled, feeling confident in his boss and the gravity of the moment. "Got it."

"It'll be epic."

"Who else is with us?" Ken asked.

"Inside? Just me. Outside? You and Sean first, then Mo and Sean later. Both prop trucks will have surveillance."

"Flower or Air-conditioning?"

"Both. AC comes first. As you'll arrive, you set the switch to fail, then disappear. Thanks for getting that repair order in a week ago."

"No worries," Ken grinned.

"Always helps to have eyes and ears wherever we can," Donovan said.

"Copy that."

"Next comes Sean who will regroup with Mo then head up to Gracie Mansion. We're sending a *condolence bouquet* for the girl. It'll come from Sion Corp."

"Nice touch."

"She'll drive. He'll deliver. Soft spot and all that."

"Copy," Ken nodded. "And then?"

"That'll bring the truck back this way." Donovan set aside his tool and poured another French press. "This time, Sean will run gear in the truck, while Mo delivers flowers."

Ken had a puzzled expression.

"Lukas' secretary. She's got a handful of years with that bastard."

"How'd you know—"

"Really?" Donovan looked at him. "Called homework."

Ken grinned.

"And the flowers come *after* my drama."

"Right," Ken nodded again. "Anything we're forgetting?"

Donovan shook his head. "I'm sure the Chief will be *somewhere* nearby. Just keep your distance."

"Copy that."

Donovan leaned across his desk, typing in a handful of keystrokes. After a new window opened, he added a long string of characters. An account window opened. He frowned. Looking at his watch, he double-checked the clock on the wall across the room.

"Okay, so he's not in any hurry. Don't guess 10:15 is anytime to start fretting. My guess is he'll have it together right after lunch."

Ken smiled like a kid at Christmas. "Which means?"

"It's *show time!*"

17

THE DEPOSIT

M<small>AYOR</small> B<small>URTON</small>, Phillip McDonough and Chief Davis were gathered in the Mayor's office. Burton stood at the window, speaking quietly while listening to someone on the phone. Davis flipped through email on his smartphone. And McDonough fidgeted with an expensive pen, absent-mindedly twirling it between his fingers like a drummer in a rock band.

"I understand, Robert. I know it will take an enormous bite out of my retirement..." Burton rolled his eyes at McDonough—who nodded, showing his support.

"Yes, but it's *Abigail*," he said, staring out the window and wishing the drama would disappear.

Davis looked up from his screen to watch his pal.

"Of course we could sell the Hampton home," he hesitated. "However, it's not likely we can move it by *tonight*."

Davis and McDonough eyeballed one another.

"Listen, Robert, this is *exactly* what both Clare and I want," he said, joining the two men and making the gesture: *I'm wrapping it up*.

"Yes, *right now*. You have the routing numbers. Call me the *instant* it's transferred. Thank you."

Burton took a seat and let out a big sigh. The two men remained quiet and distracted.

"I know he has my best interest at heart…and he's a solid financial advisor…and has been for decades, but when I say sell…I mean *Sell!*"

"It's a lot of money," Davis said.

"Really, Jacob? I didn't know that."

McDonough started to speak, but stopped.

Seeing Phil's expression, Burton said, "What? C'mon, everyone has an opinion here."

"You're doing the *absolute* right thing, Lukas. No one who knows you has any doubts. To say otherwise is not only ridiculous, but it's cold-hearted bullshit coming from someone who has *never* felt the love from a child."

Burton's shoulders relaxed. "Thank you, Phil. I appreciate that." He stared into space, then added, "I'm sorry guys. This is eating me alive. I don't give a shit about the money…" he stopped. "Well, I *do* care—but only because that's a helluva lot of money, but I don't care when my little girl's *life* is on the line."

"And you're worth a great deal more than that," McDonough said, "But you and I and this clown" he added, smacking Davis on the arm, "Hell, we've all known each other a long time and seen our share of bullshit. And as much as we both *hate* this for you, we've just got to follow through."

Davis stopped nodding. "You got no other option."

Burton looked at his hands and spun his wedding ring around. "You're right. That's exactly how I feel. And we'll catch these bastard if it's—"

Suddenly, his phone buzzed. "Mayor Burton? You have a guest here to see you," Margot Childress said. "He said it's really important."

"Who is it?" Burton was impatient.

"A…Mr. Point?"

Burton's confused frown turned into a wicked grin, as he looked at a photo on his desk.

"Would that be a Mr. *Hollow* Point?"

The three men heard Margot confirm the name again over the phone.

"Yes, sir."

"Send him in."

The two men witnessed an expression they hadn't seen in several days, as Burton stood when the door opened. Reaching out to shake, both men embraced one another like brothers, smacking each on the back.

Burton peeled away and turned to McDonough and Davis who were standing.

"*Mr. Hollow Point*," Burton laughed. "You're funny. Phil McDonough and Chief Davis, meet an old friend from my days in the force, Donovan Blair."

18

THE DONOVAN

"*THE DONOVAN*?" McDonough asked, shaking Blair's hand. "The real estate tycoon? Funny, we *hear* more about you than *see* about you."

Nodding, Blair said, "Yeah, I enjoy a lower profile."

"Impressive reputation. And impressive buildings."

"Not really all that big deal. Just tall, is all."

Davis reached out to shake hands. "Yeah, I've seen you in the papers. But I've never actually *seen* you."

"Just keeping it under the radar," Donovan said modestly. "Nice to meet you, Chief."

Turning back to Burton, he shifted gears. "Listen, buddy, I'm not going to keep you. I just I saw all the freakin' craziness on TV, what with the headlines in the papers and all…and, well, I just *had* to stop by and share my thoughts. In person."

Burton smacked him on the back. "Thanks, Donovan. That's mighty nice. And while this is certainly not the *best* time to play catch up—"

"Yeah, yeah, I know. Like I said, the *worst* timing ever. But, I don't know, I could've sent you a letter or something, but just had to let you know that I—along with *millions* of New Yorkers…are pulling for you and Clare."

"Thanks, buddy; that means a lot. And yes, our hands are full... trying to pull things together."

"Okay, fair enough," Donovan said, starting to back toward the door. "Then how about after your girl's home safe and all this wackiness has blown over, what say the three of us get together over a drink. Or five," Donovan winked.

"Sure, sure. Sounds good," Burton said, walking his guest to the door.

Donovan gripped Burton's hand. "I'm sure you'll find the bastard who's behind all this."

Burton returned the warm handshake.

"Phil? Good to meet you," Donovan said. "And Chief Davis, good to know our boy's in good hands," he nodded, patting Burton on the shoulder before waving goodbye.

"After all this is over, Clare and I'll have you over the house to spend some *real* time getting caught up. Been too long."

"We're all busy. No worries," he said at the door. "And yes, we'll do that. Gentlemen, take care."

Burton closed the door behind Blair and smiled at the floor.

"What?" McDonough asked.

"Just odd is all. Haven't seen that guy since—I don't know when. Well, except an occasional Page 6 appearance with some beautiful gal. Other than that, he's notoriously private. And done a *helluva* job building our skyline."

Burton took a seat, trying to hide a furrowed brow.

Davis pressed. "What?"

"Yeah, he's a big real estate developer, but man, like I said, it's been since we were in the Marines, that I....Wait, no, come to think of it, we saw one another at a benefit. But that's been close to a decade."

"Hollow point?" McDonough smirked.

"Yeah, quite the nickname, huh? He liked guns. Big ones. He had a temper too. In fact, that's what got him tossed."

"In the brig?" Davis asked.

"No, *out* of the Corps. Drunk and disorderly conduct, *while* threatening an officer. At gunpoint."

"Shit," Davis mumbled.

"Yeah, with a *loaded* round of…"

"Hollow point," Davis and McDonough said together.

"Bingo," he said, just as the cellphone on his desk vibrated.

Getting the phone, he read aloud, "DONE." Exhaling, he said, "Money's wired."

Both Davis and McDonough smiled.

"I guess next comes the…"

Before he could finish, a knock at the door interrupted. Margot entered with a large spray of flowers.

"Sir, *besides* all the dozens of flowers that have been arriving since yesterday—and are lining the foyer, these just came for you. Actually, *two* orders have arrived. And one was for me," she smiled. "Thank you for remembering my work anniversary."

Burton mechanically nodded, not remembering any anniversary, then said, "And?"

"The others are for you." She handed him the attached card then sat the vase on his desk.

Removing the card from the envelope, he read aloud, "Nice doing business with you, Mayor. These flowers mark your daughter's safe return home."

He looked at his two friends, then read, "You can expect her within the hour."

19

THE RUSE

ONE HOUR EARLIER—

Sean and Ken left the underground garage in a nondescript Heating & Air-Conditioning van which looked like dozens of others across the city. Sean was wearing a faded gray jumpsuit and a plain black ballcap. A thick lumberjack beard and black horn-rimmed glasses completed the look that was all the rage with hipsters.

Ken was dressed in his blues—looking like every other cop in town. However, he also wore a black windbreaker atop his uniform, and was adding a black stocking cap and sunglasses to complete the disguise.

They crossed midtown, and were at the Mayor's office in short order. Parking toward the service entrance, they found the blindspot at the corner of the building. This gave Ken a chance to exit without calling attention to himself.

"Okay, buddy," Sean said, pulling a gadget the size of a TV remote from his bag. "Here's your toy. It'll trigger the fail-switch I installed two weeks ago."

"Copy that."

"Just go to any floor—preferably his," he laughed, punching Ken's shoulder. "Geez, is that thing loaded?"

Looking down at his shoulder, he smirked, "Get to it, punk."

"Head to the equipment room—at least within 10 feet of it, push the top button, and keep walking."

"Got it."

"It'll shut down in five. With the heat like it's been lately, it won't take long."

"And I'll head straight to Burton's office," Ken said.

Nodding, Sean said, "I'll be in within minutes, with a story about someone needing help on a different floor. Nobody gives a shit how it works, they just want it cool again."

"Copy that." Ken checked his watch. "Back in 20?"

"Yeah, make it 15. It won't take me long to plant my device in his office, reset the air and get back. I'll drop you back so you can get the girl ready. I'll grab Mo and the flower truck and head uptown."

"Copy. Back in 15."

Ken removed the top layer of disguise and was out the door, around the building and up on the Mayor's floor before Sean could finish texting Mo with the details of their timeline.

INSIDE THE MAYOR'S suite of offices, Burton's secretary was on the phone and distracted, when Ken walked in with a stack of folders under his arm. He entered smiling and waving a folder at his face like a member of a Southern Baptist congregation in the middle of August.

He mouths, *Are you hot?*

Nodding ferociously, she waved for him to put the folders on her desk.

Nodding, he did a double-check and made a face.

"Can you please hold just a second?" Margaret said, putting the phone against her shoulder.

"I'm sorry," he said, turning on the charm. "I was just up this way delivering some case files when I noticed it getting hotter and hotter. I can see it's just as bad in here."

"Yes," she said, smiling and trying to read his badge. "Officer…"

"Officer Burns. I'm from the 13th, just working on a...well, that's not important. You let me take care of this heat for you..." he said, pointing to the ceiling. "On my way back downstairs. I see you have your hands full."

"Thank you, Officer Burns. I could use that," she said, returning to her call.

Before leaving, Ken could see two men with Burton. Chief Davis was one of them. He wasn't sure who the other was—as his back was to him, but judging from the man's animated gestures, he had a pretty good idea it was the attorney Phillip McDonough.

MOMENTS LATER, Sean and Ken entered the underground warehouse. One large door rolled down to close, while another slowly opened. This prevented roaming eyes from seeing inside the clandestine walls.

Mo had the next van cued up and ready to roll.

They all exit to compare notes.

"How'd it go?" Mo asked.

"Piece of cake," Scan grinned.

"What he said," Ken added, trading his uniform for a different disguise. His next performance: cabbie.

"I meant to ask, how's the post-op?" Sean asked.

"Good," Mo said. "The incision has healed nicely. All she's thinking about right now is getting home to Mommy and Daddy for her birthday party."

"Copy that," Ken said. "You two head out for delivery, I'll grab the girls and head across town. Are my other cabbies ready?"

Mo nods. "They're parked along 5th Avenue, between 79th and 86th and ready to fall in when you cross the 85th Transverse. Just give the word as you're approaching, and they'll follow you crosstown."

As Ken put on a turban, Sean tried hard not to laugh. Ken shot him a look, which made Sean raise his hands. "Sorry. But yeah, it's a good look."

Ken ignored him. "We'll cross 82nd, head up East End, drop her on 86th, and shoot back across town then split once inside the park."

"Incidentally, Margot decided on the nun outfit," Sean said, still grinning. "She thought it'd be her *good deed* for the week."

Ken couldn't help but grin. "You're just full of funny today, aren't you?"

"I try," Sean said, "She'll walk Abi up to the middle entrance to Carl Shurz park, tell her something about making a surprise appearance at her dress up party, then when Abi's out of sight, she'll pop into the tower across the street, change and hoof it to the park."

"Where one of our guys will pick her up," Ken finished.

"Okay, *clowns*, let's get this masquerade started, shall we?" Mo said, checking her watch. "We've got a lot of ground to cover, so let's get to it."

20

THE GIFT

Ken's cab arrived on East End Avenue. He spotted media trucks parked along the street in front of the Mansion. Keeping his distance, he was careful to keep it low key. Glancing up to the rearview mirror, he watched a smiling Abigail look out toward her home. He was sure she was trying to see where all the guests were hiding. Making eye contact with Margot, he found her nun outfit oddly attractive, but didn't share.

"Abigail," Ken said sweetly, "We sure have had fun hanging out with you."

She turned her attention from the crowds surrounding her home to him. "Yes, Mr. Nick, I've had fun too. When will you be at my party?"

"Soon. I have to make a couple of stops, but I'll be there very soon, okay?"

She nods.

"Okay, Abigail, let's you and I go. Now remember, I'm going to walk you to the park entrance, then go grab a few friends," Margot said. "You're going to love their costumes."

They got out of the cab and made their way to the park. She watched as Ken pulled away and the other decoy cabs followed.

Within a few yards, Margot got the sense she shouldn't go any further.

"Okay, Abigail. You go on ahead and I'll see you soon."

Abigail looked up at her and smiled. "Really?" she grinned broadly. "I wish my giraffe balloon hadn't shrunk."

Margot had promised herself she wouldn't get too attached to her. Too late. She'd fallen for this little girl and was secretly going to miss her. And worried, as well.

Smiling, she said, "Oh, I almost forgot," opening the backpack she was carrying. She pulled out a pink stuffed giraffe and handed it to Abigail.

Her eyes grew large. "Wow, that is so cool, Miss Margaret. Thank you."

"You're so welcome, Angel. I mean, Abigail."

Abigail's tiny hand squeezed Margot's hand three times. "Three squeezes means I love you," she smiled.

Margot took a deep breath in order to fight back tears. "You are too sweet. Thank you. And…I love you, too."

Scanning the perimeter again, Margot saw the crowds were a good distance away, leaned over and gave Abi a hug.

"Okay, Princess, you head on to the house and we'll see you later."

With that, she watched as Abigail walked the stone path toward her house—a path Abigail had played on hundreds of times since moving there.

Seconds later, Margot crossed the street and entered the Covenant of the Sacred Heart school. Ducking into an abandoned classroom Sean confirmed would be empty, she shed the habit, slipped into running gear, stashed the outfit in a closet, and disappeared out a back door, without notice. She was halfway to Central Park by the time Abigail had meandered through the small private park and arrived home.

Abigail stood at the front gate, staring wide-eyed at the dozens of fans and media personnel. One by one, they slowly turned to see the Mayor's daughter staring back at them. Several glanced from pictures in their hands, or those taped to the fence, then back to the girl.

As eyes bugged, and jaws dropped, Abigail said, "Is everyone here for my birthday party?"

21

THE RETURN

HYSTERICAL WITH JOY, Clare kissed Abigail over and over. Wiping tears from her face, she held her daughter at arms length to study her, then hugged her so tightly, Abigail could hardly breathe.

"Mommy, you're hurting me!"

Clare let go and straightened her clothes. "I'm so sorry, Abigail. I'm just *so* glad you're home! You're safe here with Mommy."

Several of Clare's girlfriends stood nearby, gloating at the happy sight.

"Your husband's on his way," Francine said. "He said he'd be here as soon as possible."

Oblivious to anything except having her daughter standing in front of her, Clare continued to kiss and cry and touch her little girl.

"Mommy, when does my birthday party begin?"

Clare stopped, looked at her girlfriends, and realized she had been so caught up in the latest turmoil, she had forgotten about Abigail's birthday.

"Oh, Abigail, it's going to be such a big…big party. But it's not going to be until…later today. Okay, Princess?"

Abigail nods, looking out the window at the strangers along the front gate, turned back and smiled. "Princess. That's what my new friend Miss Margaret calls me."

Clare's smile dissolved into a look of pure panic.

A CARAVAN of the Mayor's SUVs and three patrol cars were assembled and on the road within seconds of getting the call from Clare. Bypassing FDR because of the late day traffic, they hopped on Broadway, crossing over to First Avenue, then running every single light en route. Staring out the window, Burton wrung his hands.

Police Chief Davis said, "She's home. Safe. Just like we knew she would be."

Burton returned to the moment. "Yes. Thank God."

McDonough was texting on his smartphone, when his gaze shifted from the small screen to Burton and Davis. He kept typing.

"What are you thinking?" Davis asked. "Besides the obvious."

"What do you think? I can't wait to hold my little girl. I haven't slept more than a couple hours these last two days and I'm just... toast," Burton said.

McDonough continued to type. His expression, blank.

"I suppose...of course...I'll have to..." Burton began, "We'll have to get out an announcement for the press that—"

"Done," McDonough chimed in.

Burton looked at him and nodded. "And we'll have to start tracking—"

"On it," McDonough said, not looking up from his phone.

"What in the hell are you doing, Phil?" Burton barked.

"I'm putting pieces into place," McDonough said, looking back and forth from the screen to Burton. He hadn't stopped texting.

"Why don't you stop that...and just *talk* to them on the phone."

"Nah, this is easier. And faster."

"Yeah, Lukas, nobody actually *talks* anymore. My kids are the same way. Hell, they'll text to one another while they're in the same house," Davis chuckled.

Burton showed no expression to Davis, then turned to McDonough. "And?"

Phil continued to type. "And what?"

"Those plans? Care to share what you're putting into place…" Burton's expression was mixed. "For *us*?"

McDonough stopped and looked at Burton. He didn't like what he saw. "Sorry," he said, laying the phone on the seat. "It's my job, Luke. To watch your back. I'm just…watching your back."

Most people called the Mayor by his title. Close colleagues and personal friends called him Lukas. McDonough, who has been his friend for decades, had always called him Luke.

"I appreciate that. And I have some ideas of my own," Burton said. "As I'm sure the Chief here does. So, why don't we all get together on the same page," he said, looking out the window, to see what intersection they're approaching. "While we're still a dozen blocks away."

McDonough picked up his phone and began reading, while also holding up his hand to halt any conversation. Scanning a litany of incoming messages, he nodded repeatedly. "Okay. Good. Yes…" he said, continuing to scroll through messages.

Losing patience, Burton reached into a pocket for his phone.

McDonough looked up. "Okay, here we go. Good news and bad news," he said, referring to the screen.

"Let's hear it," Burton barked. "Give me the good first."

"Abigail is home."

"I know that, dammit!"

McDonough took a beat. "She's fine. Arrived at the house inside the last fifteen or so minutes. Came out of nowhere…meaning, she just appeared in front of the house. Evidently, she arrived via that pathway that cuts through the lower portion of your property."

Burton frowned. "She wasn't dropped off? No one saw her arrive? You mean to tell me—"

"She just *walked* right up to the house. No one was with her. No one saw anyone. Or any*thing* suspicious."

Burton shook his head. "Continue."

"She's unharmed. She did show up with a toy."

"What?"

"A stuffed…" he squinted at the screen. "Giraffe."

"Has it been checked for explosives or—?"

"Yes. It's just a toy. Nothing more."

Burton took a deep breath, looking to Davis. "She's fine, Mr. Mayor," Davis said, patting his knee.

"Okay, we have surveillance information being checked now," McDonough said looking to the Chief. "We're working with several people, including, of course, your precinct. And others. Footage is being scoured as we speak checking all intersections within a square mile. Maybe more. Within the Mansion, of course."

"Good," Burton said, "That's going to provide something."

"Yes, it will. Elsewhere, we are tracing the money. So far nothing."

"Is that the bad news? Have we gotten to *that* part of the program yet," Burton spat.

"No. That's still part of the good news. We're tracing it, but as you can imagine it's a sophisticated network and these criminals are pretty fucking savvy," McDonough finished, as his phone chimed several times.

"Hold on," he said, reading. "Okay, looks like the money…is… bouncing from…source to source…" McDonough slowed down and frowned. "Okay, let's move off that topic for now."

"Why? Whaddya got?" Burton asked, reaching for his phone.

"It's just that it's so hard to track. Let me move on to other news."

"Fine," Burton said, reading his phone screen.

"The screens in Times Square…were partly commandeered, partly…purchased."

"What do you mean? Exactly."

"You know they're mostly rented space…" Davis interrupted.

Both Burton and McDonough look at him. Davis stopped.

"Yes, Chief—to your point, they're purchased. And they were from a nondescript company called…" he looks back to his screen. "XYZ Media Holdings. Based in Newark."

"Let me guess—" Burton interrupts.

"Right. There is none such," McDonough said. "They paid in cash in order to—I don't know…get all the screens together? We're not sure yet. May be a moot point, anyway."

"Okay, go on," Burton sighed, looking out the window to see their location.

"As for commandeered, it looks to be just a matter of…electronic kidnapping," McDonough smiled, shaking his head.

"What's that even mean?" Burton barked.

"Wifi and…" Davis began.

"Right," McDonough answered, "Likely a sophisticated combination of electronic surveillance and interception."

Burton looked lost.

"Bottom line," McDonough said, "We won't be able to trace that. Even if we find a source, it won't be *the* source. These people are too smart for that."

"Have we hit the *bad* news yet?"

McDonough continued to scroll. "My guys have taken the footage from the park abduction. It was well edited. Even faces of bystanders were blurred out. What clothing we could see from the abductors…which wasn't much…was as generic as it gets."

"Even the clowns?" Davis asked.

McDonough smiled. "Yes, even the clowns. They're all on staff. They've had the same clown outfits for the past several years. We can't actually *see* the face of the clown who is making the balloon for Abigail."

"Shit!" Burton said, staring out the window.

"No doubt," Davis mumbled.

McDonough continued to multi-task. "The *only* thing—and it's small…we have is like *two frames* where we see the watch on the wrist of the clown."

Burton snapped his head from the window to McDonough. "And?"

"It's a big watch. A *million* guys wear it. Okay, maybe not a million. It's expensive. It's a TAG."

Davis looked at his wrist. "Like this?"

Both Burton and McDonough looked.

McDonough nodded slowly. "Yep."

Davis looked at both men.

Burton said, "I have one, too. From my days in the force."

"Okay. Let me see…if there's anything else…" McDonough said, still reading.

Burton looked at Davis and shrugged. "Well, it's *something*. And right now? I'll take something over *nothing*."

"As for any surveillance in the park…that particular area…in between two heavily traveled sections…not to mention full tree foliage…let's just say, we're not far along there."

Burton snorts.

"However, we're hopeful *someone* along the way will have cell-phone video of *something* happening," McDonough added with a phony smile.

"That's often our best source," Davis said. "Everybody has a phone; that makes nearly every person in the park a potential news reporter."

"Good point," McDonough said—his eyes yet to leave the phone screen.

"We're almost there, Mr. Mayor," the driver said.

"Thanks."

McDonough's phone rang. "Yes? Yes. Oh shit."

All eyes are on him.

"We're nearly there. I'll ring inside the hour."

Burton could barely wait for McDonough to hang up. "What?"

"Now, for the *bad* news."

22

THE SURPRISE

LUKAS BURTON SAT at the kitchen table watching his wife and daughter discuss her recent ordeal. He had never been so happy in his life. To have Abigail safely home was the single most important thing to him right now. It superseded his job.

Screw lowering crime, increasing jobs, and building a speed train to Long Island, he thought. *My daughter's home.*

Even though Burton had done all that and nearly erased a crime wave that had overtaken much of the five boroughs, and even though his potential future run for President of the United States looked good, none of that compared to having his little girl safely under his roof.

Burton thought about the $100 million dollars it took to get her back and instantly dismissed it. That amount—while not exactly a drop in the bucket, was a good chunk of his net worth. But more importantly, it paled in comparison to the love he had for his only child.

I would have spent my last dime to have her safe.

His business mates, Davis and McDonough had the same contented expression, as they watched Abigail. He was glad to have them on his team.

But why would anyone kidnap her? Whoever took her knew that stealing her was my most vulnerable point. It can't just be about money, he pondered.

The voices in the room fell distant, as his thoughts went elsewhere. His mind raced to review all the people he had crossed in his life.

Who've I pissed off so deeply they'd do this to me?

Looking at Clare, he wondered what she must be going through.

I'll find this monster, if it's the last thing I do.

"What do you mean they were nice people?" Clare asked Abigail.

I will kill whoever...wait, what?

The voices instantly returned to focus.

"What did you just say, Abi?" Lukas asked.

She turned and smiled. "I love my new giraffe, Daddy."

His smile deceived his intent.

"No, honey...I mean, *yes*, that's a lovely giraffe. But, baby, what do you mean they were nice people?"

She looked confused. Clare frowned.

"Honey, what Daddy wants to know is...tell Daddy what you told me before he got here."

"Which part, Mommy?"

"The part about who you thought these people you were visiting with...might be."

"I don't remember a lot, Mommy. Aunt Steph and I were walking in the park...I think it was this morning..." she frowned. "Maybe it was yesterday. Anyway, we were walking...and I was talking to my friends...and we saw this clown in the park. He made me a balloon...it was shaped like this," she said, holding up her new giraffe toy.

Clare and Lukas looked at one another.

Abi frowned again, "I...can't remember. I think we went home...and I took a nap," she whispered.

"And they gave you this?"

She nodded. "Miss Margaret. She's my friend."

"Miss *Margaret*? Tell me who that is...and where you met her... and..." Lukas began.

"Honey, tell Mommy and Daddy about your special new friend, *Miss Margaret*," Clare tried a softer approach.

"Miss Margaret and Mr. Nick dropped me off at the park. They're super nice people, Mommy. They let me play with all these toys. We talked and sang songs. It was really fun."

Lukas felt his heart racing. "Mr. Nick?" He asked, trying to hold his temper.

"He was nice to me."

He wanted to grab his little girl and drill her with questions, but caught himself, realizing slow movements would yield better results. He looked first to Clare, then to Phil and Jacob. He thought about how he needed to ask Stephanie how her story collaborated, except because he was so angry, he suspended her.

He wanted to do worse, but didn't.

"We should bring in Ms. Marchauex to compare details," Chief Davis suggested.

Lukas nodded, as Clare shook her head. They looked at one another.

"She's been so traumatized, Lukas," she said quietly, reaching for Lukas' hand.

"Are you kidding me, Clare?" Lukas spat.

"Absolutely. You have…no idea."

"But it would go a long way to explaining some matters," McDonough gently responded. "How about this, let's consider bringing her in…*later*."

Clare hesitated before conceding with a tiny nod.

"Mommy, when will my party start?"

Clare looked for support from her two best girlfriends, Sharon Barton and Julie Patterson. They had remained quiet across the room the whole time, but were also busy calling all their friends with young children. Sharon stepped forward.

"Clare, we have *all* the details coming together…" she winked at Clare before Abigail turned around.

"Yes, but do you think we can keep it a…*surprise*," Julie whispered very loudly.

For the past thirty minutes, both women had been frantically arranging a last minute birthday party. Given it was the Mayor and his family—at the Gracie Mansion, they had little trouble confirming a packed house. All mothers had been instructed to arrive with at least one gift—preferably, something exotic and certainly *pink.*

Abigail spun around, giggling and shouted, "Happy Birthday to me!"

As the two friends approached Abigail, Sharon took one hand, while Julie took the other.

"Clare, why don't you wrap up here and we'll get her changed. Then start getting ready for the party."

"Great idea. About the catering—"

"It's *all* taken care of," Sharon said, "All *you* have to do is enjoy having your girl home."

The three girls left the room hand in hand and went upstairs to prepare for the big event. Clare turned to the men. Her expression was tentative, as tears pooled her eyes.

"Have you heard *anything* from the *animals*…who tortured us for the past two days?"

Lukas placed his hand on hers. "No love," he answered, patting her hand. "Not yet. But you can be sure something will turn up. It always does. People like this always slip up…somewhere."

She looked at his hand on hers.

"Mrs. Burton, when I say we will continue to do everything in our power to find the perpetrators who carried out this horrific plan…" Chief Davis smiled. "You have my word."

Her smile was present, while not exactly authentic.

"He's right, Clare. We won't stop until we find them," Phil McDonough said.

Suddenly, Sharon screamed from upstairs. They all looked at one another.

"OH MY GOD!" she cried out, running down the steps. Rushing into the room, Sharon was frantic and Julie was white with fear, while Abigail had a terrified and confused expression.

"What in the world is it?" Clare cried, as panic creased her face.

Desperately trying to compose herself, Sharon slowly lifted Abigail's dress.

A perfectly straight hairline suture, the width of ballpoint pen, extended from one hip to another, just above her navel.

"Mommy?" Abigail choked out between tears. "What is it?"

Written with a *Sharpie* marker on her right ribcage, it read: *DON'T DROP HER...*

On her left ribcage, it read: *...OR BOOM!*

Attached to her navel was a small round disc the size of a dime.

"WAIT!" Chief Davis said, "It could be a *bomb!*"

Clare fainted.

Abigail screamed.

And Lukas nearly vomited.

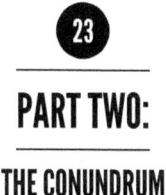

PART TWO:

THE CONUNDRUM

I STARED out the window of the private King Air 350 I leased an hour ago, thanks to Clare's Black American Express card. The eight-seat Turboprop lives in a private hangar in Asheville and is shared by three guys my age: a real estate developer, an entrepreneur who runs a local craft brewery, and a movie star who retired from Hollywood. Working privately for rich people had its share of privileges. The $3,000 an hour rate wasn't bad, considering I could bypass all the bullshit of the airlines. Besides, the faster I moved, the sooner I could get my head around Clare's desperate situation. Not to mention getting my hands around the maniac's neck who made the bad choice of endangering a friend's child.

Watching Asheville's horizon dissolve away, I spent the first twenty or so minutes of my hour-plus flight reflecting on the past thirty days. It had been one hell of a ride. My last mission hadn't gone exactly as planned or imagined.

To be honest, it went sideways.

And while my father, Lt. Colonel Randall Matheson. and his business partner, Sergeant Tony Black, made it out of Havana, Cuba alive, they would be forever different. They would both need a good bit of time in order to let their old bodies heal. And while they were in good health, what they had endured was a lot for anyone to withstand.

Randall would eventually recover from the scorpion bite, thanks to the quick thinking of Dr. Leonard Caprese.

Caprese was a man that most of us, at one time or another, thought was a traitor. He may still be an untrustworthy foe, but he did save my father's life. And just in the nick of time.

As for Black, his foot would heal; again, thanks to quick responses by Caprese. The 9mm wound Caprese fired into Black's foot ended up not being as bad as originally thought. Black was one tough SOB and he knew how to play the drama. It was smart how Caprese had the foresight to aim at the end of his foot, rather than the middle, or near the ankle. That way, Tony would suffer a bone fracture or two, but after a few weeks of rehab, he would likely only suffer a limp. At least he would still have his foot.

I now understood how Caprese needed to display some showmanship in order to prove he had no vested interest in helping the good guys.

We were the good guys. And the bad guys were a group of men who appeared to have military backgrounds. They were led by one Donovan Blair—a man they called *Scorpion*. He had escaped our reach by just seconds. I felt confident our paths would cross again. As much as I admired what seemed to be his military prowess, I felt certain he was a certifiable maniac. With connections in drug and arms trafficking, that wouldn't come as much of a surprise.

I was surprised, however, that he didn't kill any of us. One fact was certain: if our paths crossed again, I would gladly introduce him to my trusty Cheytac rifle. That way he can see what a sniper's wet dream has to say about threatening to kill me or my team.

As for the rest of us, Xeon—my favorite new soldier, disappeared to a mountain retreat for some R & R. She didn't tell us where the secret spot was, but when the time arose, it wouldn't be hard for me to find her.

Peter Cohen, a former soldier and all-around good guy, with whom we made fast friendships while working in Havana, returned to Key West. There, he would pick back up on his helicopter tour business. He said he preferred sipping splashy cocktails and flirting with tourists who wanted to see the Keys rather than fighting bad guys.

Last but not least was my best pal, Steve "Mack" McKenzie. When our new Commanding Officer demanded Mack take an official leave of absence in order to have his eye attended to, I was certain he would argue every step of the way. But he didn't. That's when I knew it was serious. Mack was lined up to have the best care by the top surgeon in the business. Fortunately, the specialist was based at the Palmer Eye Institute in Miami, not far from my dad's home. That gave Mack a regular visitor, and Pops something to do while he recovered. Doctors said that even though Mack suffered a detached retina from the gorilla who nearly knocked his eye out of socket with the butt of a rifle, he would recover in a few months.

I would enjoy teasing him about his Captain Hook eyepatch.

It was good to get back home to my mountain retreat outside Asheville, NC, and had hoped to venture out for a long hike with my trusty companion, Samson. I needed to clear my head and give my shoulder some time to heal from the gunshot I got in Havana. Evidently, fate had other plans, because that's when my cellphone rang.

I had no idea who it could be. 90% of the time, it meant work. The other 10% was social; usually Mack, who would call to discuss a mission—past or future, my brother—calling to invite me to one of his kid's sporting events, or my dad—whose rare calls involved shooting the breeze.

If it was work, it was nearly always Sergeant Major Daniel Whitestone, USMC. He was the new commanding officer who coordinated all my *under the radar* jobs. That call generally meant trouble, either for me, or for someone about to run into me. If I was lucky, it would be a lady friend.

Today, it came from a lady friend—just not one with whom I could parlay our time into an enjoyable variety of extracurricular activities. And while I could have said I didn't hear the ring, or that I was out hiking with my dog, my instincts forced me to take the call.

Within minutes after hearing Clare's voice, and getting the

lowdown on what I would be doing for the next several days, I had packed up any thoughts of taking that long hike, grabbed my Go-Bag, and left, knowing it would be awhile before my next hike.

24

THE CALM

NEW YORK'S finest Bomb Squad had been dispatched to the Mayor's home for the second time in less than a week—hopefully to disarm a situation that could end up being catastrophic. Jack Klinger, aka *Trigger*, still has his padded bomb suit on—sans the helmet. Sweat slid down his forehead. It came from the heat—both inside the suit, as well as the moment. He forced a smile, hoping to keep Abigail distracted. And in one piece.

"You're doing great, Miss Abigail," he said, gingerly holding her blouse up, trying to keep her from being exposed.

"Thank you," she whispered.

"Don't you worry. I've done this a hundred times. And really? I think it's just a silly little game people play with one another."

He smiles.

"I like games," she said, relaxing her shoulders; this let Klinger know she was starting to trust him.

"Me too. Well, not *all* games, but most. I'll be done here in just another minute," he continues to distract her, hoping the button-like device was either a receiver or a microphone and not a bomb. Sadly, he wouldn't know until it came loose from the girl. Or, they came loose from this world.

Lukas and Clare stand across the room. His arm was around her, fearing she would faint again. She held her hands over her mouth, fearing she would scream again.

They wanted to send a message to their daughter that they were close by and just as brave as she was being, so they both refused wearing bomb suits, or holding bomb shields like the police used in riots. McDonough and the Chief, on the other hand, did not refuse protection—placing themselves outside and a good distance from the house.

One could never be too safe.

A tiny LED flashlight and a fine pair of tweezer forceps helped Klinger navigate the delicate situation.

Abigail quietly whispered, "What's going to happen?"

Klinger was amazed by her calm demeanor, and wasn't sure what to say. He wasn't big on bullshitting people; however, in scenarios as delicate as these, he also felt any additional anxiety wouldn't help anyone.

"Nothing," he said, winking. "I *promise* you that."

In another minute, he has the disc removed from her navel. Then, placing it inside a see-through envelope and, as an extra safety measure, delicately placed it inside an insulated metal box. This box could would provide enough security until he got outside where he would place it inside a larger contraption. Given he couldn't figure out why there was a roughly six-inch incision across her lower belly, his face worked hard not to display anything that would excite the little girl. He had several ideas, but certainly hoped none of them would be true.

"Okay, Abigail, we're all done. Now, don't let something like this ruin your birthday party," he smiled, brushing her dress and pretending like nothing happened.

Clare approached, looking to Klinger to see if it was okay to hug her little girl.

"This appears to be a microphone," Klinger semi-bluffed. "I'll take it outside and let you know more just as soon as I can, okay?"

"Yes, yes. Thank you. *Thank you* for risking yourself…for her," Clare said.

"All in a days work, Mrs. Burton."

Gently patting Abigail on the back, he leaned down and whispered, "Happy Birthday, Abigail."

She smiled, returning his wink.

Lukas squatted down and hugged her little girl. "I love you, Abi. Daddy and Mommy are so glad you're safe."

"Me too, Daddy," she said. Seeing several of her friends arriving in the front driveway, she started to jump from excitement. This petrified them both, as the instructions on her stomach advised against this. Lukas looks to Chief Davis and Phil McDonough who have come in from outside.

"Honey, STOP!" Clare shouted, before realizing her tone was too harsh.

Abigail followed orders, and Sharon and Julie instantly arrived to her side, as if on cue.

"Abigail, how about you and I go to the kitchen to get some lemonade for these nice people..." Sharon said, nodding for Julie to head outside and intercept the incoming people. Then, turning to Clare, nods toward the vast living room. "Clare, why don't you all go in there and Julie and I will direct traffic."

Clare mouths *Thank you,* then turned to the men. "Gentlemen, shall we?"

Burton motioned for all the men to join him in the other room, just as Officer Robert Jackson, the head of the bomb division, entered the home, along with several other bomb techs.

"Mayor Burton, my apologies for not being here right away. We had an issue in Brooklyn and well, between traffic and all..."

"Not to worry, Bob. Thanks for coming. What can you tell us... if anything?"

Making their way to the living room, he began. "Well, sir, Jack Klinger brought me up to speed outside with the chip he removed. He's nearly done, but we feel certain that it's a microphone. What that tells me is they're listening—rather, *have been* listening...for whatever reason, to what's been transpiring for the past..."

"Nothing's happened...to speak of," Clare interrupted.

"Mrs. Burton," Jackson said, touching the brim of his hat, "That's good news. I'm sure they're just keeping track of her. And likely working a plan of action, based upon the number of people around her. He removed his hat, wiping his bald head with a handkerchief. "Sorry, today's been a scorcher. Heat *and* pressure. Not a great combo in our business," he said, feigning a chuckle. He wiped the soaked headband. "What's got me confused is..." he looked around nervously, "What's confusing me...are those sutures."

His dry mouth smacked. "If I were a betting man...and this *seems* completely impossible, but..."

Klinger returned. All heads turn. And Jackson stared a hole through him.

"Sir, sorry to interrupt. Uh, it *is* a tiny microphone, classically used for bugging a room, combined with a miniature radio transmitter. That pretty much means whoever is keeping track of Abigail, could *potentially* be nearby."

This stopped everyone.

Chief Davis instantly pulled a radio from his hip and started barking orders. "HQ, this is Chief Davis, give me an All Call line..." His voice faded as headed toward the front door. Spinning around, he said, "I'll be right back," then disappeared.

"I'm guessing that he's putting an APB out for anything suspicious...for several blocks." Turning to Klinger, Jackson asked, "Anything else?"

"Just that. And the fact, it's not that easy to track. I mean, you can get these..." he said, holding it up for all to see, "Online at places like *Endoacustica*. Oddly enough, they're based in Italy. And big on electronic surveillance and such."

"Okay, got it. Good work," Jackson said as he returned to the group.

Klinger interrupts, "Sir?"

Jackson spun back around.

"About that suture..."

25

THE LUCK

WE LANDED in Teterboro Airport in less than 90 minutes. Bypassing all the crowds and security bullshit was a slice of heaven. The flight was a smooth, quick ride and I got a lot of thinking done. I'd heard Clare's side of the story and assumed everything was just as it seemed. Lukas appeared to be an honorable guy—for the most part. Like most politicians, I wasn't altogether sure he could be trusted. Wholeheartedly. When I heard he was considering running for President, I'll admit I was dumbfounded. I know he's certainly smart, undoubtedly rich, and likely powerful, but does he have what it takes to run the entire country?

Not confidently certain, I thought.

I hadn't seen him since they got married nearly ten years ago, but I have kept up with him by watching the news whenever I visited New York—which wasn't all that often. I had a couple of friends who lived in the city and they kept me up to date with a lot of what was happening. And I certainly did my homework. From the first call from Clare, I started reading up on him, his staff and all the platforms he was pushing. I'd read about his keeping the crime rate the lowest it'd been in years. His tax reform proposition, while a bit *out there*, was certainly something that got the media's attention. And the news of his *Super Train* for Long Island—while being discussed for years now, looked very improbable. But then again, *Ballbreaker Burton*—his nickname as long as I can recall, pretty much summed up his tenacity to get things done. He was notorious for not taking No for an answer. His military background likely had a lot to do with that. As a Master Sergeant, he was no joke. Big, bold and ballsy. And loud. He got what he wanted and wasn't afraid to bend the rules along the way. Something tells me he had continued to use that methodology today, especially if his office was that successful. Plus, he's had two terms. The fact he handled his own and very lucrative Fund Management and Investment firm, told me he and Clare were not hurting.

At one time, Lukas was considered to be "the competition." However, Clare chose him over me and that was that. As it should be. We weren't right for one another. Despite some years between us, it was apparent she wanted to get married and have children. I, on the other hand, have been married before. Three times, actually. Who they were and where they fit into my life wasn't important now. In fact, I hardly ever thought about them. Not that I'm an asshole, just that—as they say, *that was then and this is now.*

Clare and I had a fun summertime romp in Charleston, South Carolina, where she grew up. I was doing some work there, and after mixing too much sun, surf and splashy cocktails—as she used to call them, we got waist deep in trouble.

Exiting the plane, I shook the pilot's hand and thanked him for a smooth ride and his brave service to this country. He was retired Air Force. We spent ten minutes exchanging stories, while the crew got my *arsenal of toys* from the cargo space.

Clare had arranged for a car to be waiting for me, which was a nice touch. It would take another 40 minutes to get from the airport to Midtown. That eleven-mile trip—using the Lincoln Tunnel as a conduit to get us under the Hudson River and into Hell's Kitchen, would take another 40 to 50 minutes. I had booked a room at *The Standard,* for two reasons. First, they were smack in the middle of the island—on the West Side, where I enjoyed easy access into and out of the city. Secondly, I'd stayed at one in Los Angeles and found it to be completely entertaining. They did things differently.

They should use that as their pitch, I thought.

In less than 35 minutes, I was reminded why I didn't spend much time in this city. The noise, the crowds, the traffic and the smell were enough to run me back home to the slow life and Carolina blue skies.

But that wasn't where the trouble was.

I checked in and was immediately invited to join a lovely waitress at the bar for a cocktail. I politely refused, asking her to reconsider the offer later—when I was off the clock. She ran a pink tongue across full red lips, and her seductive grin curled up into a seductive snarl. The gesture was cute.

I wonder how long she practiced that in the mirror.

Within minutes of tossing my bags in the room, I was on my way to the one place that—good, bad or indifferent, was sure to elicit a significant response.

The drive across town was unbearably slow and uneventful. I couldn't get over how many people lived and worked on an island that was only 23 square miles. Everyone trying to get from Point A to Point B in a hurry was like emptying a jar of cold honey wishing it would pour faster.

Just doesn't happen.

26

THE ASSUMPTIONS

ALL EYES WERE on Officer Klinger. He knew he had to give an honest opinion, even though there was going to be some vitally disturbing repercussions.

"I have a solid feeling..." he lowered his voice. "She has a bomb...sewn inside her."

Clare could not believe this was happening. It suddenly felt like her world cranked into slow motion. Her vision narrowed, sound dulled, and it felt as though their grand piano was sitting on her chest.

What she wanted to do was run back home to her parent's farm, where her Mom would brush her hair to comfort her, and her Daddy would do whatever it took to make everything right. She desperately wanted this nightmare to come to an end.

She could hear her own heartbeat. And wanted to scream.

"Oh no," was all she could whisper.

Lukas knew he had to be strong, but asking him to comprehend this was just entirely too much. He wanted to push down the plunger and blow this whole city sky high—obliterating anyone who could even imagine doing something as evil as this. He could feel the pressure building inside his head, like when he used to jump from planes back in the force. He wanted to hit something, or someone. He too, wanted to scream.

"Oh…my God," he spat through gritted teeth.

"I'm sorry…Mr. And Mrs. Burton. But all indications *seem* to point in that direction."

Officer Jackson had grown weary watching the last three minutes. He knew what they were feeling; he had two young boys. But as much as this stung, the sooner he made this *real*, the sooner they could work toward making it disappear, As in, fix the situation.

"Folks, I hate to be so bold, but…that's my job," Jackson said, "It *is* a bomb. There's no sugar-coating it, or wanting it to be otherwise."

He waited for that to settle in, as both Lukas and Clare slowly bounced their heads in recognition. Somehow, he felt better. The elephant in the room had been acknowledged. How to dismantle that elephant was an entirely different matter—one with which he had little experience.

"And as much as I hate to say this…and likely *shouldn't*…I'm not 100% certain how to handle this," he said, waiting for outbursts.

Nothing.

They remain dumbfounded, in shock.

"I've seen bombs attached *to* persons who were…threatening a large crowd. We've all certainly seen… or *heard* about such in the news, but this…" he hesitated, as he felt the sweat gather on his head. The moment he removed his hat, it would certainly run down his forehead and into his eyes. He sucked it up.

"We have the very best in the business here right now, in Officer Klinger. And I believe more…en route," he said, turning to Klinger for confirmation.

"Yes, sir. And I've called one other of our men. He served in Afgha—"

Suddenly, the living room door burst open, startling everyone.

"Where are they?" they heard a man shout.

Lukas instantly stood, as Police Commissioner Tom Norris barged into the room. "Mr. Mayor…Mrs. Burton," he said, shaking their hands. "I am *so* very sorry to hear the news. The wife and I just returned from vacation. Seems as though it coincided with your... dire situation. Anyhow, I just had to get here as soon as I could."

"Thank you, Commissioner," Clare said, still numb from the impact of the most recent development.

"Thanks, Tom. You came in just as we were hearing the very worst...actually."

"Holy Hell, I'm so sorry. I was so caught up in...well, what is the latest..." he caught himself and took a deep breath. "I apologize. How is Abigail? She's home safe; that's the very *best* news."

Jackson leaned forward. "Actually, Commissioner Norris, I was just explaining that Abigail...while home safe," Jackson nodded to her parents for comfort, "She is, rather, there is...a more *dire* situation at hand."

Jackson took a breath, not wanting to hear himself say it again. "She has a bomb...sewn inside her stomach."

The expression on the Commissioner's face said everything.

27

THE EAVESDROP

30 Minutes Earlier—

Scorpion relished the very moment.

It was all part of the ruse, the hustle—the plan he'd been forming for months. Years, actually. Donovan Blair longed to bring a deep pain to the man who had brought him so much pain in the past. He wanted his *opponent* to know what it felt like to have something taken away—ripped from his reach, with the knowledge that a person, and their business and finances could potentially be stolen forever.

Sitting in his lavish midtown condo with his two girlfriends Mo and Margot, Donovan was taking great joy in hearing the little girl and her rescuers provide a play-by-play of scenes he had so carefully put into motion.

He knew the New York icon was within earshot and being filled with intense anxiety. The wall of monitors—hidden behind an enormous piece of art that disappeared into the wall, was helpful in keeping Donovan abreast of a large majority of busy intersections around the city; however, they could only provide a wide angle *view* and not much *audible* detail.

Donovan caught himself frowning, listening intently to the audio being fed to the speakers overhead. The electronic transmission was thanks to Ken and Sean who were stationed at two different locations in close proximity of Gracie Mansion. Ken was just inside a post-modern mid-rise directly across the street from the Mayor's home, hidden behind floor-to-ceiling shears with just enough opening to have a high-definition camera and a very long lens pointed at the home. He was watching the house through a pair of Canon IS binoculars. They were so powerful, he could nearly count eyelashes from a distance of several city blocks.

The Gracie Towers was one of the more coveted locations in the city to live. Built in 1960, the thirty story majestic enclave provided spectacular views of the East River, Carl Schurz Park and Gracie Mansion. Wealthy tenants chose the community for its' exceptional privacy.

One such tenant was Dennis Murddock, former Deputy Chief of Staff at the Securities and Exchange Commission. Murddock was currently retired and spent most days fishing in the Keys. However, in earlier years, he had befriended Donovan after learning of their mutual love of expensive toys. When Donovan learned Murddock had placed a target on the Mayor's back, the friendship was forged. They both wanted to expose Burton's dark underbelly. The Deputy Chief gave Donovan access to his home whenever out of town, allowing Donovan to keep an eye on Burton.

Sean, on the other hand, was in a panel van across the street from the mansion, and joined by a number of news outlets covering the recent kidnapping. Posing as 1210 WSCN—an all-news station, Sean had the perfect cover, as most radio stations had a remote van full of electronics.

Bonus: he had a clear shot to all the action, and was feeding it via satellite. Donovan and company, back in the condo, had full access to the feed, thanks to the elaborate set up.

Donovan, Mo and Margot listened intently.

The first voice they heard was a bomb tech.

"You're doing great, Miss Abigail."

"Thank you."

"Don't you worry. I've done this a hundred times. And really? I think it's just a silly little game people play with one another."

Donovan snorted, "Silly little game?"

Mo patted his knee. "There, there…"

"I like games."

"Me too. Well, not all games, but most. I'll be done here in just another minute."

"Yeah, we'll see about who or what'll be *done* in another minute," Donovan smirked, leaning forward.

"Bomb boy is trying to figure out if the disc we glued to her navel is a microphone or a detonation device," Mo said.

"They'll learn soon enough," Margot mumbled, feeling slightly remorseful for putting the little girl in harm's way, but wasn't about to say anything.

"What's going to happen?"

"Nothing. I promise you that."

"Ha! Shouldn't make promises you can't keep," Donovan shouted to the ceiling.

"You tell 'em," Mo said.

"I'm *Scorpion* and *I* decide who lives and pays."

"Okay, Abigail, we're all done. Now, don't let something like this ruin your birthday party."

"Oh, baby-girl, you haven't even *seen* the best birthday present yet!" Donovan said, walking to the bar to pour a drink.

"This appears to be a microphone is all. I'll take it outside and let you know more…just as soon as I can, okay?"

"Yes, yes. Thank you, thank you for risking yourself for her."

"All in a days work, Mrs. Burton."

The voices became garbled, as it was obviously being man-handled.

"Microphone is all?" Donovan shouted to the ceiling before taking a long drink. "Oh, it's more than just a microphone. It's what lies beneath that microphone that tells the truth!"

As Donovan turned the volume of the feed down, he could hear the tech tell Abigail *Happy Birthday.* Then, the sound changed. He must have been walking outside.

Donovan held his glass up to invite the girls to join him for cocktails, as his cell pinged. Picking it up, he read a message from Sean:

Boss, keep the volume up. I'm getting the techs conversation.

Donovan texted, "COPY," and turned the volume up on the remote, waving the girls to keep it down.

"Fucking hell, that was nerve-wracking. I nearly shit my pants. But that little girl? Cool as a fuckin' cucumber."

Donovan was enjoying the voyeurism.

"Dude, you kiddin' me? That shit's INSANE."

"Who's that?" Donovan asked.

"Another tech. Nobody important," Margot said.

"Bro, you know she's packing. Probably C4, or something like it."

"Worse than C4, you pricks," Donovan snarled.

"Oh, hello sir. We were just disarming the little girl. Not sure what it is but we're guessing C4."

"Jesus Christ, son. What the fuck has this world come to?"

Donovan picked up his phone and rang Sean. He picked up on the first ring.

"Who just showed up?"

"Police Commissioner Norris," Sean said. "Looks like *everyone's* coming to the party."

Donovan chewed on the inside of his mouth. Checking his watch, he pointed to the phone intercom on the coffee table and made a circular motion at Mo.

"Hold on. I'm getting Mo to conference us all together. Hang up. We'll ring you in ten seconds."

Sean hung up, and seconds later, he said, "I'm here."

"Please hold," Mo said, dialing Ken's phone.

"Yes?"

"Hold, I'm conferencing us," Mo said.

"Copy."

A smile slowly formed on Donovan's face. "This is good. This is *really* good," he said. "Better than expected, actually."

Mo and Margot looked at one another. Seconds later, everyone was connected.

"Okay gang, we're close. With the recent addition of the Police *Commissioner,* things just got—"

"Wait!" Ken shouted into the phone. "No fucking way!"

"What?" Donovan asked.

Focusing and refocusing his binoculars, Ken spotted a familiar face. The man was getting out of a black SUV and approaching the security detail.

"What?" Donovan barked.

"There's a guy approaching the gate. Looks familiar."

Nobody said anything.

"Looks like he owns the place."

Donovan couldn't see as much detail from the security camera he had covering the mansion, as his two men could see from their position.

"Sean, can you see?"

"Copy, sir," Sean said. "I see the guy Ken's talking about. Not familiar to me."

"*Shit,* it's that guy who was chasing you in Havana," Ken said. "Remember when I snagged you off the tarmac? It's him!"

Donovan nearly dropped his drink.

28

THE REUNION

As I ARRIVED on the East Side, I was surprised to see the number of people still camped out in and around Gracie Mansion. TV and Radio trucks lined the streets. Reporters were either shooting their stand-ups, or smoking in clusters. The front fence was covered in photos, balloons and candles, as a homage to Abigail. It was touching and unnerving at the same time—feeling more like a sign of things to come and less like a sign of hope.

My personal radar was humming and I wasn't entirely sure why. If I said I wasn't nervous, I'd be lying. Yes, it was a new assignment. That always had me a bit on edge. But the anxiety, for lack of a better term, was coming from the fact I hadn't seen Clare in nearly a decade. The time I had seen her before that, she and I were naked —for three days straight.

Now, I'm in New York trying to help find the sick bastard who stole her kid. I was pretty sure what the Burtons had witnessed was not the end of it. What I couldn't get over was how she was kidnapped. You'd think with all the security they had, this sort of thing could never happen.

But it did.

The clown at the front security gate evidently didn't get word I was coming. Either that, or he wanted to show how hard he was.

The slack-fitting suit and comfortable shoes showed me he wasn't serious. But I let it go and waited patiently for him to ring the house.

Moments later, the guard begrudgingly returned my ID and nodded toward the house. Walking the long driveway gave me the opportunity to case the property. Besides the front gate, there appeared to be a back gate. From what I could see, there wasn't any traffic there. Made me wonder if any security was covering their *six*.

I stopped to light a cigarette—a move as much about buying time to survey the property as anything. My sunglasses helped provide extra cover as I made a mental inventory of the vehicles parked along the front, as well as the number of type of reporters. I also scanned treetops for lights and/or cameras. I saw some lights wired into the trees, but only two cameras—one in the front, and one back.

I was about to head in when something clawed at the back of my mind. On the off chance anyone was watching me, I took out my cellphone and held it up to send a message. I wasn't actually typing, but taking a picture of the vehicles parked along the side gate. I recognized the CBS affiliate truck. Their satellite dish was raised—obviously beaming the scene back to their studios on the West Side. Everyone knew the radio station, 1010 WINS; they'd been around forever—literally as long as there was news being broadcast in this city. There was a plainclothes van that caught my attention. But they had a reporter sporting a CNN jacket and microphone badge. I let it go.

Wait.

There was a radio station van. WSCN and the digits 1210 parked further away, across the street. Why so far away? Secondly, I didn't see any reporter who matched their logo.

Off the top of my head, I didn't recall there being a 1210 signal in New York, or New Jersey—which, according to the side of the van, was their office location.

I did a quick Google check.

WSCN was in Duluth, *Minnesota*. Also, 1210 was in Philadelphia, not New York.

Okay, that could be a weird coincidence, I thought. *But I don't believe in coincidences.*

I let it go. For now.

My sixth sense must have been on high alert, because the hair was standing on the back of my neck—the same way when you know someone is watching you. I scanned the perimeter slowly. With so many buildings, and so many windows, it would be practically impossible to see anyone. And if they were on a rooftop—say with either a sniper rifle or binoculars, then my chances diminished even further. There were three high-rises within spitting distance. Two of the buildings had a minimum of thirty stories. The third was shorter. Wouldn't be much luck there—unless I had a second set of eyes.

Mack had been in the back of my mind since I lifted off the tarmac in Asheville. I knew he was under doctor's orders to lay low, but one thing neither Mack nor myself did very well was to lay low—especially when there was action in the cue.

Or a life in the balance.

I knew he would have to show up eventually, so I suppose it would be better to plant the idea of his making plans to be here sooner rather than later.

He can always say no.

I flipped through the photos I just took, making sure they were clear. At the same time, I flipped an imaginary coin in my head, trying to decide if I was going to call him.

Heads, I call him. Tails, I leave him alone.

The security slack at the gate hadn't taken his eyes from me since I arrived. I couldn't decide if he was trying to play a hard-ass, or he was bored. I didn't give a shit either way. Even if he hadn't let me through, I'd have gotten in—one way or the other. I cut him a smirk and he finally unglued his eyes from me. Stubbing out my cigarette, I start toward the house, figuring I could always call Mack and discuss those pictures later. Right now, I wanted to see what sort of beehive I was about to step into.

Fuck it, I thought at the last second—stopping just shy of the porch, and dialed his number. While the phone rang, I scanned the media entourage again.

Something's off.

Ring.

Most perps will hang around to watch their dumbass antics.

Ring.

I had the strongest feeling that was the case here.

Mack answered with a laugh, "Miss me already?"

"Yeah, never the same without your slack ass around. How's the eye, Captain Mack?"

"You worked long and hard on that one, huh?"

"Uh huh. Seriously, how's it going?"

"You mean my eye, the fact I'm laying around getting fatter by the day, or life in general?"

It's weird how much I love this guy. When you're friends with someone as long as we've been, it's hard to imagine life without them. The fact he's *saved* my life more than half-dozen times was nothing to sneeze at.

"Let me guess. You need my magical personality nearby to keep you company."

"Something like that," I said, looking at windows in the buildings across the street.

"Listen, Carter. I'd do just about anything right now to get off the couch and back into the shit. You know that. So, just give me the details and I'm there."

A window caught my eye—high above the street and directly across from where I stood.

"Not so fast. I do *not* want to be the one who puts you behind the eight ball."

"Why start worrying about that shit now, bro?"

I'm just about to divert my attention to another building when a flash caught my eye.

"I *knew* it," I grunt, lighting another smoke.

"What?"

"I'll bet you dollars to donuts I'm being followed—watched, anyway."

"Where?"

"What?" I answer, distracted.

"Where's the perp?"

"Across the street," I say, counting floors. "Fifteen stories up."

"How can you tell?" Mack asked, knowing it was a waste of time to question me.

I turned my head in another direction, while keeping my eyes on him.

"Caught a reflection. Also, standing there too long for my comfort."

"Copy that."

I could hear Mack moving around.

"His mistake was having that curtain pulled back so…" I began.

"Woah. Okay, there you go. He pulled it."

"Made you?"

"Yup. Gotta have glasses on. Or a scope."

"Glasses. Not on the roof, not a scope."

"Of course," I said, appreciating how Mack's mind worked.

"Okay, here's the deal. Straight up. I'm heading in. Time to face the music and see what kind of idiots we're dealing with. Why don't you—"

"Packing now," he interrupted. "Was checking flights as you babbled on."

"Smart ass."

"What I do best. You head in. I'll be there…"

"What?"

"Just calculating shit."

"Shut up 'n call the office for my bird. Save all that *bullshit*. You kidding me?"

"Hey, I don't take anything for…"

"Save the heroics for when you get here and save my bacon. Again."

We wound down, he rung off, I banged out a text to the pilot, and headed in.

Time to peel another layer.

29

THE DIVERSION

DONOVAN WAS PACING the room like an expectant father. Mo sat on the couch—her eyes shifting from the wall of TV screens to Donovan. Lost in thought, he stared out the window. Margot was in the kitchen, pulling together food.

Mo said, "Donovan?"

"Yeah."

"To me—it feels like it was only a matter of time. Right?"

Donovan knew she was right; it was the elephant in the room—the fact Carter was going to show up. While he wasn't sure how, he knew it was inevitable. He had watched the way the soldier handled conflict in Havana.

You don't handle that much pressure, with those many distracting variables and not be a mental machine.

He noticed the way he withstood pain. It wasn't likely you could be put through situations as Carter had—surviving that much pain, and not come out the other side broken.

I'll never forget the look in his eyes when I threatened to kill his father in cold blood, right in front of his face.

He knew if he and Carter were to switch places and Carter threatened his father, Donovan would search the earth to find him, then slowly tear him apart, limb by limb.

Donovan understood that look. And now, with this foe in front of him once again—in his own backyard, he not only *felt* that look, but had the strong feeling things were about to get complicated.

"Sure," Donovan said quietly.

His girls knew him better than most. And with Ken and Sean not in the room, he could be more transparent; even though it wasn't his favorite emotion.

"It's okay. We're good," he bluffed. "He's just one guy. And we...*I*...have the upper hand."

"Exactly," Mo said, looking to Margot—who tossed her head toward Donovan.

"Baby, we've got this," Margot said. "You've done all your homework. Nobody can touch you."

Donovan spun around, flashing his part-charming, part-maniacal grin they loved.

"Hashtag-Boom!" he said, merging social media with his love of all things explosive.

"That's our man," Mo said.

"Just a momentary lapse of reasoning, girls," Donovan said. "We're about to launch the next phase of our master plan and there's not a god-damned thing that jarhead can do about it!"

They laughed.

"Even if I'm a jarhead, too," he laughed. "And proud of it."

"Okay, Ken and Sean have eyes on our target. We've just added an element that'll make things all the more interesting. And 48 hours from now, we'll be rich 'n happy. While *someone* will be poor 'n dead."

Donovan took a cellphone from his pocket and dialed a number. He started to speak before realizing he had reached an answering machine. Checking the screen to be sure he had the right number, he waited for the beep.

"Hey, Caprese, been awhile. I'm in the middle of a sizable nego-tiation...that's right up your alley. And could benefit you. Call me."

. . .

KEN HAD PULLED the curtains way back in order to see Carter more clearly. He had watched the stranger from the moment he arrived to the moment he disappeared inside. And while he didn't know him—outside of the Cuba gig, he knew from Donovan's reaction something was up. It didn't take a rocket scientist to realize Donovan had a beef with him. Ken felt fairly certain Donovan would kill him the next time he saw him. Even more, Ken knew he'd have to learn more, and the sooner he did that, the further ahead he would be. Being in front of a situation with Donovan—not an easy position to manage, would go miles toward making him richer than he'd ever imagined.

He took out his cellphone and called Sean.

Sean answered on the first ring. "Yeah?"

"Man, you got that thing taped to the side of your head?"

"Sorta," Sean replies. "Whassup?"

"Where does Donovan know that guy from?"

"The guy we just made?"

"Yeah. He's the one we saw in Cuba. But what the hell's he doing there?"

"I don't know," Sean grunted, "Why?"

"Well, I was called in to grab Donovan, and *that* guy, shot at us. Luckily, he missed my chopper, but only by inches."

Ken continued to watch the stranger, and mumbled, "Coulda ended a *whole lot* differently."

"Sounds like it."

"But you don't have any—"

"Nope, but I can find out," Sean said.

"Nah, I'll do it. Probably got better resources than you. More, anyway."

Sean didn't appreciate the slam, but let it go.

"How's your angle? The trees are blocking a lot of my view."

"I've got a straight shot through the front gate and up to the house," Sean grinned. "I can't see *in* the house, but then neither of us have x-ray vision, right?"

"Okay, no big. Guess we'll just sit tight until…"

Ken's phone pinged. Checking the screen, he said, "Speak of the devil. Gotta go."

Sean sat for a moment, stewing over Ken's attitude. He knew he was Donovan's *boy*, and was making more money than him, but there wasn't nothing he could do about it. Except play along.

Just then, his phone rang. "Yeah?"

"Hey, we're hooking up a three-way. Hold on," Mo said.

Seconds passed, before the three were connected. Donovan was the first to speak. "Okay, guys, we know who's in there now, it's time to plan our next steps. If we deliver the message *now,* we'll be in the strongest position possible, *especially* now that Carter's with them. I'd call that a bonus round."

"Nice, boss," Ken said.

Sean asked, "Hey boss, you want me to deliver the message and get out?"

"Are you positioned well?"

"Not *exactly*. There were several vehicles here but—"

"But will it do?"

Sean didn't want to complicate matters, or piss Donovan off, so he went with it. "Yeah I'm in a good position."

"Then proceed as planned," he said, "And Ken?"

"Yes?"

"You've got the stronger cover, and the best view. Stay put."

"Copy that," Ken said, going back to the window and pulling the curtains open far enough to see everything, including Sean.

"Sean, drop 'n dash. We'll see you back here. I've got your next gig already lined up."

"Got it."

"And Ken, you keep an eye on Sean. See that he gets out of there. Any complications, call me right away. Keep your eyes peeled. I want those people to stay put."

Donovan disconnected.

Sean's position, while not perfectly placed in front of the gate, was okay for what was to come next. He went to the back of the van, rolled back a rubber floor mat, unlocked a handle, and lifted a panel in the floorboard. Seeing the street immediately beneath him, he took a flat metal box and gently placed it on the ground directly below the van. Sticking his head down and out of the opening, he double-checked the undercarriage to be sure he would clear the box as he pulled away.

Happy with that, he set the timer to 2:00 minutes, closed and locked the floorboard lid, covered the space with the mat, climbed back into the front and pulled away.

30

THE CHAOS

I WAS GREETED at the front door by who I had to assume was the housekeeper. She was a short, plump, African-American woman with a gentle smile, but stern vibe.

Opening the door, she looked me up and down then offered an automatic and inauthentic smile. "Mr. Matheson?"

"Yes. But you can call me Carter."

"Fine, Mr. Carter. Everyone is in the drawing room. Mrs. Burton is expecting you. Can I get you something to drink?"

"No, thank you. I'm fine."

Nodding, she hesitated, as though waiting for a cue.

"May I ask who's in there?" I tossed a nod toward the closed door.

"Certainly. Besides Mr. and Mrs. Burton, Police Commissioner Tom Norris, along with Chief of Police, Jacob Davis, and Mr. Phil McDonough, the Mayor's personal attorney. There is also a press secretary, or something like that, in attendance. I'm sorry, but I didn't get her name."

Her voice was as perfectly polished as her demeanor.

"Good," I said, waiting for her to usher me in. "Are we waiting for someone else?"

"I don't believe so," she said, looking in the direction of

upstairs.

"Who's upstairs?"

She hesitated before answering. "Two of Clare's—I mean, Mrs. Burton's close friends. A Mrs. Patterson and a Ms. Barton."

I knew Abigail was here, but wondering why this woman was acting so squirrelly.

"And Abigail?"

"Oh, yes, Miss Abigail is with them," she said, fidgeting. "They're preparing for Abigail's birthday party."

"Can I join the others now?" I smiled, nodding toward the closed doors.

"Of course. This way," she said, ushering me through the grand foyer and to the drawing room, sliding open tall mahogany pocket doors.

The first face I saw was Clare's. She was as beautiful as she had ever been. Maybe more so—even after ten years.

And one child kidnapping.

Lukas was locked in conversation with a tall officer in the corner. They all stopped and turned to stare, as I entered. Watching Clare, I recalled her being the quintessential host, and thus, she kicked into instant dramatics. She always was one for making everyone feel special; thus, the melodramatic introductions, complete with names, titles, years in their positions and anything else that would paint the very best of pictures of each person and their contributions. While informative, it felt contrived, which made me wonder if it was nervous energy, or a stalling tactic.

I went with nerves. The fact that all the men in the room had served our country would make this more palatable. We all exchanged nods; however, the intense look from Lukas was not only disconcerting, but made for awkward energy.

Clare came directly to me, without hesitation. "Hello, Carter."

"Hello yourself."

"You look fit."

"Thanks. You, too," I smiled.

"You always were a good liar."

"Calling it like I see it. And I see a beautiful woman who hasn't changed a lick in a decade."

She blushed. "Oh, you can save that cool demeanor and devilish grin for the other girls. I'm quite taken."

"I know. But ya' can't blame a guy for trying."

Shaking her head, she kissed my cheek, whispering, "Always the charmer."

"If it works…"

She turned to show the room it was all business. "Okay, before 'his majesty' comes over and breaks up our social hour, let me get you up to speed."

"I'm here to serve and protect. In any way possible."

I watched her let that sink in, before I add my most charming grin.

"Right. Well, this false sense of calm I'm displaying is merely masking a neurotic and devastating terror I feel deep within."

Placing a hand in the small of her back, I said, "Your little girl is home safe. She'll be fine. *You'll* be fine."

I glanced over just as Lukas was heading toward us. Clare made distance between us.

"Thank you, Carter," she said loudly. "I'm sure Abigail will be very excited to meet you. I've told her—"

Lukas interrupted with his hand out. "Carter. Been too long. Good of you to come."

"Glad to be here," I lied, extending my hand.

"I would say I'm happy to see you, but I'd be lying," he smirked.

"Understood, Mayor."

After an awkward moment, he said, "Actually, considering this…mess, and the fact you're good at dealing with situations like this, I guess I'm *somewhat* glad to see you."

"Fair enough. And off-topic, what's this I hear about your running for President?"

His surprised expression and brief glance at Clare was humorous.

"Well, I have a good many people who believe I can do it."

"Crazier things have happened," I smiled.

"Who knows? Presidents have come from all sorts of backgrounds."

"You mean like New York's real estate tycoon with the prime-time TV show?"

"Don't get me started," he rolled his eyes, as he slapped his hands together.

Clare held up a hand to stop him. "Lukas, to address the *elephant*...and get it out of the way, I *had* to call Carter. When I saw that things were escalating and your schedule was so busy, I just—"

Ignoring her with a wave, Lukas shifted his energy to include the others in the room. "It's fine, Clare. I just don't like surprises."

Two men stepped forward and we spent a moment getting acquainted. Soon, we were covering details about how the Mayor's daughter was kidnapped—with Lukas briefly explaining how he had paid with offshore accounts and such. Then, as though he was the hero of it all, he spoke about how his girl was returned quickly and without incident.

I found the rapid payoff odd, but said nothing.

My hunch was one of three scenarios. First, whoever did this was clearly one sick bastard who needed some attention. And money. Secondly, I was confident the *mastermind* behind this would want more money, or something as equally important. Thirdly, this was about more than just money. I was getting a hit about revenge, or jealousy. Or, as my gut was saying, *All the above.*

"Look, I'm here to *help* solve a case," I said, looking at the Chief and the Commissioner. "I can't do it alone—just as none of you can. It's become quickly evident we are dealing with a person, or persons, with a unique skill set; one that includes kidnapping. And while remaining practically non-existent—so far, my job over the hours to several days will be to find who is behind this. And we will. Together."

"Good. Let's hear your thoughts," Lukas said, looking at Clare then me.

"First, let's see if I've got all the details I need."

"Shoot," Chief Davis said.

"Abigail was kidnapped less than 72 hours ago. Broad daylight. Middle of Central Park."

Lukas and Claire nod.

"Well, not actually in the *middle*..." Clare nervously said.

"Right," I said, "But not far from the Zoo. Closer to Fifth Avenue."

A nod.

"And her nanny, Ms. Marcheaux? She's been with you for awhile. So, she's a trusted member—"

"Several years. She's family," Clare said emphatically. "We trust her implicitly, right Lukas?"

I instantly knew from his expression they were in disagreement.

"Yes, of course."

Whatever, I thought. "And this took place around ten o'clock in the morning."

Another set of nods.

"Carter, I appreciate your showing up here and sharing all your knowledge with us," Chief Davis began, "But could you...would you mind letting us all focus on the incident *immediately* at hand?"

I looked at him, allowing my silence to do the talking, before adding, "Sure, Chief..." I looked to his badge—even though I knew. "Davis."

"Good."

"And the *immediate* incident?" I asked.

He stared at me, before releasing an oversized sigh. "She has a *bomb* inside her stomach."

My mind yelled, *Holy Shit.*

My face showed, *Oh, okay.*

I said, "Tell me more."

31

THE MONEY

THE NEXT THREE MINUTES WOULD CHANGE EVERYTHING.

Police Commissioner Norris' phone rang at the same time Chief Davis' walkie-talkie squawked. Seconds later, a bomb tech with the city barged in the front door and ran into the room where we were gathered.

Breathing heavily, his face read: terror. "Chief, Commissioner, Mr. Mayor? You're going to want to see this."

We all looked at one another.

"NOW!" he shouted, waving us to follow him to the front porch.

Outside, in the middle of the yard and surrounded by a half-dozen bomb techs and policemen, was a large metal box, the size of a carryon suitcase. Matte black and with a plain handle, it looked fairly innocuous.

A bomb tech with *Klinger* printed on his vest said, "This was discovered by a reporter a few minutes ago. It was left by the curb, not quite a block away. Because of the news, one of them ran and got me."

"I thought you were headed back to the precinct," Chief Davis said.

"Not so much. I just kept having a feeling like I should hang out."

Impatient, Commissioner Norris said, "Son, get to it."

"Yes, sir. My robot ran a thorough examination. It's just a box with a note inside."

"And?" Chief Davis said.

"And, uh…an odd *prop*, Sir."

"What do you mean prop?" I said, leaning forward.

Klinger jerked his head toward me, looked to the Chief.

"He's one of us," he said. "Carter Matheson meet Officer Jack Klinger."

"Carter's one of the best shooters in the Corp. And expert at finding people."

"Honor, Sir," he said, looking barely old enough to drive—much less dismantle bombs for a living. He picked up the box to show us the prop.

It was a children's doll, but with a hollow chasm where her stomach would be.

Lukas reached for Clare, as she started to faint.

"As you can see, this doll had a firecracker, or maybe an M-80, inserted into her stomach. It's…well, *prank* isn't the right word."

"Got it," I said, motioning to move things along.

He handed me the doll. After looking it over, I passed it to Commissioner Norris. "What else was in there?"

He handed me a cellphone and an envelope.

"They've both been dusted for prints," Klinger said.

I looked up with raised eyebrows. He shook his head. I mumbled, "Not a surprise, I suppose.

Since the envelope was addressed to *Mayor Burton*, I handed it over and examined the phone, and grunted, "Generic burner."

I pushed the power button and the screen lit up. It read and I said, "Expect a call."

Lukas read the letter aloud, "And here you thought we were done. Almost. Thanks for the $100. Glad your girl is safe. Now, for part two."

"What?" Clare gasped.

"Honey, please," he said gently, before continuing. "You will wire us a second $100,000,000 by 6AM/EST this Friday."

Lukas' jaw dropped—the color quickly disappearing from his face. He looked to Phil McDonough, before taking a deep breath. No doubt, trying to remain calm for Clare, he continued to read.

"Deposit *exactly* as before, or if by 6:01 we don't have our money, the next sound you hear will be your last...as we detonate the bomb inside your daughter."

32

THE PARTNER

MACK KNEW he had to get up and running as quickly as possible. For Carter to call and reach out to him—after his doctor gave explicit orders not to do anything for at least a month, he knew Carter needed his help. And frankly, he liked that. Besides, he could only binge-watch so many shows. After *Longmire, House of Cards, Man in the High Castle* and *Game of Thrones* were complete, what else would he do besides take long walks, go fishing, or have an occasional rendezvous with a past or present lady friend. Worst of all, he wasn't allowed to hit the gym because he couldn't exert substantial pressure due to the eye injury.

Just as he told Carter, his *GoBag* was packed. He would get to the hangar and be on a flight before Carter sat down for his next meal. With only thirty minutes left before he landed at Teterboro, he ran through a number of items on his list.

He was sure Carter had packed his *Cheytec* rifle. Mack did the same—along with enough ammo to fight off a small army. He had learned long ago one could never pack too much ammo—especially if they were flying private, as Carter and Mack did most of the time. He also brought along a pair of Canon binoculars. They were the best made and both he and Carter never scrimped on anything that was instrumental in allowing them to see, hear, or shoot their targets.

Mack had his Mac laptop open and was scouring the island of Manhattan, using Google's latest map app and their 3D technology. He was fascinated how he could zoom in to buildings and streets and see them in such detail. One of the added benefits of being among the elite of Special Ops, was having access to inside secrets.

James Bond, just more probable.

One app he was especially fond of was *SynthCity,* a program that took surveillance to the next level. Along with that, he carried a pair of the next generation *Oculus* goggles. Given his passion for technology—plus the fact he had friends in R & D in Silicon Valley, he was able to get his hands on the latest toys in development. With these two elements—along with a thermal adapter, he would be able to see things most others could only dream about.

He had spent too many hours researching weapons, and besides sniper rifles—which was obvious, he enjoyed the latest in handguns. Much of the new technology allowed you to print your own arsenal on a 3D printer. The possibilities were endless. At the same time, it provided a good deal more dangerous opportunities for lunatics to be armed in ways we never thought possible a few decades ago.

An offshoot of his weapons fixation was explosives. He had certainly heard of, and worked with C4, a plastic composition made popular decades ago. It was used by the Army to blow up enemy compounds. Needless to say, it had dozens of uses, but was bulky. K5 was a new product some companies had been adapting from a number of different compositions. However, it had the reputation of being unstable at times. In fact, in certain temperatures, it would explode when it wasn't supposed to.

Then there was M6, a military propellant used in firing heavy artillery. It also had challenges with stability. On more than several occasions, it was reported to have *not* worked in times when it was absolutely necessary—not a good situation when a person, or group, was depending on an impenetrable force in their path to be removed.

The latest concoction of choice, used mostly by terrorists, was a compound that went by the initials: TATP. It lived in an acetone peroxide base and utilized an easily accessible collection of over-the-counter products. That easy accessibility, along with its' inexpensive price tag, made for a quick and easy destructible soup. A group of his pals outside Silicon Valley, affectionately known as lab rats, were working on merging TATP—something they referred to as *tater tots,* and putting it in a liquid form. That way, it would pass the sniffing dogs at airports, could be concealed in every day bottles, and be more easily transported anywhere.

Mack looked up a few places Carter had mentioned on the phone, in order to be instantly acclimated upon landing. He double-checked his email, and saw he was staying at the same hotel as Carter. He had heard about *The Standard*—known for being a swinger's paradise—at least in LA.

Taking out his cellphone, he typed a short text to a car service he had told Carter about. The driver was an old friend from the Corps who had returned to his hometown of Brooklyn, and set up shop with the help of friends in the security world.

Within seconds he had a confirmation text.

Another thing off my list, Mack thought, as he swiped through his phone, searching for four pals who lived in or near New York.

Two were twin brothers. Ty and Thomas Svenson who both worked for NYPD. As former Marines, they suffered from PTSD. After returning home, they took up body-building as a way to channel their aggressions and serve their bigger mission: killing bad guys on the streets rather than trying to put them behind bars. They felt that removing them from society was better than wasting taxpayers money trying to rehabilitate them.

Next was Ko Yoshi, a Japanese tech wizard, nicknamed, Koi—as in fish. When he wasn't developing complex websites with uber encryption, he was designing algorithms for satellites in space. His hobby, Mack recalled, was working with miniature communications —be it either cell phones, or radio transmitters.

His last contact was a guy Carter had met on a job out West. Pete Norelli was a cop. He was a helluva character. Mack liked him, both for his no-bullshit attitude and his nose for finding people. He and Carter had that talent in common, as both were relentless hunters.

Taking the last minutes before hitting Manhattan, he pushed his seat back and tried to relax his eyes. The calm before the storm was a place he relished. And he knew that in very short order, his life, Carter's life, and potentially the lives of many more would be placed in the path of danger.

But he wasn't afraid. He was never afraid. After all, this is was what he signed up for.

Looking out the window, he whispered, "*Semper Fi.*"

33

THE CLUE

AFTER THE POLICE, the Mayor's family, and I recovered from the news we just received on the front lawn of Gracie Mansion, we were back inside. I began designing a strategy which included getting prepared for next steps, while guaranteeing one little girl would live to see another birthday. That beautiful girl was sitting in the living room and surrounded by her parents, police personnel and myself.

I had to help her feel secure, even in this most insecure of situations.

"Abigail, I know this seems complicated, but I have a really good feeling about you."

"Yeah?"

"Yep. I think all this fuss…is nothing you can't handle. Would you agree?"

Her smooth forehead wrinkled. "I think so."

"After all, *someone* who just turned…*ten years old…*" I began, watching her tiny grin break into a cheek-to-cheek smile. "Well, that special person is a big enough girl to handle just about anything. Wouldn't you say, Mom?" I said, looking to Clare.

Even deep inside an emotional quagmire, she beamed with

pride. To those close to her, that smile was a mask that cloaked the horror she was feeling.

Mother and daughter exchanged looks. I had a good idea this was one of very few sweet moments this family had seen in several days.

Abigail had been nervously squeezing her toy giraffe the entire time we spoke. It was obvious she was trying to appear brave. And even though I just met her, I was proud of her.

"Abigail, there are a lot of silly people in this world. And those silly people do some really silly things. And sometimes those silly things…well, they turn into mean things. Does that make sense?"

I felt as long as we kept the room peaceful, she would remain calm.

"Yes I do, Mr. Carter."

While I don't have children—nor likely ever will, I certainly had a soft spot for Abigail. She was just one year older than the niece I lost in a tragic accident not very long ago.

Another story for another day.

"You're so polite, Abigail. But how about you call me Carter? Just Carter."

"Okay, Just Carter."

I knew right there, we were going to get along just fine.

"Abigail, like I said, there are a lot of people in this world who are…mixed up," I said, touching my head. "You know? Up here."

Looking to her giraffe, she gave a small nod. The room patiently. If I rushed this part, I was afraid she'd get spooked. And that spooked feeling could not only upset her mentally, but physically. And that *physical part* was something we didn't want to mess with.

"Abigail, some of those mixed up people do really bad things. We don't know why. Maybe it's like when kids bully one another at school. Does that happen in your school?"

"It happens a lot," she whispered. "Not to me, but some of my friends."

She was engaging and this was good. I think her parents were more terrified than she was.

"My new friend Miss Margaret said that bullies are just scared people," she said very quietly.

I enjoyed watching her smile, as she rubbed the fake fur of the giraffe.

"Who's Miss Margaret, Abigail? Is that one of your teachers?"

Shaking her head, she looked up at me. "It's the lady who gave me this giraffe. I really like her."

I looked from Abigail to Clare.

"That was her *friend*..." Clare said with an odd expression. "The person she stayed with for a couple days."

"And Mr. Nick. He was nice, too."

Then it clicked.

Holy shit. Why hasn't anyone talked about the captors?

My expression must have said it all, because everyone wanted to speak at once.

"*Those* were the people who had her for a *sleepover*," Lukas said.

"We're looking into that, but we need *more*," Chief Davis said, nodding toward Abigail.

I can't believe this shit, I thought. *Mack's gotta get here now.*

"That's good," I said, smiling and stroking her giraffe.

"Abigail, how many other *friends* were you staying with?" Police Commissioner Norris asked.

"That's a good question, Mr. Commissioner. Thank you," I said, smiling at him before turning to Abigail. "Yes, Abigail, how many people were you hanging out with?"

Her bright blue eyes shot up to the ceiling and to the left, just as we do when trying to recall a memory.

"There was two more. No, three."

"Really? That's...something. What were their names?"

"Uh...the other woman was Miss Kitty. And there was...a...Mr. Scott."

I held my breath, expecting this to be a turning point. When she hesitated, I nudged her. "Was there one person who kinda led the group, maybe he was the *party* host—is that what you call it, Clare?" I turned to her, nodding for reinforcement.

"Yes, Carter. That's a party host. Just like Miss Barton and Miss Patterson, right honey?"

Abigail was practically giggling now, as she looked across the room for the two women. They were standing at the doorway listening. Both waved to Abigail—who returned the gesture.

"Abigail, who was the...party host?"

"Mr. Smith! He was nice. He has a really nice home. It's big. And white."

White?

"Like the White House?"

"You're silly, Mr. Carter. That's where the President lives. Mr. Smith's place looks like..." she touched her chin like she was deep in thought. "Like a museum."

In a city of 13 million people, with hundreds of thousands of buildings—shouldn't be too hard to find, I thought.

"Good, Abigail. Like a museum. What was outside those windows?"

"All the windows had curtains. But I peeked one time...when they all thought I was taking a nap. I wanted to know where we were."

"Smart girl. And you peeked where?"

"Out the window. They told me that it was really bright outside and they needed to keep the windows covered so it would stay cool."

I looked from the Chief to the Commissioner to Phil McDonough and back to Abigail.

"But they stayed closed all the time."

Both Lukas and Clare were hanging on her every word.

"And what did you see?"

Petting her giraffe, she looked at me and smiled. "We were really, really high. It was like that time Mommy and Daddy took me to..." she turned to Lukas. "Daddy, what was that place we went on vacation...in that big tower...in the really green city."

Frowning, Lukas tried to recall. Then, he and Clare simultaneously said, "Seattle."

"The space needle! Yes, that was a couple summers ago," Lukas answered.

"The *space* needle. That's neat," I leaned forward. "Abigail, tell me one more thing. Can you remember *anything special* around you…when you were peeking out that window? It could be a building, or a sign, or…*anything.*"

She shook her head quickly, not giving it much thought. I waited. As she started to fidget—clearly ready to get on with her party, I thought, *At least we've got something.*

Trying a different tactic, I slumped, pushing out my bottom lip.

"When's my birthday party? And why are you pouting, Just Carter?"

"Soon, honey. In just a few minutes?" Clare interrupted. "Right, Carter?"

"Right, Abigail. Soon. And I'm pouting because I really, *really* want to try and figure out where you were staying with your friends, Miss Margaret, Miss Kitty, and Mr. Smith. It would *reeeeeeally* help me figure all this silliness out."

Seeing she clearly ready to celebrate her party, I decided I had to be happy with this crumb, so I stood. "Thank you, Abigail. And again…Happy Birthday," I said, giving her a small peck on her cheek.

"Thank you, Just Carter," she giggled, took Clare's hand.

"Let's get on with the show," Clare said with a crooked smile over her shoulder, as they started walking away.

Suddenly, Abigail stopped, spun around—like she just heard a secret and pulled Clare's arm toward me. "I remember now, Mr. Carter. I saw a lot of water. Just like the river…right outside our house," she said, pointing toward the East River.

Bingo!

34

THE LETDOWN

THE DAY WAS GETTING LATE. People were emotionally drained. And Abigail's nap time was sneaking up on her. It had been a tough day and it was time we took a different tact—something that needed to be put into motion.

"I think the best idea for all of us..." I said, looking at Lukas, Clare, the Chief, the Commissioner, Phil and Clare's two girlfriends. "Is for the family to call it a day and get some rest. The rest of us will discuss more over dinner. Then, tomorrow, we can face this with a fresh mind."

It was obvious everyone was glad to hear that. With a combined sigh of relief, each stood.

"Good idea," Lukas said.

"Sounds like a plan," Chief Davis said, absently brushing his cap before putting it on.

"Clare, we want you to know..." Police Commissioner Norris stood, reaching out to take Clare's hand, "We will do whatever it takes to help make this difficult time less so. Don't hesitate to call me for anything."

"Thank you, Commissioner. The fact you've been here by our side through so much of this...well, I can never thank you enough."

"I've got some things to tie up and run past my partner..." I checked my watch, "Who is waiting to decompress with me back at the hotel." Squatting down to Abigail's level, "Abigail, you have been the bravest young lady I have ever met."

"Thanks," she yawned. "Will I see you tomorrow, Mr. Carter?"

"You bet. Now, get some rest so we can plan some fun events for your birthday. I think it's a good idea that your Mommy and Daddy delayed the party until this weekend."

"It's going to be even *bigger* and *better* than before!" Clare said.

Eyes wide with excitement, Abigail said, "Really?"

We watched as the enthusiasm rekindled in her eyes. Clare knew this is exactly what Abigail needed.

"This way we'll have time to invite even *more* people and plan a party *twice* as big," Clare laughed.

Abigail was ecstatic with the thought. "Can we have a pony ride in the backyard, and a clown to make balloon animals for my friends, like they do in the park?

Looking to one another, Lukas and Clare say, "Sure."

"For right now, let's get you ready for an early bedtime," Clare said, waving her two friends over. "Aunt Sharon and Aunt Julie will help you get ready and I'll be up in just one minute, okay?"

The rest of us made our way to the grand foyer for a few closing thoughts.

"The best advice I can think of is to get rest," I said. "Then, first thing tomorrow, we get Abigail to the hospital for x-rays."

"Agreed," Lukas said.

"Of course," Clare said quietly. "We need some peace of mind."

Looking to Clare and Lukas, I tried to think of the best way to say what was on my mind.

Clare must have seen my struggle and said, "Just spit it out, Carter. You're in the thick of it now."

"Right. Here's the thing. We have to be honest with each other and about Abigail's current state. We don't know exactly what this maniac has done. I have a good idea, but we can't be certain. Yes, she has to remain calm and stable. No sudden moves. No…"

Glancing up, Clare looked like she was about to lose her shit. I said, "I'm sorry. Maybe, I shouldn't be speaking so—"

"No, Carter. It's fine. Just alarming. I understand the situation. But I'm a mother. It's all so unbelievable."

Lukas wrapped his arm around Clare's shoulder. "It is. But you're a strong person, Clare."

"Both of you are," I added. "And have to remain that way…for just a little longer."

Phil McDonough, who had been quietly observing, finally spoke. "Let's take her to Presbyterian. It's the best, and if we need *special eyes* on it, I know someone over at Cornell that'll have insight."

"Good," I said, turning to the Phil, "We really need someone special to handle this. *Without* fanfare."

"Trust me, I've got the people. She'll be in the best of hands," McDonough said, turning to Lukas. "And *we* have to discuss where to get the extra hundred."

As I walked to the corner to hail a cab, Phil's car pulled up. Rolling down his window, he said, "Want a ride?"

Not sure why, but I hesitated, not really in the mood to make small talk. And with an attorney, no less.

"C'mon, you don't want to ride in a smelly cab," he said, waving us toward his car. "You're in midtown right?"

At the moment, I had no idea how he'd know that, but I didn't show that I cared. "Yeah. Meatpacking district."

"Good. I'm heading in that general direction."

I started for the door, but his driver beat me to it. Expressionless, he held the door.

"I'm at the Standard."

He gave a terse nod, and I got in. The inside of his car smelled like an expensive cigar. Or twenty.

There was an awkward silence before McDonough spoke. "Quite a pickle we're in, huh?" he said nonchalantly.

"Yeah, I'd call it a…*pickle.*"

He snorted, "More like a pile of *shit.*"

Not sure why, but I had an odd feeling Phil was playing both sides of the fence. I played along. "How's that?"

"Well, this isn't just a random occurrence, right?"

I said nothing.

"I mean, we *both* know that."

You just keep talking.

"Someone comes outta nowhere…kidnaps the Mayor's daughter…and demands not just $100-million dollars, but comes back for a *second helping*?" He shook his head. "Why $200 million dollars?"

He took a cigar from a built-in humidor—in the partition between the driver and us, and motioned for me to have one.

"No thanks."

"C'mon, Carter, enjoy. This box of smokes cost more than you made last year," he grinned.

"Doubtful," I said, reaching in and taking two. "I'll smoke it later. With my business partner. We've got a long night ahead."

He laughed, "Fair enough."

"And what makes you call it bullshit?"

"Just what I said. *Two* trips to the Mayor's bank? With what appears to be a backup plan with catastrophic ramifications?"

Nothing.

"Something smells bad."

"Could be your cigar."

Rolling one between his stubby fingers, he said, "*Cohibe Behike*. Cuban. Very nice."

While I don't know much about cigars, I know a good one when I smell it. And I have heard of that brand. And they did cost a lot. *But not my last year's salary. Dick.*

After several blue rings disappeared, he continued, "I want to know what *your gut* says, you know…about this situation. So far, anyway."

I didn't have the time, nor the patience to drill down on matters I still had to decipher. This was intel I was only going to share with Mack. I wasn't interested in spinning hypotheses to someone I just met.

But given he and Lukas were pals, I had to give him something.

"I guess…something feels fishy. As in…unusually *familiar*. But what? And who? No idea. But that's why I'm here. My job is to find the guy behind this bullshit. And bring him down. Ideally, inside the next…" I looked at my watch, "40-plus hours."

McDonough blew a thick blue ring toward a slightly open window. It hung in mid-air, floating in slow motion, before rapidly disappearing out the slit.

"Good. That's what we need…a man of action," he said, before getting quiet for several minutes.

The ride seemed longer and slower with the silence. But I was in no hurry to talk.

"When's the last time you saw Clare, Carter?" he asked, looking straight ahead.

The balls on this guy.

"Too long," I played along.

From the corner of my eye, I saw his head turn in my direction. I just kept looking out the window.

35

THE DISTRACTION

THE RESTAURANT DONOVAN had chosen for the team to celebrate was a favorite among many in-the-know New Yorkers. Claiming the phrase "sushi nirvana" by a number of prestigious reviewers, made getting a reservation at *Sushi Nakashima* next to impossible. However, given Donovan was friends with Chef Daiki Nakashima, who often reserved the entire restaurant for close friends, made snagging coveted seats at the tiny restaurant a breeze. It also helped that one of Donovan's two girlfriends, Mo Wang, had at one time shared "social time" with Chef Nakashima.

Donovan had booked the entire place for just the five of them, allowing them to be staged in the center. Hidden shades were pulled to cover the front window. It wasn't that they needed the extra privacy, but more Donovan didn't want roaming eyes to see them all in one place at the same time—something they rarely did.

Tonight, *Scorpion* was elated with the way his plan had taken shape. His astrological sign was Gemini, and tonight he felt both the angel and the devil sitting atop his shoulders. Free-flowing bottles of sake certainly helped elevate his heightened sense of elation. In fact, they were finishing their third bottle of *Dassai Beyond Junmai Daiginjo* Sake and were only halfway through the meal. At $1300 a bottle and four-figures per person for dinner, Donovan felt like a rich kid in the best candy store.

In a couple of days, he thought, *my wealth will reach an all-time high.*

He lifted a glass to toast. "Here's to you and here's to me and if we ever disagree, then fuck you all and here's to me!"

Laughing, they clinked glasses.

"That's classy, love," Mo said, kissing him.

"I'll second that," Margo said, pulling his face to hers, also kissing him.

After the laughter died, Donovan said, "Guess the ball's in his court now."

"And his balls…in our hands," Mo said.

"Nice," Margo added.

Sean asked, "So, who *is* this Carter guy?"

"Just some jarhead," Donovan said.

"Who is *supposedly* a killing machine," Mo adds. "Although I didn't see any of that when we ran into him in Havana."

Donovan smirked. "Yeah, but we got the jump on him."

Ken smirked.

"What?" Donovan asked, pouring himself another glass.

Ken punched Sean's arm. "You know Chris Kyle? The Navy Seal? The one who has, or rather *had* the record for the largest number of confirmed kills."

"Yea, wasn't he shot at a shooting range by some whack job *after* coming home from duty?"

"That's the one. 160 kills. All time high."

"Shit."

"Carter?" Ken raised his eyebrows. "141."

Sean raised his eyebrows, but didn't say anything. Ken slammed a shot of sake.

"He also had two tours of duty. Decorated both times. Between he and his sidekick—a guy named Mack, they've *saved* more lives than they've taken."

"Impressive," Sean said.

"Plus his old man's a retired Lieutenant Colonel in the Marines. And his sidekick is a retired Sergeant. With a Medal of Honor."

Margo leaned forward. "So, what's so special about this Carter?"

"Couple things, I guess," Ken said. "You know the Top 10 sniper shots in history?"

Margo shook her head.

"*Shooter,* one of my favorite films," Sean said to Margo. "Marky Mark."

They fist bump.

"Well, Carter's number 11."

"Shit," Sean said.

Donovan had been fidgeting with his chopsticks since the Carter conversation began, and was growing impatient with the discussion being taken away from him. He leaned forward, resting elbows on the table.

"Okay, so what's the other thing about our *Boy Wonder?*" Donovan spat.

Ken saw Donovan's reaction and didn't want to pour gasoline on the fire, so he took another mouthful of sushi.

"C'mon, *Mr. Reference Manual*...don't let me down now," Donovan smirked.

Wiping his mouth, Ken stared at Donovan. "You're the one always telling me to know the enemy."

Donovan waved him to continue.

"Okay. He's a hunter. And according to his background report— which I got my eyes on, thanks to a pal inside, he can find anyone... or pretty much anything he wants to find. Whatever it takes."

Donovan swallowed, but didn't allow his expression to shift. "And now, he's hunting me," Donovan growled. "Well, *us,* actually."

The group looked at one another. And kept sipping.

"That's cool," Donovan said calmly, leaning back in his chair and popping his neck from side to side. "We're gonna be his *toughest* target yet."

"Copy that boss," Ken smiled.

As Donovan raised his glass, the others joined.

"Here's to the *toughest*...*most* *tenacious*...*most* *talented* *targets*...to never get caught."

EXITING THE RESTAURANT, Donovan and Nakashima embraced. Bowing, Donovan said, "Gochiso sama deshita."

Nakashima bowed, smiled and said, "Come again. There's always more."

Leaving, Mo whispered the translation, "It was quite a feast."

As everyone gathered curbside at the short parade of Escalades, preparing to say goodbye for the night, Donovan said, "Okay, one more quick thing before we call it. I've got to take a short trip out of town. But I'll be back this time tomorrow...if not sooner."

Both Sean and Ken start to say something.

"Hold on," Donovan holds up his hands. "Just some quick business in Havana. In the meantime, Mo, I want you to double-back to confirm no loose ends on Time Square screens. I'm certain their snooping will start there. Margo, you keep a low profile. You spent the lion share of time with the girl..." he paused. "On second thought, you go with me."

Margo and Mo eyeball one another, but in a mocking way.

"All right, we'll even the score later," he winked to them both. "Sean, you keep tabs on Gracie Mansion. Your choice whether you want to live in the van, or in the penthouse across the street."

"Got it."

"And Ken, you see what, if anything, you can learn about the nanny. Who knows, maybe our good Mayor would like her to disappear—given she *lost* his daughter in broad daylight."

"A vacation, or...?"

Donovan measures his response. "I'm thinking the big exit, as she's the only one—besides Abigail that's seen all of us. And I do mean *all* of us." He let that sink in. "But, we can play it by ear."

Margo said, "Speaking of Abi, are we really...I mean, if the Mayor doesn't come through with the money...are we really going to—"

"What do *you* think?" He said, staring at her, then scanning the faces of his team.

Silence.

The maniacal laugh that came next was abrupt, making the girls nervous. They weren't sure if he was being dramatic, or was actually insane.

"There's no way in hell Burton will let anything...and I mean *anything* come between he and his *only* daughter. I know the guy. Really well. I knew his wife. The *first* one. And he can be a tremendous son of a bitch. But here's the funny thing...Burton never wanted children. *That* was the problem with his first wife. But then he met this *Southern Belle,* and had a daughter. Well, that changed everything. So, trust me when I say, he will do *anything* to keep that little girl safe."

"So...why just $200 million?" Sean asked.

"What?" Donovan barked.

"I mean, he's worth, what..." he said, turning to Ken.

"Something like one-point-five billion. I think."

Mo said, "Actually, *just* shy of two."

Donovan looked at her. "That's my girl. Not only a tasty figure, but a head for figures."

Sean asked, "Okay, two billion. Why not more?"

"All two?" Donovan grinned.

They all nod in unison. Then, there's a long silence.

"Because pigs get fat and hogs get slaughtered."

No one said anything for a moment, then smiles spread across each face until everyone was laughing.

36

THE DECOMPRESSION

PHIL MCDONOUGH and I arrived at West 13th & Washington Streets, where *The Standard* straddled the High Line. As much as I was a Southern boy at heart, I liked the funky hotel with a chill vibe. Even the rooftop bar was cool, although a bit crazy. Which is exactly what Mack and I intended to do—get crazy, once I left McDonough's traveling humidor.

He was still on the phone as we arrived. His hush talk had gotten annoying about twenty minutes ago. Now, as I reached for the door to get out, he grabbed my arm.

"Wait," he said to me, then "Hold on," to the phone.

I looked down at his hand on my arm. He let it go.

"Sorry, Carter. I had to take this...and didn't mean to be rude. Whaddya say we circle back around first thing, huh? I can have a car pick you up, if you'd like."

"Thanks, but I'm good. See you at Presbyterian, or, I don't know...later in the day?"

"I'll be at Presby by 8, but have a court case at 10. I'll see you then, or we can get together later. Whatever works for you. Happy to help any way I can."

"I'll let you know."

He said, "Good" and was back on the phone before the door

closed. I thanked the driver for getting my door with a head nod. He was as expressionless as the moment we started.

New York my ass.

AFTER SEVERAL COLD BEERS knocked the road dust from our throats, Mack and I started catching up on personal matters.

"So, you *can* or you can't see yet?" I said.

"I can," Mack said, lifting the patch to show me his eyeball was in fine form—well, besides the sclera being bright red.

Mack had gone to wearing the eyepatch full time, as he said the ladies dug it.

"You're insane," I said, smacking him on the back.

"True. And while it's not 100%, it's 90," he said, taking a drink, but fiddling with a cocktail napkin.

I've known him long enough to know that was a clear sign for *I'm trying to decide if I should tell you something.* So, I waited. Watched the crowd for a minute. Spotted a few hotties. Then ignored them. And looked out at the skyline.

"So, I was thinking...about calling Teresa again," he finally said.

I grinned—more inside my head than outside my face. "Really?" I said, playing coy but enjoying seeing him squirm. He knew I had my eyes on her, but then we both knew she was a fickle gal.

"Mack, that's an infatuation with no future," I said.

"Yeah, prolly so," he said, swirling the last drops of beer in the bottom of his bottle. The *second* sign he still had stuff to say.

"And?"

"And what?"

"And what does *she*...think about your...seeing her again?"

He finished the last of the beer and motioned to the bartender for another. "Look, let's just get to talking about why I'm here."

The beer arrived. He took a healthy drink. And I waited.

"Tasty, is it? You good?" I smirked. "C'mon, spill it."

He took another gulp, then leaned closer. "Okay, smart ass. She told me that—and I quote, 'My heart is with Carter, but my body is with you,' unquote."

I couldn't help but chuckle. He had it so bad. But I knew exactly what it was. Because I had had it, too. "Okay. I get it. You play it the way you think's best. Our friendship will outlast everything else."

We clinked bottles and finished our beers.

I said, "Good talk," tossed a $100 dollar bill on the bar, winked at the overly-tattooed, yet underly-intelligent waitress with a skirt that left nothing to the imagination, and we made our way downstairs.

THE NOISE WAS TOO MUCH, we were too tired, and despite the fact we didn't want to appear *bromantic*, we did want to be able to hear one another talk. Besides, I needed food and I knew the *Standard Grill* served until 3am. Checking my watch, I figured we had just enough time to feed the beast within. So, sliding into an oversized leather booth in the corner, we ordered *Steak Frittes* with extra mayo—otherwise known as *meat with a side of artery-clogger.*

On a more serious note, Mack went on to share how my dad had developed an infection from the scorpion bite he'd gotten over a month ago. The guy named *Scorpion* we met in Havana dropped his pet killer down my old man's shirt. Needless to say, *both* scorpions disappeared shortly thereafter. The good news was that after some hefty antibiotics, Pops was mending nicely. As for his full-time bodyguard Mr. Black, he was walking with a limp.

We finished "family business" by wrapping up with an update on Xeon—the remaining soldier in our Cuban rescue mission. Word was she had been reassigned to an undercover gig back in Havana. This time, she was on point to intercept intel that was passing through town. We didn't think it was about a group setting up shop. At least, that was the word *under* the street. We weren't sure *when* we'd see her again, but I mentioned we should get her up here to help, and how cool it would be not only to see her again, but how much we could use her ass-kicking *machismo*. We wrapped up our *girl talk* with a mention of our she reminded us of Gina Carano in *Haywire*—a movie that was a favorite of ours.

The steak and fries were perfect. The beer was overly expensive, but deliciously cold. We both pushed away from the table, rubbing our bellies like two old men.

Mack cut to the chase. "How about you bullet-point me what you have, and I'll stop you when I need details. Cool?"

"No other way, right?"

We clinked glasses.

"Here's what I know," I began. "First, our guy knows explosives. That puts him in one of several categories."

"Right."

"Terrorist, demolition, or hobbyist."

Mack nods.

"It's a team. I'd say anywhere between three and six. The lead could be military. And potentially rich."

"Why do you say that?"

"Which part?"

"Well, I get the three to six. It would take at least that to orchestrate the park snatch. The screaming nanny," he said, holding up one finger, "The clown," adding a second finger, "And the blind guy," he finished with a third.

"First grade shit, right?"

"Exactly. Plus, another couple for transpo or surveillance puts it at six."

"We both know military would create this sort of precision. Timing's everything, right? Also, being rich's a given. Takes money to make money."

Nodding all along, Mack said, "This isn't a hobbyist, or a terrorist. Too big for a weekend warrior, and too small for a terrorist."

"My thinking exactly. Moving on. My money's on one of three opponents. You'll come to the same conclusion."

"Shoot."

"My gut says it's someone he knows; either someone he's worked with, or *works* with. Could've been someone in the force with him, someone he stepped on—or over, but had to have pissed off."

"Revenge," Mack nodded. "Logical."

I finished the last of the fries in front of us. "Something keeps nagging at me: *No one* saw *anything* out of the *ordinary?*" I punched for emphasis. "I get the park. It's *Central* Park. And I get it, yeah nobody wants to get involved, but there's always *someone* who comes forward with some cellphone video."

"Nothing?"

I shook my head. "Whoever it is or was, had or has, is *jonesing* to hurt Burton."

"Makes sense."

"Hurt Burton," I chuckled. "Sounds like Halliburton."

Mack gave me a deadpan look.

"The briefcase maker?"

Nothing.

"Never mind."

"You're losing it, bro—terrible thing to waste," Mack smirked.

"Funny. But what I'm losing is *sleep.*"

"Why don't we say, for the sake of argument sake, it's a group *outside* the country: Taliban, Isis, the Chinese—someone with plenty of money and or position, who wants to get even. Or something to gain like—"

"Right, right. *And* don't forget the *political* angle, especially given he's now wanting to run for freakin' President!"

He gave me a high-five.

"Okay, so let's think. What's Burton *really* got, besides money and *potential* future power. Meaning, there are plenty of other rich politicians to hit. Richer, even."

"Copy that," Mack sipped. "I'm sticking with local."

"Agreed," I grinned. "Also, according to Abigail, we know she —and by that I mean *they*…were in a tower."

"Oh, I *guess* that helps?" Mack grinned. "We're only in a *city* of towers."

"And there was water. Smart ass."

Mack laughed. "Again, *two* rivers? East and Hudson."

"I know. But this is more than we had 24 hours ago."

"I'm going with the East River," Mack said. "Going with the proximity factor. Sounds like they're watching the Burton's every move."

"I can see why you'd say that. But I'm going with the Hudson."

"Of course," he smirked.

"He wouldn't shit in his own backyard. And, it would double the danger."

"Okay."

"Let's also talk about the surgery technique."

"Yeah, right." He leaned forward. "Tell me about *that*."

"Could be a surgeon—"

"A disgruntled doctor wants to get even for a botched tummy tuck," Mack burst out laughing.

I smacked his arm. "Or the perp could be a seamstress. Or rather, seamster?" I said half-joking.

"And we're back to military," he said, finishing another beer. "Remember, you can sew."

"Yeah, buttons."

"Fuck that. Remember the time we were in Wrightsville Beach following that East Coast drug dealer and one of his jokers came at me with a knife, and opened my thigh?"

"Yeah, but that—"

"But nothing," he interrupted. "You took out fishing line, a hook and sewed me up."

"Point is: this guy's precise," I leaned forward. "The opening on that little girl? It was *ruler* straight…razor thin…and meticulously precise. We'll know more what lies beneath…" I looked at my watch, "In a couple of hours."

"Okay," Mack held up his hands in surrender. "Got it. What else?"

I got the attention of our bartender and scribbled in the air. "We gotta crash. I'm toast. And we gotta start early."

"Anything else we're missing?"

I released a big exhale, sat back and stretched my neck from side to side. "Well, we know the team, or someone inside the team, has got to be pretty tech savvy. Or connected."

"Why's that? Screens in Times Square?"

"While certainly not impossible, that shit takes tech, planning and again, *large* money."

Mack scratched his chin. "Guessing local, right?"

"Reading my mind, brother."

The waiter delivered the check. I tossed my Platinum Amex and a $50 bill toward the waiter before Mack could even touch his pockets.

"Thanks."

"Whatever."

"Let's go back to Lukas himself, getting away from the who... and hit the *why*."

"Solid call. We know he's an asshole."

Mack snorted. "How's that?"

I cut him a look. "Really? Marines? Top of his class? Leader of the pack? Clawed and scratched his way to the top of the financial markets the second he bounced from the Corps. Everyone knows he's the first guy to do whatever it takes to turn his opponents, or his teammates, into a freakin' ladder—catapulting him to whatever top he's aiming for."

The waiter returned with the bill and disappeared with a wink and a nod.

"Yeah, I was reading up on the flight here. Notorious business-man, has made millions upon millions."

"Uh, try *billions*. Nearly two, anyway."

"Yeah? Geez," Mack shook his head. "Okay. And from what I read, he didn't make those bucks by making friends."

"Copy that," I said, putting away the receipt and motioning for us to leave.

"Hold it. Let me just finish this beer," Mack said.

"Oh, sorry."

"I got something," Mack grinned, finishing his beer.

"What?"

"Could be a shooter, except I haven't heard any mention of guns *except* when you called the other day. You thought you saw a sniper in the window across the street."

"Yeah, no," I said, picking my teeth with the edge of a sugar pack. "That was a fluke. Probably some old lady wondering what was happening at the Mayor's house."

"Okay, one last thing," Mack said, rolling a cocktail napkin into the shape of a cigarette. "Why his daughter? Why not the wife?"

"Go on."

"Wouldn't his wife be a stronger target? She's from old money and quite the socialite, right?" Mack scrunched his face like a boy trying to pronounce something tough.

"Good point. On both counts."

"Also, why *two* asks? I mean, why the $100-million, *then* a second hun? Why not just…half-a-billion?"

"Funny, Phil McDonough asked the same thing. I've wondered, too."

"And lastly…"

"Finally," I said, standing.

"Lastly…" Mack stood, taking the patch from his eye and tucking it into his shirt pocket. "Why a bomb, if—" he said, stumbling on the table leg. "IF there really IS a bomb."

We both stopped, and looked around to see we are the last two in the place.

"I hadn't spent much time thinking about there *not* being a bomb. I just assumed so," I mumbled. "Guess we'll know soon enough."

"See?"

I swatted the air—pushing aside his idea. It had merit, but just kinda off.

At the elevator, I punched the button and turned to Mack, raising consecutive fingers. "My gut? One, it *is* a bomb. Two, it's someone he knows. And three, someone in his office, likely close to him, helped set the whole damn thing up."

37

THE PILLOWTALK

IN THE DARK, during the last moments of consciousness, Lukas and Clare were lying next to one another, pondering the complexities of the past several days. The only comfort they had at the moment was knowing Abi slept peacefully in the room next to theirs. That, and the fact, there were armed policemen surrounding the house. While that gave Lukas comfort, it did nothing but distract Clare. She tried to put it out of her mind.

A baby monitor captured Abigail's shallow breathing. It felt familiar and comforting to Clare, but her mind raced, considering what the next dozen hours had in store.

"Clare?" Lukas whispered.

I thought he was asleep.

"Yes?"

"Why didn't you tell me about Carter?"

I knew it.

"Like I said, you were busy. And things were moving so fast that—"

"But Clare," he interrupted, "I am your husband."

Really? I didn't know that.

"Of course, honey."

"I'm here for you. And Abi. I would do *anything* for the two of you."

Then show us the attention we need.

"I know that."

He sighed heavily—not interested in underlying issues.

Carter makes me feel safe.

"I was just scared," she whispered.

"But I'd move heaven and earth to be certain you both were safe."

I don't want to get into this.

"Honey, I need *at least* a couple hours of sleep. You do, too."

"Clare, please don't shut me out. Let me help."

You could help by stop talking, so I could sleep.

They shared a long silence.

"But you reached out to him first," his voice nearly cracked.

Carter understands me.

"But my heart and daughter are here."

"And me?"

Can I just get some peace?

"Yes. Of course."

"You know we may need to…liquidate some things."

Are you trying to fuck with my head?

"I'm sure we will. What are your thoughts?"

Another long silence.

"Actually, *either* the house in the Hamptons…and the boat…" he trailed off.

Shit.

"Or?"

"The house and rental property in Charleston."

Now, you're fucking with me!

"What?" She gasped, sitting up in bed. "My *childhood* home? It's been in my family for generations. Besides, Mom still lives there!"

He put his hand on her back, and gently rubbed it. "Okay. The Hampton house. Plus, we still have this home."

Not like it's ours.

"Right," she sighed, lying back down.

"We just need to remember…of the many things to consider… especially with my running for President."

Unbelievable.

"You sure there's a real chance at that? I mean—"

"I'm *very* confident. We stand a *very* good chance. It's early, but we'll see."

Just make my baby girl safe, first.

"For now, it's all about Abigail."

You better believe it.

"So, I don't have to worry?"

"No, dear. Certainly not," he whispered.

Bullshit!

"How can we be sure there won't be *another* note…asking for *more* money?"

"Because I'm sure the NYPD will find the bastards."

Rolling onto her side, she put her back to him.

If anyone will find them, it'll be Carter.

"I hope you're right."

"And yes, we will use Carter's help," he said. "I just want to… lead the efforts."

Like everything else.

"I know you do."

He let out a long deep breath, "It's going to be fine."

Please stop taking.

"Good night," she whispered.

He began snoring.

Finally!

TWO HOURS LATER—

Awaking from a nightmare, Clare sat up in bed, trying to gather her bearings. She looked around. All appeared safe in her home. Lukas quietly snored next to her, and she could hear Abigail's heavy breathing on the baby monitor sitting on her nightstand. She took several deep breaths, in an attempt to lower her heart rate.

In the dream, she had been standing in the middle of Central Park shackled to a park bench. There were neither trees, nor people around—just Abigail and Lukas, riding wooden ponies on an enormous merry-go-round. As circus clowns chased them, Abigail screamed for Lukas to take the bomb out of her tummy. Lukas' face was full of panic because his hands were tied to the pole supporting the pony he was riding. Suddenly, she saw Carter riding toward her on a large white horse, dressed in all black.

Doesn't take a genius to figure that meaning.

She quietly slid from bed and into a pair of slippers, making her way down the hall toward Abigail's bedroom. The door was slightly ajar, so she stuck her head in, saw her little girl was safe and sleeping soundly. Considering returning to bed, she instead had a strong need to hear Carter's voice.

Tiptoeing down the stairs, she was startled by a security guard by their front door. He took a step forward.

"Sorry, couldn't sleep," she said, smiling and pointing toward the kitchen. "Just going to get something to drink."

"Of course, ma'am. Sorry to startle you, and good night," the officer said, returning to his post.

In the kitchen, she filled a glass with ice and went to her home office. Pouring a large splash of vodka, she removed her private cellphone from the desk drawer. Staring at the phone, then double-checking the time on a walk clock, she saw it was just after three. Wondering if it was a good idea to call, she took a long sip of courage.

I've got nothing to lose—he's already here.

Staring out at the East River, she wondered how life may have turned out differently.

Worse case scenario, he picks up and I say I couldn't sleep.

She shook her head, thinking how childish she was being.

I wanted to know if you've learned anything yet, I could say.

She frowned, thinking he'd see right through her.

What are you doing?

She finished the vodka and opened the desk drawer, then stopped.

"Fuck it," she whispered, dialing the number.

After four rings, it went to voicemail.

"This is Carter. Tell me what you need. I may get back to you. We'll see. Here comes the tone—"

Just as she started to leave a message, something caught the corner of her eye.

BEEEEEEP.

She spun around to see Lukas standing at the door.

38

THE DREAM

4:20AM/EST —

Carter drives down a long and winding road, somewhere in the mountains of what looks to be Northern California. Tall mountains are on the right; the Pacific Ocean, on the left. He is driving an enormous Cadillac convertible from the late '50's. It's red with a white leather interior. The hood looked twice as long as he remembered.

"Lying Eyes" by The Eagles is playing on the radio.

As Carter reaches over to turn up the volume, he sees there was no radio in the dashboard. Instead, the sound was coming from a tiny stage that sat atop the car's dashboard.

Looking more closely, he saw the stage was a miniature replica of the Hollywood Bowl. And The Eagles were playing on that stage.

Something out of the corner of his eye caught his attention.

Mack was riding alongside the Cadillac on a huge Harley Davidson motorcycle, wearing an Elvis outfit, complete with The King's signature sunglasses and chewing on an enormous cigar, smiling like the cheshire cat in Alice in Wonderland.

They drove, looking at one another from time to time, but saying nothing.

Suddenly, both Clare and his part-time girlfriend, Teresa, simultaneously appeared in the backseat. As they watch the scenery pass by, he made eye contact with them in the rearview mirror. They both looked at him seductively, but said nothing.

Carter looked out to the horizon, over the ocean, and saw a storm brewing. It was full of dark clouds and lightening. The ocean was becoming more turbulent by the second.

Looking back to the road in front of him, he slammed the brakes to avoid hitting a man standing in the middle of the road.

From the waist up, it was the man he saw in Havana. Donovan Blair. But from the waist down, his body was an enormous scorpion. His huge Popeye-like arms held his father in one hand and Abigail in the other.

Hearing a scream behind him, he spun around to see Lukas sitting on the top of the back seat with Clare straddled between his legs. He had a machete to her neck.

Yelling at Carter in slow motion, Clare reached out for his help, but no sound was coming from her mouth. Carter tried to grab her, but his hands were tied to the steering wheel.

Suddenly, a thunderclap in the distance grabbed his attention, and he turned to see waves climbing higher and higher, threatening to crash the shore.

Another bright flash—like lightning, caused the scene to change. Now, they were all in the middle of a desert. And instead of sitting in a Cadillac, he now sat in a barber's chair.

Off in the distance, he saw his partner Xeon approaching. She was riding an enormous white Arabian horse, and dressed like Xena —Warrior Princess, holding a huge sword. As she came to a stop, her horse stood on back legs and appeared to whinny, but there is no sound.

Then, she froze in place, as the ground shook beneath their feet, and a phone rang in the distance.

Ring, Ring...Ring, Ring.

Each ring got louder, until the last ring nearly deafened him.

Looking down, tree roots were growing up and out of the ground like snakes, wrapping around his ankles and pulling him into what appeared to be quicksand.

A nearby gunshot caused him to look from the quicksand at his feet, to the direction of the noise.

Two men, Dr. Leonard Caprese and Ashgar Debashi, approached, riding horses just like Xeon. Caprese was laughing, but Debashi was pure white, while his eyes were black and dead.

Jumping off his horse, Caprese began dueling with Xeon and Mack—the Elvis impersonator, as Debashi slowly melted into a puddle of blood.

Carter closed his eyes, trying to force himself awake. When he opened them, he was in the middle of what looked like a frozen tundra.

Standing twenty feet in front of him was Abigail with a long wire that hung from underneath her shirt. The wire disappeared into the distance, for as far as he could see. His gaze followed the wire, but then noticed how the wire returned from far in the distance, circled back around, and stopped at his feet, where an old-fashioned dynamite plunger sat.

With his hand glued to the top of the plunger, he looked up to see fear in Abigail's eyes.

Carter suddenly felt a crushing pain in his chest—as an invisible force began pushing his hand down on the handle of the plunger. He fought desperately.

In an instant, the Eagles song, the thunder, and a gunshot came to a crashing halt, as she opened her mouth and screamed as the plunger slid down to make contact with the box.

SUDDENLY, I awoke, lying on the floor, face down and still dressed. Sitting up, I saw I had knocked over a small dining table and a bucket of ice. Squinting at the clock on the bedside table, it read 5:55. The early morning light was just beginning to break the horizon.

Rubbing the side of my face—which was partially numb, my

head felt like someone had driven an iron stake through one temple and exited the other side. Standing, I walked to a full-length window and stared out at the High Line, the Hudson River, and over into New Jersey.

It all felt oddly familiar, as I whispered, "Damn."

39

THE HANGOVER

STANDING IN THE SHOWER, the oversized shower-head beat the crap out of the top of my skull and the back of my neck. I lost track of the number of beers Mack and I had consumed last night, but I was sure it was more than a half-dozen—maybe eight. Judging from the handful of tiny bottles scattered on the floor across the room, I evidently had enjoyed some Tequila, after returning to my room.

Going down, it was all great. However, this morning, the after effects hung around my neck like a boat anchor.

I had about 20 minutes before Mack would be tapping on my door, and I was going to take every second of time to soak my head and refuel. Turning on the shower at full capacity, I let the room fill with steam, went to the mini-bar, and took every bottle of water, Gatorade and Red Bull they had. Before climbing back into the shower, I washed down two *Goody* powder packets with a small *Gatorade* and ordered room service, asking for two pots of coffee— telling them to delivery even if there was no answer.

I then sent a text to Mack: *In shower. Come over. Coffee's here.*

The next 19 minutes was dedicated to massive hydration.

The images of last nights nightmare flickered on and off in my head like a broken fluorescent bulb. I didn't have the immediate wherewithal to make a great deal of sense from it, but I had several good ideas that would intermittently drop through the grate of my subconscious. I had to assume some of those ideas would settle into a semblance of rational thought soon enough.

One thing came to mind: while I wasn't 100% sure what was residing in Abigail's belly, there was no way any of us could take any chances, and given we were all gathering at the hospital shortly, that was all I could focus on.

Well, that and the throbbing heartbeat I felt between my ears.

MACK and I sat in silence for a five full minutes, sipping coffee and watching the sunrise. All the windows were as open as they could be. The breeze felt great and the coffee was slowly bringing me back to life. Mack had the presence of mind to order a dozen eggs and a pound of bacon for the two of us. He wasn't in much better shape than I, but given we didn't do this often, we didn't care. The pain would be a distant memory, soon enough.

"Did you sleep as poorly as I did?" Mack asked.

"You don't have to yell."

He chuckled.

"I don't remember, but the fucked up dream that woke me…"

"Yeah?"

"Let's just say, I need to call that therapist our former CO recommended when we got back from Afghanistan."

"That sucked," he snorted.

"You have no idea." Deep breath. "I'll share some of it in between locations today—just for your amusement, but for now…" I said, looking around the room. "Do you have the keys?"

"Huh? What keys?" he asked.

"To the truck."

He grinned."What truck?"

"The one parked on the back of my head."

"Never get tired of that one."

"Me either."

. . .

MINUTES LATER, I was climbing into a black Yukon Denali with tinted and bulletproofed windows. Mack and I were being driven by one of our preferred drivers. His name was Ko Yoshi. He went by the name, Koi—as in fish.

He occasionally worked as a bodyguard, when he wasn't driving politicians, starlets, or television anchors in and around town. Standing just under six feet and packing 200 pounds of solid muscle, he had a look that said, *Don't fuck with me.*

Don't let the kind eyes fool you, he would often say.

"Hey Koi," I shouted through the window that separated us. "Mack tells me you have some mad skills."

Koi pulled a pair of Oakley sunglasses down his nose. Looking at us in the rearview, he said, "That's a fair assessment. Depending on what you mean by *mad*," he grinned.

Mack and I eyeballed one another.

"Tell Carter about what you were doing back in the Corps."

Koi shook his head to imply, *Not important.* But when Mack gave him "the look," Koi complied.

"My thing was Intel, Recon, Cell Comm. If you had to keep a secret, find a secret, or hear a secret…well, that was my shit."

Mack and I looked at one another and grinned. He said, "His shit could come in handy."

"Yep."

"My official skills are boring," Koi said, maneuvering city traffic like our enormous SUV was a scooter. "Cloud-based services, security encryption, and I dabbled in miniaturization."

"So, what are you doing playing taxi driver?" I asked.

Smiling, he said, "I'm my own boss. Work when I like. Don't answer to anyone, and make stupid money. Get tipped even stupider."

"Wait, did you say *miniaturization?*"

"Yeah. Why?"

I looked at Mack and smirked, "You thinking what I am?"

This time, he answered, "Yep."

I took a long swig from an overpriced bottle of water—starting to feel normal again, and felt pretty certain I was going to make it out of the day alive.

"So, a few things managed to settle into the soup," I tapped the side of my head—feeling the caffeine kicking in.

"That'll help, C. I've had a few thoughts myself. Possibly because I *didn't* drink half the mini-bar after I returned to *my* room," he grinned.

"Very funny. Then you go first, while I drink another gallon of water," I said, reaching for more.

"Last night you said a few things that made a lot of sense. Like a team. Which is a given. Also, I've been noodling on the money angle."

"Yeah?"

"I mean, the $100-mil, then the *next* $100. That was *always* part of the plan."

I nod.

"And while I think he could've just made the bounty a cool billion, I think it was to *toy* with Burton. Push his buttons. Increase the pain."

"Copy that."

"So, I guess the biggest question is…who does he know—and I *have* to believe it's one person who has pushed him so far that he's willing to burn for all the counts coming his way."

Finishing my water, I turned the air-conditioning vent in the direction of my face and said, "I'm 100% in agreement, and think we're going to know…inside the hour."

"Hey guys," Koi shouted from the front seat. "What's this I hear about the Mayor's daughter getting stuffed with TATP, or some derivative?"

Mack and I shook our heads at one another.

"Who said anything about TATP?" I asked.

"Just a hunch," he said—his eyes, not leaving the traffic in front of him.

"It's not public, is it?" I mumbled. "That she's packed full of explosives?"

"Not to my knowledge," Mack said quietly.

"Gents, I'm right here. I can hear you."

"Oh, I forgot to tell you. Our boy, Koi, *also* dabbled in explosives, back in the day," Mack said.

"Oh, really?"

"Yeah, wasn't my thing," he chirped from the front seat. "Made me too nervous. But doesn't mean I don't know how they work."

Scratching my three-day growth, I said, "Looks like we have a new team member."

As Mack grinned, Koi said, "Copy that."

40

THE DETOUR

DONOVAN AND MARGO LANDED LATE LAST NIGHT IN HAVANA. He was worn out, she was stressed out, and their time was running out. Abigail's life hung in the balance, and the only person who could control whether she lived or died was her father. While Donovan thought she was cute, she meant nothing to him—as nothing would stand in the way of his getting what he wanted.

This job was to be his last gamble. After he got even with his old pal, and after pocketing his winnings into an offshore account, he would go legit.

As legit as a drug czar can be, he thought. *More was never enough.*

They were staying at the *Hotel Ambos Mundos* in downtown Havana. While it wasn't *The W*, it was nice for this country. Besides, he couldn't stay at his former haunt—it had undergone some devastating renovations.

Donovan had converted an abandoned silo of the former nuclear power plant in Cienfuegos into a home, and the lower level of the compound into a multi-million dollar drug factory. However, thanks to Carter Matheson and his entourage of *jarhead* lunatics, it was blown to pieces in an air raid. And what wasn't destroyed was confiscated and destroyed by either local officials or Carter's network of drug enforcers.

I'll simply build another one.

Of course, he would need some help; thus, the reason he was back in Cuba meeting with the man who controlled the majority of the marijuana and cocaine going into the States and out of Mexico, Guatemala, Honduras, Nicaragua, El Salvador and Costa Rica, as well as Cuba.

Donovan wanted a piece of that pie. It would be the perfect compliment to the development of his next generation of ecstasy. He also was looking to compliment his arsenal of wares by discussing artillery.

El Diablo, better known as *The Devil,* was one of the richest and most deadly drug czars the world had ever known. He bypassed Pablo Escobar, one of the richest and most famous drug dealers of all time. Escobar's net worth was $25 billion. *El Diablo* was worth closer to $35 billion. It was extremely important that Donovan work a deal with the devil in order to keep his network of drug trafficking successful.

IT WAS STILL early as Donovan sat on the balcony, sipping coffee and watching the early morning traffic start to pick up. He wanted to get the day started—the sooner he could get this meeting complete, the sooner he could get back to New York and put the next phase into motion.

"You ready?" Donovan asked Margo who was getting ready in the other room.

"Just five more minutes," she answered through a partially open bathroom door.

Donovan checked his watch. His patience was thinning. He was about to rush things along, when his phone rang. Looking at the screen, he found a number he didn't recognize, and paused—wondering whether or not to answer it.

"Hello?"

"Is this *Scorpion?*"

"Who is this?"

"I'm calling on behalf of El Diablo. There's been a slight change of plans, he wants you—"

"Wait," Donovan interrupted. "I'm here to see El Diablo. No one else. And I'm not taking a phone call from someone who is calling *for* him."

There was silence, followed by a muffled man's voice. "Hold on."

Several seconds passed.

"Donovan Blair, how are you, my friend?"

It was El Diablo. The false charm oozed from the other end of the phone.

"I'm well. And you?"

"*Muy excelente!* And my apologies. I certainly should have called you myself. Now, that I have you on the phone, let me suggest you come to my home in Cancun."

Donovan frowned. "I flew *here*. We said we would meet in Havana. And that's—"

"I know, Donovan. I'm so sorry. Something came up last night and I simply couldn't get there. My private jet is sitting on the tarmac at Jose Marti International. And I have a driver already at your hotel. Please, oblige me, won't you?"

"El Diablo, I appreciate your—"

"Think nothing of it," he interrupted. "Now, take me up on my hospitality, okay? You'll be at the airport in less than fifteen minutes, here in forty, and back before the end of day. Promise."

"I don't have the extra time. I must return—"

"Understood," he interrupted again, "Looking forward to seeing you."

Before Donovan could respond, the line went dead.

Margot stood behind Donovan, biting a nail. "What is it?"

"He wants me to go to his home in Cancun."

"Mexico?" she blurted.

"Yes," he absently nodded, trying to figure out what the drug lord was up to.

"Is that strange? Should we be worried?"

"Yes. And no. And perhaps." He bit the inside of his lip. "Here's what we're going to do. You're going to stay here—"

"No, no," she shook her head, getting her bag and starting toward the door.

"NO! Listen to me. He doesn't know you're with me. Things could get... sideways. And frankly, it may just complicate things. Besides, you'll be safer here."

"Are you...sure?"

"Yes. Go down to the pool. Relax. Get some sun. I'll be there inside an hour, do my deal and be back in time for lunch. We'll hop a flight shortly thereafter and be back in the city by dinner."

"Okay," she said, walking over and kissing him. "If you say so. And I'll—"

"Let the others know, yes. Please," he smiled, then walked to the window. There was a black town car at the front door. A man in a light suit, sunglasses and a fedora stood by the car smoking a cigarette—staring at the window.

WITHIN MINUTES, Donovan was in the car and on his way to the airport. Margo ordered a drink at the outdoor bar, then settled onto a chaise lounge near the deep end of the pool.

A moment later, a dark-skinned man strolled across the opposite end and sat in a chair under the shade of a large umbrella.

She looked up and managed an uncomfortable and inauthentic smile, just before a waiter delivered her drink.

The stranger lifted his glass in her direction and took a sip, offering a tiny smile behind sunglasses that gave nothing away.

41

THE EXAMINATION

WE ARRIVED AT PRESBYTERIAN HOSPITAL and were escorted by two of New York's finest to Abigail's examination room. The front steps, the lobby, and the hallway of her floor were all lined with a host of officers. Lukas, with the help of Chief Davis, had pulled out all the stops.

It was just after 8 when we arrived. It looked as though the procedure had just gotten started, so we quietly entered a darkened room where Clare, Lukas and Phil McDonough were gathered on this side of a thick window of glass.

"Hi, Clare," I said, touching her arm. Shaking Lukas' hand, we moved into the room. I nodded to Phil McDonough—who returned a pleasant if not nonchalant gesture.

"Carter, thank you for coming today. This will mean a great deal to Abigail," Clare said, working diligently to hold back the tears. Lukas gave a nod of agreement.

I turned to see Abigail exiting an enormous MRI machine. The way the light caught her face and hair, along with the white gown, made her look like an angel. The thought of anyone doing such a despicable thing to such a sweet girl made my blood boil.

I'm going to make the fucker suffer—in a very distinctive way.

Mack must have sensed my reaction, because he looked at me

with an expression of solidarity.

The door opened and a nurse entered. Her badge said *Megan*, and her posture said *business*. She was short and lovely, with bright blue eyes and an inviting smile.

"Mr. Mayor, Mrs. Burton, Abigail did just fine. She was a real trooper. We have the top MRI technicians and radiologists in the country working on this, so we should have all the results you need within the next 30 minutes. Maybe less. In the meantime, we're moving her to the next room, if you'd like to join us."

She smiled, extending her hand in the direction of the next room like a game show hostess. Mack, Koi and I followed the others like happy sheep.

WE SPENT the next twenty minutes getting a detailed description of how the machine worked, followed by what this specialist saw inside Abigail. He went into verbose detail, showing us X-rays on the light board, describing what the difference in tonal colors of each mass meant. While a bit overdone for my "cut-to-the-chase taste," it certainly gave us a broad perspective of what we were looking at.

He was a patient doctor, full of enthusiasm for his craft, as well as showing us his vast knowledge.

The room was a good fifteen degrees cooler than outside which didn't hurt, given my state. The temperature and the ten gallons of fluid I had consumed since leaving the hotel, was making for the perfect hangover recovery.

It was my turn to examine things and I began formulating a plan which would provide a grain of solution. I made sure before we came in that Mack and Koi were perfectly free to jump in at any time, offering ideas, concepts or solutions during our visit. Their simultaneous nods provided all the assurance I needed to know that my bacon was covered.

In the process, I had noticed Koi off to the side during this whole process, looking closely at the X-rays—so closely, in fact, his nose was within three inches of the light-box.

"While I'm no expert in X-rays or hiding small items inside people," I smiled at Abigail like she doesn't hear me talk about the gruesome event she's had to endure. "I'd say someone is playing a silly trick, wouldn't you, Mr. Koi?"

I purposely pulled him into the conversation—not just because he knew what the hell he was doing—which I respected, but because he had a way of making people feel comfortable, which was exactly what Abigail needed right now.

He stepped squatted down and extended his size eleven to her tiny size four hand. Shaking, he smiled, "Nice to meet you, Miss Abigail."

"Nice to meet you…Mr. Interesting Name," she giggled.

"Just think of a fish, in a pond—the orange and white colored ones. Have you ever seen a koi pond?"

Her eyes lit up. "Yes, Daddy took me to Japan when I was younger."

Instant bond—we were in.

A FEW MINUTES OF BONDING, a few of my asking questions about anything else she could remember—which was negligble at best, and we were ready to go. About that time, the doctor suggested she get dressed and have something to eat. Given she had fasted, and was starting to wilt, we decided his suggestion was a good idea for *everyone*.

About ready to leave, Abigail approached—holding Clare's hand, and showed me with a big grin.

"Mr. Carter, I did remember something when I was laying in that tube machine," she practically giggled.

I knelt down. "What's that, Miss Abigail."

She started her explanation with a furrowed brow. "It's funny because I keep thinking I remember little bits of things…kinda like after you wake up from a bad dream, you know?"

"Yes. Little bits and pieces. Sometimes they're funny. Sometimes they're not. And what bits and pieces were you remembering, you smart little lady."

Where the sweet side of Carter was coming from, I had no idea, but I went with it. Even Mack looked at me like, *Who are you?*

"Laying in that tunnel…I remembered when I first got to Mr. Smith's house. It was dark and cold with high ceilings."

I was confused, as it didn't sound like the same description as before. "Like what?"

"Hmm…I'm not sure, but there weren't any windows. And the lights…" she turned back toward the examining room, "They were like in there. Over the tube machine."

Operating room?

"Well, that's funny, because I thought you said the other day the place you stayed, you know—with all your new friends, was light and bright, with lots of windows. And you said the curtains were closed."

She frowned, but I could see a light of recognition. "Yeah, I know. It's kinda like I said, Mr. Carter—"

"Little bits and pieces," we said at the same time, which made us laugh.

"But at first I was in that dark place…with those lights…and later I'm in another brighter place. The one with all the TV screens. It was awesome. Okay, that's it."

What? I thought. "What do you mean? About all those TV screens."

"In the living room, Mr. Smith had a big wall of TV screens. It was, uh, like when Mommy and Daddy watch the news with that white-haired man."

I had to stop and think. I looked at Lukas and Clare.

"Oh, you mean, Mr. Pelley?" she asked Abigail. "On CBS?"

Abigail nodded, as Clare said, "We're news nuts."

I returned my attention to Abigail. It was a *big* clue. "Abigail, that's *really* good. That's a LOT more than just…bits and pieces, right?"

Proud of herself, she smiled. "Yes, it is, Mr. Carter. And I'll keep practicing, but right now, I'm hungry!"

We high-fived, shared goodbyes and she started for the exit, pulling Clare by the hand.

"Clare, Lukas, my guys and will grab lunch, then meet at your office. Lukas, say about an hour?"

"Sure. I'll run them home, and meet you at my office in 60—"

"Let's make it 90," McDonough interjected. "We've still got to talk about…" he rubbed his fingers together.

"Right. Make that 90. Thanks."

In an outer room, we stopped to discuss. Mack started. "There's a *lot* there, Lucky. We now have two places. No windows? A basement. And—"

"Or warehouse," I interrupted.

"Copy. And a wall of screens? There's your *hi-tech* angle."

I mumbled, "That leaves a lot…but it *gives* us a lot."

"Girl just needs some time is all," Mack said.

"Hell, there's no telling how much drugs they gave her. Think about it—drug to grab her, drug to cut her open, drug her to heal up, drug her to keep her quiet."

"And then she shows up at Mommy and Daddy's full of…*whatever*…and they drug her to keep her chill so she doesn't blow Grace Mansion."

I noticed Koi pondering something. "What's up, Koi? You got an idea?"

"Not sure exactly what, but…let me run this by you."

Mack said, "Shoot."

"There's a delicate two-part situation here. Judging from the masse—my guess, capsules, I'd say perhaps a powder and a liquid one. Most likely connected. And while they may not do much on their own, when they're united—perhaps with a charge, that's when you have…well, *action*."

I looked at Mack. He shrugged.

Koi continued, "They look to be in sausage-like tubes resting just under the transverse colon—uh, large intestine. Without an X-ray, you wouldn't see it. And my guess is that the trigger, for lack of a better term, is tucked up behind it."

Mack spoke up. "How's it triggered?"

"And," I interrupted, "How far would you need to be to do so?"

"Remote control," Koi said to Mack, before turning to me. "And as far as you like."

"Shit."

"Exactly," Koi replied. "My educated guess? Maybe a phone. That way they could potentially monitor the action *and* conversations, as well as *trigger* it by dialing a number."

We all looked at one another. I shook my head.

"Tell me, was there a phone given to the Mayor, or his wife, or anyone for that matter?"

"Yeah," I nodded, emphatically.

"Shit," Koi whispered. "Well, that's the trigger. I'm gonna guess you have to keep the phone nearby to wait for instructions, but it could also be the exact thing that's used to—"

"Got it," I said.

"And *potentially* worse?" Koi said, with an odd expression.

"What?" I groaned.

"I wouldn't touch any of the buttons. No matter what."

"Great," I said, waving to leave. "Let's go."

Koi said, "You guys drag your heels, I'll pull the beast around."

With that he was out the door, as Mack and I looked at one another. Just then, something clicked.

"Wait," I said, pulling him out the door. "Watch this. Surgeon skills, right?"

He nods.

"Explosives knowledge, right?"

Another nod.

"Surveillance and recon strategies—"

"And overseas banking, a *team* of professionals with him…" he interrupted.

"Not to mention someone with a real axe to grind. It's a reach, but I think you'll see what I'm getting at—"

"Someone who used to work with, or be *led by*…"

"Bingo."

Koi had already pulled around and was at the curb, standing at the opened doors, and about to say something when I held up a hand. Pointing a finger in Mack's face, I said, "Wait for it."

With a shit-eating grin across his face, Mack said, "Scorpion!"

42

THE SCORPION

"HOW IN THE *HELL* DID I NOT SEE THIS BEFORE?"

I had shouted way too loudly for such a tight space. The SUV was big, but I was loud. The guys looked at me like I was crazy.

"What?" Mack snorted. "How the hell didn't *I* see it? *I'm* the smart one in this group."

We were so busy high-fiving we didn't see Koi in the front seat trying to get our attention. "Excuse me, can you please...excuse me," he said in an effeminate voice.

"What is it *Koi Pond*?"

His smile turned to a frown, as he tapped the brakes so hard, he threw Mack off balance. "I told you *not* to call me that."

"Or?" Mack taunted.

"Or, I won't continue giving you the family discount on back waxes."

I asked Mack, "Where'd you find this guy?"

"Long story."

"Okay, gents, let's turn it down a notch," I said, "At least until tonight when we can *turn it back up.*"

"Just tell me one thing," Koi said from the front seat. "Who the *freak* is Scorpion?"

I took a deep breath, enjoying the fact we were on to something.

"I'll tell you the whole thing, but first, let's pick a lunch spot. We've got about an hour, so we need something good, but on the faster side."

"Just not cheap," Mack said.

"Guys," Koi said. "Stop the *Oscar and Felix*. I've got an idea." Dialing a number, he held up a hand. "Hey, it's me. Can you fit me plus two in?" Beat. "Like *now*?" Looking at us in the rearview, he gave a nod. "Yes, put us in the box seats. Thanks."

Next, he said something in Japanese, laughed, and hung up, before turning to us. "You girls just sit back and relax. It's handled."

WITHIN MINUTES, we were standing outside a tall one-story nondescript building, squeezed between a sleek hotel on one side and an expensive woman's shoe store on the other. The building had the color and texture of stone; like a tall, skinny boulder, but with no windows.

"What's this place?" Mack said.

"Welcome to *Koi*," Koi said.

"Seriously?"

"Doesn't look like much," Mack added.

Koi just grinned, shook his head and waved for us to follow.

The enormous door was made of rusted iron and had no handle. Lifting a thin stainless blade that looked like a mail slot, Koi pushed a tiny button. Within seconds, the door opened, pivoting on a center pole, and we were greeted by a very attractive Geisha girl. A pleasant smile, a small bow, and we were invited in.

"Damn near feels like a brothel," Mack smirked.

"Oh, it's *full* of sin," Koi grinned, bowing to the hostess and looking at us to suggest the same. As we entered, *Miss Geisha* gestured for us to leave our shoes on a wooden shelf. And to put on cork flip-flops.

"One size fits all?"

"Does it *look* like a shoe store?" I said.

A sushi bar was positioned in the middle of the room, surrounded by small tables, and I estimated the room to seat about thirty or forty people. The ambiance was breathtaking. One wall was made of rough stone with a subtle waterfall. Lit from behind, the water fell on grey pebbles. Another wall was live bamboo trees, appearing to grow from the floor. They were moving slowly, as though a breeze blew through them. The back wall was frosted glass, top to bottom. The ceiling looked like a real sky, complete with slow moving clouds.

But the best part was the floor—which resembled a stone garden with a serpentine path made of thick glass. Below it was a waterway, which held enormous koi fish. They meandered under the floor and through the entire restaurant.

FIFTY MINUTES LATER, we waved off the geisha girl, holding up the sign for *time out*. Mack had eaten twenty-five or thirty different pieces of fish—all of which was flown in that morning.

"I've eaten in some of the best restaurants in the world," I began. "And this was by far the best sushi I've ever eaten, Koi. Your place," I asked, putting a last piece of Toro in my mouth.

Koi shook his head, "It's my father's. And was his. And so on."

"Well, it's unbelievable."

"Should be," Koi smiled, nodding for the geisha waitress. "Memberships are by invitation only."

I reached for my wallet.

Koi waved me away, shaking his head. "No."

"But…"

"You're my guest. Besides, you fools are letting me play in your sandbox. Speaking of—before we bounce, tell me more this *Scorpion* fella."

I leaned on my elbows, looking around to see only a few patrons remained.

"Not to worry. An unspoken rule of this club—*what is said here, stays here.*"

Mack and I looked at one another. "Okay, while I—*we*, aren't 100% it's Scorpion, it's a damn strong hunch. Think about how all the elements fit. And while I'm still unclear of the *motive*, it *feels* like his handiwork. Again, from what I have learned of him."

"To play devil's advocate—which I rarely do, it could just be a super coincidence," Mack said.

I start to speak but he interrupted me.

"And I know—you don't believe in coincidences, but for the sake of argument, it could be *anyone*. Maybe it's 'cause just a month ago we were all nearly killed by him."

I let Mack's words sink in, as the three of us looked at one another.

"True. And the one thing I've not spent much if any time looking into—because this invite came out of nowhere, is his affiliation with Lukas. But we can find that."

They both nodded, as Koi spoke. "I can help there. Just...well, I'll explain later."

"You're on," I said to Koi, then turned to Mack. "And you've got a point. He nearly smoked us all. Why he didn't, I still can't figure out. I mean, we had him dead to rights—with Dad nearly dead from the scorpion bite, Black just shy of gone—thanks to the gunshot wound, and *you*...practically blinded by one of his thugs."

"Not to mention our blowing his meg-million dollar operation sky high," Mack said.

"Yeah, you can be sure he'll be looking to get us back for that."

"What's that?" Koi asked.

"Long story, but the short of it? We were in Havana," Mack said, nodding to me, "Me and this clown were bringing his Pops and a pal back home, when we called in some *Apache* help to level his compound."

Koi raises his eyebrows. "What was inside?"

"Grass and X, pretty much. Acres of underground labs in an abandoned nuclear power plant."

"What the *fuck*?" Koi mumbled.

"Truly impressive," I said, "But toast in less than three minutes. That jackass was behind the eight ball by the time we called our pals into place."

"You shoulda seen this cat run," Mack laughed. "Disappeared into thin air."

"What I *do* know is we're less than 36 hours from…"

"That's still a lot of time, if you ask me," Koi said.

I looked at him. "Really? Cause to *me* that means," I held up a finger, "We have to *find* him," I raised a second finger, "We have to *disarm* the bomb," I added a third finger, "Because if not, he'll *certainly* pull this prank again."

"You think?"

"We know," Mack said.

"And if not him, then the Governor, or the President."

"Nah, he'd never get close enough to the President's kids."

"You shitting me?" I barked. "You ever seen the Mayor's detail?"

"Yeah, a *nanny,*" Koi snapped.

Mack and I looked at one another.

"No."

Koi nods.

"What?" Mack asked. "He's *got* to have a large detail."

"Just the nanny," Koi said, slowly shaking his head. "Well, for the most part. Otherwise, a couple suits that shadow him. In big crowds."

As I let that sink in, I stared at the fish swimming under our table.

Then it hit me and I snapped my finger. "He's got someone *on the inside!*"

"Dirty cops," Mack snarled.

"Oh boy," Koi said.

I looked Mack dead in the eye. "And you know the only other person we haven't said a *friggin'* word about?"

"Who?"

"Think about it. The one other person with us in Havana."

The light went on.

"*Caprese.*"

I nod. "Makes sense, right?"

"Fuckin' A," Mack said, spreading that grin across his face when all the pieces come together.

Standing, I motioned to move out. "Don't be surprised if it's some twisted triangle," I said, heading for the door. "After all, they were buds in Havana—"

"What do you mean?" Koi asked, stopping to bow to the Chef. We followed suit.

"Something we didn't mention. Caprese—that's *Dr. Leonard Caprese,* is a Whip in the Senate. He's also on the..." I motioned air-quotes, "Advisory Board of Foreign Relations. And has a penchant for two things—besides exotic homes all over the world. Guns and money."

"Holy *shit,*" Koi said, handing us our shoes.

"You bet. When we met him in Nicaragua—"

"What?" Koi interrupted.

"Yeah, met him there with a cat named Ashgar Debashi. A Saudi King, or some shit. They were trading guns for names and locations of high-ranking individuals at the G8 Summit."

"Playing both sides," Koi said, holding the door open for us.

Stepping outside, we were bombarded by loud noise and bright daylight.

"Damn," Mack said. "That was some *cocoon.*"

The car had already been pulled to the curb. Tipping the valet, Koi reached for our doors.

"Dude, we can get our own doors," I smirked. "Seriously."

"No shit," Mack snorted. "You're not our *man servant.*"

"Oh, I didn't say that," I said, turning to Mack. "I just said we could get our own doors."

Koi stared at us, deadpan. "Really?"

43

THE EVIL

DONOVAN'S DRIVE from the hotel to the airport was uneventful. The flight to Cancun was quick. And the drive to El Diablo's home, alongside two bodyguards, was silent. They made it to the Cancun International Airport in less than 35 minutes.

El Diablo's home was a veritable compound, complete with nine-foot high walls, an armed and well-lit front gate with security tower, located in the far northwest corner. Passing through the gate, security didn't stop there, as there were soldiers roaming various parts of the five-acre compound. Most, if not all of the guards were armed with either Uzi or AK-47 machine guns. Given Donovan was a former Marine and grew up around guns his whole life, his eye was highly trained in artillery.

These guys are prepared, he thought. *And little chance I'd make it out alive, if I piss him off.*

A SHORT, plump and polite Hispanic woman dressed in a maid's uniform greeted Donovan at the door. Speaking perfect English, she made pleasantries before inviting Donovan to follow her. They meandered through a house that he estimated to be between fifteen and twenty thousand square feet. It was elegantly appointed with exquisite furniture, the walls were adorned with handsome art and big game trophies, and there were security cameras and emergency floodlights in nearly every ceiling corner of every room.

Donovan and his two oversized guard companions—both of whom hung back behind him several feet, eventually approached the pool located at the back of the massive home. The Olympic-sized pool was adorned with an enormous fountain in the middle, hot tubs at either end, and was further outfitted with an assortment of barely-clad women of various ethnicities lounging around the pool.

The moment El Diablo saw Donovan, he stood, smiled and started toward him, extending his arms wide, as though asking for a hug.

Donovan reached out to shake his hand.

"Mi hombre, c'mon, give your pal a big hug," El Diablo said, wrapping his arms around Donovan and squeezing him tightly.

Donovan was surprised to feel the man's strength—especially given most photographs he had seen over the years depicted him as appearing soft and much heavier. This was in fact the first time they'd met face to face—having only communicated via a secure phone.

"Quite a spread you have," is all Donovan came up with—still hungover from a late night.

"Thank you. It's probably not as nice as the *high-rises* you build in Manhattan, but it will do. I'm sure your home is magnificent, yes?"

"It's nice," Donovan said modestly, doing everything he could to keep the conversation cool and steady. After all, this man had a notorious reputation for being extremely violent; just another reason his current *kindness* had Donovan on edge. He knew he was being sized up, by the way El Diablo looked at him.

"Is everything alright?" El Diablo asked, squinting in the hot midday sun.

"Yes, of course," he answered, remaining neutral.

"Then why are you sweating so?"

Donovan looked down to see his armpits were soaked.

"How about because it's hotter than *fuck*," he chuckled, trying a different approach.

Cocking his head to the side, El Diablo started to grin, then punched Donovan in the gut—knocking the air from him.

El Diablo laughed hysterically, and Donovan caught his breath, acting like it was no big deal.

"Come on, my friend, I'm fucking with you," he continued to chuckle, looking to his bodyguards, encouraging them to follow along.

Which they did. On cue.

"Come with me," El Diablo said, motioning to an enormous wrought-iron table across the patio.

Two enormous umbrellas covered the area—which was good, because the heat seemed to continually increase. El Diablo motioned for the guards to pull their chairs, then clapped at two women who were in the deep end.

"Angelique, Saphoro, drinks. Now!"

They jumped from the pool, slipped on shoe,s and practically ran to the house.

"They're so beautiful..." El Diablo said, "But much too stupid for my tastes. I like *intelligent* women."

Donovan gave a nod and took a seat.

"Sure, they must have perfect bodies—the more to please me, but they should be able to keep me on my toes, too. Agreed?"

Donovan gave a smile and a nod, placating his adversary, while scanning the property—on the off chance he needed to get out quickly.

Right, he thought. *I'd be shot dead. Then buried in the mangroves before cocktail hour was done.*

Both girls returned with trays—each held a pitcher, salt-rimmed glasses, and a bottle of expensive tequila.

"Let's have some drinks. And then we'll talk business."

Donovan wasn't crazy about that idea because he was still trying to get over last nights drinking binge, and secondly, he felt confident he would pass out if he had another drink. However, he knew better than to disagree, and played along.

"Tell me something, El Diablo. Why did you change the location for our meeting? We agreed to meet in Havana."

The man skipped the pitcher of margaritas and instead poured two shots—one for himself, the other for his guest.

Smiling, he said, "I trust no one, my friend. And let's just say... something didn't feel right."

"What do you suppose that was?"

The man shrugged his shoulder. "Need salt and a lime. Or, can you take it like a man?"

Donovan sneered. "What do you think?"

"Good!"

They clinked glasses, took the shot, then slammed the glasses on the table.

El Diablo poured another, and they repeated.

Then, another.

And another.

And yet, another.

Donovan could ordinarily hold his own—when he didn't mix alcohols. However, at the moment—between the hangover and the heat, he was hanging on for dear life.

And hoping he wouldn't puke.

"Okay, El Diablo, I get it. You can drink. So can I. But seriously, let's get down to business."

In a blink, Donovan realized that wasn't the best way to...dance with *The Devil.*

El Diablo stared at Donovan, taking his time to wipe his mouth with a linen napkin. Sliding back from the table, he took a deep breath and meticulously brushed his pants and smoothed his linen Guayabera. El Diablo loved his fine shirts.

"Okay, my friend. Let's get to business. Evidently, my hospitality *bores* you."

Oh, shit. Not the way to make friends with the enemy.

"Not bored, my friend. Just...well, to be honest, I'm terribly *hungover,*" he grinned. "You see, I was out late with my team. And I suppose we drank too much, you know, celebrating some new business."

Think, think.

"Business…that I want to bring to *you*."

El Diablo squinted like Clint Eastwood in an old western.

"Perhaps *one* more—then we get down to business," Donovan smiled.

El Diablo's frown slowly morphed into a shit-eating grin.

"Just *one* more?" he said, grinning.

"Sure. I can go one more."

Reaching over, El Diablo slid the shot glasses out of the way, then took two large margarita glasses from the ice bucket and set them down. Reaching for the bottle of tequila, he poured them both large drinks. So large, that the tequila poured right to the rim.

El Diablo's stare only left Donovan's eyes once—making sure he didn't spill the booze.

Donovan didn't blink, and taking a long deep breath, he summoned his inner frat boy.

As El Diablo slid one glass toward his guest, and the other toward himself and said in a low growl, "Here's to your life. May it be long. Prosperous. Or both."

Donovan touched the glass to his adversary's and each man drank. The whole glass. In one gulp. And without flinching.

Setting his glass down, El Diablo reached over to shake. "Now, for business. Tell me what it is you want."

Without missing a beat, Donovan began, "$30 million. Split between grass and coke. 50/50."

El Diablo looked across his compound, lost in thought. "I thought you had a grass lab in Havana."

While Donovan felt certain that exact fact had been kept a secret, he didn't want his expressions to give anything away. Besides, given the devil knows everything, Donovan was pretty sure his situation had become common knowledge, so he kept moving forward.

"Yeah, well, we ran into some…let's say inconvenient circumstances."

His opponent smirked. "You mean the Feds who leveled it?"

Shit.

"Yeah, well, not the *Feds,* but..." he said, reaching in his pocket, whereupon two bodyguards instantly stepped forward, placing their hands on their guns.

Donovan froze, and El Diablo waved them away, nodding.

Flipping through photos on his phone, Donovan pulled up a photo and handed it to El Diablo. "Look at the carnage these clowns caused."

El Diablo looked at the photos and made a noise: *"Tsk, tsk, tsk..."*

Donovan wasn't amused.

El Diablo was expressionless. "That's a shame."

Then, taking a cellphone from his pocket, he likewise swiped the screen several times, looking for a photo. Finding it, he smiled and handed the phone to Donovan. "Since it's show and tell time, look at this."

Donovan looked at a photo of what appeared to be a destroyed lab—not unlike his own. Swiping the screen, there were a couple of photos of dead people. He said, "What happened?"

"Looks like my competition thought they could enter one of my farms and steal from me, and then kill nearly a dozen of my workers," El Diablo let out a long, deep sigh. "They were like...family."

"I'm sorry to see that happen," Donovan said, waiting a long beat before asking, "So, can you help me?"

El Diablo stared at Donovan for a long, quiet, and nerve-wracking moment, before answering.

"Sure. But the price is now $60 million."

Caught off guard, Donovan barked, "Are you crazy?"

"What's the phrase you gringos use? P-O-D-B," he smiled. "And the split it *60/40.*"

44

THE DEVIL

"PRICE OF DOING BUSINESS. OF COURSE," DONOVAN GRINNED.

He knew he had to play it cool because he had a second order to fill. Which he needed to mention. Right about now.

"I also need AK's. A *lot* of them. My stash was in that same compound," he said, tapping his phone.

"How many?"

"I believe our agreed price was $1,000 per gun. And I need fifteen thousand. With matching ammo."

El Diablo whistled.

Donovan's stomach was beginning to perform somersaults.

Hang in there, he told himself. *It'll all be over soon.*

"My Washington connection needs some overseas assistance," he grinned, wiping sweat from his brow.

"I would say so," El Diablo said quietly, taking an ice cube from the bucket and sliding it across his forehead. "What are you planning? The takeover of a small country?" He chuckled.

"Yeah, something like that. Can we do that for $20 million?" Donovan asked, reaching for an ice cube—also running it across his forehead.

El Diablo enjoyed watching his opponent sweat—both metaphorically and physically. He liked being in the driver's seat.

He also figured the last drink would push one of them over the edge. However, it wouldn't be him.

He planted a smile on his face, before delivering a second blow.

"Yes. For $40 million."

"What the fuck!"

Donovan was furious, as that amount would now take the first $100 million he got from Burton—a sum he designated specifically to this next gamble, and significantly affect, and leverage his cash flow on a number of investments—ones in which he didn't plan on tapping for private capital. Also, he had yet to secure the additional money he was expecting, and with Carter now in the picture, there were added complications to consider. His new nemesis seemed to have found a way to get in his way. And he didn't like it.

Both men stared into the distance in opposite directions. One needed what the other had, while the other likely had no need at all. It was a different sort of chess and Donovan had to make a move.

El Diablo picked up his cellphone and slowly, methodically swiped through it.

"Here's another photo," he said, handing over the phone. "This is some of our other business acquaintances. Those three pictures best tell the story."

He watched Donovan's reaction when he saw the first photograph.

It was a pile of bodies facedown in an enormous pool of blood.

Donovan swallowed.

"We were moving a lot of products offshore on that boat…if you want to call it a boat," El Diablo choked out a guttural laugh. "Swipe to the next one."

Donovan swiped. The next photo had been aimed at the men's bare feet.

"And they killed *more* of your men?"

El Diablo gave a languorous nod, still staring at his opponent.

"Actually, those were *their* men who were caught taking…" he motioned for Donovan to swipe again, "More than we wanted to give."

Donovan swiped. This time, the photo was taken from a closer angle and showed a dozen severed heads laying on the floor of the boat. In the background, two men were in the process of cutting heads from the remaining bodies.

Suddenly, Donovan jumped up and ran to a nearby patch of grass, violently vomiting on a flowerbed—spraying his shoes at the time.

El Diablo watched the humiliated Donovan finish emptying his stomach. He picked up a table napkin and walked over to Donovan.

Entirely too close to his face, El Diablo said, "So, tell me, is that number too *rich* for you to stomach, *Señor Blair?*"

Donovan took the napkin, wiped his mouth and managed to choke out a quiet, "No. I just need some time."

Donovan knew he was in a tight place, but he needed to get back to New York in order to seal the deal with Burton. That way he could secure the cash he needed to get his drug business back up and running. Atop that, Caprese needed guns for his sources, and that markup was to help cover his bet. Plus, Donovan had committed to supplying substantial funds for an upcoming Presidential campaign. To none other than Mayor Burton—the one from which all the evil stew was brewing.

"I need to return to New York and get things…moved around."

El Diablo nodded toward the house. "I know that price tag is a handsome one, my friend, but I have costs, too. Tell you what, close this deal right now—before you leave, and I'll drop that 100 to 75 mil. Just as my way of saying no hard feelings. El Diablo isn't a *complete bitch,*" he laughed.

Donovan knew the deal stunk and it was overpriced, but a twenty-five-percent savings was nothing to sneeze at. He could get his hands on that right now. Then again, he could also go to other sources; people with whom he wouldn't have to be concerned about losing his head.

Checking his watch, he had just over 24 hours before the Burton deal closed—one way or the other. He felt supremely comfortable of two things: Burton had the money and would not hesitate paying the ransom. Secondly, within 15 minutes of getting the wire transfer, he would be able to pay this maniac back—plus a *Vig*, as needed. Then, he could be on to his next adventure.

Within twenty minutes, Donovan had gotten on the phone and transferred $75 million to El Diablo's offshore account. While it tweaked his stomach—because he hated paying the surcharges for something as stupid as insulting his opponent, it was a necessary evil. He watched as El Diablo typed a long series of numbers on his computer, stared at the screen and then smiled—like a child getting his favorite toy at Christmas.

"Done," he said, extending a hand to Donovan. "Pleasure doing business with you. I'll arrange for your three shipments to go out first thing next week."

Donovan needed it sooner, but he felt an argument would only press buttons he shouldn't push. And with that, he gave a nod and started toward the door.

"Right now, I need to get back to Havana, and then home."

As soon as he said that, he realized he'd made a mistake.

"Really?" El Diablo said with such accentuated drama. "Why must you divert to Havana…if you're in such a hurry. Please, allow my pilot to take you directly to the city. It would be my pleasure," he said, smiling and patting him on the back. "It's the least I can do…for such a good *friend* as you."

"I…have to get my things in the hotel. My briefcase and such," Donovan bluffed.

As Donovan, El Diablo and three bodyguards made their way through the vast living room, El Diablo reached in his pocket.

"Tell me…*Scorpion*…are you sure you're not returning to Havana to retrieve this?"

Swiping the screen, he handed the phone to Donovan.

Looking at the screen, his stomach nearly emptied again, as he saw Margot, completely naked and spread eagle—her hands and feet, tied to the four-poster bed that she and Donovan had shared last night. Standing over her was a huge dark-skinned man, holding an enormous stainless machete at her throat.

Breathing heavily, Donovan lifted his head and faced his opponent and growled, "You evil *fuck*."

El Diablo smiled. "This very rich—as you put put it, *evil fuck* —thanks in part to you, has a second deal for you. You arrogant *prick*. You wire me $100 million dollars inside the next 24 hours, or my friend—one evil Mr. Salazar, will *first* remove both arms and legs, *before* cutting her head off. Then, after slicing her open, will deliver her bloody remains in a garbage bag to the front door of your handsome...*big city* home."

Donovan didn't budge—his eyes, remaining locked on El Diablo.

"And just in case *that's* not enough...we'll do the same to your *other* girlfriend, Mo. Followed by Mr. Dawson...and Mr. Burns."

Donovan was speechless.

Stepping forward, El Diablo was so close Donovan could smell the tequila on the man's breath.

"That, my friend, is what it's like *to dance with The Devil.*"

45

THE CONFERENCE

WE PULLED up to the front of City Hall then sat in the truck a few minutes. I wanted to make sure we were all dialed in. There was going to come a point in our conversations it would likely get steamed. And with tensions high, emotions even higher, and my working alongside people I didn't particularly trust, I thought it best to run over a few things.

"Hey, before we go in there, I just wanna say as much as I *feel* we're close to knowing where to chase this lead...I can't be sure. So, needless to say, eyes and ears on full alert."

Mack said, "You feeling good?"

"Huh? You mean my hangover? Or my overall head in the game."

He grinned. "Both?"

"Hangovers gone. My head? Still percolating. I'm confident of where we're going. Things *seem* to be coming together. My nerves are pretty good—even with this ticking time bomb...so to speak."

"Nice choice of words," Mack smirked.

"No doubt," Koi added.

"Yeah, well, I'm doing my best, *ladies.*"

We sat for a moment and observed our surroundings. Mack and I had worked enough surveillance details that we were good at

"I see that," I said, turning to walk up the steps.

"So's the van," Koi said.

"Yep," I snorted. "We've just been made."

46

THE EAVESDROP

THIRTY MINUTES EARLIER—

KEN AND SEAN HAD TAKEN IT UPON THEMSELVES TO FOLLOW CARTER. Donovan had told them to split time between watching Gracie Mansion, as well as keeping tabs on Carter and his sidekick. But they were told specifically to keep their distance, as Carter was known to be an extremely keen hunter.

Ken's ego ignored the suggestion, while Sean had grown bored with spending hours upon hours sitting in a van on the street. He welcomed any movement. So, they met up for a quick slice of pizza near the courthouse, then drove over to sit outside the Mayor's office, knowing Carter and company would be heading over around lunch.

Ken had stopped by the penthouse to pick up his binoculars and a radio package, before meeting up. Sean had stopped to take a shower, given he'd spent the last couple of days glued to his fake radio van. They arrived just minutes before they spotted the black SUV they had pegged as Carter's.

"Shit!" Ken barked over the radio, causing Sean to pull the earpiece from his ear.

"Geez, I can hear you just fine."

"I told you we were running late. Now, we're too vulnerable. That jackass'll spot us in a blink."

"Maybe not. Let's just make the best of it," Sean said, circling the block. "At least you're not driving something as conspicuous as *this*."

"Whatever. Those things are parked around this building day and night. You'll be fine."

Sean found a spot near the back of the lot, replacing a TV van from the local NBC affiliate. He was able to slide into place just as Carter's SUV arrived. Ken, on the other hand, ended up parking too close for comfort, but didn't feel it was too be a big deal, given he had an unmarked car. One they hadn't been seen before.

"Okay, I'm in place. Looks like they're all there," Ken radioed Sean. "Copy?"

"Copy," Sean replied. "I've got a long lens facing out the front, and the dish on the roof will pick them up…in a second."

"Can you hear them?"

Sean tested the mic, cranked the volume, but got nothing. The muffled hum suggested they may have some sort of interference mechanism in place. That made Sean assume the SUV was rigged for tight security.

"Nah, they've got a surveillance block up. I'll catch them when they get out."

They waited while the men talked inside the truck.

Several minutes passed, when Sean finally said, "So, Ken, you think the Mayor's gonna go through with this?"

"It's his friggin' daughter, for Christ's sake. Course he's going to pony up."

"But…what if he doesn't?"

"Are you shitting me? You know exactly what Donovan—"

"Wait! They're getting out," Sean shouted.

"*Hey, Koi, stand still a sec,*" Carter said over the air.

"Copy that," Ken said.

"*See that radio van over my left shoulder? It's your 2 o'clock.*"

"Copy that. What's that...Jersey's Best News, WSCN, 1210 AM?"

"Right. It's bullshit. Remember me telling you about it before you got here? It was parked outside Gracie."

"Are you fucking kidding me?" Sean shouted.

"Shut it!" Ken barked in to his ear.

"There is no 1210 AM in this area And certainly no WSCN in Jersey."

Sean threw his headphones down, popping an earpiece off. The shrill feedback made Ken flinch.

"...does that cop in the unmarked to your 3 o'clock look familiar?"

"They've spotted me," Ken said, "I knew I shoulda stayed across the street. *Fuck!*"

Sean was trying to fix his headphones.

"Can you believe this shit?" Ken barked.

"And, that's a Troopers car, right?"

No answer.

"Sean, can you read me?"

Nothing.

"Looks like—yeah, it could be Ken Dawson. And affirmative; that's a State Trooper's car."

Sean finally put the headphones back on, adjusting the microphone. "What the fuck?" Sean said, as he got his headphones on.

"Right?" Ken barked into his mic.

"Yeah, huge. A boxer and bodybuilder."

"Oh shit, they have *so* made us," Sean whined. "What do you want to do?"

Ken was fuming. He was better than this. He let their getting rushed jam him up.

"Hold on," Ken barked, listening.

"Mack, change this up. Go back to the truck, grab something, anything and bring it back. Make it look important."

"What in the hell?" Sean said. "Are they—"

"Shut the fuck up!" Ken barked.

"*...take the glasses from my bag, then see if he's not wearing a wire. While you're at it, scope inside that van....*"

"Shit! Now they've got *me*. What do you wanna do?"

Both listened.

"*...that's a State Trooper's car, but he's a city cop...Could belong to his boyfriend.*"

"I'll show you my boyfriend, you *fuck*. It's called a 9 millimeter *Glock!*"

"I say we get outta here," Sean spat. "We've got nothing to gain now. And if they come over to me, I can't get out fast enough."

"They're not gonna do that, trust me. So they've made us. Doesn't matter. We did like we were supposed to."

"*...it's the same group I drive around. Just better money.*"

"Who is that little fucker, anyway?" Ken mumbled.

"His dad runs a swanky membership-only sushi club in midtown."

"How'd you know that?"

"I like sushi."

"Hold it!" Ken said, watching Mack return from the SUV.

"*Yeah, he's got a wire. And he's working a phone. Feels like he's talking...*"

"We're out," Ken said, "See you back at the tower." He backed out and was gone, as Carter ground out a cigarette. Sean managed to slip out the lot and into the alley. The last thing he heard was, "*Yep. We've just been made.*"

Sean snorted, "Yeah, us too."

47

THE GEMINI

DONOVAN LANDED AT NEWARK, was met by his private helicopter, and was en route to Manhattan with no delays. Quiet with his thoughts, he feared for his life. While not one for maudlin sentimentality, nor ever accused of being "sensitive," the latest situation had him genuinely off balance. His mind replayed the photographs El Diablo had shown him. The bloody, headless bodies, and the photo of Margo held at knifepoint. He couldn't imagine what she was suffering right now. But he was certain he would do whatever it took to bring her home safely.

That fucking lunatic, he thought. *I knew he was a sadistic maniac, but I had no idea...* he stopped, trying to erase the images from his mind.

Within minutes, he was dropped at *Air Pegasus*—the helipad on 30th Street, then driven home by a private service. Now, safely ensconced in his high-security steel and glass ivory tower, he entered his living room—immediately walking to the bar to pour a drink, before heading into his office.

He checked to see if his opponent Caprese had yet make a move on the chessboard. Nothing. When he pressed a button, an enormous *Jackson Pollack* painting slid to the side, revealing a bank of television screens and security monitors. His eyes darted from a stock ticker to a news station, where he scanned a few headlines, then made a quick check of the weather channel—more by habit than anything else. Finally, he settled back on *MSNBC,* turning up the volume to see what the markets were doing.

He had a lot of capital liquidation to accomplish.

Exhaling a deep breath, Donovan realized his shoulders had relaxed for the first time since he arrived at El Diablo's compound. Looking to the row of *Mont Blanc* clocks directly above the door, he saw six time zones, but centered his focus on his own. It was just after 4 o'clock. He had just about 26 hours before his deal with Burton came due. Looking at the clock representing Los Angeles— or Cancun, as the case was, he only had 29 hours to get El Diablo his money.

What was I thinking, he pondered, *You want to play the big leagues, you have to pay the big leagues.*

Donovan was smart enough to figure it out. After all, he'd fought in Afghanistan, as well as a number of other duties, and faced life-threatening situations every day. He was a trained solder. There was nothing he couldn't stand up to. Nor get away from. His tactical background was legit. His lack of fear had served him well. And his ability to lead teams was his strong suit.

Besides my discharge.

Those memories came flooding back with a vengeance.

It was Burton's fault, he thought, wondering how he'd let all this mess happen.

If I hadn't been drinking. And shit like that.

Knowing he now had not one, but *two* clocks ticking made his head spin, his stomach turn, and his thirst grow. While he couldn't drink too much, he figured just one more would be okay.

Lost in thought, he hadn't heard Mo open the front door, and it wasn't until she was standing at the door, that he jumped.

"Baby, are you alright?" She said, walking to his desk and leaning over for a kiss. He kissed her quickly, then stood, walking to the window.

"What's wrong?"

"Huh?"

"You never greet me like…" She looked around. "Where's Margot?"

He turned, stared, and for the first time since knowing her, he fought back tears.

"She's in trouble, Mo."

"Donovan, what sort of trouble?"

He shook his head for several minutes, before returning to his desk. Emptying his drink, he buried his face in his hands.

While not scared, Mo was unnerved. She had only seen Donovan show emotion one other time, the entire time she had known him. And they had been together for nearly ten years. Sure, other girls had come and gone, but they were just "extra sauce on his main entree," as he enjoyed putting it. She had always gone along with it, because she genuinely cared for him. Likewise, she had an affinity for "straddling the sexual fence," thus the occasional three-way.

"We were in Havana. On business. It was—"

"El Diablo?"

He nodded, waiting before looking up at her.

"I told you he was—"

"Mo, this isn't the time to correct me. I knew, rather, I know what I'm doing. If you and I are going to create the world we're planning, some very…extreme measures must take place."

She shook her head. "You're not telling me, are you…that she's still there?"

With a sigh, he took his cellphone out, unlocked the screen and showed her the photo.

Screaming, "Holy shit!" She said, "What's going on, Donovan?"

"What? It's the *one* thing I hadn't thoroughly worked through."

"What the fuck!" she screamed again—tears, filling her eyes.

He tried to ignore her. But couldn't.

"She was the *one* person who stood, or rather *stands*, to put us in the worst position. That little girl can identify her better—faster, than any of us. And it's because of how she allowed herself to get… too close."

"What are you saying?"

"You saw the way she took to her—the way she didn't keep her distance. I tried to tell her—"

"It's because she wants a child, Donovan. It's not hard to understand."

"But with *this* lifestyle it's hard to."

"Listen to me. Part of it? Is her age. She's ready. And part of it is her love of family—something the three of us have."

Donovan accidentally rolled his eyes, then tried to play it off.

"I get it, and I…*want* that. It's just that…right now, this is more important. *Way* more important."

Shaking her head, she mumbled, "Unbelievable."

He gave a snort.

"I told you *I'd* be willing to share—"

Holding up his hands, he tried to keep from shouting. "Stop! Just…I can't get into that right now." He walked to the window then began to pace.

"*Please* tell me you're going to do whatever it takes to get her home—that you're NOT going to leave her there…in the hands of that barbarian!"

"Of course not. Ken and I will head down as soon as we get this other taken care of."

"Donovan, we have everything we could ever need—money, homes, power—"

"Please, Mo! You know me better than anyone. And you know…it's *never* enough."

He froze, staring at her. Taking and releasing a deep breath, he walked to his desk, opened a drawer and took out a cellphone.

"Do you realize this tiny piece of electronics…is the one and only thing standing between you and I having literally *anything* we want? *This* is the key to our future?"

Suddenly, a knock at the front door startled them. They turned to see Ken and Sean enter.

"Welcome back," Ken said casually.

"Yeah, not now," Donovan spat, putting the cellphone back in the drawer and locking it. "Looks like we've got a bit of a problem," he said, "Take a load off, grab a drink and wait in the living room. Be there in a minute."

They tossed a nod and left.

Donovan faced Mo, taking her by both shoulders and pulling her close.

"Babe, we are so *very* close to having this done. And yes, she's in the shit. But I've got a plan. Let's stay focused, keep strong…and everything is going to work out perfectly. We've done it all right… and now it's just a matter of a few hours standing between us, and ridiculous financial freedom. Not to mention, I'm about to push that prick *Diablo* aside. Then, you and I will go down in history as the modern day *Bonnie & Clyde* of the Underground. At the same time, we will *rule* this town with an iron fist, building more towers and more net worth…than anyone has ever seen."

"Bonnie and Clyde? We? What about the *three* of us?"

He said nothing, and instead, walked back to his desk, sat and spun to stare out at the city he was obsessed with conquering.

In that moment, Mo knew Donovan had crossed a line. She could see it in his eyes. And while she loved, believed in and would follow him, she also knew his incessant drive for *more* would be his downfall. His methodical planning and near-perfect timing had somehow gone astray. She wasn't sure if he some occasional drug use—using the very products with whom he poisoned his clients, had baked his reasoning. Or, if the level of his thirst for power had grown to a size he could no longer control. Perhaps it was seeing his other lover in harm's way—knowing it was *his* fault that caused him such massive guilt.

That was the weakest of the choices, she felt.

Familiar with astrology, she saw the *Gemini* in him more clearly now; perhaps more than ever before. Their dual nature, symbolized by twins, represented exchange of ideas and trade. They were also believed to be adaptable and flexible, sometimes to the point of being two different personalities. There were other thinkers who believed people with this sign lived in a world of duality, sometimes so convoluted by extremes, they lost touch with reality.

That was what she was seeing more of these past few days.

Either way, she had to do something. Be true to him as best she could, and watch out for him and the team so they could all get out of this alive, or do everything in her power to stay *one step ahead* of him—just in case things went sideways, as she felt they were destined to do.

She could be as ruthless as he had once been. Likewise, she came from nothing, and had worked extremely hard to get to where she was today. And while he may be ruthless and money-hungry, she was not willing to risk her life for him, or anyone. Not anymore.

Metaphorically, the tiny hole in their boat had sprung a leak, and her fear was that small hole could just as easily turn into a gaping chasm, and drown them, if they weren't careful.

Turning from the window, she forced a smile and spoke to him softly from across the room.

"Okay."

He turned, sighed and quietly said, "Trust me?"

"I trust you," she said, letting him feel her loyalty. "Let's do this."

"Let's do this," he smiled.

AFTER DONOVAN HEARD the update on the whereabouts of Carter and his crew, and got a pulse on where things stood, he went into a full explanation of exactly what had taken place since they last spoke over dinner. Fifteen minutes later, Ken, Sean and Mo sat with an expression that teetered between horror and anger. It took a long moment before the lively discussion began.

"So, when do you and I head out to execute every one of these *motherfuckers*?" Ken said so calmly even Donovan was unnerved.

Donovan admired his enthusiasm and knew his immediate reaction was to pack up as many explosives as they had on hand, jump a plane, and hit Cancun—to not only execute them all, but level their entire compound to the ground.

"There's just one thing," Donovan began. "Actually, more than one, but for this example, it will suffice."

"What?"

"He…literally *is*…the devil."

"So?" Ken said expressionless.

"He has *no* conscience."

"And?"

"And, we're so outnumbered…it isn't even funny."

Losing patience, Ken barked, "And your point is?"

Donovan, while appreciating the bravado, was getting annoyed.

"My point is that he's *heavily* armed…with an *army* of men. And his network *vastly* outweighs ours. And let's not forget the fact, that by our working alongside him—in whatever capacity that may be, it will make all of us *incredibly* wealthy. As in…for *decades* to come."

Sean finally spoke, "I like that."

Ken turned to him and frowned. "Shut the fuck up, Sean. You couldn't fight your way out of a schoolyard scrap—on your best day. These people are fucking killing machines. You eavesdrop on *conversations* for a living and occasionally help build explosives. But there's *never* been a time, I've seen, where you've held a gun and actually killed someone in cold blood."

Sean took the heat, before quietly saying, "Then now's the time. Because I got no problem killing anyone who fucks with Margo."

The room was still.

"Okay then. Looks like we're all on the same page," Donovan said, looking for reassurances from Mo who sat showing no expression.

"Mo?"

"Yeah?"

"You in?"

"Yes."

"Really?"

She looked to Ken, to Sean, and finally to Donovan, then extended a fist. They each obliged with a fist bump.

Looking back to Donovan, a grin grew on her face. "Bring it."

48

THE CONFERENCE

We entered Lukas Burton's office, which was lavish and had pretty much everything you would expect a big-time mayor in the number one city in the world to have.

Phil McDonough and Lukas were sitting opposite one another in chairs in front of his enormous desk. Phil smoked a cigar, while Lukas drank coffee. They stood, as we entered. I couldn't help but notice an odd expression on Phil's face.

"Hello, gentlemen," Lukas said, crossing to shake our hands. His demeanor was much more chill than before; like we were pals now.

"Mayor," I nod. "This is Mack, uh, Steve MacKenzie. My business partner."

They shook hands, as Phil stood off to the side, with a nod of hello.

"And Ko Yoshi. He's one of our...special detectives."

They exchanged nods and a smile.

I watched Lukas—a bit surprised by his coolness, but then again, I suppose he had given in to that place where there was only so much you can do.

"So, I'm guessing you've made progress in pulling the funds

together," I asked him—as much for gauging where we stood on delivery times and places, as I was interested if he had been able to liquidate whatever assets were needed. I noted how closely Phil watched Mack and myself.

"Almost. Phil and I were just putting the finishing touches on that. It's taking longer than expected."

"Really?" Mack said, "Last time I tried to raise a million bucks is was nothing."

Everyone chuckled except me. I knew Mack was trying to break the ice, but I was ready to spank this bitch.

"True, Steve," Lukas said, waving us to take a seat.

"You can call me Mack. Most do," he said, taking a place next to the window, forgoing a chair.

"Fine, *Mack*," Lukas said, "Can I offer you gentlemen anything?"

"No, we're fine. In fact, what do you say we just get down to business?" I said, taking the pad and pen Mack gave me earlier.

"We're still working on several leads as to who we think could be behind this," I began. "And was wondering if we could run a few things past you, Lukas." Turning to Phil, I said, "And you, Phil; in case you have some inside info you think could help."

"Of course," Phil said, releasing a thick cloud of smoke toward the ceiling.

Koi instantly coughed.

"Sorry, is this bothering you?"

Koi nods, and Mack said, "Do you mind?"

"Of course not," he complied, stubbing it out and carrying the ashtray to the window ledge where Mack stood.

"Okay, let's start with motives," I said, looking at my empty pad. "We tried to examine every possible angle of whoever we thought could be remotely involved."

"Of course," Lukas replied, pouring a coffee from the tray between us.

I watched as Lukas poured a second cup, glancing to Mack in the back of the room. Standing by a large credenza, Mack was searching the room for clues—looking at books, awards, certificates, and any photos that decorated the back wall.

Lukas and Phil paid him no attention.

"Let's start with former employees. Anyone who used to work with you—maybe someone who was either disgruntled, insubordinate, or otherwise."

Lukas stared at the ceiling. "You know, I've been in this office for a decade…and frankly, there's no one that fits that description. With the exception of maybe someone who was just lazy and didn't carry their share of workload. But honestly, they wouldn't have lasted long. Other than that, nobody comes to mind."

Looking at Mack, he shrugged and slowly meandered toward Lukas' desk.

"Okay," I continued, "How about current liaisons, or better yet —opponents, who might be fighting anything you're currently endorsing, raising money for, or perhaps topics that may just have the ire of the people."

"Are you kidding, Carter? Take a number," he laughed, smacking Phil's leg.

"No kidding," Phil said, laughing along with Lukas. "We'd be here all day. Hell, all month!"

"Okay, well, we could talk about my proposed High-Speed Long Island Train, or the Gambling Casino in the works for Riker's Island. I'm sure there are *plenty* of people who want to give me an earful for those deals."

"Or worse," Phil joked.

"Yeah, or worse. There's what, 47.8% of people who do *not* want to see me run for President. There's one guy, a Senator from Wisconsin who has it out for me, saying that it was time we had a President who wouldn't be controlled by clandestine, uber wealthy 'one-percenters' dictating which puppet would carry out which personal agenda."

"Oh yeah, Gerald Blackwell. He's got it bad for you."

"Only because *he* isn't one of those people who stand to gain what we…" he pointed between he and Phil, "Can offer him."

As they laughed, I looked to Mack who shook his head. I faked a laugh-along, just to appease them, but in reality, just wanted to bitch slap Lukas's face and knee Phil in the nuts—that is, *before* introducing *Mr. Cheytec* to whomever was behind this. Instead, I pressed on, scribbling random notes.

"Well, that's only been done for decades, right?" I said mostly under my breath, which made Lukas and Phil look at me like I just farted.

Mack was now looking out the window, standing behind Lukas' desk.

"Okay, how about someone who holds a personal grudge against you. Anyone you can think of?"

Lukas looked from Phil to Mack to Koi and then to me.

"You mean like you?" Lukas said with a deadpan expression.

He and Phil shared a chuckle, but their levity was grating on my nerves.

"Not really, Lukas. After all, it was your wife that called *me*. Something about not wanting to wait…until it was…too late."

His next expression said I took him down a notch.

"Besides, we haven't communicated—not *once*, in that time. And that was, what, a decade ago, when you got married."

Lukas applied a fake smile, as Phil said, "He got you there, brother."

Just then, I looked up to see Mack nodding toward something on his desk. I confirmed with a tiny nod and walked toward the desk, saying, "Anyone who might owe you money…or maybe *you* owe them money?"

Burton's frown said he was digging deep, but he ended up shaking his head, "Not that I can think of."

At his desk, I saw the picture Mack alerted me to. It was a photo of he and Clare at their wedding. That was next to a family photo.

But the third was what Mack saw. And pointed out.

In the photo, Lukas was standing in the middle of four men, all dressed in desert fatigues, apparently somewhere in the Middle East.

That's when I noticed a familiar face. And my heart skipped a beat.

"Tell me, Lukas, who are these guys?" I asked, picking up the frame and looking at it more closely, before handing it to him.

He stood, reaching out for the frame, then said, "Oh, that's my troop. We were in the shit together."

He and Phil simultaneously said, "*Oorah!*"

Mack and I look at one another and said, "*Semper Fi.*"

Everyone stopped in place.

"So, there's you and Phil…" I led.

"Yeah, we all had nicknames—just like you, *Lucky.*" Then, looking to Mack, he asked, "What's your nickname?"

"Mack," he said, expressionless.

"Original," Phil smirked.

"So, there's Phil—aka *Fat Crayon*, Pete Norelli is *Radio*, Donovan Blair, aka *Hollow Point* and…"

Mack and I exchanged looks.

"…the one ethnic in the bunch, Hector Gonzalez, aka *Tequila*. And of course, me."

"And your nickname?" Mack asked.

"Snake," he said, rolling up a sleeve to reveal a rattlesnake tattoo that went from his wrist, along his forearm, to wrap around the bottom of his bicep. A USMC crest was emblazoned on the snake's rattler.

"Of course."

"We were a salty bunch. The only one who didn't make it was Hector. He stepped on an IED. Was gone before he blinked."

Phil made the sign of the cross, and I looked at Mack, before asking, "So, who's this *Hollow Point* character?"

"Oh, he was a pistol," Lukas began.

"More like a *prick*," Phil said.

"There's that. A good soldier. Had a lot of skills."

"Like what?"

"Well, besides being a good leader and an ammunitions expert, he was a handy helluva guy."

"What do you mean?" Mack asked, taking the picture from Lukas.

"Well, he was sort of the *McGiver* type. Whatever situation he

DAVID TEMPLE

got into…he got himself out of. Plus, he was good with a gun, and even better with a knife. And cocky as *hell*."

Everyone was silent.

"Why?"

I motioned for Mack to hand me the frame. "This guy you call *Hollow Point*?"

"Yeah?"

"We know him as *Scorpion*."

"What?" Lukas had an appalled look on his face.

"Wait. You mean the drug dealer that surfaces now and again? The guy they can't seem to catch?" Phil asked.

"Uh huh," I grunted.

"No way," Lukas said, shaking his head. "That's Donovan Blair, the real estate—"

"*Scorpion*."

"No, no…the *Real Estate* Tycoon. Here in town," Lukas was genuinely dumbfounded. "Only one of the biggest developers in the city."

"Also known as *The Donovan*," Phil added. "And crazy as it sounds, rumors have him running for President, too."

They both guffawed.

"Ridiculous, right? But don't be surprised if he helps *fund* some people who may be running for that same office," Lukas said, fist bumping Phil.

I shook my head. "No. That's Donovan Blair, aka the *Scorpion*, and we ran into him—and were nearly killed by, he and his Japanese girlfriend while investigating a kidnapping in Havana, Cuba."

"Carter, you've got the wrong guy. Seriously," Lukas said. "He's a legit real estate guy."

I shook my head very slowly, for effect.

His face went slack. "You're shitting me." Then, the color drained from his tanned face.

"What?" I asked.

Lukas took a deep breath, rubbed his forehead and eyes hard. "You remember when you were asking the questions before? About

224

anyone in our past? Well, he crossed my mind, but I guess I just…buried it."

"And?"

Scratching his chin, he grew an embarrassed expression. "I guess I *may* have had something to do with his getting kicked out of the Corps."

49

THE REVELATION

"WHAT THE FUCK?" I SHOUTED. "And you don't think that may have *something* to do with someone in your past who held something against you?"

"Oh, boy," Phil mumbled, shaking his head repeatedly.

I motioned for everyone to sit and huddle.

"Give me the story, Lukas. The *whole* story. And don't miss a *stinkin'* detail."

After a deep sigh and tentative glance to Phil, Lukas began.

"Donovan had a real problem with his temper. And he liked to drink. So, often on furlough, he'd have too much to drink, get all riled up with us and a lot of other people…and, well, he'd get out of hand," he stopped to scratch his chin. "Can't believe I'd forgotten so much of this. He was a team leader, and like I said, he was good with guns. Knew a lot about them, and strangely enough, always carried a single .45 caliber bullet in his pocket. We never knew why, but he always did," he glanced to Phil then turned back to me. "That's how he got his nickname. Because of the—"

"Hollow point," Mack said.

Lukas turned to Mack. "Right. 185 grain, to be exact. Showy, but…we never forgot the message," he snorted, turning back to me. "So, all of us have way too many days on duty—on tour, when we *finally* get some time off. Soon, we're pouring drinks and striking up some poker. We all liked to play poker. But Donovan? He *loved* to play poker. But *hated* to lose. He was really good, too. So, one night, some Private—much too drunk for his own good or our safety, dared Blair to slam some shots—who was *clearly* over the limit, but he did anyway. Again, 'cause it all about competing. And as you can imagine, the intensity of the game increased, stakes got higher, guys fell out, etc. About that time, this Master Sergeant, who was just passing through and wanted to have a couple drinks to blow off some , well long story short—after too many *more* drinks and much higher stakes, there were only a couple of us left. Sarge played a hand, and Donovan—thinking he was cheating, got super pissed and—"

"You're killing me," Mack said.

"Okay, so the night's over, everyone's heading back to the barracks, when Donovan—much too drunk to be doing anything besides sleep, goes back to his bunk to get that one *hollow point* and put it in his gun before setting out to get him some."

I half-whispered, "No.

"Yes," he shook his head. "He went to the Officer's bunks, called him outside…and Donovan proceeds to point the gun right at his forehead, cocks the gun and calls Master Sergeant a cheater."

"Holy shit," Koi said.

"Yeah, brutal. Since the Sarge owed me one, I asked him if he'd drop the charges. But later, because of details that surfaced—people who were provoked and put into uncomfortable positions…you know how it is, anyway upon further reflection, and some resistance from a *higher stack of bars*, I went back to the Master Sergeant and said Donovan was a threat. *And* that it wasn't the first time something like that had happened. They asked what I thought was best and I said he's got to go."

"And?" Mack leaned in.

"And he was discharged."

"DD?" Koi asked.

Lukas nodded. "Dishonorable discharge."

"And you didn't..." I hesitated for effect. "Remember any of this? Earlier...when all this shit was going down?"

"Not really. Not until you started drilling down. I guess because we actually became good friends after that...well, not great friends, but—"

"But you don't think someone like *Hollow Point* or rather, *Scorpion,* or whatever he's calling himself these days—"

"Donovan."

"Yeah, Lukas, I got that. But this guy isn't the type of guy who would hold a grudge against you?"

He shrugged.

What a tool, I thought, but only said, "Well, *that's* our guy."

"Hundred percent," Mack added.

"Where is he now?" Koi asked, "I mean, if he's New York's biggest real estate tycoon, he's got to be very public. Where's his office?"

"He only owns four of the tallest, most luxurious towers in town," Phil said.

"And that's the thing," Lukas said. "He's super private. Rarely makes Page 6. Only shows up to events at their opening ceremony, if even then."

Mack and I eyeballed one another.

Getting better by the minute, I thought. "And his company?"

"It's called Scion Corp."

"Shit," I said, scribbling notes. "Aka *Gold pot.*"

"I *think* he lives in midtown—possibly in one of his towers. Like I say, he's not an out and about guy."

"Anything *else,*" Mack asked, clearly getting tired of pulling teeth.

"Yeah, he's got a helicopter. I should know—he bought it from me when I upgraded."

"Where's it parked?"

"On the Westside."

I'm looking at my notes, when something pinged the back of my head.

"WSCN?" I said, looking at Mack.

"Yeah, the radio van," he grinned.

"That's one thing. But here's another," I smirked, turning the pad to show Lukas two words: SCION CORP.

"Yeah?" he said.

Scribbling, I said, "One's abbreviated, but rearrange the letters…and you've got…"

I turned the pad around. I had scratched out SCION CORP, and next to it wrote: *SCORPION.*

"Oh shit," Lukas mumbled.

"Oh yeah."

ONCE EVERYONE FELT confident that our Donovan Blair and *Scorpion* was one in the same, and the man ever-so-likely responsible for kidnapping the Mayor's daughter, our job became infinitely easier. As easy as finding a needle in a haystack of steel towers.

As we began to make closing comments, I had a couple of things still nagging me and said, "Lukas? Or Phil. Can either of you tell me if anyone has access to this office besides you and your secretary."

Lukas shook his head, "No one. Except the cleaning staff, but there are only two people who have a key. If one can't make it, the other covers the office. It's always been that way. And both of them have worked here for nearly thirty years."

I stood and walked to the door. Opening it, I asked his secretary to join us. As she entered, they looked at one another.

Entering, Margaret Childress asked, "How may I help?"

"You've worked here for how long?" I asked.

"Twenty-five years—two terms with our honorable Mayor Burton," she smiled, "Plus, five years before him."

"Thank you. Just one more thing."

"Yes?"

"Have you seen, or has anyone…out of the ordinary, stopped into this office, say in the past week?"

She thinks, and was about to dismiss it, when she looked at a vase of flowers on Burton's desk.

"Yes, actually. Besides a florist—which isn't all that unusual, but they never enter this office, there was a Police Officer. And frankly, I don't recall ever seeing around here before. Of course, there are thousands on our force, but rarely do they come to *this* office. And if they did, they would nearly always be accompanied by Chief Davis."

We all looked to one another.

"It didn't seem that odd at the time," she shrugged.

"By the way, where's the Chief?" Mack asked.

"His wife fell yesterday and fractured her hip. He's at St. Luke's with her," she said.

Mack nodded. "So, that officer you mentioned….was he tall and well built?"

Smiling, she said, "Yes, actually. And had a deep southern accent."

"Southern?" I said. "That seems…out of place, doesn't it?"

"I thought the same thing, too. I remember because it was hot that day—evidently the air-conditioning went out, and he stopped in to say he'd help take care of it."

Grinning, I looked to Mack. "That's good information."

"No doubt," he said. Turning to her, he asked, "Anything else?"

"Yes. Something else…just a bit odd I suppose," she said. "Because an air-conditioning repairman arrived in…just minutes."

"It's New York, everything happens fast here, right?" Mack smiled.

"Not *that* fast," she said. "No, it was *less* than five minutes. I'm fairly certain about that."

"But that's also strange. The AC *never* goes out here," Phil said, looking at Lukas.

"Yeah, not in the ten years I've been here," Lukas said. "Not once."

Shit!

Looking at Mack, I dropped and shook my head with an expression of, *Can't believe I didn't think about it.* Pointing to both ears , I made a circle in the air—our signal for *audio surveillance.*

As I began walking around the room, Mack kept the chatter going, by turning back to her. "Mrs. Childress, is it?"

"Yes."

"Tell us everything that happened that day," Mack said, as I started looking inside table lamps and around phones.

"So, he said he'd call for service. The serviceman came, checked the thermostats on my wall, came in here to check on *this* wall." She pointed to the device on the wall. "Then he smiled and left."

I was about to wave her off, when my hand rubbed against something on the lip of a bronze statue sitting on the corner of Lukas' desk. The figure was a miniature version of the Wall Street Bull. Peeking underneath the tail, I couldn't help but grin as I removed a black disc the size of a shirt button from beneath the bull's balls. Holding it up for all to see., I put my index finger to my lips, motioning for Mack to keep talking.

"So, Mrs. Childress, do you know this repair service to be reputable," Mack said, nodding adamantly.

Next, I removed a Zippo lighter from my pocket.

"Yes, absolutely," she said, as I pulled the lighter mechanism out and buried the microphone inside the felt fluid reservoir.

"Thank you," I said, shoving it back into and closing the stainless lid with the familiar *clink*, putting it into my pocket. "And *this* is how they knew your every conversation, Mayor."

He shook his head , as Phil rolled his eyes.

"So, on my count, I'd say, we've got Donovan, the cop…"

"Ken Dawson," Koi interrupted.

"Right, the *bad* cop, plus the radio van guy—who's likely the AC guy, too."

"And the hysterical Central Park Mom, who was likely played by—I think Donovan called her Mo, whom we met in Cuba," I said more to Mack than anyone else.

Lukas stood. "Carter, can Phil and I have two minutes?"

I glanced at Mack. "Sure, let's go burn one," I said, heading for the door. "Back in ten."

. . .

STEPPING out on the front steps, I lit a smoke. "Everybody with me?"

Nodding, Koi took out gum and stuck it in his mouth.

"Absolutely," Mack said. "Nice stuff back there. Never crossed my mind about a *bug*, but makes sense."

"Right? I kept thinking, how do these guys seem to anticipate their every move. Then it came to me. If it's not someone on the inside, it's got to be at least someone *listening* on the inside."

"And nothing saying it's *not* an inside job," Koi said.

"True."

Mack stared into the distance.

"What it is, pal?"

"Couple things. I'm with you on Donovan and the three others. Makes total sense. But why would this 'real estate tycoon' also be a drug dealer? Seems wacky, huh?"

I shrugged. "I guess so. Sometimes a nut-job's just a nut-job."

"True. When we met him, he seemed all about the business. Drugs, that is. And yet, he's still *legit*."

"Sometimes the *front* has a dark back."

"What?"

"I don't know, dude. I'm toast. I feel like I've been awake for 72 hours."

"We practically have."

"Speaking of, where are we on the *countdown*," Koi asked, using air-quotes.

Mack and I looked at one another.

"You know, although we don't actually *speak* Japanese, we don't need the added interpretation of hand gestures to understand our...*native tongue*."

"Smart ass," Koi smirked.

"But to your point," I checked my watch, "Less than 20 away."

BACK UPSTAIRS, Lukas was sitting at his desk, while Phil stood by the window, stubbing out a cigar. As we entered, Lukas waved for us to have a seat.

"Carter, while I've done pretty much everything I can to get my funds together, and will have it *all* in place, I have a proposition for you." He looked to Phil who came around and leaned against the desk. "While I'm a rich man, and can certainly afford this…ransom, I want to up the ante."

I listened.

"I don't know what you were expecting when Clare called on you to help find our daughter, but I want to make it *specifically* worth your while to catch this…barbarian," he hesitated. "Still hard to believe it's Donovan, but, well, I guess we never really know people…do we?"

"I wasn't expecting to do anything but help a friend. And for the record, and as much as I'm not 100% convinced you're the best thing for Clare, you are her husband. She chose you. I'm good with that. But I didn't, nor do I ever, help people with an expectation to gain anything in return."

He looked bewildered.

"No fooling," Mack said. "That's my boy."

"And PS? Same goes for him," I tossed my thumb at Mack. "He's on my ticket."

"That certainly makes what I'm about to say…all the more *poignant.*"

We watched.

"Carter, I will pay you $10 million dollars in cash…when you bring my daughter to safety."

My jaw wanted to drop, but I needed to stay cool—as there was still plenty of danger in play.

"And by that I mean, *disarm* the device. And *guarantee* she's no longer in danger."

As the five of us exchanged looks, he said, "As for *how* you do it, I don't care. My thinking? By whatever means necessary. And the way I see it? You'll not only be doing Clare and me the biggest service, but you'll be helping this great city. And frankly, the entire country."

"Okay, before you get all sentimentally patriotic 'n shit —I'm in."

By his expression, I'd say it was the first time he relaxed all day.

"But," I barked, pointing at him for emphasis, "Before *we* begin, you're going to shake on this deal—in front of these guys. I know it's old school, but that's me."

Grinning, he shook my hand.

MACK, KOI AND I WERE OUT OF HIS OFFICE, in the SUV, and leaving the parking lot when I said, "Damn."

"Yep," Mack said.

"You said it," Koi added.

"Gents, I think our mission just amped up."

Just then, Koi reached over, punched a button, and cranked up *Thunderstruck* by AC/DC.

I grinned, "Perfect."

50

THE DUALITY

THE MEETING with his team had gone as well as Donovan could have expected, given the circumstances. They appeared to have bought his story and were willing to follow him back into the shit. However, he wasn't convinced it was the best play. His mind raced as he thought of Margo and the danger she was in. He pondered how he and his team were going to rescue her—a feat that seemed impossible. And he envisioned all the money he would have this time tomorrow. On top of this nightmare, he had a Special Ops crazy man hot on his trail. And if Donovan knew Lukas Burton as well as he felt he did, Lukas would be engaging Carter to do his dirty work.

Burton didn't get to where he was, and to where he was headed, by being a nice guy who played by the rules. Burton and he were not only soldiers together, but had become real friends—brothers, even. But over a decade ago, when Burton learned Clare was dating him and Donovan at the same time, all bets were off.

One of Donovan's premiere strengths was patience. Burton never counted on that. When Donovan wanted something, time was not important.

Whatever it takes, had always been his motto. He was willing to spend months if not *years* crafting a scenario which would not only bring the egomaniacal blowhard Burton tumbling to the ground, but one that would take what was most important from him: his wife and little girl.

But if he played the game well, one of two things would happen for Donovan; either he would do considerable damage to Burton's net worth, humiliating him in the process, or worse, rid himself of Burton for good. The problem with the latter plan was that both Clare and Abigail would be sacrificed as "collateral damage."

Donovan knew he was a broken man.

As long as he could remember, he had seen life through a cracked lens. Growing up with nothing; with a father who told him he would never amount to anything, and a mother who slept around —either to entertain herself or to make ends meet, he didn't get the sort of start many of his comrades had enjoyed. Early on, he promised himself that as soon as he was old enough he would run away and join a group where he could belong.

That group was The Marines.

His plan was to study under the tutelage of someone he could respect. He would fight the bad guys, killing for all the right reasons. He had also imagined that somewhere along the way, he would meet a woman who could provide him the love and acceptance he so desperately sought. So, when he met Clare one hot summer in Charleston—while on temporary duty for his battalion, he was certain he had met his dream girl. However, in retrospect, circumstances were different than his imagination had created.

Yes, they had met at a swanky enlisted party her father managed. Yes, they were hobnobbing among the elite her socialite mother orchestrated. And yes, one night they both became entirely over-served, thanks to an open bar. But between the summer air, her sexy attitude, and a sultry ambiance, they fell down a tempestuous rabbit hole that got complicated entirely too fast.

What Donovan didn't know was his rugged good looks and undeniable masculine swagger—while intoxicating to Clare, was mild competition for a Rhodes scholar soldier-on-the-rise whose collective sights were set on a more affluent and influential future. Between her brains and beauty, and their magnetic connection, she was exactly what that man wanted. Consequently, because of her youth and restrictive upbringing—which resulted in her entertaining several men simultaneously, she was the target of many a man's attention—including Burton.

About the time Donovan and Burton's professional friendship had bonded in the same military camp, and Burton and Clare's committed relationship had become singularly formed, their three way dalliance was accidentally exposed by Clare to a large circle of her parent's socialite friends during yet another cocktail-soaked soirée. Both her mother and grandmother periodically chastised Clare for not becoming "one of those women."

He recalled hearing them say, "A woman of your background shouldn't entertain multiple men whose level of commitment was as deep as the cocktails we hold at dinner parties."

Clare always laughed it off, knowing they were "old fashioned," while she was "romantically progressive."

All three women were right.

When Donovan started to infringe upon Burton's plans, and his hot-headed antics had risen to a crescendo, Burton used the inflamed situation as the perfect alibi to make Donovan disappear—all under the auspices of his being an *out-of-control maniac*.

After his discharge, *Hollow Point* became *Scorpion* and began systematically plotting the ultimate revenge—eventually making certain that Burton's future would one day sting badly.

Donovan felt numb.

He stared out at the tips of towers, many of which he helped build in one way or the other. Likewise, hundreds and perhaps thousands of those whom inhabited them were now addicts, thanks to the chemical dependency to which he had introduced them.

I like living high—both in the sky and in my mind.

However, a sad reality had set in: he had run out of patience. The "other half of himself" was starting to show its twisted face. He had felt this transformation before. Likewise, he knew if not careful, things would get very ugly. Very fast.

His eyes went from staring at the FedEx envelope on his desk, to the elaborate chessboard next to his couch, to the view of Manhattan outside his window. The colors were beginning to drain from the day, but his energy was increasing. His nerves were getting rattled, but his courage was getting stronger. The calculated plays of the board were blurring with those on the street, and the package in front of him begged to be opened.

As the "Abigail Deadline" was looming, he found his palms sweating and his heart racing. Wondering what play would come next, he fought the urge to say sell everything and disappear to an exotic island off the coast of Asia.

That feeling will pass as quickly as it arrived.

He stared at the FedEx package, contemplating its contents. Given it had arrived from Mexico, had a bulge that disfigured it, and was addressed to *Mr. Scorpion Blair,* he had an idea of what it contained.

His stomach tightened, as he picked up the package.

Inside, he found a metal bandaid box. It was sealed with duct tape. The front of the envelope which accompanied it read:

FOR YOUR OWN SAFETY, READ THIS FIRST.

Is it a bomb? Am I being fed my own medicine?

Ripping the envelope open, he pulled out a sheet of paper.

Hello Scorpion,

You would be smart to deliver my money as soon as you can. Otherwise, more of this will be coming your way. And at this rate, it will take a lot of packages.

Remember when you borrowed money from me to start your own business? Remember when I said I would share my wealth with someone as industrious as you. Remember how I said I would do that IF you pay me back and never double-cross me? Well, you have yet to pay me back, and that feels like a double-cross.

There are plenty of drugs, guns, money and power to go around for everybody. Don't get greedy. But if you must, know there is also plenty of evil in the world. And if you choose that path, that evil will rain down on you with such a vengeance you won't have enough energy to catch up.

In closing, give me the past and present money you owe me, or be prepared to give me your life and those of everyone you know.

-El Diablo

Donovan tossed the paper aside and pressed his palms into both sides of his head.

"Shit!"

He stared at the package, wishing it away.

No such luck.

Picking it up, he smelled the container; feeling confident if it were explosives, he would detect it.

Nothing.

Pulling the tape off, he checked the lid for a trigger, even though he knew it wasn't a bomb.

He would gain nothing by killing me now.

Turning the can upside down, he shook it.

Out fell a bloody bandage, and he unwrapped it.

Margo's middle finger.

51

THE WHIP

DR. LEONARD CAPRESE, a highly educated man from prestigious heritage, sat in his handsomely appointed Washington, D.C. office, admiring his office full of impressive plaques on the wall, signifying membership and achievement in all sorts of committees, boards and organizations. A vast number of expensively framed photographs included him arm in arm with presidents, dignitaries, royalty, influencers, politicians, and several powerful, yet secretive men who were less-than-silent members of groups few knew about, yet held positions of immense control.

As a Whip in the Senate, he had a good deal of influence.

He was second in the party hierarchy behind the majority leader. He liked that power. His duties included making sure members were positioned in DC and in the chamber during crucial votes, as he helped forecast how members would vote. He liked that persuasion. His job was to alert party leaders to shifting congressional opinions, and he would often distribute information on pending amendments or bills. He liked that presence.

Having climbed the corporate and political ladder over the years, Leonard's experience taught him a great many things. First and foremost, while all men are created equal—most men are equally corrupt. He had seen it more than he cared to recall—every day, in fact, and in every level of government. However, there wasn't any judgment on his part; after all, as far as he was concerned, it was merely a way of doing business. It was *his* way of doing business.

Caprese had more than a dozen times used his power of influence and persuasion on matters of international matters, and with international leaders who were—as many would say, beneath the law. He felt those men were more *beyond* the law—as beneath implied they would play by some rules while attempting to remain under the radar.

Most men he dealt with operated in a sphere of influence that transcended the law. In fact, Caprese's position allowed him to sit upon the proverbial fence of right and wrong, and in a world of black and white, he chose the "grey in-between." He felt that was a position that always worked in his favor, and in doing so, had created great wealth for him.

Conversely, he also became more dangerous.

When one chose to exist inside such a dangerous world, one had to spend their days looking over shoulders, covering tracks, keeping journals of conversations, and duplicating computer files—storing them securely.

And forever wondering when the shoe would drop.

Because as was always the case in gambling, you may have a winning streak, but that streak eventually sputtered, or worse— came crashing to a halt.

Perhaps one of the most impressive attributes about Caprese was his mental stamina. He could look at a chessboard and be able to see not one or two, or even three or four—but often five and six moves ahead of his opponent. As a formidable adversary, there were few people he had met who could match his calculative power.

One such person was business acquaintance, Donovan Blair.

They had met a decade ago at a gala in Manhattan. Blair was celebrating the erection of his latest super tower. Caprese was celebrating his new-found position in DC. Their paths crossed, thanks to mutual billionaires with whom they were doing business. Over several *Cohiba Behike* cigars and one too many bottles of *Louis XIII*

Remy Martin Black Cognac, they formed a friendship that would benefit both in their respective lines of work.

One particular night set them back nearly a quarter-million dollars for dinner and post-dining enjoyment. But it was worth it, because it was when Caprese came to clearly realize no matter how much money one had—it was truly never enough.

He knew with great certainty Donovan felt the same way.

It was a year or so later when Donovan was setting up another one of his many businesses—this time outside Havana, Cuba, where they would again form an alliance. Things were going fine, as they were both printing money. Donovan was creating a vast supply of drugs in Cuba, Nicaragua and Mexico, while buying guns and ammunition in various black markets then selling them to and through Caprese to Middle East countries. Caprese was working his own alliances by selling guns for information. But always information for position.

Together, they formed a formidable alliance.

Caprese crossed his office and stood over his intricate chessboard—a gift from his billionaire friend. They had matching sets; both of which were ridiculously expensive. Each also had a tiny camera mounted in the ceiling directly above their boards allowing them to constantly stream their games live, via the web—playing one another in real time, any time of the day or night.

He enjoyed this on-going game they played, and had been studying Donovan's opening play. The move was called the *Ruy Lopez*—one of the greatest and perhaps more complex openings in chess. Caprese knew and respected the move because if white played the lines correctly, they would carry an advantage in double king-pawn openings. The move was commonly seen in games played at the grandmaster level. And in many ways, Caprese had come to admit Donovan was indeed a grandmaster.

His mind shifted from the board in front of him to a memory just a month or so ago, when a business deal with Donovan in Havana, Cuba went sideways.

Staring down the barrel of a gun pointed directly at his face by his friend and business partner caused him not only to worry, but to reconsider their business relationship. As much as he enjoyed aligning himself with the *Scorpion,* he knew it came with the risk of eventually being stung.

Caprese pondered the reasons he had chosen to do business in that country with this man who many considered to be as ruthless a killer as he was a ruthless businessman.

There were three.

First, Caprese needed a base of operation for some of his "off-shore dealings" which included a plane hangar. This, he shared with Blair. Secondly, Blair wanted Caprese to be a conduit of drugs to the high-pressure world of politics, feeding the very rich with the finest versions of his sophisticated synthetic derivative of X, as well as Columbian Coke and Mexican Pot—all of which were coming through the portal of Havana. Third, Blair agreed to help fund the political running of Caprese when that time came. And while Caprese wasn't sure his office of choice would be President of the United States, he was certainly going to get as close to that pinnacle of power as was possile.

For now, those details, like many others, remained a secret. Caprese was good at keeping secrets. It was woven into the fabric of who he was. Secrets made for power covered the tracks of powerful people and opened the doors of influence like few elements in life.

He learned this lesson in a profound way when a deal went south with influential contacts from the Middle East. He was vacationing at his home in Nicaragua; a lavish, remote and distant location to all sorts of espionage, when he first met Carter Matheson. The soldier and several of his men infiltrated his cozy compound while tracking some of his constituents. Fortunately, minutes after his capture, Caprese's widespread connections allowed him to escape, using Carter's men as pieces in his game of mental chess. Shortly thereafter, when Carter came looking for them, Caprese would once again be two moves ahead. His ingenuity would allow him to yet again escape while retaining his position.

Caprese stared out his office window which overlooked several of Washington's well-known monuments. They reminded him of what this country stood for: power, control, and freedom. He enjoyed his life because it too was full of power, control *and* freedom. He helped sway votes, influence people, and steal ideas—while directing people and decisions for political gain. His position would eventually allow him to take his place at a table with one of the best seats in the house, while leading the strongest country in the world.

Controlling those around him, he used his relationships like chess pieces on an elaborate board. And that fed the hungry beast within. He used his relationship with Blair to amass great wealth. He used his relationship with Burton to infiltrate the world's wealthiest influencers who lived in New York City, where he could nudge open doors for Burton's influencers, which in turn would help them slide Burton into the right position when needed. He used his relationship with Phillip McDonough, one of the most powerful and connected attorneys in the free world, for the sole purpose of *power management.* Caprese knew there would come a time when he would hit a wall and need someone to cut a way through that wall.

Thanks to quick thinking amidst a heated situation in Cuba, he would use his relationship with Carter for one specific purpose. He was confident Carter would eventually go after Donovan Blair, the man whose pet scorpion nearly poisoned his father. Saving the lives of Carter, his father, and two other of his team, was the best thing Caprese could have done. He also knew Carter was a soldier first. This made him an ally. But a volatile one. That Donovan escaped and left them all behind showed Caprese the reality of Blair's *true* reputation and the *insecurity* of their friendship.

Caprese knew that in the high stakes game of corruption, someone somewhere would at some time fall. And because of the debt owed him, Caprese felt confident when the time came, he could count on Carter to permanently remove a chess piece—aka man, on Caprese's board.

That would allow him the ultimate checkmate.

Observing the board in front of him, Caprese realized days had passed since his last play, and he was ready to make his next move.

He considered the *Morphy Defense*—a move that would put him inside the perimeter of destroying his opponent.

His hand hovered over his Knight, but stopped.

Taking a cellphone from his pocket, he dialed a number and waited for a five-tone confirmation.

Beep-beep...Beep-beep-beeeeeeep.

His eyes shifted back to the chessboard.

Smiling, he entered a six-character security key, then waited for the call to connect.

After three rings, a message played: "*If you've reached this message and I haven't answered, you know what to do.*"

The pause before the tone was just enough time for him to decide his next move.

52

THE PREPARATION

MACK, Koi and I sat on the outdoor patio of *The Standard*. We figured there was just enough time to grab a quick bite before we hunkered down for what was likely to be a non-stop run at the clock. Driving across town had given me a chance to follow up with the one contact responsible for helping with the security footage in Central Park. The officer had originally hoped to locate any security camera footage that could lead us to the *park clown, hysterical mother* and *blind guy* from the kidnapping.

Nothing significant turned up, as the lack of clarity screwed our chances.

Koi had spent his time following up on tech connections with nerds who worked for the company who handled the Times Square jumbo screens. Again, nothing traceable.

Mack had secured a thumb drive from Chief Davis which proved to be invaluable. Loading it on our laptop, we were able to see an aerial view of the entire island. Imagine *Google 3D Maps,* but better. Evidently, his office had worked with NASA and a corp of engineers and software techs who provided a bird's eye view of Manhattan. Thousands of cameras mounted at nearly every intersection worked with the software, giving us incredible time-saving views. The only thing we couldn't see was *inside* homes, because of privacy issues.

We would find a way around that.

Here's what we now knew with near certainty: Donovan lived in one of four towers which included: *The Apex* in the Wall Street district of downtown, *The Ambassador,* located on the east side of midtown, *The Avalon,* located in Hell's Kitchen on the opposite side of midtown, and *The Avenue* which was located on the Upper Eastside, on Park Avenue east of Central Park.

The four structures were glass and steel and among the tallest buildings in Manhattan. Each was built as 80% residences, with retail and/or offices in the remaining 20%. Both midtown structures had rooftop pools complete with terraces and balconies, while the remaining two structures were self-enclosed with little to no operational windows and no balconies. These were significant factors when it came to access.

We would find a way around that.

As we began examining potential elimination procedures—given our narrowing band of time, Koi suggested he didn't see Donovan living in the *The Avenue.*

"It just seems too *foofaloofa* for him," Koi said.

I couldn't help but chuckle. Mack took it one better.

"What the *fuck* is—what'd you say...*Foo-foo-loo-foo*?" he cackled.

"Something like that," Koi dismissed. "Means fancy."

"Then why not just say fancy?"

I waved, "Keep going." I wanted to hear his reasoning.

"He's a tough guy. Military. Meat 'n potatoes. He wouldn't go for that nose in the air snob factor."

"Okay, I see your point. And actually agree. Okay, we mark that one off." I drew a line through my list.

Washing down a last bite of his sandwich with a beer, Mack wiped his mouth on the back of his arm. "I say we nix Wall Street."

Koi and I looked at one another. I asked, "Why's that, partner?"

"Similar reasoning. Too *stuffy* for him. Plus, according to the blueprints we got, there's no outside egress. Something tells me he's gotta feel the outside. He may build and live in these big, cold steel structures, but he's gotta feel nature."

"Very *sensitive* of you, Mack," I grinned. "And I like your reasoning. It'd be the exact reason you and I'd never live in a building like this."

"Oh, hell, I'd never live in a tower period. Better yet, I'd never live in this city, are you kidding me? But IF I did…it would have to have a balcony. *And* a rooftop pool. Surrounded by beautiful women, of course."

"Okay, we've got the picture."

"What's your pick, Carter?" Koi asked.

At that same moment, I thought about what Mack just said, which confirmed my choice. "The Avalon."

Mack grinned, as they looked at one another. "I wanna hear this."

"I'll show you," I said, waving over the tall brunette waitress— who I've enjoyed watching since we arrived.

"Yes?" she smiled.

"Would you be a love and put this on my room. 1813. And add $100 for yourself. Thanks."

Before she could answer, we were heading to the elevator.

ARRIVING ON THE ROOF, I directed my partners to join me to the northeast corner, where we were able to scan the skyline for 360 degrees. I hadn't been up here yet, but judging from an app on my phone and the software Mack shared, I had a good feeling what we would find.

"First of all, good hunches on the Park Avenue and Wall Street towers, Gents. I completely agree. My money's on this one. Here's why. It's in Hell's Kitchen—which fits our guy's personality, right?"

They nod.

"Secondly," I faced West, "Look at the points of entry. You've got the Holland and Lincoln Tunnels, plus the George Washington Bridge on this side of town. The Brooklyn Bridge on that side," I said, pointing in that direction. "So, it provides easy access in and out of the city. The other locations are more complicated. My opinion, anyway."

"Okay, I'm with you," Mack said. "So, where's—"

"Right behind you," I interrupted, taking his shoulder and spinning him in that direction. In the distance, stood dozens of tall structures. I pointed to one in particular.

"This hotel stands 18 stories. The first really tall one is on 42nd Street, just past the *Javits Convention Center*, at the mouth of the Lincoln Tunnel. It's 46 stories. The one next door is called Silver Suites, and it goes 62."

"Geez," Mack said.

"Crazy, right? These buildings are something else: full-service, indoor and outdoor pools, blah-blah. Now, go another ten blocks and you'll see the Avalon. See it?" I pointed. "The one with the silver band around the top. See how it's catching the light. Like I say, good access, convenient, and the tallest residential building on the West Side—at 77 stories."

"Living high, huh?" Mack toyed with the pun.

"And guess what happens to be just one block from his building —about 19 blocks from us right now?"

"Burton mentioned something Burton about—"

"A helicopter," I snapped. "The Pegasus Heliport, right there," I pointed.

"*Totally* get it. With you 100% now," Mack said.

I could see Koi's wheels turning. "Ditto."

"Solid recon, bro," Mack grinned. "And coming together faster than I'd thought."

"Me too," I said.

Koi said, "What's next?"

"Glad you asked."

53

THE MISTAKE

As Ken entered Donovan's condo, he nodded to Mo who was sitting in a chaise lounge by the window. "What's up, Mo?"

"Just thinking," she smiled.

"Okay..." he checked his watch, "And where are we on the countdown?"

Her smile disappeared, as she spun to face the window. "I don't know. 15, 16 hours?"

He approached, having a good idea what was bothering her. "Margo," he whispered.

She turned.

"We're going to find her. Promise."

She looked up at him, then in the direction of Donovan's office, and back to him. "*We*. As in you and me? Or, as in...the team?"

Before he could answer, she added, "Because personally? I think it's going to be you and me. That's the *we* I see."

Ken was used to closing people off and compartmentalizing his emotions. Part of that was just what guys did. The other part; while he wasn't much for showing emotions, he genuinely felt for her. Leaning closer, he squeezed her shoulder.

"Then it will be the *us*...we."

She knew him well enough that was a big deal for him. She was also confident that even as much as she loved Donovan, she may not be able to count on him, and felt confident she could count on Ken. She took great comfort in that.

"She's my girlfriend, too," she said quietly.

He wiped a tear from her cheek and smile. "I know. Your heart's so big, you have to share it with two."

She stood and hugged him. "That is the sweetest thing ever. Especially coming from a lug like you," she giggled in his ear. "FYI, he's in the office. In that dark place."

As long as Ken had known Donovan, he had never seen Donovan appear beaten. This guy grew up with adversity, and had faced danger square in the face without ever blinking. Ken had also seen him kill a man with his bare hands, feeling pretty sure Donovan's heartbeat never shifted a beat. Donovan could be cold as ice, hard as steel, but every once in a while, they would see him do something so incredibly kind it was hard to believe he was the same man.

Ken also knew you had to always watch your *six,* as Donovan primarily looked out for himself. It was common knowledge everyone was well paid, but when push came to shove, you had to have your own *exit strategy.*

Mo had shared the Havana story where, at the last minute, Donovan nearly walked away, leaving her behind. But he didn't. As to why he didn't kill the soldiers he and Caprese were holding captive—Ken would never know.

Part of what he chalked up to Donovan's split personality.

Before knocking, Ken peeked through the half open door. Donovan sat at his desk staring at what looked to be a finger. He was stroking it. Tapping on the door, Donovan concealed his surprise and quickly grabbed the remote, turning up the volume on his bank of televisions.

"Come in," he said nonchalantly.

"Hey, boss."

"What's up?"

"Just checking to see where we are on things."

Donovan caught Ken looking at the finger on his desk, and said, "Son of a bitch," under his breath.

"We'll get her back."

Donovan stood to stretch. "Yeah, we will. Hey, you have any idea where that clown Carter is?"

"Last I saw him, he and his team were leaving City Hall. Looked like—"

"That's when they made you?"

Ken wasn't completely surprised Donovan knew, but figured it best to keep things open. "Yeah. Sean and I were running behind and got…kinda pinned in."

"Kinda? Or were?" He waved him off. "Never mind. What's done is done. He'd have found you sooner or later. All of us. That's what he does."

With a nod, Ken kept quiet.

"In fact, it's just a matter of time before he shows up," he looked around. "Doubt he'll get past my security, but who the fuck knows. We got other things to worry about."

Ken was debating whether to push the El Diablo conversation, feeling like the team could be approaching a divide. Being a good soldier that he was, he wanted to keep the morale high and the objective in sight.

As Ken said, "Donovan, I'm thinking…" Donovan looked up from his desk, with that unnerving stare.

"I'm thinking given you've got the girl's deal…you know, in the bag…why don't you let me and Mo bug out and find Margo."

Donovan sat and stared for what felt like an eternity, before finally saying, "That's not the *worst* idea. And I see your logic— two heads are better than one, plus I've got this under control, *and* we all want her back," he said, rubbing his face then staring out the window.

Ken calculated they had been at this countdown for 33 hours, and nerves were shot, Donovan was tired, and Ken could feel cracks in the foundation.

He waited.

Donovan could feel pressure building in his skull—it felt like climbing a high-speed elevator to the top of a hundred story building. His eyes burned from the heat bubbling inside. And his stomach was wrenched—feeling like someone reached in through his belly and was twisting his internal organs into a cluster of knots.

"Yeah, really not a bad idea," Donovan stood. "So, why not do this…why don't you grab your GoBag…along with Mo and Sean… and catch the next FUCKING PLANE out of here to GOD KNOWS WHERE!"

Stepping closer, he shouted, "And when you *GET* THERE, *after* you've BEGGED FOR YOUR LIFE, you can ask EL DIABLO if he would *kindly* turn Margot over to you, and *spare* your life, and just, you know, *forgive* the debt I *currently* OWE HIM—which is, oh, about 100 TIMES what I pay you IN A YEAR!"

With that, Donovan took a seat and spun his chair around, leaving Ken to stare at his back.

DOWNSTAIRS, Mo was running on a treadmill—huffing it. As he walked in, Ken estimated her to be running about a six-minute mile. She saw his reflection in the mirrored wall and pushed a button to slow down. Taking a towel, she wiped her face and— slowing to catch her breath, gasped, "Hey."

"Hey."

"Uh oh," she frowned. "What's eating you?"

He fiddled with the tail of his shirt that was uncharacteristically untucked.

"You gonna sew a button on that ratty shirt, or you wanna tell me why you interrupted my workout."

He grinned, shaking his head. "That's rich," he said, heading back toward the door.

"Hey, what is it?"

He stopped, took a dramatic breath, then walked back over— getting right up in her face.

"I don't know about you, but I've just about had it with his… maniacal antics. I know he's got a lot of pressure on him. I get it. And I know he's deep into that prick *Diablo*, but he made that choice! What I don't need is to be talked down to, or disrespected just because I don't jump to his every command. And another thing; I personally think *he's starting to lose his fuckin' mind!*"

Expressionless, she whispered, "I agree. Look, I love him. Truly. Always have, most likely always will. But shit, he's starting to get weak at the seams and frankly, I don't need it."

Ken stared at her, surprised.

"And not that it matters to many, but I really care about Margot. She's the girlfriend I never had."

He smirked.

"Fuck you," she said, punching him in the gut. "I don't expect you to understand. I can't help I like to ride both sides of the seesaw."

"No, I get it."

"I seriously don't think..." she hesitated—thinking she heard him coming down the stairs. "I don't think he's going to try and save her."

"Same here. Which is why—"

"You know what I think?"

"What?"

"I think he's going to take the money from Lukas...and bounce."

He stared at her.

"And I mean...the *big* bounce. Cash in what he can and...disappear."

She looked past Ken, waiting to hear anything.

Nothing.

"I mean...*poof.* Not take me along, *not* Margot, and certainly not you."

"Thanks."

"Shut up. Like you'd go anyway," she said, wiping the sweat from her arms. "You have enough money stashed away, right?"

He nods.

"Then get on your way. Stop being a double-agent. You'd be a *great* cop."

He smiled.

"That is, if you'd *stop* killing people."

"I don't—"

"Busting your balls, *Sarge.* But seriously, you could stay a cop, get away from this corruption and have a nice life. Or, go the other way and follow Donovan. Or just do your *own* thing. Hell, I'd work with you."

"Really?"

"What? Fuck no. I'm made for this. With this brain…" she tapped her head, "And this body…*plus,* a bank account that'd choke most people?"

"Okay, stop."

"I know. I'm a bitch. What I'm saying is—which is what you *want* to say, but you're a chicken shit…let's go find her!"

54

THE REMOVAL

THE MAN they called *The Devil* stood over Margo observing her beautiful physique. Even though she was bloody and bruising, and missing a finger, he thought she was lovely. He didn't get pleasure from hurting someone like this, but sometimes drastic measures were required.

When a man takes something that isn't his, or is dishonorable, then circumstances change. El Diablo was a businessman first ,and foremost.

The saying he had learned as a young boy was true: If you give someone an inch, they will take a mile.

Donovan had borrowed from him, not returned what was his, and then had the *cojones* to ask for more. If El Diablo let this go, his reputation would be damaged, his word would mean nothing, and his pockets would be empty.

The woman before him looked like every other woman he used for his pleasure. She was beautiful and seemed to be smart, given their short conversations. She took the removal of her finger better than he expected; most people passed out. She didn't. He had learned through the years if you can suffer the break, enduring the cutting was easier. She was smart not to watch.

Salazar was very large, particularly ugly, and ridiculously

strong. He was also dumb. But with that ignorance came a childlike innocence. How that characteristic helped in situations like this was he worked quickly to clean and sew the wound. He may be cold, but he was not completely heartless. That quality bothered El Diablo at first, but soon he came to realize that his *destruction machine* had a way of keeping loose ends tight.

"I'm sorry you have to suffer, Miss Margo. But it is your man's fault," El Diablo said with a gentle tone. "My opinion? He appears to be…*loco.* And I can't, nor will I take any risky chances with my money. I have a business to run. I'm sure you understand."

She was tied to a table, which made it impossible for her to move. Being gagged with a piece of her own clothing made things quieter, too.

Her tear-filled eyes shifted between Salazar and his sharp tool, to El Diablo and his cold eyes. She was using every ounce of strength to appeal to his mercy. But she was afraid it was to no avail. He had already laid out what was going to happen, and there was no sign of help on the way.

Given she had already lost a finger told her the cartel leader wasn't one to bluff. And what he would remove next was anyone's guess. Her mind scanned her body. Strangely, she hoped it would be another finger or toe—not an entire appendage, like an arm or leg.

El Diablo's eyes shifted from Salazar To Margot. Again, his eyes scanned the beautiful body. She sensed his desire to violate her.

If all he wants to do is fuck me—do it, she thought. *Just don't kill me.*

Then, as if he had lost interest in tormenting her, El Diablo gave a nod to his tormentor. Salazar picked up the machete and a stone and began sharpening it. The sound made her skin crawl—like nail on a chalkboard. She could feel gooseflesh appear on her soft skin, and she caught El Diablo watching the involuntary reaction ripple down her legs and arms.

He smiled. And her heart raced, coursing blood through veins at the speed of light.

If I don't slow my heartbeat, I'll bleed out too fast.

Wondering what was running through the *butcher's* mind, she couldn't help but look at his massive and scarred hands. Her gaze shifted to his arms. They were as big as most men's legs, and his shoulders looked as though they could carry a tree. Oddly enough, his eyes were a blend of cold detachment and warm sympathy.

Salazar wondered what was going through her mind, as he watched her beautiful eyes twitch back and forth between he and El Diablo. His mind drifted to all the carnage he had carried out over the years. His job was like carving an animal for a meal. Men were one thing, but hurting women was the only place he had a weak spot.

Each woman reminded him of his sisters. And his mother. He tried to shut their memories from his mind when he performed his work. As much as he wanted to just hurt this stranger and not permanently disfigure her, he couldn't lose this job. Besides, if El Diablo was going to watch, then doing a procedure in front of his boss meant he had to remain distant and cold. Salazar was paid well and received many gifts by doing his bosses wet work.

Removing a finger was easy. For the victim, they just had to adjust to their daily rituals. But removing this next body part would make life miserable for a lady as pretty as this.

Salazar liked keeping his weapons in top shape, and sharpening his machete took time. While butchering his enemies, he often watched El Diablo's eyes to see if he would wince. He never did. Salazar wondered if the bottle of tequila the man drank a day would cause him to be sick at the procedure. It didn't. He had seen his boss kill a man inches from his own face and never change his expression.

El Diablo was a cold man.

As Salazar was about to begin, El Diablo held up his hand. "On second thought, let's wait. Give my friend a few more hours. Then we'll send the next message."

With that, El Diablo patted Margo on the leg and walked away, saying over his shoulder, "Take a dinner break, Salazar. She's not going anywhere."

Pulling the tape from her face, Salazar removed the cloth from her mouth, and brushed her hair aside.

"Thank you," she whispered. She wasn't sure if it was her imagination, but it seemed like she saw a tiny smile appear at the corner of the monster's mouth. He walked away, without a word.

MARGO LAID THERE for at least twenty minutes, trying to lower her heart rate. She tried to imagine a way of escape. But looking at her bound wrists and ankles, the possibility seemed hopeless. Knowing the close call she just missed—as well as what to come, she chose to focus elsewhere, holding on to any singular hope of survival.

As twisted and complicated a man as Donovan was, she was sure he would come back for her—and if not him, certainly her other lover.

NO LESS THAN an hour later and waking from a deep sleep, Margo was startled to see Salazar standing over her. Holding a bottle of liquid and a gauze wrap, he was staring at her body. When she started to speak, he dropped the wrap and slammed his hand down on her mouth. Unscrewing the cap on the bottle with his teeth, he poured a large amount of liquid onto the gauze, set the bottle down and pressed the gauze over her nose until she passed out.

The last thing she heard was, "Sorry."

55

PART THREE:

THE PREPARATION

MACK and I went to our rooms, grabbed our rifles, then headed downstairs. It was hard to hide a rifle, so we stopped at the luggage valet and monetarily commandeered a golf club traveler. They fit fine.

Koi bypassed the Valet stand with a special card in his visor he flipped down at just the right moment. We hopped in and drove uptown to Hell's Kitchen. We called his Cadillac Escalade *Road Sub* because it was nearly the size of a submarine, and had all the bells, whistles and space one needed to live comfortably.

"You guys want some face paint…maybe wear your night goggles 'n shit?" Koi chuckled.

We ignored him.

Arriving at *The Sky* condos on 42nd, we made our way to the rooftop like we owned the place. Within minutes, we reached the Penthouse and found a large pool, a dozen cabanas, Jacuzzi, a bar and a one-hole putting green. No one stopped us—that is, until we ran into an unusually large man who was apparently a bodyguard, a lifeguard, or both.

As we approached, Mr. No-Neck held up a fat hand.

"Excuse me, guys, but can I see your keycards?"

Checking his name-tag, I began with the obvious, pulling my Special Operatives ID badge, to complete the ruse.

"Hi Stewart, I and my partners are part of a security detail commissioned by Mayor Lukas Burton himself."

He stared. I continued.

"Given it's Memorial Day Weekend, and we're *all* proud of the service provided by our men and women of the Armed Forces, he has asked us to watch over this particular area for *obvious* reasons."

Evidently the emphasis on obvious—wasn't. Instead, he lifted an eyebrow, cocked his head and ever-so-eloquently said, "Huh?"

Things were going to be just fine.

"Did you see the aircraft carrier parked—at the end of this block?" I asked.

"Oh yeah. Thought it was part of a new exhibit. Like the one right next to it."

"You mean the *Intrepid Sea, Air & Space Museum*?"

"Yeah. It's cool."

"Uh, no. That's a *museum*. While *this* is for real."

"Cool. Okay. Head on up."

ON THE ROOF, it was easy to see we had a nearly perfect line of sight to Donovan's building—with the exception of just one problem. We were on the 62nd floor; 63rd, if we counted the extra ten feet of roof.

Donovan's *Avalon* reached 77 stories.

That meant we were fourteen floors shy of being even; more, if we needed to look *down* on the target—which would be ideal.

I looked to Mack. He shrugged.

"At this distance..." I said, leaning over to do a quick count of blocks, "The variables include wind—*duh*, ricochet potential, and worse, *passing through* and landing in some place...that it shouldn't."

"Or some*one*."

"And there's that."

Scanning the horizon, I spotted any number of buildings that were as tall, or taller, and having surveyed the island thoroughly, I had gotten very familiar with structures. It was the sort of research I developed during my early training.

In the past, there had been times where I would fly into a DMZ with 30 minutes of prep time, need to locate a station, in proximity to my target, know the weather—outside my control, along with the targets' movement—inside my control, then sit and wait for hours. Sometimes days.

"We can still go from inside his camp," Mack said quietly, also scanning the terrain of skyscrapers.

"True. I just want us to have all the options possible."

As long as I've known Mack, he has never once questioned where my head was. He knew, instinctively and intellectually, I would quantify and consider every possible option. 99% of the time, we only had *one shot*. And that shot had to matter.

"You know what?"

"Huh?"

"Here's what we'll do," I said, laying the rifle down and replacing the caps on both ends of the scope, "We'll set up shop here. You and me. Then, we'll get Koi inside—"

"But they've seen me," Koi said.

"Copy that. However, they haven't see you…as a *woman*."

"What?"

Even Mack was confused. "Lucky, yeah, he's kinda handsome, but he's sure as hell not *pretty*."

I grinned at them both. "Yeah, but I've got an idea."

"This should be good," Mack blew a kiss to Koi. "Game on."

"Yup, time for Plan B…*ladies*."

56

THE COMPLICATION

CLARE SAT on Abigail's bedside, patting her forehead with a cool cloth. Abi had a severe fever, after spending a fair amount of time vomiting earlier in the morning. Clare immediately called their personal doctor, asking if he could make a home visit. He was there in 30 minutes.

While both she and the doctor knew it had to do with whatever chemicals had been placed inside her belly, she chose not to talk with her daughter about it. Instead, she directed the conversations toward *bad Chinese* food—trying to soothe her fears. The doctor gave her a sedative to keep her calm.

Between her girl being sick, her husband liquidating a large portion of their assets, and her heart being torn between too many thoughts and too much stress, she felt like she needed to talk to someone. Lukas was at the office, and her other option was Carter.

Calling her best girlfriend, Sharon Barton, she quickly brought her up to speed, asked her to come sit with her, and that she owed her "big time." Sharon agreed and was instantly in a cab and on her way. She lived on Madison and 85th so she was just a half dozen blocks away. Waiting for her to arrive, she slipped down to her office, lit a cigarette and stared at her cellphone.

I gain nothing by calling him, she thought. *It's insane to think that anything...*

The phone rang. "Clare? It's Carter. You hanging in there?"

Oh my God, that's insane.

"Yes. I'm good. I mean, hanging in there. Sorry, it's just..." she shook her head, feeling like a schoolgirl with a crush.

"What? I'm sorry, Clare, I'm on a rooftop, the traffic noise is crazy. But, I just wanted to check in on you."

Her heart was racing. *Stop it.*

"Thank you. We're good. Well, Abigail isn't exactly."

"What? What's wrong?"

"She's got a fever. Doctor said it's likely...an infusion of the chemicals in her tummy."

Clare tried to stop the tears, but with the recent bad news, she was afraid she was reaching her limit of pain. "Sorry," she said, "Just catching my breath. The doctor thinks that there's a *possibility* ...that if we don't operate soon—removing whatever is inside her... she could—"

"Clare, please be brave. Be strong. We are moving as quickly as possible to bring this nightmare to a close. Abigail is going to be okay. I *promise.*"

"I know, Carter. I believe you're doing everything you can. That's just your way..." she said quietly, fighting back the tears and the emotions. "But I'm afraid—"

"What? I'm so sorry Clare. I forget how loud this city is. Listen, I've got to keep moving. Lots to do in too little time. I just wanted you to know we're on deck and in charge. You have nothing to worry about. I'll ring back shortly, okay?"

In that sentence, she felt all the stress melt away and caught herself smiling. "Okay. Yes. And thank you. I'll tell Abigail...and Lukas you said hello." Shaking her head, she rolled her eyes.

"Be brave, Clare. You always were and always will be."

57

THE COLLUSION

Dr. Leonard Caprese was my next call. I couldn't decide whether I had been dreading to talk *to* him, or dreading a call *from* him. Either way, I knew the connection we had made would help us all in the end. And even though I wasn't exactly sure what he could offer, I had a strong hunch it would be powerful. While he could be divisive among his political constituents, he was a keen strategist—as Mack and I had quickly learned. And while what he was doing "on the side" wasn't always legal, neither were many tasks I performed.

Besides, I owed him for saving my father's life.

Dialing Caprese's private line, it instantly went to voicemail. I left a message and waited. As I recalled, his method was to screen, strategize and respond. And just like clockwork, my phone rang.

"It's Carter."

"Of course it is. Who else would it be?" Caprese said in a warm tone. "Hello, my friend."

"Hello. As much as I'd like to spend time catching up, I have to move rather quickly. Can you talk?"

"Understood. Time is money. And yes, I can. Just tell me what you need. And shall I assume it involves one Donovan Blair?"

Nice, already one step ahead.

"Exactly. And given you know that, how much else do you know? Are you familiar with Mayor Burton and—"

"His daughter, Abigail? Yes, I'm aware of a great deal, Carter. Let's just call that part of my business."

In that moment, I admired his approach. He made no bones about what he had done or currently does. He seemed to use the system to his advantage.

But in the end, don't we all?

"Understood. Then, you know she's in grave danger, he's over a sizable barrel and we're literally sitting on…"

"A time bomb," he interrupted. "Just so you know—as we have no secrets, I help Mayor Burton in his, let's say *political ambitions*. And I help Donovan—your *Scorpion*, in his *financial ambitions*. Plus, I am fully aware of your *military ambitions*."

Gotta admit, this guy's buttoned up.

"And you, have your business ambitions—borrowing your train of thought. And that helps facilitate all of the above."

We chuckled. "I like the way you think, Carter. It's refreshing to speak with someone who doesn't shy away from calling people out on their stuff."

"Thanks. I think."

"You're welcome. I'm sure."

"Given this information, you know we're just hours from some potentially devastating ramifications, as it pertains to Abigail and her parents. And you must know Donovan holds the key, or rather, *some* sort of device that's the trigger. And finally, and I don't care who has how much money, or needs to exchange however much money, but all I know is my job is to save a little girls life, and potentially the lives of many other people."

"Yes, to all the above. Now, in the interest of time, let me share several quick points I am confident will be *extremely* helpful to you."

"Good."

"And just know that it's going to cost you."

"Right," I snorted.

"Handsomely."

"No shit."

CAPRESE and I spoke for nearly thirty minutes. I had no idea how entrenched he was in so many aspects of this group of people. The *six degrees of separation* was insane. In fact, it was much more like two degrees.

"Do you know…of course you know a man by the name of El Diablo. The most notorious drug lord since Escobar."

"Yes," I said.

"His kingdom, for lack of a better term, is growing so rapidly and is so large that…frankly, it's hard to comprehend. He's now responsible for…well, you didn't ask for all that. Simply put, he's the *real* threat. Not that Donovan isn't—he's a nasty fellow, but he's also a very shrewd businessman. That is, up until now."

"How's that?"

"I've known Donovan a long time. Just about as long as I've known Lukas, Phil McDonough and a few other usual suspects."

Interesting he mentions McDonough.

"From the Corps?"

"Yes. But that's a longer story…for another time."

"Copy that."

"Donovan, I sincerely believe, is planning an exit strategy."

"How?"

"That's the 200-million dollar question, isn't it? Maybe he's had enough, maybe *you* and others like you have gotten too close to his…legit business. My money's on the fact he wants to replace El Diablo."

Caught off-guard, I couldn't help but snort. "That's not going to happen. Not with Diablo's infrastructure."

"Certainly," he said quietly. "That man…*is* the devil."

"I've heard."

"It's true."

Feeling the pressure of time, I pushed. "Leonard, we need to—"

"I'll make this short. Donovan owes El Diablo a great deal of money. Part of that money was for the compound he ran in Havana

—where we last met. The other part is for services for other clients."

"Two quick questions. One of those clients is you, right?"

"Yes."

"Secondly, why is Donovan approaching someone as dangerous as El Diablo for money?"

"Donovan's got so much of his capital in real estate, and he simply got over-leveraged. Plus, he wants to align with El Diablo, after a fashion, in order to see his network, learn his methods and eventually—"

"Take over?"

"Yes."

"Insane."

"And *that,* my friend, is the *key* to Donovan."

"Insanity?"

"Perhaps not *certifiable,* but certainly on the fringe."

I just recalled his being discharged from the Corps. "Wait! Something just clicked."

"Okay."

"Is this…rather, does all this go back to *Lukas?*"

"What do you mean, exactly?"

"Lukas systematically orchestrated Donovan's discharge from the Corp. While Donovan orchestrated the kidnapping of Lukas' daughter. And, as we all now know, he orchestrated the planting of the *bomb.*"

"I'm still with you."

"So, my question," I took a deep breath, "Does all of this have to do with getting back at Lukas, while the *money* is to pay back El Diablo?"

"Yes. And launch his own initiative. Lukas, that is, not El Diablo—although, I'm sure he has his own plans. And traps."

"Demented."

"Indeed. And thoroughly planned. Every step of the way."

While all of this was insane, it was beginning to crystallize.

"The thing is," Caprese said, "Right now, El Diablo is holding

Donovan's girlfriend hostage—as a checkmate position, if you will."

I just saw her through my scope not thirty minutes ago.

"What? No, she's here in New York. Mo Wang, right?"

"Yes. And no."

"What? C'mon, Leonard, chop chop."

"Mo Wang is Donovan's longtime girlfriend. Margo Wheeler is Donovan's *other* girlfriend. And Mo's *other* lover."

"What?"

"Donovan and Mo have been together since University days. Mo wants anything Donovan wants. So when they met Margo—on holiday a year or so ago, they decided to make it—"

"A three-some. Got it. But what do you mean El Diablo is holding her hostage?"

"Donovan went to Havana to close a deal. Margot went with him, although I'm not sure why. That's when El Diablo decided to hold Margot as *security*."

"Shit, this has gotten complicated."

"Yes, it has."

"So, with Donovan holding his finger on one trigger, and Diablo's on another—"

"Now you see what I mean by *checkmate*."

"Yep."

"So, how may I be of service to you?"

"You're in DC, right?"

"Correct."

"I need you here *now*. I'll have a private Leer ready for you at Dulles…" I checked my watch, "In less than 30. And have you arrive inside an hour. I'm not really asking—"

"Understood. I can do that. It's just going to—"

"Cost me, I *know*. Not to worry; we *both* have a great deal to gain. See you shortly."

Ringing off, I look to see Mack across the roof and nod him over. He had been following the weather, and keeping tabs on the crowd downstairs.

"You've been eyeballing your *Ares* like an expectant father," I said. "You know what time it is."

"Funny. Just wondering what kinda shit we were about to get into."

"You have no idea."

58

THE WILDCARD

AFTER COMPLETING the conversation with Caprese and strategizing with Mack, we both decided the idea I was cooking might work. Given the insane circumstances, and a clock that was ticking too fast for my liking, I decided to throw a Hail Mary.

The third call I made was to an ally—someone who could help us pull off a ruse like this. We had worked together twice before. Actually, the first time we met was part of a recon mission in Nicaragua. The second time was part of the rescue team I engaged to find my father and his business partner in Havana.

Her codename was Xeon, and she's one of the best soldiers I've ever met. Her strategic mind and defense skills are off the charts. The fact she is smart and beautiful just added to her arsenal of tricks. Last we spoke, she was off to a mountain retreat for some downtime.

She picked up on the second ring.

"Carter, don't you know I've got better things to do than to come babysit you?"

We both enjoyed a good laugh.

"Yeah, I'm sure you've got more important things to do, like—"

"Yeah, yeah, you've only ever called me twice, and both times were for a favor. So, what is it you need this time?"

As much as I enjoyed her busting my chops, we had to make tracks, so I cut to the chase.

"Stop whatever you're doing and come help me kill a bad guy."

"You're just trying to get me hot."

I snorted, "True."

"Well, joy. I have nothing else to do…well, except *relax*."

"Remember the guy who had your father and—"

"Scorpion?" her tone quickly changed.

"Yeah."

"What the hell? You've got a lead on him? Where *are* you? And when—"

"Hold on!" I laughed. "Yes, we've got *more* than a lead. I'm in New York City, and I need you now!"

"Why didn't you say so?"

"You still in Denver?"

"No. I was, but dad wanted me to visit, so I've been here in Miami for a couple days."

"Perfect, that'll save us an hour or two."

But it's not fast enough.

"Do this. Call Randall. Get him to hook you up with his corporate jet. That'll save you an hour of airport hassle and another 30 minutes or more in flight time."

"Copy that."

Randall was Lt. Colonel "Bulldog" Matheson. My father. And even though he was retired, he never stopped moving, or telling people what to do. His best asset was he his prime connecttion.

That, and he could move mountains quickly.

"I'd call, but I just don't have the time to answer a hundred questions about what I'm doing. Besides, if he were here, he'd kill Donovan himself. And frankly, I want that pleasure."

"Don't we all?"

"You'll stand a chance of getting closer to him than any of us, so get here, pronto!"

"You want to tell me a bit more, or you just gonna *surprise* me?"

"Let's just say we've got a lot of ground to cover and time is not our friend."

"Yeah, so what's new, Carter? Seems to be your *SOP*."

"True, but that's why they pay us the big bucks."

"Yeah, right."

"Speaking of—you'll be paid *handsomely* for this one."

"I'm all ears."

I FILLED her in on just a few of the finer details, told her who Koi was to our team, and how he would be at Teterboro waiting for her. She confirmed she would be up to speed and ready to roll inside the next two hours and change. I disconnected and took the next two minutes to connect the dots for Mack—he had strings to pull.

While I made a fourth call.

59

THE BLACKMAIL

LUKAS BURTON SAT in his home office, sipping a scotch while nervously talking on the phone. Clare was in the adjacent living room attending to Abigail who was lying under a stack of covers on the couch. The office door was closed and Lukas spoke in hushed tones. On the other end of the phone was Phil McDonough.

"Lukas, what do you mean it's not coming together like you thought."

"Exactly that," Lukas said too loudly, then spoke quietly. "Between all the funds I pumped into the presidential campaign— most of which are nearly gone, along with some investments— many of which haven't gone exactly as planned, I'm behind in liquid assets."

Neither said anything.

"Trying to pull additional funds together that quickly—in less than 24 hours, would take too much—"

"Stop a second," Phil said. "We've known one another a long time. We've seen plenty of shit before. And we'll get through this. Just tell me…*how far* behind?"

Silence.

"Luke?"

"I'm maxed out. Only thing I can think of is...offer a different number?"

Phil suppressed a chuckle.

"What?"

"This maniac is not going to negotiate."

"Look. I just don't have the net worth that...well...everyone thinks I do. Not the way it used to be, anyway. That number's tough. At least right *now*."

More silence.

"Do you suppose...you could help?"

That question made Phil uncomfortable. He wanted to help his friend, but if he's *that far* behind, he wasn't sure what he could do.

"I'm not sure I'd have enough to make a difference."

Lukas let out a heavy sigh.

"I'm confident Carter's got this. The whole purpose of trying to pull this money together was *just in case* our natural born killer lost his touch," Phil said.

"Washington assures me—"

"Whatever!" Phil interrupted. "They always do. Look, not to be a buzz kill, but a narrow miss is still a miss. Everyone has an off day."

"Are you *trying* to make me feel worse?"

"Sorry."

"How about you buy the Hampton house?"

That surprised Phil. "What?"

"It's 20 acres, waterfront, has its own mini golf course, two pools, and a six car garage. Market value's $150. I'd sell it to you for...$125."

Phil let himself imagine the compound he could cultivate.

"I don't know. That's still a lot..."

"Phil! You're the highest paid attorney in all of New York; hell, in the *country*. You can afford it. And you've been talking for years about getting out of the city. Besides, you *love* that house."

Fact was he did. In fact, nearly every trip out to visit, he tried to imagine living on a spread like that. *Interesting.*

"I do," he grinned—considered how he could buy it, then turn around and sell it for a tidy profit, if worse came to worse.

"I know it's just a bump, but 125's the amount I'm short."

I have to do something.

"Okay, but you don't have to take a bath on it."

"Done!"

"Shit, what's Clare going to say? She adores that place."

Lukas snorted, "Seriously? Besides that, we have a cabin in the Catskills, a lodge in Aspen, not to mention her childhood home in Charleston—which her mother still lives in. We don't need it all. And I'm tired of being over-leveraged."

"Kinda crazy given your business," Phil said quietly.

"I heard that," he sighed. "Shit happens."

"But you and me; we're good?" Phil asked.

"Yes."

"And IF Carter takes Donovan down…"

"A deal's a deal. Of course, if he *does* complete this mission, perhaps you could go easy on the spread."

ON THE WAY HOME, Phil called Ken Dawson, asking him to meet him at the office for a short conversation. Ken told him he was on the opposite side of town and had a meeting shortly.

They agreed to meet halfway at Madison Square Park.

In short order, Phil's car arrived at the park, and had his driver park on the street facing the Flatiron Building. He smoked a Cuban while he waited. Within minutes, Ken arrived on a *Ducati 959 Pani-gale.* Removing his gloves, he placed them inside his helmet and walked toward the Escalade. The darkened rear passenger window lowered, as a billow of smoke poured out.

"How do you breathe in there?"

"How do you ride that thing laying down?" Phil smirked.

Ken walked around and got in. "What's up?"

"I know you've got a commitment, so I'll make it quick. I need your help."

"Okay."

"It's about the Burton kidnapping."

Ken nodded.

"The Mayor and I have brought in someone to help find the people who kidnapped his daughter."

"Right."

"And after the ransom was paid, they're holding her *remotely hostage* for an additional amount of money."

"How much?"

"Total? 200 million."

Ken whistled.

"Right. And if they don't pay up, they'll detonate. You can imagine the rest. And you know how it works."

Ken remained expressionless.

"Given that I orchestrated your current position…when no one would touch you because of your background…"

Ken reached for the door.

"Wait…a minute. That's never once been spoken of, I'm just—"

"Trying to *blackmail* me now?"

"No. Help you…as you help me…help the Mayor."

"Jesus, that sounds like a self-help pitch."

Phil dropped his cigar out the window. Adjusting his shirt cuffs, he caressed his expensive cufflinks and released a deep sigh.

"I know you're working with Donovan Blair."

As hard as he tried, Ken couldn't hide his expression. Phil found it priceless.

"Then why the *fuck* are you toying with me."

"Because you're here with me."

"Okay, we can keep this pissing match up, or—"

"Here's the deal. One thing I don't question about you, oddly enough, is your loyalty. You were loyal to your country, you are loyal—for the most part, to the Blue. And you've shown some periodic loyalty to me. I think you'd agree, I've watched out for you from time to time."

Ken remained silent.

"I know you have to make next to nothing in the force. You're *maybe* making a hundred-thou contracting for Donovan. But what I'm proposing—*strictly* between you and me *only*. Understood?"

Ken managed a tiny nod.

"Good. I'm proposing a chance to make some..." he grinned. "Well, let's just call it *silly* money."

He started breathing again. "I'm listening."

"All you have to do is help Carter and his pal get to Donovan. *Before* he does something stupid."

"And?"

"And I'm willing to pay you $2 million. Cash."

Phil was pretty sure he saw a light in Ken's eyes.

"What's the catch?"

"None, actually. Just help Carter. In any way he asks,. And upon completion, I'll deliver my end of the bargain. And in any form you like. Cash, in person, or to a bank, offshore."

"You wearing a wire?" Ken asked, leaning over to pat him down.

"Very funny," he said, but opened his suit coat anyway.

"Maybe this whole thing?" he looked around.

"Neither," Phil snorts. "You have my word."

"And this deal is strictly between you and me? Nobody else. Not even Lukas."

"That is correct. NObody."

"I don't know. Why do I feel like you're a dirty attorney—working both sides."

He shook his head with a look of disappointment. "You mean much like a...dirty cop—working both sides?"

They remained expressionless.

"The chance you take."

Ken held his stare for another 30 seconds.

"It's two *million* dollars, Kenneth. Could go a long way to doing whatever the hell you want," Phil said, looking at his watch.

Ken looked out the window, still silent. He knew he was in a tight spot. He owed Donovan a lot. But he was also tired of his bull-shit. And just as he witnessed earlier in the day, he was getting tired of wondering when the keg was going to blow.

Like Mo said, he'll disappear without as much as a thought of me.

Phil patted both knees like he was about to wrap it up and said, "Look. You know what kind of man Donovan is. He'll double-back or double-cross. Just the kind of prick he is. Both you and your partners will be left behind, and nobody will get a dime. After all, *he* made the deal...not you."

Ken fiddled with his gloves, looking from Phil to the driver and then out the window. He finally leaned forward to speak.

"And I answer only to Carter? And he keeps all this *completely* tight."

"100%."

Ken ground his jaw. "I'll need some help."

"I figured as much. So, I'm including an extra million for your team. But that numbers up to you. Spread it any way you like, but that's all there is. Your two, plus one."

Ken took a beat then gave a nod. "I'm in."

Letting out a long sigh, Phil reached out to shake. "Deal?"

"Really?" Ken frowned.

Phil didn't budge until Ken shook his hand.

"Call me old fashioned," Phil grinned, as they shook.

As Ken started to get out, Phil grabbed his arm.

"Carter will ring you inside the next 30. The call will show up as *NYC Waste Management.* Take it."

Ken stepped out, put on his gloves, and turned back to the window that was still open. "You better not fuck me."

"What fun would that be," Phil smiled, closing the window. "We're such good friends."

60

THE BETRAYAL

DONOVAN COULDN'T SIT STILL.

His nerves had been on edge all day.

He had checked his accounts no less than a dozen times.

In the last hour.

Nothing.

He wanted to call and make a ridiculous threat.

Instead, he chose to save drama as a last resort.

When he designed the trigger device with Sean, he wondered if it would be better to trigger the bomb by calling—using a distinct tone to set off the explosion, or triggering by a shortwave burst, located nearby. He passed on that idea because if he blew an entire city block, he didn't want to be within 10 miles of the line of fire.

He went with dial tone.

What they didn't know was if they called any number less than seven digits—such as 911, the bomb would detonate. It was an insane option—he knew that, but he learned long ago if you only had one go-round in life, it was best to shoot for the moon.

Donovan was wondering if he had been too tough on Ken. After all, Ken busted his ass and never complained. And while Donovan paid him very well—much better than playing toy cop, he should let him in for a bigger piece of the pie.

That is, *if* Donovan felt that he could trust him.

Picking up his cellphone, he rang his phone.

Ken and Mo were in the basement raiding an overly stocked arsenal of weapons. Since they controlled the inventory, it was easy to secure enough weapons to outfit a small army.

As Ken's phone rang, he looked from the screen to Mo.

"It's Donovan."

For a second, she looked spooked, then shrugged it off.

"Answer it. We're just *checking inventory.*"

"Right." He picked up. "Donovan, what's up?"

"Listen, I'm sorry about earlier. I kinda flew off the handle. You're out there busting your hump for me and the team, and here I am busting your balls."

"No big. We're all under a great deal of stress."

Just then, Mo dropped a cartridge on the concrete floor. The noise echoed through the room.

"Okay, cool," Donovan said, "What was that?"

"Nothing. Just uh…" he hesitated, looking at Mo, wide-eyed.

She motioned *polishing the rifle.*

"Just polishing my rifle. You know me; always want to keep things in tip-top shape."

Smirking, he made a face. Grinning, she shook her head.

"Good point. Say, you wanna join me and Mo for dinner?"

She shook her head quickly.

"Uh, nah. I'm grabbing beers with some pals."

"Speaking of…have you seen her?"

"Uh, no. Haven't seen her since around 3? She said something about working out with a friend."

Donovan let the silence hang for a minute.

"Well, tomorrow's the big day. Money should hit the account by 6AM…and we'll all be sitting pretty."

At that moment, Ken knew he should have let it go, but he couldn't resist. "Just curious about something."

"Yeah, what's that?"

"How are you, you know, planning to split the money up?"

More silence.

Wondered how long it would take for the buzzards to circled, he thought. Donovan hadn't shared how or what he was planning to pay any of them.

"I'm thinking a couple hun each?" Donovan replied, waiting to hear Ken's response.

That's it? "Yeah? Sounds good."

Mo gestured, *Wrap it up.*

"Listen, Donovan, I've gotta bounce. My pal just texted me. See you at 0600?"

"Sure. See you in the morning."

As they hung up, Ken high-fived Mo. They finished packing rifles, ammo and an assortment of highly explosive toys in the back of a truck.

What they didn't know was Donovan had recently installed hidden cameras in the equipment room.

And had been watching them the entire time.

61

THE PLAN

IN LESS THAN THIRTY MINUTES, Ken and Mo were sitting in a dark corner of *Jake's Saloon,* a Hell's Kitchen landmark. It had been a favorite of Ken's for many summers, as a go-to place where several of his cop pals, and a couple of the beat reporters from CBS met after work. Most people didn't know his double-life, but then, he didn't know theirs.

Before their chairs were warm, he and Mo were greeted by the owner, Jimmy Cahill, who approached with drinks in hand.

"Whadya say, kids?" Jimmy chirped, setting down two Guinness pints.

"Good, Jimmy. Just unwinding and meeting a friend," Ken said.

"Best place to do it," Jimmy winks. "Your usual burger?"

Ken patted his stomach, "Nah, watching my waistline. Just drinks."

"Yeah, watching mine too," Jimmy laughed, "But it's going in the other direction."

Mo leaned in and kissed Jimmy on the cheek. "Thanks for the drink, you sexy beast."

"Yeah, right. You see a sexy beast—introduce me, will ya?" he laughed, walking away to seat new customers.

Ken saw Sean enter and waved him over.

"What's the deal?" Sean asked.

Ken and Mo looked at one another then to him, but said nothing.

"What?" he asked again, taking a chair.

Ken said, "You interested in making some money?"

"You interested in asking stupid questions," Sean smirked.

"Seriously."

"I *am* serious. What up?"

"Keep your skirt on *Shauna,*" Mo joked. "We have an option for you."

"Who doesn't like options?"

"First, answer me this," Ken started. "You happy working for Donovan?"

Sean cut them both a look. "Is that a trick question?"

"Just answer," Mo frowned.

"Yeah, I guess. For the most part. It's certainly…interesting."

Leaning forward, Mo asked, "But how *interesting* is your bank account?"

"It's okay. Gig's not as dangerous as I *thought* it'd be."

"Not yet," Ken said.

"For the record, I know your bank account," Mo smiled, licking the creamy beer foam from her top lip.

"No, you don't," Sean said with a crooked look.

"Uh, really? You'll recall I'm sleeping with the boss. I know everyone's take. You make $125,000, minus bonuses—as of last year."

He shook his head and whispered, "Fuck."

"Whatever. Not important. Our proposal is this," Ken lowered his voice. "Help us…help this Carter guy take down Donovan, *if* he's the shit they say he is, and for helping, we'll pay you a quarter-million dollars. *Double* what you get paid in a year. For two days work."

Sean was speechless.

Jimmy appeared with a third Guinness and patted Sean on the back. "First one's on me," he said, "Just promise you'll buy your friends a round, will ya?"

Sean nodded, as Jimmy disappeared. He took a huge gulp, set the glass down, and wiped his lips. "Okay, you got my attention."

They smiled and Ken leaned closer. "Now, there's a *second* part of our mission…which is to fly to Cancun, find El Diablo, and rescue Margot, then return home. Hopefully without getting killed."

Sean looked at them like they were crazy. Then, he finished the last sip, set the glass down and said, "I may not be the *sharpest* knife in the drawer, but I'm not stupid."

"Okay, we get it," Mo said, finishing her beer.

"Yeah, just thought we'd ask," Ken looked at Mo, suggesting they leave.

"Yeah, time to bounce," she said, starting to slide from the booth.

Sean stopped them. "Whoa. Just a second," he said, looking around. "So, $250,000 for me to help you two…and Carter…take down Donovan." He looked around. "What's the second part pay?"

"Ten," Mo said quietly.

"Ten-thousand?" Sean frowned.

Ken shook his head. "Ten million."

Sean's eyebrows raised, as his jaw dropped. "Go to Cancun, find Margot, and bring her home…for $10-million?"

Ken leaned forward. "And *kill* El Diablo."

Not taking her eyes from Sean, Mo pointed to Ken. "What he said."

Sean was quiet for a long beat, before saying, "What if I want to do both?"

Grinning, Ken said, "You greedy little bastard."

"I like your style," Mo smirked.

"You get the 250 for helping us out here in New York," Ken said, "But the three of us *split* the ten to fly to Cancun and take care of the other. There will be expenses and shit, but for easy math call it three-million…*apiece.*"

"Plus the 250?" Sean grinned. "Oh, I'm *so* in."

"Cool deal. Now, let's get outta here," Ken said, dropping a $50 on the table.

Sean grabbed his arm. "One last question. Who's putting up the bounty on their heads?"

They sat back down.

Ken nodded to Mo.

"Not sure who's paying Carter and his group. All I know is someone inside the system is paying us *cash* to help take Donovan down."

"And there's an outside *government* source," Ken interrupts, "Who wants to remain anonymous, who's putting the up the money to take out El Diablo."

"Dang," Sean whispered.

62

THE MERGER

THANKS TO CONNECTIONS to Burton's office and Chief Davis, I had managed to sequester the entire roof, as well as the "game room" below from the manager. That made things more private, allowing us to move smoothly and quickly. Given the sun wouldn't set for another half hour or so was it's own version of blessing and curse.

The good news for us was the humidity would soon drop, the wind was expected to slow, and *if* we were being watched, their visibility of us would decline. That would help the potential shot.

The bad news was our visibility would soon decrease, people would be harder to spot, and rain was looming in the distance. That would make for the opposite scenario.

Xeon and Caprese had arrived, and were downstairs with Koi. Mack and I were upstairs standing over a large sheet of paper, sketching out different scenarios for our upcoming plan. There were three different plans of attack: distract to confuse, snare to capture, or shoot to kill.

Obviously, the last choice would be the most dangerous. It would involve my taking out Donovan from this vantage point. Since I was sitting at 63 stories and Donovan's penthouse was 77 stories, I would have a 14-story disadvantage. However, at that distance, those numbers of floors were not as critical—as an "even playing field" was created, due to trajectory. However, the biggest challenge was a two-headed beast: distance and wind. There is a phenomenon in the city where "wind tunnels" were created between buildings, and they happened more on the East-to-West Streets than the North-to-South Avenues. I'm not entirely sure why, but it was true.

Manhattan was laid out in a grid. The area was bounded by 14th Street in the south and 110th Street in the north, and from river to river. Traveling north/south (street to street), 20 blocks is about one mile. And while 20 blocks equaled a mile, the distance between two avenues—east/west, was greater than the distance between 2 blocks.

My round would be traveling from 42nd Street to the target at 52nd Street. I would be shooting in the direction of avenues, not streets. Given a mile is 1,760 yards and we were somewhere over half of that away, Mack and I calculated it to be between 800 and 1,000 yards. My record for a bull's eye is 1,764 yards, so this shouldn't be too tough.

However, when you figure in the wind tunnel effect, my efficiency could drop as much as 30 to 40%. And we haven't even figured in the thickness of the plate glass windows of Donovan's penthouse. Bottom line: with the caliber of round I would be shooting, there was a much better than average chance of my hitting my target.

I brought my Cheytac M200 with me. The round was a .408/305 grain cartridge, and had an initial muzzle velocity of 3500 FPS. I was confident it had more than enough power to do what I needed.

The question that remained was: would the east/west 'wind tunnel effect' mixed with the 'heat bumps'—those wafts of residual heat which got absorbed into the asphalt during the day and released at night by the back-force pressure from the subway trains below, affect the shot.

All these elements, along with the reflection of bright lights from nearby Times Square—which bounced off of acres of glass buildings, made the shot all the more challenging.

. . .

To mix things up, I had Koi reach out to an independent fireworks company. This, after recently learning it was popular for firework barges to travel up and down either the Hudson or East rivers throughout the year, letting off short light shows. Several of those vendors were hired by companies to celebrate all sorts of event, or honor special occasions. We told them our parent company was in town to celebrate an enormous takeover and we were anxious to get —we couldn't help the pun, a big bang for our buck. After negotiating a small fortune, our primary diversion was now in place.

Just as I was about to orchestrate next steps, I saw Xeon, Leonard Caprese and Koi coming off the elevator. She looked great. Caprese looked business. And Koi looked interesting.

"Long time, Lucky," Xeon said, giving me a bear hug. Her perfume and breasts pressing against me provided a pleasant distraction.

"Too long?" I said, smiling like an idiot. It was great to have her with us.

"Original," she said, nodding to her shorter partner. "Koi pond here, said—"

"Don't call me that, *Freon,*" Koi smirked.

"Hey, kids, keep it down?" I said, reaching out to shake Leonard's hand.

"Good to see you again, Carter," he smiled.

"Likewise. Seems our paths just keep crossing, huh?" I winked.

"I suppose The Gods have big plans for us."

"You took the words right out of my mouth."

Over the next twenty minutes, I filled everyone in on the ordeal which had taken place during the past 48 hours, and covered as many details as quickly as possible. Koi filled Xeon in with tech issues, Mack added colorful language, and Caprese drank it all in— watching and listening without an interruption. Mack and I described the multiple moving pieces and how everything needed to be well orchestrated. If all went as planned, we should get out of it alive, while delivering one hell of a punch.

Checking my watch, I knew it was time to see if our latest allies were going to play along. So, I searched then dialed the number Phil gave me.

We were about to merge forces on both sides of the fence.

Hey, this could work.

63

THE ORCHESTRATION

THE NEXT THIRTY minutes went better than expected. And while I was hopeful, I felt equally skeptical. Ken and I didn't as much strike a deal, as we chose to agree on two things: helping to save Abigail's life, and giving Donovan a taste of his own medicine. Kcn told us that as much as he considered himself loyal, he was tired of being treated as second rate. Whether he was genuine, was anyone's guess. I just rolled with it.

We had too much to do in too little time to spend much energy worrying about what we had little control over.

Kind of like life, I mused, only to myself.

Inside the last 48 hours, I had come to learn the only person with zero interest in Clare's daughter was Donovan.

Big surprise.

I also learned Margot, one of the other team members, was somewhere between Cuba and Mexico, fighting for her life. We would address that later, but for now, the clock was our enemy, as a little girls' life was in our hands.

Another directive I had to focus upon was keeping Lukas and Clare out of harms way, while keeping collateral damage to a minimum. The coming together of two opposing groups—Donovan's and mine, was going to work. Merging opposing forces had worked in battle through the generations, and this was going to be no different.

AFTER SURVEYING our location for the past hour plus, something still didn't feel quite right. Long ago, I had learned to trust my gut. Always. So, Mack and I began plans to vacate the premises and move closer. Since I had no real idea of Donovan's hidden agendas —some of which could include additional firepower, I thought it best to remove us from this *public* space, and instead try to find an *industrial* application, instead.

Reaching out to Chief Davis, he alerted us to a nondescript tower which housed an array of public utilities—mainly, electricity reserves and cell towers. The best part was the top looked like a cross between an old southern church tower and a double bell laid on its side. Sounded crazy, but it gave me a much better vantage point to Donovan's tower. By trimming three and a half blocks off the distance, while gaining an extra five stories, and providing a 45-degree angle versus a nearly straight-on shot, it gave me a host of advantages.

First, we removed the danger of civilian's exposure. Second, the angle would decrease several of what I called atmospheric challenges; wind tunnels and heat bumps. Third, and most importantly, I had a better shot. An added bonus was we had better cover. We lost about twenty minutes in the move, but it was worth it. Gathering on the rooftop, we learned a few things. The power vents over our heads were ridiculously loud, making communication nearly impossible. We would have to rely on hand signals.

The two teams gathered one floor below.

From this location, we could at least discuss details without screaming at the top of our lungs. The downside, we couldn't keep an eye on Donovan's lair. Koi explained that if I could give him ten minutes, he would run a line from a several *GoPro* cameras that would be mounted on the lip of the rooftop, to an oversized display in the ante room where we were located. I told him to hurry.

"Okay, gang," I said, looking at both teams. "Some would say this arrangement was unorthodox, but who gives a shit, right? We're here for two reasons and two reasons only. Save Abigail's life, and drop Donovan Blair like a dirty shirt. IF we can take him without incident, great. But for my money? I would just as soon as turn his melon into a red cloud."

"And at this distance," Mack said, nodding toward my rifle, "And with the heat you're holding—you'll get your wish."

Nothing would make me happier, I thought, nodding at Mack.

My $10-mil deal was to kill *or* capture. Anything short of that would result in another chase and no payout. My patience was spent, and I had no intention of letting this scumbag do any more damage. We were losing minutes, so I cut to the chase.

"Here's what I need. Sean tells me Donovan called inside the last 20 minutes. My guess, and his, Donovan wants to build up his fortress—alleviating any surprises."

"Good luck with that, *bitch*," Xeon said.

Everyone enjoyed a momentary chuckle.

"Sean, you'll lead Xeon and Koi into the building. Thanks to you, Koi has the blueprints of the building—more importantly, the dimensions of the elevator shaft and elevator interior. His bag of tricks are going to hide their presence during the time you're in getting your assignment."

Koi comes barging in the door, trying to catch his breath.

"A little out of shape, *Koi pond*?" Xeon smirked.

Koi ignored her and approached me. "I've got the cams and monitor. I'll have it up and running in less than 10."

I checked my watch. "Okay, but sit tight for two more. I'm almost done."

"Copy that."

"As soon as Sean leaves the condo, all three come back down. That's when the good Doctor moves into place," I say, nodding to Caprese.

"I spoke with Donovan an hour ago," Caprese said. "We had an *interesting* conversation. Let's just say, he's getting nervous. He wouldn't admit it, but I've known him long enough to know his moves."

"Chess master, right?"

"Yes. In fact, I made a strategic move just before I left. It should put him into a tailspin."

"Chess—putting a psychotic killer into a tailspin?" Xeon frowned. "Interesting."

"You have no idea," Caprese said. He takes it *very* seriously."

"No shit," Ken said without expression. "He'll sit and stare at that board for hours at a time. No moves—just stare."

Caprese enjoyed that with a tiny grin.

"Okay, once they're out, Caprese you're in. Your whole mission is to stir his pot. Get him off center. Talk your money deal, the possibility of Burton's backing out, and El Diablo. I don't need to tell you how to do your job."

"That should fuck him up pretty good," Mack said.

Caprese quietly said, "I've got just the recipe."

"Good. Next, it could be a waiting game—that is, until some more *brilliance* comes my way," I joked.

Mack chimed in. "Seriously, it's going to come together fine. Main thing is we're all on one team...and will be coming at him from both inside *and* outside his camp."

Holding his gear up, Koi asked, "Can I go ahead, now?"

"Yeah, fire in the hole," I said, reaching for a pack of smokes. "Let's give him time to get that going, and in the meantime...burn 'em if you've got 'em."

"Lucky, *you* are the only one stupid enough to still be smoking," Xeon said. "Those things'll kill you."

I stared at her—giving a thought to not having one, then said, "Something eventually will."

With that, I motioned for Mack to join me on the roof.

WE STOOD at the very edge of the roofline, watching the lights of Time Square flash like an amusement park. Facing west, I focused my attention on Donovan's building, as we tried to enjoy the calm before the storm.

"Think this'll work?" Mack finally said.

Blowing a cloud of smoke, I scanned the horizon, observing the acres of glass and steel.

"Yeah. I do. It feels a bit...*Mission Impossible*...but like they say about the lottery—you can't win if you don't play."

Taking a pack of gum from his pocket and unwrapping several sticks, he shoved them in his mouth and said, "You're such a philosopher, Lucky. And do you mean the *film*, or the overused axiom?"

"See? You're more than just a pretty face."

Xeon came out the fire door and headed our way, stopping to watch Koi running a backup wire for the monitor downstairs.

"Don't even," he said, heading toward the door. She shrugged and approached us. "Interrupting you love birds?"

"You know us so well," Mack grinned.

"You trust these cats?"

"No real options at the moment," I said. "Besides, they're getting paid *very* well."

"Not as well as *you*," Mack said. "But well."

My phone rang. The screen read: Clare.

I held up a hand to excuse me. "I gotta take this. Mack, you know what to do."

My stomach sank, wondering if Abigail was in danger.

"Copy that."

Heading for the door, I answered, "What's up?"

"I know I said I wouldn't call, but Carter I'm scared."

64

THE SETUP

OUR BLACK SUV ARRIVED and parked a half block shy of the 77-story *Avalon* skyscraper on 54th Street. Putting the SUV into park, Koi spun around to face Sean, Xeon and Caprese.

"Okay, Sean, this is your world. We'll follow your lead. I'm guessing security cameras will catch all of us as we enter, right?"

"Yeah, but best to let me enter first, I'll break off to the left toward the elevators, while you two enter and do your thing. Make it two beats after me, and head to the *right*. If anyone wonders, it'll look like you're heading to the club room."

Sean looked to Leonard. "Dr. Caprese, you just sit tight until you see us completely clear the building."

Caprese nods.

"Back to your point, Koi, the cameras are in the far corners of both the entrance and the lobby space right at the elevators. The entrance poses no problem, as they face toward the street, where the others cover the lobby. There's a slight blind spot to either side of the elevators. You'll see three massive pillars that reach two stories. After you've changed, just circle back toward the elevators right as they open. Just to play stupid—for lack of a better term, I'll flip my phone out and take a selfie. I'll have the flash on and it will temporarily blind the security camera, which is directly over the door. It's wide angle, so it covers most of the elevator. As soon as you see the flash, jump in. You'll have about three-maybe-four seconds to put up your screens."

"Copy that," Xeon said. Koi nods.

"You're going to have to move *really* fast, as the iris adjusts. Even *if* Donovan's watching, he'll think it's a glitch. I mean, who knows, given he'll have seen two drunken *lovebirds* enter moments before, but two *guards* enter the elevator seconds later—he won't give it a thought."

"And if he does?"

"Well, guess we're screwed. Given this is a *direct flight* to the penthouse, you can't get off at a different floor."

Xeon and Koi looked at one another and shrugged.

"Good. It'll take us about three minutes and change to get to the top floor. No more than four."

"So, no one can get on and stop us?" Koi asked.

"No, this is an express elevator," he said, revealing an e-card on his keyring. "Takes us right to 77. One of the best things is it doesn't empty directly into the unit. There's a fancy mini-lobby, complete with art and pricey furniture—you know, for show. We just go up, exit, and either knock or go right in. Needless to say, you'll stay where you are, doing what you're going to do."

They both confirmed with nods.

"One last thing. I'll punch the first floor button, sending the elevator back down. This will give you both a chance to do what you need and get out. Just be aware that Donovan often walks his guests to the elevator."

"And if we are there?" Xeon said.

"He'll spot it…and it'll get pretty freakin' tricky."

65

THE GAMBLE

"WHAT?"

I shouted—my voice, echoing off the concrete room.

"Her temperature is 104," Clare whimpered. "She's coming in and out of consciousness. The doctor said he's going to have to do something *soon*. Or else."

"Is he there now?"

"No, he was called out to an emergency, but told me he will be happy to come back if we need him. And that he would need an hour or so before that could happen. He also said we may want to, or rather, *must* consider operating. He said whatever is inside her is…" she began to sob, and I could hear Lukas on the other end consoling her.

I could make out an occasional remark—as she raised her voice, but because of the muffled sounds, I couldn't understand everything.

"Clare?"

Nothing, so I checked my signal.

"Carter? It's Lukas. Sorry about that. I know you have your hands full. She's…hysterical."

My stomach felt like it was bouncing against my ribcage in slow motion.

I can't stand seeing children hurt.

"I understand."

That response was something I learned a long time ago—taught to me by my mother. It had become a phrase I used many times—usually when listening to women describes their feelings. Interestingly enough, I rarely had a clue what they were trying to say.

"Dr. Simms, our family doctor, said it's urgent," Lukas' voice broke.

"As in?"

"As in...inside the next several hours, if she doesn't get strategic help, he feels certain she will die."

His voice broke again, as his breathing became heavy, when he said, "We either operate...and risk not only her life, but the lives of others—that is *if* this doctor would be willing to take that chance."

Waiting, I thought, *I can't imagine being in their place.*

"Frankly, I think his leaving for an emergency was his *big* exit."

I felt for Lukas. He had about as much as he could handle. All my thoughts of jealousy, or whatever else evaporated in that moment. Abigail's safety trumped everything.

"Lukas, I'm so very sorry."

"I know, Carter. I haven't doubted that for an instant, and frankly, after going through all this *bullshit*, I promise bygones will be bygones."

I could hear Clare crying in the background. It sounded like someone throwing a cat against a wall.

"Is that?" I ask absently.

"Yes."

I took a deep breath and said, "Lukas, this is going to sound insensitive, or callous, or I don't know, but is there any way you can give me..."

I stopped, as something just pinged the back of my mind.

"Carter?"

It was a gamble. A big one. But it could be SO worth it.

"Lukas, you have to listen to me," I said, checking my watch.

We had somewhere between four and five hours before the

deadline. My head starting pounding in time with my heart—which was racing.

Chill the hell out, I thought, taking several deep breaths.

"Look. I know this is a lot to ask, but I need you to trust me."

"What is it?"

"It's either a long shot, or it could also be the perfect solution to get Abigail out of harm's way."

"What do you need? And, Carter…there's a damn wide chasm between long shot or perfect solution, don't you think?"

He's right. I could be insane. We're down to hours before the deadline, but minutes if not seconds could stand between Abigail living or dying.

"Carter? C'mon, I've got *you* negotiating with me on one end, and my wife melting down on the other. I need to hear your idea."

Go for it.

"Okay. Give me *one* hour. If inside 60 minutes, I can't make this happen. I'll ring you at 60 minutes and one second and…I'll perform the operation myself. We'll do it in a remote location so no one is injured. And trust me, I know how to handle a knife."

There was a long silence on the other end, except for the faint sounds of Clare's whimpering in the background, and I said, "Lukas?"

His voice cracked as he said, "Carter, I…can't believe you'd… there's no way in the world…"

"Stop. Nothing's happened yet."

"I know, but just the *suggestion*—"

"Lukas, this *Oprah* moment is great, but I have to pull my shit together inside the next 59 minutes…or else."

66

THE SHAFT

SEAN LEAD the way toward the massive glass doors of *The Avalon*. Xeon and Koi—looking like club rats, stumbled in, arms around one another, as they headed across the room toward the clubroom, but away from the watchful eye of closed circuit cameras.

Standing at the elevator, Sean held his hand over the button, while looking around casually, giving his accomplices enough time to step into a valet closet that was closed. He counted to ten, and then pushed the button. Fortunately, the elevator was on 77th floor, which gave them another couple of minutes. In that amount of time, he removed two mini-bottles of cheap whiskey from his pocket and chugged one. The other, he *spilled* on his shirt. He then took a cellphone from his other pocket and held it down to his side.

The elevator car arrived and he took one more look to the side before he entered. Placing his foot inside the path of the doors, he added a little swagger to his movements, holding up the camera and striking a pose.

FLASH!

He counted: *one-thousand-one, one-thousand-two...*

Pushing him aside, they stepped in, dropped a cartridge the width of the car, and quickly unrolled their respective screens, from floor to ceiling.

The screens were made from a mylar material that became stiff once it was extended. This would allow them to "disappear" behind it, with just the width of their bodies between it and the side walls of the elevator car. From the security camera's viewpoint—given the convex nature, it would be hard to see that the elevator car had shrunk by a couple of feet.

Koi instantly went to work on his side, removing the electronics panel where the floor buttons were housed. Although this elevator would travel as an Express to the 77th floor when using a keycard, all the remaining buttons were fully operational.

His job was to install a switch that, once activated, would return the elevator to the first floor and keep it there. This way, if the opportunity arose, Donovan would not be able to escape. He would be able to take the stairs, but that would take a long time. His only other escape was the roof. That would require outside help.

Later that night and with device in hand, Dr. Caprese would trigger the switch, upon his departure.

The 37 button flashed, as they were passing the halfway point.

Xeon, on the other side of the car, was removing four stainless steel screws with a small power drill. She would have to get the plate off, lift herself up onto the roof of the elevator and position herself, then return the plate back to its original position.

"Forty floors to go, people."

"Copy," Koi said, struggling to get the switch mounted behind the plate.

He had the luxury of replacing all the screws upon his descent.

"Copy," Xeon said, halfway through the opening. She didn't have the same luxury, as she had to get the plate into place by the time the door opened, in case Donovan was there to greet Sean.

Sean could feel the sweat pouring down his brow and into his eyes, and thought, *Be ready for anything.*

Just as the roof panel clicked back into place, the elevator door opened.

Donovan exited his condo, briskly walking the ten paces it took to cross the foyer.

Thinking quickly, Sean slammed against the doorframe, simultaneously pushing the ONE button. With his right hand, he covered his mouth, extending his left arm toward Donovan's chest.

"Get the fuck outta the way, I'm gonna puke!" he shouted, shoving Donovan aside and running straight for the bathroom down the hallway.

Before rounding the corner, he quickly look back at Donovan who was watching the elevator doors close. As Donovan turned to head back in, Sean was in the bathroom puking—thanks to two fingers being shoved down his throat.

I never liked whiskey anyway.

67

THE EYE

DONOVAN WAS STANDING against the front edge of his desk, as Sean walked into the room. Dramatically wiping his mouth with a towel, he continued the drunken ruse.

"Damn! Guess I had more than I thought."

"What the fuck do you think you're doing showing up for business *drunk*?" Donovan's stare always had the same affect: to instill pure terror in his victims.

Sean spotted the familiar black box with clear lid on Donovan's desk. He had learned in his short tenure working for *Scorpion* that when you pissed him off, or pushed him too far, he would often break out one of his many pet scorpions.

And it never ended up good.

He tried to ignore that and instead focusing his attention on getting in, getting what he needed, and getting out alive.

"I saw you come in," Donovan said, expressionless.

"Yeah?" he replied calmly.

"I also saw some others enter the building shortly after you."

"Yeah, from the smell of them, I'd say we were at the same bar," he chuckled.

"Why are you laughing? Your condition is not funny. It's...*pathetic*."

Stay calm. Don't let him see you crack.

"C'mon, Donovan. I was out getting over-served when you called."

Donovan looked at his watch. "Did I not say we were on the clock until the delivery was made?"

Sean swallowed. The bile in the back of his throat still burned, as he answered. "Yes, Sir. I just didn't think that—"

"You just didn't THINK!" Donovan shouted, slamming his knuckles down on the desk. "And why did you send the elevator back down? We never send the elevator back down, especially when we know it's a short visit."

"I don't know. I guess I bumped it," he exhaled, rubbing his face.

Donovan stared at him for a full minute, before looking to his chessboard. As he started to walk around his desk, Sean quickly looked to the security monitor, and saw Koi exiting the elevator then the front door.

As Donovan turned, he caught Sean staring at the monitor. "What are you looking at?" he barked.

"Uh, just saw those two drunks I came in with. They fell through the front door," he grinned.

Shaking his head, Donovan said, "I expect more from you, Sean. You can't get anywhere in life doing stupid shit like this."

Donovan walked back to his chessboard. Staring at it, he frowned, scratching his three-day beard, and said, "Take a seat." He didn't look up.

"Yes, Sir."

Sean's stomach gurgled, disturbing the uncomfortable silence. Trying to play nice, he asked, "You working on a move?" He knew this man could kill him at any time—just for the fun of it. It had been known to happen.

Just then, Sean's eyes fell to another monitor. It was then he realized that particular screen had a different viewpoint. And given he was largely responsible for installing most of the electronics in Donovan's condo, he was perplexed he didn't know this one.

That's the sub-basement, where heavy artillery and...

The screen suddenly went black, and his eyes instantly returned to his boss.

Donovan had that *look* in his evil eyes.

Oh shit.

68

THE BITE

I FOUND myself pacing the rooftop, wondering where the hell Sean was. Checking my watch for the umpteenth time, I caught Mack out of the corner of my eye.

"Carter, you've looked at that thing exactly *ten times* in the last 60 seconds. That's once every six seconds."

I stared before saying, "Were you always that fast with math?"

"Smartass."

My cellphone rang. "Yeah?"

"What the fuck, Lucky?" Xeon barked.

"What do you mean, *you* left him there. Where is he?"

"Still in there! We've been sitting here 20 minutes. He assured me he'd be out in ten, *maybe* fifteen."

"Do you know why Donovan called him?" I asked, putting her on speakerphone so that Mack and Ken could hear her.

"Something about setting up a camera on Burton's property."

Stepping forward, Ken smacked my arm. "We had a contingency plan. Several, actually. One of them involved getting more cameras in and around his property. He actually wanted us to get one inside the house, but, well, you can guess that became impossible."

Nodding, I was trying to make the most of the situation. That's when a piece of the puzzle clicked into place, and I grinned.

"What the fuck are you smiling at?" Mack smirked.

"Hello? Anyone there," Xeon said over the phone.

"Xeon, tell me *exactly* where you're located," I said.

"Well, unfortunately, I'm on the roof of the elevator car, waiting to get back up and provide cover for Sean, just like you asked me to do."

"But you're down on level one, right?"

"Copy that," she said.

I looked at Mack, then to Ken—who asked, "What?"

"Bear with me a second," I said, motioning for them to follow me to the corner of the roof.

I walked to my rifle, which was on a half-roof shelf—five feet above us, laying atop a stack of thick blankets I confiscated from the hotel. The gun was in *Go-Mode,* complete with scope and a spare clip. Mack's position was beside it. I picked up his pair of binoculars and we made our way to the very far corner. It was the best vantage point— besides my rifle perch, given our conditions. Looking through the glass, I could see Donovan—or rather his back, as he stood by his desk.

I couldn't see Sean.

"Get out of the way, freak," I mumbled to myself.

"Hang in there, buddy," Mack mumbled.

"Tell me, Ken. Now that we're all playing on the same team and working for the same man. Sorta," I began.

"Yeah?"

"Where did y'all perform the operation on Abigail? I'm crazy for having not asked that yet."

"In the basement," he answered matter-of-factly.

Knowing that basements often had inferior signal strength, I had an idea.

"Is there anything, I don't know, *extra special* about this basement?"

Ken squinted. "Well, it's two levels deep."

Nothing to write home about.

"But that's *below* two other parking levels."

Okay, better.

"Carter, I'm still here, you know that right?"

"Yes," I answered Xeon, turning to Ken, "I'm going to guess—given his demented mind and obscene practices—not to mention a bunker of artillery, he must have supreme, uh, secrecy."

"Oh, hell yeah. That *bunker,* as you put it, is not only four stories underground, but the walls are three feet thick."

I looked at Mack. "That's what's been digging at me."

"Hate it when that happens. Puts you in such a mood," Mack smirked. "You thinking what I am?"

"Of course."

"Carter?" Xeon started—her radio crackling. "You want me to stay put, or try and make my way back up?"

Looking at Mack, I shook my head. "Girl, you are crazy. Scaling 77 stories, while admiral, is ridiculous. But thanks for the suggestion. Just hold tight."

"Copy that."

We chuckled, not because she was silly, but because she had bigger balls than any of us.

"Impressive," Ken grinned.

"You have no idea," Mack said. "She could drop you without breaking a sweat."

"Doubt that."

Did he just flex when he said that?

"Don't," I said.

"What?" Ken asked.

"Doubt her. She could," I said, looking back through the glass. "Oh shit."

"What?" Mack asked.

I handed him the glasses.

"Oh shit."

"What?" Ken asked.

"What the hell's going on," Xeon chimed in.

Mack handed back the glasses.

"Looks like your boy pissed off Donovan," I said, handing Ken the glasses.

Adjusting the eyepiece, he scanned the property until he found it and mumbled, "Son of a bitch." He handed them back to Mack and spat, "Sick fucking bastard."

While I wasn't sure, my guess was that Donovan dropped one of his "pets" down Sean's shirt.

"Same thing he did to my dad in Havana. Luckily, we got him out of there in time."

"Time to move," Mack said, "Like *now!*"

"You said it. Mack, get Koi on the phone. We have to patch in everyone. Xeon, I need you to do something…complicated."

"Copy that."

"Give me ten seconds for a phone patch."

Moving the pieces in my mind, I knew exactly what had to happen next—that is, if I was going to keep my promise to Lukas.

Which is exactly what I intended.

69

THE SWITCH

THE ENTIRE TEAM WAS PATCHED IN, except Sean, unfortunately. Using my Sat-phone gave us the ability to merge up to a dozen calls with zero latency, while providing complete privacy. While I didn't know Sean's condition, I knew we couldn't do anything but move our pieces into position as quickly as possible. We only had two hours until daylight, and less time to save Abigail's life.

We had relocated to the lower level, because the ventilation fans had kicked back in, making it harder to hear. Thanks to Koi's handiwork, we had several cameras watching our *six*. It was working well, as I had one eye on Donovan's tower, and the other on my team in front of me.

"Okay, listen up everybody, we've got to move quickly. Donovan has become a live wire, putting one of our team in jeopardy. Dr. Caprese, you on?"

"Yes, Carter. I'm here."

"Okay, I need you to go in there *now*. Work the magic you've rehearsed. Fortunately, the elevator is there for you. Koi's got you rigged for sound, so we'll hear your every word. And not to worry, I've got your six."

"Thanks, Carter. I'm leaving now."

With that, I heard Koi's SUV chime, as the door opened and Caprese got out.

Caprese had called Donovan while we were assembling all the players for the phone call. And while I felt certain we'd lost one member, we were about to gain an ally that could help seal our deal.

"Lukas, Clare, are you there?"

"It's Clare, Carter. Lukas is getting the police escort in place."

"Good."

"And a couple of friends have come over and are helping me with Abigail."

My stomach tightened as I thought, *She did nothing to deserve this.*

"Clare, be straight with me. Is she okay…well, enough to do this?"

"Yes. I told her *Uncle Carter* needed her to be strong and brave."

Damn, that's sweet.

"Okay, good. Please tell her I've got a super big surprise for her if she can hang with me for just *one more hour*, okay? Can you do that for me?"

"Yes, I will. And she can do it. Don't worry."

"Now, don't forget, you're both a part of this, and you'll both be *perfectly safe*. Not a worry in the world. You have my word."

"I trust you, Carter. We all do."

"Okay, ring off and get over here as quickly as you can. Mack gave Lukas all the details."

I waited for the disconnection tone, just to make sure she was okay.

"Xeon, remember when I said you were in for something complicated?"

"Copy that."

"Well, since we're one man short, and things have gotten complicated, I'm gonna need you to be in two places at once."

"What's that?"

"Hold a sec," I said, turning to Ken. "I need you to get moving now. You're going to have to get into the building, without being seen by Donovan, get into the basement and start prepping it. While it won't be perfect, we've simply run out of time. I have a hunch that the finer details won't matter."

"Copy that," Ken perked up.

I grabbed his arm and stared him in the eye. "One more thing, while I'd prefer to have *you* in arm's length from Donovan, something tells me—instinct I guess, that by now he's made you. So, you'll have to handle the Burton's downstairs. Koi will be there to rig the electronics. Right Koi?" I asked.

"Copy that, Carter. If he can get me inside the main frame, I can get this working. I really needed Sean, but I *think* I can manage. I'm sure Ken will have something for me."

Ken confirmed with a nod.

"Lastly, Xeon, you're going to *have* to get to the roof. I know it's insane, but with this little hiccup, Caprese now upstairs, and the elevator frozen there—"

"Hey Carter," Koi interrupted, "I set the elevator to lock in the *up* position so it could be ready for Sean or whoever. But I *should* be able to switch it to come back down and get Xeon up there."

Love when a plan comes together.

"Excellent, Koi. Nice work. Make that happen, and you're my hero. Hear that, Xeon? We just saved you climbing a 77 story rope."

"I'll get you back, Lucky," her voice—echoing off the elevator shaft, "Trust me."

Mack laughed, "Oh, she will."

"Okay, Koi you'll get her up and in place to watch Caprese, *and* our surprise guest," I said, winking at Mack.

He confirmed with a salute.

"By the way, Xeon, if you want to plant some of those *daisies* that Farmer Carter brought you from the farm, it may help matters," Koi said.

I frowned, not knowing what he meant, but had too many things to worry about. Turning to Ken, I said, "You know what Mack and I are up to.., so a lot rides on you."

"Got it," he said to me, then into the phone, "Hey, Xeon, I'm on my way."

"Copy that. Soldier."

I looked at Mack. He read my mind. Then, more from habit than anything, I signed off with, "Lucky Strikes!"

IN THE NEXT MOMENT, Mack and I realized the fans on the roof that had been periodically drowning out our voices had finally stopped. We looked at one another and went back upstairs.

In those few quiet moments, Mack and I stood in the warm summer air, listening to the infrequent sirens and big city traffic.

Oddly enough, we enjoyed the moment. We had learned through dozen of years and many tours of duty—along with a number of near-death experiences, that often the quietest moments occurred just before the worst catastrophes.

That thought—while not comforting, caused us to stand firm, knowing it would likely be the case...once again.

70

THE FOX

It was times like these when you saw the results of solid planning and substantial teamwork. Two teams, with completely different agendas, had come together to form a new set of the same. And the two things which hung in the balance were the life of a little girl and money.

One represented all that was good and sweet with the world, while the other was often seen as the root of all evil. There were those who subscribed to the belief that the only thing which separated these two elements were their intrinsic *value*. For once you removed the value, its worth was as meaningless as the space it occupied.

Mack and I were in position on the top of the building that housed *Audercomm Inc.* It was a 68-story building home to several things: an international software company, a medical device company, and a telecom company that oversaw a number of internet, cellular and satellite systems. But all we really cared about was that it was tall, nondescript, and didn't have any inhabitants on the upper floors between the hours of 11:30PM and 6:00AM, seven days a week. There was no house-cleaning being performed, and no late-night workers padding their hours. There were only two security guards—both of whom worked on the main floor.

The only other movement was a robot—one designated to each of the remaining 64 working floors, transmitting live video feeds and temperature readings via Wi-Fi to ground floor security.

In other words, at 5:55AM, we were alone.

Fortunately for me, the sky was deeply overcast, providing us extra cover, while keeping light to a minimum. It also meant the lights inside buildings—like that of *The Avalon,* would remain on for another 30 minutes or so.

The entire team had radios and earpieces. This way, we could all communicate without hassle. That is, except Ken and Koi in the basement, and occasionally Xeon, inside the elevator shafts.

Koi, being the *boy wonder* he is, was able to tap into a monitor feed into the main frame of communications. This meant the video and audio which was feeding to upstairs from deep within the bowels of the building could be seen and heard in the master control room of the building. Unfortunately, all that same information could also be fed to the Penthouse. We had to take a chance Donovan was not watching at the moment, while we prepared.

We had commandeered the building's security crew, replacing them with several of New York City's finest. However, in the Penthouse, it was anyone's guess. Without the assistance of Sean—who I learned all but single-handedly wired Donovan's entire place, we were slightly behind the eight ball.

With binoculars, I spotted the Mayor's parade of cars as they were heading west on 57th Avenue, passing CBS studios at the corner of 10th Avenue. They were just about to hang a left onto 11th Avenue, when I rang Lukas.

He picked up before the first ring completed. "Hi, Carter, what's up?"

"On the off-chance Donovan's got any surveillance covering 11th Avenue—which I'm sure he does, how about having your squad cars break away just as they round the corner, or certainly before you reach the building. Have them all park on the *north* side of all the surrounding buildings, say mid-block."

"Will do."

"Also, you'll see Koi's black SUV in front. Park right behind it. You've got on a vest, right?"

"Yes."

"Nervous?"

"Hell no. I've been in deeper shit than this. You know that."

"Good."

"Besides, my daughter's right beside me and..." he lowered his voice, "What kind of a chicken shit would I look like if I didn't act as brave as her hero, *Uncle Carter.*"

"You're killing me, Lukas."

"It's true."

"Give her a kiss for me. We'll have all three of you safe and sound in no time. Don't you worry."

"Copy that."

"Tough thing is...you're the only one in harm's way."

He was silent for a long beat—then, "Let's go."

"Yes, sir, Mr. Mayor."

LUKAS WOULD TAKE the elevator up by himself, but Xeon would be within ten feet and watching his *six* at all times. Wearing a vest, he would be safer. With a wire, he would be connected. Sporting a .45 Browning with ACP rounds in the small of his back, he would be loaded. And with his trusty .9mm Glock 26 in a holster on his angle, he would have backup.

Fully prepared, he was ready to use whatever means necessary. And that was if *I* didn't complete my mission.

"Lukas, just to confirm," I began, "The moment you step out of your vehicle, you'll be fully exposed. However, there will be no less than 4 agents escorting your vehicle around the building to Loading Dock C, as in Charlie. Once there, they'll take Clare and Abigail to meet Mr. Dawson just inside the first door of the loading dock. He'll stay inside the door to avoid the surveillance cameras; however, the moment he sees your vehicle enter the lot, he'll shut off any extra lights for the time it takes your girls to get from the car to the dock's edge."

"Will they be—"

"Yes," I interrupted, "They *will be* exposed. *However*, we have two officers standing by. There's *no* need to worry."

"Copy that."

"Once inside, Ken will take them downstairs and get them in place. We've taken the liberty to decorate, if you will, their room and we feel confident you'll be pleased."

"That's up to you."

"Not to worry, Lukas. It's all good. The minute you get the word from me, you enter the building through the revolving door and straight to the elevator, immediately to your *left*. Push 77 and you're on your way. You'll arrive in less than four minutes."

"What if the elevator's not there."

"It will be."

"But what if—"

"Then you're fucked. Copy that?"

"Affirmative," Lukas said.

"Remember, Caprese and Donovan should be on good terms and likely discussing Caprese's deal, just like old times. When the door opens and they see you, that's when the party begins."

"Yippee," Lukas joked.

"Humor. That's good. Just one more thing: once you exit the elevator, walk straight to the only door you'll see. It'll be about ten paces. It should be unlocked. Just go right in like you own the place. You probably will someday."

That was the only chuckle I would hear from Lukas for the next several hours.

"How long before—"

"Let's just say, I'll be listening before anything happens. It shouldn't be long. And if anything gets squirrelly? Well, it'll all just happen…a whole lot faster."

"Got it."

"And Lukas?"

"Yeah, Carter."

"Whatever you do, and I know you know this, but for the love of money, do not, I repeat, do NOT—"

"Look in your direction," he barked.

"Smart soldier."

"Didn't get the stripes for being handsome."

"Copy that."

71

THE BEAT

THE NEXT EIGHT TO nine minutes were the worst. Because they were the very last pieces of the move before Checkmate.

Clare and Abigail were in place and wired for sound.

Lukas was climbing a glass tube in a world of steel and concrete at a speed most cars on the streets of Manhattan never reached during drive time.

Xeon was suspended somewhere between the roof of an elevator car and the underneath side of the building's roof, moving with the deftness of a cat, waiting for just the right time to pounce.

And Ken, after putting Clare and Abigail in place, would make his way up to the 76th floor, through a catacomb-like structure, eventually accessing an alternate entrance to a deathtrap.

THE ELEVATOR DOORS opened and Lukas took a slow and deep breath, stepped out and walked to the main door. Reaching for the doorknob, he entered just like he owned the place.

The look on Donovan's face was priceless.

The rehearsed look on Caprese's face was believable.

"Hello gentlemen, sorry to barge in on you two, but…"

In the time it took Lukas to cross the threshold, Donovan had reached into a desktop cigar box and withdrawn a stainless steel .45 caliber pistol.

Lukas raised his hands and looked dumbfounded. "What the hell, Donovan?"

Donovan stood staring. The look of confusion on his face was palpable. He may be a good drug dealer, but he was a bad actor. Lowering the gun to his side—but not disengaging the trigger, a strange smile creased his face.

"What are you doing here, Lukas?"

Lukas looked to Caprese who held a surprised look on his face. "Who's this?"

"What do you mean, who's this? You know exactly who this is."

"Uh, no, I don't," Lukas said, selling it well.

"It's Caprese."

Lukas looks surprised. "Leonard Caprese?"

Caprese nodded.

"We've only spoken on the phone. And only a few times at that," Lukas said.

"Alright, either you're full of shit…and only a fairl actor, or… you're both fucking with me."

"Donovan, I simply thought I'd come down here and talk man to man, you know, just work this whole thing out," Lukas said, before looking at Sean—who was slumped over in a chair. "Who's that?"

"Who are YOU to come into my home asking all the questions?" Donovan shouted.

"Okay, okay. Not my business. I don't give a shit anyway. I'm just here to settle this thing and give you your money."

Donovan stared at Lukas.

Lukas returned the stare-down.

Which lasted for a good thirty-seconds, before Lukas relaxed his stance and took a step forward.

Donovan flinched, moving his gun just enough to make Lukas stop.

"Just…stand…there. Let's the three of us…remain calm."

LESS THAN SEVEN BLOCKS AWAY, I had the back of Donovan's head centered in my scope. Mack was beside me, reading the wind, distance and *guesstimating* the humidity.

"Winds are out of the north, northeast…five knots," he said quietly.

"Copy," I said, not moving a muscle.

My finger rested on the front of the trigger guard, and I waited.

"Attention team. Sean's down. Burton is inside," I quietly said.

A whisper of *Copy*, returned from Xeon, then Ken, then Koi.

Koi's voice crackled, as he was highjacking a circuitous signal from below ground. There was an outside chance Koi would miss some, if not all, of the commands.

Some shit's just beyond my control.

"Xeon, do you copy?"

"Copy."

"Where are you? What do you see?"

"I'm in the ceiling, just above the entranceway. I can't see them, but I can hear them. I *am* able to drop in on them. Just give the word."

"Copy."

"Ken, do you copy?"

Silence.

"Ken, do you copy?"

Another several seconds of silence passed, before I hear, "Copy. Sorry, I'm in between floors. About to climb an elevator shaft just above 76. Should arrive inside 5 minutes."

"Copy."

"Koi, is the transmission ready?"

There was some crackling followed by intermittent words. I waited.

"Car…we have a…-ion…it's goi…to be…-conds bef…I ca…"

Shit.

"Koi, listen up. Your signal is choppy. We can't hear you.

Maybe you can hear me. I'm moving forward. Just do what we rehearsed. It'll be fine. Click twice if you copy."

Silence.

"Koi, your signal is choppy. We're moving forward. Do as rehearsed. Click twice if you copy."

Click. Click.

"Copy that. Now, we wait. Everyone? Stand by."

72

THE SHOT

DONOVAN LEANED AGAINST HIS DESK. His arms were crossed and he looked more relaxed. His gun, however, was nearby—laying on the desk beside him.

"I can see you're trying to figure it out, right?" Lukas asked with a comfortable, easy smile.

"Well…" Donovan began, looking from Caprese to Lukas. "I suppose once that pest Carter got involved, the—how shall I say this, *game* had to take on a different tact."

His eyes darted from the chessboard to Caprese—who smiled.

"Your last move, Leonard, was quite the *strategic* one."

Caprese's smile didn't shift.

"You have me in a perplexing position."

"That's what the game is all about," Caprese quietly said. "Isn't it?"

"True," Donovan grinned. "Position. Power. Control. Strategy. All things I really like."

He looked at his watch, then confirmed the time by checking the row of clocks on the far wall. "Well, gentlemen," he said, walking around his desk. "It's two minutes to six. And the time has come to see what we're made of, yes?"

He sat in his chair and awakened his bank of computer screens, with the tap of the keyboard.

"The markets have already opened in Europe," he said, momentarily distracted by several news tickers scrolling across his screen."

Leonard glanced at Caprese. They exchanged looks. Lukas shifted his attention to the security monitors on the screen behind Donovan.

Evidently, Donovan had not yet seen what was happening right under his nose. As Donovan looked up, Lukas' eyes had shifted back to his opponent.

"Tell me something, Donovan," Lukas asked. "Why'd you have to get so greedy?"

"You mean with the...*dual standoff?*" he smiled.

Looking to Caprese, Donovan said, "It was actually a move I learned from our friend here, Dr. Caprese. It involves incorporating two rooks, or two knights, or two of any piece, for that matter, and using them to box in your opponent."

"You've gotten good at that over the years, Donovan," Caprese said. His voice and body language was non-threatening, and nearly comforting.

"Thank you. Learned from the best," Donovan smirked. "Or was it *you* that learned from *this* best?" he frowned.

"I'd say we're equally matched."

Donovan laughed. "That's rich coming from you, *Doctor*. Whatever that title even means. While you're an excellent opponent, you're far from being as cut-throat as I."

"And you're proud of that, aren't you?"

Donovan shrugged off the question, turning his attention to the news tickers that crawled along the bottom of the monitors of his trading desk. "Markets won't open here for another few hours, but it won't matter," he said, typing in a long series of keystrokes, watching for the screen to display his accounts, periodically checking his watch.

Lukas looked at the clock on the wall: 6:00 AM.

Donovan's carefree attitude slowly dissolved into a blank stare. He didn't budge.

Lukas glanced at the monitor behind Donovan. Clare and Abigail sat perfectly still in chairs in the center of what looked to be Abigail's bedroom.

Caprese started to take step toward Sean.

"HOLD IT! What are you doing?" Donovan barked, abruptly standing.

"Just wanted to see if I can help this young man," Caprese said.

"He's dead, you idiot. My favorite scorpion finished him off an hour ago."

Wanting to throw him off balance, Caprese took another step.

In a flash, Donovan picked up his gun, pointed it directly at Caprese, and held it for a second, before shifting to aim at Sean's body.

He fired three rounds into him. *Tap-Tap, Tap.*

The first shot went to this heart, the second to his right lung, and the third—directly between his eyebrows.

A perfect kill.

"WHAT THE HELL?" MACK SHOUTED.

He had been watching the sky for light and cloud shifts when the shots nearly blew his eardrums.

"It's Donovan making a point. Everyone's fine," I said to Mack, adding, "Everyone stand down. It's Donovan acting stupid. Stand by."

Click, click.

Click, click.

Click...

All three team members had checked in. The last was Koi. Evidently, he's still having communication challenges. I continued to follow Donovan's every move, not letting his head stray from my crosshairs.

THE SMELL OF GUNPOWDER FILLED THE AIR.

Caprese slowly uncovered his ears—not accustomed to that

sound. Lukas didn't flinch. Without any expression, Donovan held the firing position for several more seconds, before laying the gun down and swiveling back to his computer screens.

Lukas checked the time. It was 6:04. He looked to Donovan—whose expression was now one of anger. Donovan's nostrils flared, as his breathing increased.

He slowly stood. "What sort of game are you playing, *Mayor*? I control this board!" Donovan said, slowly making his way around the desk, not taking his eyes off of Lukas.

Lukas didn't move, but instead allowed a tiny smile to appear, further antagonizing his foe.

"What…in the name of sanity…are you doing?" Donovan asked. "It's only money. Yours. But it will soon be mine. And the score will be settled."

Feeling as though he had nothing to lose, Lukas spat, "Will it, *Hollow Point*?"

Donovan squinted.

"I mean, *Scorpion.*"

Donovan ground his jaw.

"When will *any* score ever get settled? In war? No. Over religion? Never. In a battle for supremacy? Not going to happen. We're officers—we know that."

Donovan didn't blink.

"Well, *one* of us is a *retired* officer. The *other* is a…" He stopped to see if Donovan would fill in the blank.

Donovan ever-so-slowly shook his head.

Lukas continued with the punctuation, "Is a…*Dishonorably discharged*…soldier."

Donovan was furious.

Lukas knew he was playing with fire, but didn't care. He had a point to make. And a bad man to destroy.

"You are about to make…the worst mistake…of your life," Donovan said, relishing every word. He reached for his gun and slid it into the back of his waistband, then went around the desk—taking a key from his pocket, and unlocked the top drawer.

· · ·

"ATTENTION TEAM. We are in lockdown. Stand by," I said quietly, slowly moving my finger from the trigger guard to the trigger.

"Winds have shifted. Looks like a slight swell. Left, point one," Mack said gently.

I adjusted the scope with my left hand.

Reposition.

I took a long deep breath and slowly released it.

Easing my mind, I saw nothing but Donovan's head.

"Target locked," I whispered.

DONOVAN STOOD JUST feet from Lukas, holding a cellphone in his hand. He accentuated his words with the phone, pointing it toward Lukas. "*You* didn't honor our deal. *You* don't care about your daughter. And money is *your* master," Donovan spat the phrases as declarations.

Lukas shook his head. "That's where you're wrong, Donovan. We didn't *have* a deal. And I *do* care about my daughter. More than anything. And newsflash? Money is *not* my master."

They stared at one another.

Challengers facing a duel, awaiting the final bullet.

"And in the ever so glorious end…" Lukas said with exacting precision, "I got the girl."

That was the breaking point.

"Yeah? Well, you can kiss her goodbye!" Donovan shouted, raising the phone in the air—his thumb positioned over the one button that could end the lives of Lukas' girls.

"WAIT!" Lukas shouted.

A TINY BEAD of sweat inched down my forehead, crawling toward the one eye that demanded most of my attention. I willed it away, fearing it will interfere with the job at hand.

No such luck.

"Mack," I whispered.

"Yeah?"

"My forehead. Right eye."

"Got it," he said, taking his handkerchief and delicately dabbing my forehead, catching the bead. He then gently wiped the rest of my forehead.

"Thanks."

"Yup."

LUKAS WAS LOOKING over Donovan's shoulder, toward the bank of security monitors.

Donovan shook his head and grinned. "Really, Lukas?"

Lukas continued to stare at the monitors. "Donovan, trust me. I have no reason but to help end this catastrophe. Just look," he said, nodding to the screens.

Donovan backed away from Lukas, and looked to the monitors. Frowning, he whispered, "What the hell?"

"I had someone from the precinct feed a line here. It's a satellite feed from Abigail's bedroom. She wants to say something to you."

I WAS GENTLY LEANING on my favorite Cheytac M200 *Intervention*. Ranked among the very best sniper rifles in the world, its accuracy was unparalleled, engaging targets 2,500 yards and beyond, while delivering greater accuracy than any other cartridge in the world.

Inside the barrel sat a .408/.375 grain bullet, with a muzzle velocity made for stable transonic flight. The low recoil, extremely fast time-to-target and ballistic tip with solid core, made precise shooting flawless.

The nickname for my killing machine was *The Peacemaker*.

Mack and I could see the light starting to shift, and knew if the clouds broke, we could be in a world of shit.

I kept my head down, and my eye glued to the scope.

"Buddy, much more time and we'll lose the contrast on that glass," Mack said quietly.

"It won't be long now," I whispered.

. . .

DONOVAN FOCUSED INTENTLY ON CLARE AND ABIGAIL.

With one hand, he turned the audio up on the control board. With the other, he aimed the gun at the center of Lukas' chest—his eyes, shifting from Caprese to Lukas, then back to the screen.

"Daddy?" Abigail said, coughing and crying, but performing perfectly for the camera.

"Can she hear us?" Lukas asked.

Donovan nods, watching the screen and stepping closer to examine the details of the room.

The confused look on his face made Caprese smile. "It doesn't look like a little girl's room," Donovan said.

"How would you know?"

"Daddy, why does this man want to hurt me?" Abigail whimpered over the speaker.

With this, our team was trying to appeal to whatever remaining thread of decency this lunatic might possibly have.

No such luck.

We knew time was running out. The light was increasing, the minutes—passing. Lukas needed to do something quickly.

Making sure that Donovan wasn't looking, Lukas looked at Caprese, nodding toward the chess board.

Caprese gave a whisper of a nod then loudly said, "Donovan, tell me, how's it feel to *lose...so...badly?*"

Caught off guard, Donovan turned his head, looking first to Lukas—who pointed his thumb at Caprese.

Once their eyes locked, Caprese tossed his chin toward the chess board. "Look for yourself."

Donovan frowned, but being an obsessive competitor, couldn't help but approach the board. He studied it for several moments— knowing Caprese's move had been good, but Donovan had made an intuitive counter play. He looked from the board to Caprese.

Caprese relished the tiny frown that creased Donovan's brow. He further enjoyed, on a much deeper level, how Donovan would secretly appreciate what he would say next.

"Knight to C4."

Donovan's head whipped back to the board and stared. The room was so still you could practically hear a heart beat.

Or was that a tiny catch in the back of Donovan's throat.

Caprese had been waiting for months to say just one word. "*Checkmate.*"

Donovan's nostrils flared, and just when Lukas thought he had reached his boiling point, he went in for the kill.

"Maybe not in this order, Donovan, but how does it feel to... lose the game...all that money...*and*," Lukas paused for effect—nodding toward the monitors, "The woman of your dreams?"

The evil stare Lukas and so many others had come to know whenever *Scorpion* was about to strike had finally arrived.

"Fuck you, Lukas," he growled, raising the phone then pushing the button.

Nothing happened.

His head whipped in the direction of the monitors, and he pushed it again.

And again, nothing changed.

"What?" he barked, pressing the button repeatedly.

Abigail and Clare waved at the camera, but Clare—just behind her daughter, held up her middle finger.

"They're right under your nose," Lukas said, pointing to the floor.

Time seemed to stand still.

But only for a second.

THANKS TO A STEADY HAND and the good eye of my trusty spotter of 20-plus years, Mack calculated we were roughly 2,900 feet from our target.

Since the round I had chambered would be traveling at a speed of nearly 3,800 *feet per second,* the bullet should reach the target in *less* than one second from...

NOW!

. . .

LUKAS, CAPRESE AND DONOVAN DIDN'T HAVE TIME TO REACT.

From the time it registered anything was different, Scorpion's head exploded and disappeared into a fine pink mist.

Donovan Blair was dead and down before the shattered glass of his penthouse window hit the floor.

73

THE END

BEFORE LUKAS and Clare had the ambulance rush Abigail off to Presbyterian Children's Hospital for surgery, we stood by and shared a moment. I was encouraged, but certainly nervous and sad. Watching her frail body fight the infection the past few days, along with handling the psychological turmoil Donovan had put her through, nearly broke my heart.

The one thing that gave me strength was when she grabbed my pinkie finger and said, "You're my hero, Uncle Carter."

That made everything worth it.

We had it on excellent authority, she would be just fine. Evidently, her high temperature was the result of an infection—not because of leakage of any sort of explosive chemicals, but just that —an innocuous infection.

Saying goodbye to Lukas and Clare didn't feel as permanent as I would have expected, and observing Lukas in action—especially at the end when he stood up to Donovan, gave me a new respect for him. He told me about some soul-searching he had been doing, and how he had come to some extreme conclusions—several of which was influenced by Phil McDonough, who had shown up at the end of the ordeal. After spending entirely too much time whispering into

Lukas' ear, Lukas could only say that he and his campaign had run into some "indiscreet complications."

We left it at that.

Watching Clare cling to her little girl, support her complicated husband—all the while fighting feelings she had for me for entirely too long, made our goodbye a sweet, yet melancholic dance. Hugging goodbye and holding one another too close and for too long didn't make our triangle any easier. However, the three of us knew the score—both the past and the present, and were willing to handle it as best we could.

I made it easier for her by saying something vague about being anxious to get home to *my gal.*

LATER, as we stood atop *The Avalon,* Mack and our team took a long-deserved and much-anticipated sigh of relief, as the NYPD, the FBI, the CIA and several other non-initialed agencies blanketed the two-story condo of the late Donovan "Scorpion" Blair.

The sudden shift in the weather made for a dramatic conclusion to the moment, as a last minute breeze blew the dark clouds east toward Long Island, making way for blue skies and bright sun.

Even the two-degree difference made the day feel different.

It was hard to believe that all the chaos and tension, suffering and pain had taken place over just the past 48 hours. To several of us, it felt more like 48 days.

After several minutes of enjoying the scenery of the city and surrounding boroughs, the silence was broken.

"That was freakin' intense," Mack said.

Mack had stood by my side hundreds of times over the years. And this moment, like all the others, was no different, as I couldn't imagine stepping into harm's way with anyone else. He was simply the best friend a man could have.

"Thanks, buddy," I winked.

"Wouldn't miss a minute, bro," he said, leaning closer. "And gonna be a *helluva* pay day, too."

"You said it."

Xeon and Ken were on the terrace below, and from our view, their body language suggested a budding romance. With her, I felt sure it was just another flirt. Even amidst all the mayhem, she found the time to charm a guy.

As they headed our way, I looked around for one of our missing.

"Hey, Mack?"

"Yeah?"

"Where's Caprese?"

Mack swiveled his head in one direction and then the other.

"What the—?" he said under his breath.

"Just as I expected. The *suits* show up…" I say, nodding toward two CIA members on the terrace below, "And he finds a *convenient agenda* to attend to."

Mack shook his head. "Well, at least we know one thing."

"What's that?"

"We're *sure* to see him again. He owes us *a lot* of money."

"Yeah, come to think of it, so does Lukas," I said, chewing the inside of my lip. "Maybe we'll have to hang out an extra couple days."

Grinning, Mack shrugged, "Hey, I got money in the bank, and plenty of time on my hands."

As Koi, Xeon and Ken approached, I was curious to see what they were cooking.

"I'd say that went pretty well," Xeon said, throwing her shoulders back and sharing the view.

"You mean the part where Donovan's head evaporated?" Mack smirked.

"Never liked that guy," Ken mumbled. "Never stopped talking about chess."

"Speaking of; Caprese got the last move, but Lukas got the last word," I grinned.

"And you got the last shot," Mack said, high-fiving me, then the rest of the team.

"Don't know about you guys," I said, stretching like a cat in the noonday sun, "But I could eat some eggs, a pound of bacon, alongside some biscuits 'n gravy."

"The southern boy has come to play," Xeon said.

"What's next for you guys?" Koi asked, looking to each of us.

"The minute you guys pay me," Ken said, "I'm flying to Mexico, where I'll hunt down *El Diablo*, cut his throat, piss on his corpse and shoot every bodyguard within a hundred yards. Then, I'll find Margo and bring her home."

"Damn!" Xeon raised her eyebrows. "If you need some help, I got some free time."

I looked from Mack to Koi and the three of us shrugged. "Speaking of, whatever happened to Mo?" I asked.

"Guess we lost track of her," Mack said. "We *have* been a little busy."

"She couldn't take not knowing where Margot was," Ken said. "Something about her being the only person who ever loved her. And something I found odd? She said that while she loved Donovan, she never really *liked* him."

We decided the civilized thing to do was to return to the spot where many of us started, so we headed back to the *The Standard*.

As everyone plopped into chairs in the outdoor bar, I spoke with the same waitress I had met two days earlier. Within minutes, she was returning to our table, carrying a bottle of *Casamigos Tequila* and a tray of shot glasses.

"How about a toast?" I asked.

The group shouted, "Let's hear it!"

After drinks are poured, everyone stood and raised their glass.

"Let others boast of clique or clan, there's no prouder boast of man than this: I am American. Where one can raise from any grade, and few are warriors by trade, but all are soldiers ready made, to fight for dear Old Glory."

As I pointed my glass to each of my comrades, we drank, slammed down our glasses and shouted, "*Hooah!*"

THE END?

Look for the next Carter Matheson thriller when he returns for ACHILLES HEEL, Coming 2021.
And if you would like to read any of my other thrillers, please visit my website at: DavidTempleBooks.com

ABOUT THE AUTHOR

David Temple is the author of the Carter Matheson thriller series. *Lucky Strikes* was the first novella, written during the NaNoWriMo Competition. Next came, *Behind The 8 Ball,* another NaNoWri Mo competition. By the next year, David decided to increase the punch, writing his first full-length thriller, *Knuckle Down,* and making it number three in the series. This third edition has undergone a rewrite and a cover makeover.

Look for David's other books, **The Poser**, a new thriller series starring Detective Pat Norelli, and **Devour**, a psychological thriller, available now.

David took his first self-published book, *Discovering Grace*, and after adapting it to screenplay, renamed it *Chasing Grace*, where it became the award-winning independent film. David raised all funding, then produced, directed, and starred in the film. It is now available to watch on many On-demand services around the world.

David and wife Tammy live in a beach town north of San Diego.

Please connect with David by joining his newsletter. There you learn of his future books, as well as find out which books he plans to turn into a Film or TV series!

DavidTempleBooks.com